ZOË FOSTER BLAKE is the author of seventeen books, spanning novels, beauty, relationship advice and children's picture books. Her novel, *The Wrong Girl*, was turned into a network TV series, and her first picture book, *No One Likes a Fart*, won the ABIA picture book of the year. In 2014, after a decade spent as a beauty journalist, Zoë created a skincare line, Go-To. She lives in Sydney with her husband, two children and a lot of SPF.

THINGS will calm DOWN SOON

ZOË FOSTER BLAKE

Atlantic Books
Australia

First published in 2024

Atlantic Books Australia
Cammeraygal Country
83 Alexander Street
Crows Nest NSW 2065
Australia
Phone: (61 2) 8425 0100
Email: info@allenandunwin.com
Web: www.allenandunwin.com

Atlantic Books Australia acknowledges the Traditional Owners of the Country on which we live and work. We pay our respects to all Aboriginal and Torres Strait Islander Elders, past and present.

A catalogue record for this book is available from the National Library of Australia

ISBN 978 1 92292 802 3

Set in 12/18 pt Janson Text LT Pro by Bookhouse, Sydney
Printed and bound in Australia by the Opus Group

10 9 8 7 6 5 4 3 2 1

MIX
Paper | Supporting
responsible forestry
FSC® C001695

The paper in this book is FSC® certified. FSC® promotes environmentally responsible, socially beneficial and economically viable management of the world's forests.

In loving memory of Karen Crawford

Part One

OCTOBER

KIT DEEPLY REGRETTED ASKING RAMONA to wash her hair. Ramona's off-duty look, her Real-Life Hair, was curly, fine, overly processed and, because of all the peroxide, in terrible shape—classic Famous Girl Hair. Washing it on a drizzly, humid morning was creating a real pain in Kit's arse. She'd blow-dried it carefully with only minimal product for hold but could see the waves marching right back in. According to the brief, in this part of the film clip Ramona was meant to look like 'the librarian after she'd taken off her spectacles and shaken out her bun'. Kit had learned from her many years of working with directors, brands and advertising agencies that this meant straight hair; curls were reserved for the nerd or the nosy mum from next door.

'You're bein' a bit sassy up there, babes,' Ramona remarked as Kit tugged at her hair.

'Sorry, I'm just . . .' Kit took a breath to keep her cool and smiled. It was bad form to bring stress or anxiety onto set. Kit took pride in her ability to maintain a calm, professional presence around the talent and crew. 'Don't you worry,' she said. 'It's all in hand.' Kit combed Ramona's hair gently as she considered which products and tools would achieve the result she was after. Too heavy and the whole thing would flop. Too light and the halo of frizz would bloom. Too sticky and the curls would return with fury.

'Washing it always makes it foul,' Ramona observed.

'I hate clean hair more than anyone,' Kit told her, 'but yours was unsalvageable. What I *need* is second-day hair,' Kit murmured to herself. 'Not clean, not dirty, in between.' She picked up some mousse, looked at it, then put it back. She did the same with a tube of smoothing balm, then a can of texture spray, before folding her arms and pursing her lips in concentration.

'Why is there no product that does this?' she muttered to herself. 'I swear, it's the foundation of every look . . .' She mixed a small amount of styling crème with a few spritzes of sea salt spray and applied it to Ramona's mid-lengths and ends. It was one of a few quick fixes she'd developed to fake slightly dirty hair without spending an hour styling it.

'Shit,' she said under her breath, sensing immediately she'd used too much product.

'You good, hon?' Ramona asked as she scrolled mindlessly on her phone.

Kit laughed mirthlessly. 'Yep, I just need a product that doesn't exist.'

'So invent it,' Ramona said.

'I'm not able to conjure unfortunately.'

'No but, babes, for real. I've heard you say a *zillion* times you don't have the right product, so why don't you make it?' Ramona said this as though it were the most obvious thing in the world.

It was true. Kit had found herself in this situation countless times, had spent a ridiculous amount of money sourcing products from all around the world, yet not a single one had been able to deliver the one incredibly specific hair texture she needed. *Nothing* could give her the perfect level of tousled separation that was soft, not crunchy, making the hair feel and look lived in, but not *too* lived in.

'I'm sure it exists,' Kit said. 'I just haven't found it.'

'What are you *looking* for, though, when you're buying all this shit?' Ramona gestured towards the battalion of products lined up on the table before them. 'Like, what actual *words* describe it?'

Kit shrugged helplessly. 'I don't know. I'm probably over-thinking it.'

'Yeah, totally,' Ramona scoffed. 'I mean, you've been styling for twenty years—'

'Ten, thank you, I'm not *that* old,' Kit interjected.

'—and never found it, but, of course, it must exist, right?' Ramona pushed. She raised a brow at Kit in the mirror.

'I suppose you have a point,' Kit said slowly.

'Do it!' Ramona said. 'You've been building up a fan base for years on YouTube and Insta; you're, like, *pro*-level experienced; you style celebs . . . if that's not a golden ticket to starting your own brand, I dunno what is. Do the damn thing.'

Ramona went back to her phone and Kit turned on her curling wand. As she waited for it to heat up, she mindlessly smoothed the same section of Ramona's hair over and over again with her fingers. Make a product? How did you even do that? How did you *literally* get something in a tube or a pump and put it on shelves? It seemed impossible, a completely mind-boggling concept.

Portia, Ramona's latest stylist, appeared, her bike shorts and oversized jumper channelling Princess Diana, her mood channelling Satan.

'Ramona, honey, we have a bit of a *situation* and need you in wardrobe. Kit, sorry, I need Rom for ten.'

'I only have'—Kit checked her watch—'twenty minutes, and I need all of them before BJ takes her for make-up. I'm sorry.' Kit was unfailingly polite, but her days of deferring to other people's invented crises were long behind her.

'It's a Catelyn request,' Portia said, pulling out the big guns.

'I can talk to her if you like,' Kit said brightly.

'But she's busy,' Portia shot back. Catelyn was the director, after all; she outranked everyone.

'Catelyn understands we all have a job to do,' Kit replied.

Portia, with no more weapons to deploy, stared at her. 'What am I supposed to tell her?' she asked.

'That Kit said Ramona would be there as soon as hair was done,' Kit said, smiling.

'Thanks, babes,' added Ramona, winking at Portia.

Portia's eyes narrowed as she looked from Ramona to Kit, suspicious of collusion, before walking out.

'God, I love you,' Ramona said. 'No one *ever* protects my time, you know? My whole life is "come here, do this, be this, wear this, say this" . . . I can't even take a dump without people telling me to hurry up.'

Kit looked at Ramona. Despite her youth, her expression was weary, jaded. Ramona, a striking multi-instrument prodigy with an immense online following, had morphed into Ramona 2.0, a Pretty Girl pop singer, at fifteen. Like anyone who achieved fame early, she had lived a thousand lives in her twenty-six years. She jetted between her Sydney and LA homes, travelled the world, performed to sell-out stadiums, and dated race-car drivers, rappers and actors.

'Can you take a break after this shoot?' Kit asked.

'Nah, we start the tour week after next—not that *you* care,' Ramona sulked.

'You know I'd love to go with you, but I just can't do this one,' Kit replied, mentally congratulating herself for having accepted a gig on a huge TV network ad campaign almost a year ago. Kit loved Ramona, but she did *not* love touring. She was too old to be sleeping on buses or in a different three-star motel every night. She wanted to go home each night to her own bed and, ideally, Ari in it—and he was actually going to be around for the next little while, because his next gig was Sydney-based. This realisation took Kit by surprise; for the first time in a long while, she was factoring a man into her plans. Did that mean she *like*-liked Ari? Or was it just that she was quietly leaning towards a more normal existence, one that involved fewer four am Ubers to the airport, and more morning sex and weekend brunching? Not even her ex—Jackson, that grub—had been able to push her career to number two. Work was everything to Kit. She *loved* it. She could film a hair tutorial at seven am, be on set from nine to nine, stay up till midnight replying to comments online, and do it all again the next day, no problem. Doing hair never felt like work for her; it was creative, it was interesting, and it was always changing.

But what was next for her? she mused, as she blow-dried Ramona's hair, and Ramona tried again and again to get a good photo of her nail art for Instagram. Kit had done the shows in Milan and Paris, she'd worked on global ad campaigns, she'd done Oscar-winners and *Vogue* covers. Since she'd started out sweeping hair on the salon floor at sixteen, she had worked so hard, and been so driven, that she had reached the top of the industry in Australia. So . . . where to now?

Her best friend Maggie thought Kit should move to NYC and try her luck there, but that was only because it was Maggie's own dream, and now she had two kids and cursed herself for not taking her chance when she had it. But moving overseas didn't hold any appeal for Kit: she'd done stints in both London and LA and had missed Sydney terribly. Being a full-time creative director for a brand had felt so restrictive; she wasn't looking to do that again in a hurry. So what was it? What could she do with everything she'd learned, all the contacts she'd made? She *could* start a hair academy, she supposed, she did love educating people, but that felt like a bridge too far. Besides, both her doctor and osteo had made it clear that her lower-back pain—which had her chomping anti-inflammatories all day during busy periods—would worsen if she continued to stand for ten hours a day. *But what was she supposed to do?!* You couldn't *not* stand all day in this profession.

Seeing Kit lost in her thoughts, Ramona pounced. 'You're thinking about it, aren't you, babes?'

'What's that?' said Kit, as she began softly tonging waves into sections, tugging at their ends to loosen the curl before it set. She *should've* used mousse, she realised. No, actually, she *should've* used sea salt spray and *then* tonged. She felt the time ticking past and started to feel the pinch of pressure. In a sick way, she thrived on it. She placed the tongs down carefully, always as far away from the talent as possible, and began rifling through one of the many black kit bags arranged neatly in her large suitcase. She spied the one she was looking for, and thanked the gods as she unzipped it and pulled the hair pieces out. She would place a row of weave under the top layer of Ramona's hair, which would bulk up the hair and mask the wave starting to return.

'Making your own shit, girl, John Frieda-style!' Ramona reminded her, oblivious to Kit's urgent focus on her hair.

'I could do with whatever I'm supposedly inventing right now, that's for sure,' Kit said.

'Oh my god,' said Ramona, dropping her phone to her lap and looking wide-eyed at Kit in the mirror.

'What? What is it?' asked Kit. Had she accidentally burned Ramona somehow?

'Fluro's dad owns a pharmacy chain!' Ramona frowned. 'I can't remember the name. It's the red one at all the airports . . .'

'I know the one,' said Kit through the pins in her mouth. Fluro was Ramona's current boyfriend, a baby-faced rapper who wore pigtails and only drank sherry.

'Well, they have their own in-house brand. They make every-thing: skin care, hair care, tampons, fucking toothpaste, the works. They could make it for you!'

As Kit absorbed this information, the first assistant director, Joel, came over, clipboard in hand, eyebrows raised dangerously high. 'Ready to go, ladies? Wardrobe need Ramona and we're already running behind.' As if a single shoot in history ever ran on time.

'All done!' said Kit cheerfully, pushing the last pin into place.

Ramona stood up, and her assistant Maddi magically appeared from a crack in the floor, or perhaps an air vent, to take her phone and drink from her. Ramona turned and pointed a finger at Kit. 'This conversation is not finished.'

'Go, go!' Kit said, laughing as she ushered her out.

A text from Toni, Kit's manager: *darling are you on set xxoo*

Toni always checked in on her when she was working a well-paying gig. Not because she was concerned about punctuality, but because Toni knew Kit had no real need for her anymore. Kit only worked with a handful of clients, and she could easily save twenty percent commission on every gig if she dumped her manager. And so Toni overcompensated with unnecessary texts and check-ins, to remind Kit of how useful she was. It had the opposite effect.

Kit punched in a thumbs up emoji and hit send then sat on the stool Ramona had just vacated, brows furrowed in thought. Was Ramona right? Could Kit actually make this happen? Create her own line? How did you even begin something like that? Did she just write a brief and hand it over to the manufacturing people and they would make it? She felt a crackle of excitement mingled with nerves . . . *her own product*. It felt strangely urgent, like if she didn't grab hold of this idea and get working on it straight away, it would disappear, or someone would steal it. She would write some notes as soon as she got home tonight. Just for herself, just to see if this had legs.

She stood up with a groan—damn her lower back—and had begun to tidy away her things when her phone beeped. She glanced at it.

if you rub a magic lamp tonight pls wish for me to be able to come home tomorrow

Ari! Her heart skipped a beat. Smiling to herself, she wrote, *Oh no! I did, and already wished for Adrien Brody. So sorry. X*

WHAT, he replied.

She grinned. Was she thirty or sixteen?

He wrote: *u might have to find him a babysitter cos I AM coming home tomorrow*

And then: *and I'm gonna eat u right up*

Kit sucked in a breath, feeling a wave of heat spread up the back of her neck. *For real??* she typed. He wasn't due home for another week.

I wanted to surprise u my god I miss u

Kit closed her eyes, feeling a gooey smile spread across her face.

Come to mine? I'll be wrapped by 6 latest.

His response was immediate: *wild horses xxx*

2

AFTER FOUR WEEKS OF FILMING under the Mexican sun, Ari's brown skin had deepened to a rich maple syrup. This made his grey-yellow eyes even brighter, and his physique appear more toned. He grew up in Wānaka, New Zealand, and was therefore legally required to excel at mountain biking, hiking and kayaking, all of which kept him fit and lithe, but he looked different, Kit realised. There was definition. Bulk.

'Whoa, Jackman, you been working out?' she asked with a smile, as he lay face down, naked, next to her in bed. He'd had a buzz cut and let a wash of stubble grow in; the kind of glow-up pretty sitcom boys had when they landed their first action franchise.

'Why? Does it show? It is hot?' he demanded, immediately sitting up and flexing a heavily tattooed arm. Despite having lived and travelled all over the world since he was nineteen as an in-demand director of photography, his New Zealand accent was still extremely thick, to Kit's delight.

'You're always hot,' she said, smiling. 'The problem is you know it.'

'But does it turn you on? I did it to turn you on.' He winked lasciviously.

Even if it *did* turn her on (and it did), she was completely spent. He had walked in the door and led her straight to the bedroom, her meticulous dinner prep wilting in the kitchen as they fucked urgently and hungrily to make up for lost time.

'You definitely didn't do it for me,' Kit said, 'but it works with your preference for hotpants.'

Ari was extremely self-assured when it came to fashion. His most recent theme—and he did dress in themes—was 1980s camp counsellor: Converse high tops and tube socks, short shorts and a crew-neck t-shirt. Dad cap and vintage sweatshirt tied around his neck optional.

'Well *you* look absolutely fuck-a-riffic as always,' he said, giving her arse a little squeeze. 'Body of a twenty-two-year-old. My god.'

'Hang on,' she chided playfully. 'It was body of an *eighteen-*year-old last time.'

'That's what I meant,' he said, coming closer to kiss her. 'You're a superbabe. A pocket rocket with a filthy mind. *Stunning* combo. And I love this hair; you *know* I love this hair.' He took some of her long, dark, straight hair in his fingers and twirled it gently.

Kit herself had amped up the training lately, not that she would admit it to Ari. She was only thirty, but with him being twenty-six and so annoyingly attractive she felt the pressure: the hot selfies and sexy FaceTimes were hard work, even with low lighting and filters. She'd bought expensive, itchy, lace lingerie because her seamless nude undies didn't cut it for long-distance smut sending—only to discover he had a thing for white cotton undies. She'd even gone back to bikini waxing, something she'd ditched the instant she broke up with Jackson two years ago. During the six years they'd been together, her personal grooming was utterly perfect. He had a 'thing' about chipped nail polish, so she always had fresh gels. He had a 'thing' about fake tan, so she never wore it. He had a 'thing' about pubic hair, so she removed it. She finally snapped when Jackson gave her a kit to fix the scratches on her car for her twenty-eighth birthday. Maggie wasn't surprised. She said that women's lives were bound to seven-year cycles, that turning twenty-eight was when you become a woman proper and found out who you were—but Kit reckoned it was when she'd discovered who *Jackson* was: a complete garbage person.

'I was so bored, baby,' Ari said, propping himself up on one elbow. 'Had to find something to fill my time since my lady love was all the way back here.'

'Don't tell me you were working out with Jason Momoa?' she said in disbelief.

'He asked if I wanted to train with him and his beast of a PT; what kind of egg would say no to that?'

'Well, *I* wouldn't—he's dreamy,' Kit said.

'He'd love you. *Everyone* would.' He waited a beat. 'Will you do this murder-y snow movie with me in Norway in January? Come on. I can get you a gig doing hair on set . . . Think of the *adventure*! Me all cute in a hand-knitted beanie! Fish for breakfast!'

Kit smiled. Ari was always trying to persuade her to tag along with him. He thought the idea was romantic and exciting, but he failed to take into consideration her already full career and life. It wasn't completely his fault; they'd met while shooting a celebrity tourism campaign in outback Western Australia earlier in the year, and Ari thought it would always be like that if they were working the same job. But Kit knew that was a uniquely special moment. Dream crew, incredible location, weather and talent . . . Ari was a dynamic, charming burst of energy and spunk in a crew of avuncular blokes in their fifties. They had hung out the entire fifteen days, having fun, making each other laugh. When he kissed her by the fire at the wrap party, both drunk, both feeling the high of accomplishment, she let herself go with it, even though she had a firm rule about hooking up with crew. Kit told herself it was just a moment in time, the school camp factor, that Ari was far too gorgeous, extroverted and pansexual to ever be anything more than a hook-up, but he'd called the night they got back to Sydney and said the conditions were perfect for kayaking the next morning, and he would pick her up at seven am. They'd been seeing each other ever since. Ten months and counting.

'I'll think about it,' she said noncommittally.

'You're lying,' he said.

'You're right; I'm absolutely not coming to Norway,' she confirmed with a cheeky smile. 'Are you hungry? I made dinner—well, I've prepped it, but it's all ready to go.'

Ari looked at his watch and sighed. 'I am hungry, but my window has closed.'

'Your what?' she asked.

'My feeding window.'

'What are you, a tiger at the zoo?'

'I'm fasting.'

Kit just looked at him, waiting for more of an explanation.

'It's what Hollywood hunks do to stay looking so good: they don't eat for, like, eighteen hours a day.'

His eagerness to try new things, his refusal to accept boredom or routine and his unflagging curiosity were some of the qualities Kit admired most in Ari, but they also exhausted her, and made her feel dull and introverted by comparison. *His* idea of the perfect night after a fifteen-hour shoot was to have a loud dinner at a cool new restaurant with the very same people he had just spent all day with. Hers was to get home as fast as possible, remove all restrictions (bra, shoes, jewellery), wash and put her kit away, change into soft clothes, order some comfort food, pour a wine, double screen with social media and any strain of *The Real Housewives*, and speak to no one.

'Okay, so you're not eating because of your cool new brotocol,' Kit said as she slipped into her favourite silk robe (covered in lemons and leaves—she'd splurged on it when she'd been flown to Capri to do a private client's wedding), 'but *I* am, so come to the kitchen and keep me company while I cook.'

'What are your plans for tomorrow?' he asked, flipping onto his back, rubbing his eyes.

'Not much, I'm just going to do some work,' she said casually.

'Shoot?' he asked.

'No, no shoot. I'm, well'—she took a breath—'I'm actually working on a business plan to make my own hair products.'

'What?!' he sat up. He was genuinely interested in Kit's career, something she never took for granted after years of Jackson's indifference when she tried to discuss what she was doing or hoped to do. Jackson told people she was a hairdresser, which infuriated her, and which she knew he did for just that reason.

But Ari and Kit had formed a friendship before they fucked; it made a difference. They both liked each other and respected each other's work. Plus, Ari was in the same industry, so she didn't need to colour in the background.

'It's a long conversation and I am too hungry right now . . .' she said.

'Headline?' Ari raised his brows.

'Okay,' she said, giving in to her excitement. She leaned against the doorframe. 'Basically, there are styling products that don't exist and I really, really wish they did. So, I want to make them.' She told him about her conversation with Ramona, noticing her heart pick up speed. It had started to feel like a real thing, an actual possibility: the idea had *life force*.

Ari sat up, his face serious. 'This makes *so* much sense. You've seen a gap in the market, and now you're going to fill it. *That's* where the big ideas start, the Amazon and Apple ideas. Oh man, I heard a great podcast by this guy, um . . . I can't remember his name. Anyway, you've got to listen, it's about *this moment exactly*. He says the thing everyone gets wrong is they don't protect their idea properly; like, you've got to be *so* gentle with it, let it grow safely, like a little seedling, you know? Don't tell anyone until it's ready. Don't even tell *me*, to be honest.'

There was no one else Kit had thought to tell, except Maggie. Maybe Toni eventually, but this felt like something Kit needed to keep from her for now. Toni was too aggressive, too inter-fering. She already felt innately protective.

'Yep, good talk,' Kit said, nodding.

'Who's going to buy it?' he probed.

'Honestly? Anyone. *Everyone*. Whether they were never taught how to style their hair, or don't have the time to learn,' she said.

'I want to make the looks I do for campaigns and red carpets accessible for everyone. Make it super simple. Foolproof.'

'I love it,' he said. 'There's no one better at making tricky stuff achievable. Look how many superfans you have on the socials already! It's your gift.'

'Thank you . . .' She smiled. 'What do I have to lose, right?'

'Money,' he said, deadpan. '*All* your money.'

Kit laughed. 'Oh, I'm going to start tiny, don't worry about that.'

Kit did *not* throw money around. She tallied every dollar that came in and had put away half of her income since moving out of home at sixteen. She didn't splurge on designer clothes or live in a fancy flat. When she made really big coin doing influencer gigs or working on extended brand campaigns, she placed the entire amount straight into her long-term saving account without it even hitting her everyday account. Maggie, who would buy a nine-dollar punnet of blueberries without thinking twice, teased Kit mercilessly about her modest living, but Kit was unapologetic about her need for a financial safety net—a result of having grown up without one.

Kit told herself she was not going all in, just dipping a toe in the water, but the financial risk still spooked her. But maybe this was what she'd been saving for all these years; maybe *this* was the rainy day.

'Thank you for being excited with me,' she said quietly.

'Thank you for giving me a Ferrari when you're a tycoon,' Ari joked. But then he turned serious. 'You have the idea. You have the experience. You have the credentials. I'd buy it.'

Kit felt almost giddy. She loved having Ari's focus; his radar was never off. He'd worked with some of the biggest people and brands in the world: Patagonia, Tame Impala, Nike . . . He knew his shit.

'Got a name?' he asked, as he flipped his legs over the side of the bed and reached for his underwear.

'No, but in my head I call it Second Day Hair. That's the holy grail of texture for me, the thing we stylists want—and I reckon most people want the same thing, even if they don't know how to articulate it: second-day hair. It falls perfectly, it looks better, it's not too clean, not too dirty, it's just cool and undone and, I don't know, *sexy*.'

'Second Day Hair,' he said, trying it out, nodding slowly. 'It's good.' He stood up, revealing he'd put her black lace underwear on instead of his own.

She shook her head, smiling. 'Come on, I'm starving.'

Kit turned to walk the five steps out the bedroom door to the kitchen. She'd found her tiny Bondi apartment the day after she and Jackson had broken up, when she was in urgent need of a place to live. She *adored* it. It was cheap, cute and always felt safe and cosy. It was a corner apartment in an old red-brick block of six, and had giant, fully opening, probably illegal windows on all sides of that corner, which housed the kitchen and dining nook. She had views down to the beach, a giant gum tree outside, and her neighbours had generously covered their entire exterior in pink and purple bougainvilleas. Her home was her happy place, quiet and central to everything— and she loved living alone. It felt empowering and peaceful, and she didn't need to worry about waking anyone with her four am starts. She missed Ari when he was away, and they spent most nights together when he was in town, but she had no desire to live with him or anyone. She was becoming a bit of a loner, she realised, but she was really, really okay with that.

Ari sauntered into the kitchen, now wearing his own under-pants and a thin vintage white tee advertising a garage in St Louis, and plonked himself down on one of the bar stools.

'Found a gorgeous new playlist,' he said, scrolling on his phone.

A few seconds later, an upbeat, psychedelic Colombian beat began playing through Kit's speakers.

'*Fuck* that smells delicious,' he murmured, as Kit fried sliced garlic in butter.

'There's plenty to go around . . .' His fasting had ruined her vision of them sharing a meal and the good bottle of chianti she'd bought.

Ari tilted his head to one side, thinking. His resolve was spaghetti-strong at best. 'I suppose one night won't hurt.'

'Atta boy,' she said.

Kit opened the wine and poured a generous serve into two tumblers, handing one to Ari.

He looked into her eyes and tipped his tumbler towards hers so they could clink. 'To good sex, good times and one *helluva* good business idea.'

Taking a sip, she watched Ari: seeing how he enjoyed the wine and music, and the universe in general, all beauty and ease, reminded her of why she found him so attractive, so magnetic. As did everyone else. They'd had the talk and had agreed not to sleep with other people while they were together, but she knew the monogamy would bore him eventually—at which point they would say their farewells. For now, though, Kit was enjoying herself. She hadn't had fun or sex like this in years.

'What's going on in your nog?' he asked, placing his wine on the bench. He had the perceptive skills of a psychologist, which Kit found both wonderful and unnerving.

'Just wondering if you managed to keep it in your pants over there,' she said, returning to the stovetop to check on the pasta.

He nodded. 'Of course!' He stood up and walked over to her, hugging her tight from behind as she tossed the pasta in a pan with lemon, rocket and ricotta. 'It's easy to behave because I adore you, and I want to be with you. You don't need me, you *choose* me, and I just find that so hot.'

'I promise I'll *never* need you,' she joked, but she meant it. She was determined to stay liquid, ambivalent, untethered. One day he'd run free, and Kit would find someone who wanted to settle down and do The Things You Were Supposed To Do. She was not immune to the biological clock ticking away inside her, but she was far from clucky. She had Maggie's kids if she wanted to play with a small, dependent human. Anyway, she didn't have time for all that stuff—she was about to start a business.

3

MARCH

'JESUS, THAT SMELLS *AMAAAAZING*,' MAGGIE said, eyes closed, swooning.

'Ignore the smell,' Kit said. 'It's wrong.'

'But it *isn't*!' Maggie took another huge sniff of the product in her hair.

'I didn't ask for fragrance yet,' Kit told her. 'He's just ad-libbed it . . . Don't you reckon it smells like car air freshener?'

'No way. *I* think it's hot. Tacky hot; you know, Victoria's Secret-candle hot. Makes me feel all young and horny. Like I'm off to a blue light disco to make out with Luke Owens.' Maggie grinned.

'Okay, noted,' Kit said. 'But what I actually need to know is if it's giving your freshly washed hair good texture and shape.'

She worked a tiny bit more of the cream through her best friend's hair. It started off well, taking nicely to the hair and

22

creating soft texture, but within seconds she could see that it was going to be too heavy. Sure enough, after a bit more styling, Maggie's hair fell flat. But Kit wouldn't lead the witness.

'Okay, go have a look in the mirror. What do you reckon?'

'Well,' Maggie said as she stood in front of the chubby blue-framed mirror in her living room, holding up the treated section of her deep red hair as if it was coated in lard; her ability to mask her repulsion was a D– at best. 'It looks like I never wash my hair,' she said.

'I *knew* it was too heavy. He's gone overboard with the silicones. Let's try the next one . . .' Kit rummaged around in a giant Ziploc bag filled with small tubes that looked identical save for the numbers on the tiny label. She selected sample 19H.

'Am I really the best person for you to be using as a tester?' Maggie asked, flopping back down into the orange armchair Kit was using as her salon chair. Maggie's home was a wild blend of incredible vintage finds—she favoured the seventies—and globally recognised icons she had invested in carefully over the years. Her expression was doubtful. 'I mean, I'm not exactly your target audience, am I?' Maggie gestured to her clothes: oatmeal-coloured tracksuit pants with several visible stains and a baggy black t-shirt emblazoned with the words BURGERS HAVE FEELINGS TOO—likely her husband Sam's, given his position as CEO at vegan 'meat' company, Veat. Maggie and Sam had met cracking heads on a trampoline at a party in primary school, became childhood sweethearts, broke up to sleep around at uni, then got married at twenty-three.

'My love,' Kit exclaimed, 'you are *exactly* my target! Women who don't know how to do their hair, have no time and want it to look cool.'

'I *meant* because I'm already perfect.' Maggie raised one brow wryly. She wore no make-up, but she'd had her eyebrows tattooed before having Beau, so despite an otherwise very pale canvas, they were still there: thick, dark, slightly menacing.

'No, but seriously, I'm not trying to make something for people who already have a pile of hair products and tools, and who watch online tutorials—though obviously I'll take them if they're interested. I'm trying to make something easy, something that cuts out five other products. It just *does the thing*, you know?'

'What's the thing?' Maggie asked.

'Easy, good hair! *Cool* hair. Hair with a hangover . . . Like it was styled perfectly yesterday, so *today* it's all lived in and sexy.'

Maggie snorted. 'Why do I need good hair? I don't go anywhere or do anything. I am not a functioning member of society. I'm just a housebound pig, snuffling around for toast and coffee.'

'HEY!' Kit said with force, and love, looking directly into her friend's tired eyes. 'You are the *best* member of society I know. You're in a moment, and it's fucked. But it will pass. We are going to get you through this, okay? And honestly, having hair you love will help. Look good, feel better, et cetera et cetera.'

'I was so good after Dyl, wasn't I?' said Maggie, her voice strained and nostalgic. 'Remember we went to see the Rolling Stones when she was two weeks old? And I was great? And look at me now . . .' She covered her eyes with her hands. 'They all told me the second one ruins you. I didn't listen.'

Maggie, when unencumbered by a sleep-resistant newborn, was the embodiment of self-love and optimism. A human sunbeam, a humming ball of colour, creativity and spontaneity, and a profoundly reliable source of high energy. Of course, she didn't feel like herself. Kit leaned over and kissed her friend on the cheek.

'Oh, and my hair is a lie, don't forget,' Maggie said. 'I had keratin before I had the baby. Oh! Why don't you try it on Dylan's hair? *She* has the hair you want: long and straight and perfect, goddamn her.'

Dylan was Maggie's four-year-old daughter. She looked like something out of a 1978 knitting catalogue, all turned-up nose, big brown eyes and long, thick honey hair with a home-cut blunt fringe. Despite Maggie's attempts to get her to wear black, Vans and take up smoking, she was a loyal and passionate devotee to the church of unicorns, tutus and rainbows. It annoyed Maggie immensely, especially the plastic, glittery debris her daughter left around the house. Dylan, who existed to teach Maggie many lessons, picked up on that, and ran even harder with her sparkly sartorial ball.

'Is it appropriate to test hair products on children?' Kit wondered.

'She's a *human*,' Maggie reminded her, 'not a fucking lab bunny. Hair is dead anyway—you of all people should know that.'

Kit sighed and glanced at the notes she'd been jotting down on her phone. 'No point; these samples blow. One legitimately felt like toothpaste. I don't know how much clearer I can be on my brief.'

'Is this guy your only option?' Maggie asked. 'Can you find someone else?'

'Hey,' Kit said abruptly. 'Am I mad for doing this? Most businesses fail . . . Am I going to lose all the money I put in? It could chew up all my savings—that freaks me out.'

'Well . . .' Maggie said, reaching under her t-shirt to grab her left boob a few times. 'Sorry, it felt hot, be just my luck to get fucking mastitis again a day after finishing antibiotics . . . Listen, I'm obviously going to tell you that you'll crush it, because I'm your number one fan, but honestly, you have as much chance as everyone else, don't you?'

'Yeah,' Kit said, exhaling slowly.

'It's simple, right? You've got to *really* believe in what you're making. Make it *good*. And then work really fucking hard to let people know it exists. That's how I see it.'

'You're right,' Kit said, nodding slowly.

'*Do* you really believe in it?' Maggie asked, squinting at her friend. 'Cos if you do, it *will* work. I've never met a bigger perfectionist, or more of a control freak, or someone more ambitious. I'd probably hate you if I didn't love you, you little type A monster.'

'Aw, that's cute,' Kit said facetiously.

'It *does* kinda feel like all arrows were pointing this way, though?' Maggie went on. 'I mean, Australian Stylist of the Year at twenty-one. It was in the stars . . .'

'Twenty-four,' Kit corrected. 'But yeah, maybe. It does have a sense of inevitability, now I think about it.'

'Okay, so just being devil's advocate, there are, like, a *million* other products already out there made by really big companies with infinity money that are super established and can wipe you out.'

'Thank you,' Kit said. 'I'm well aware.'

'But you think people will choose your product over all those others?' Maggie raised her eyebrows.

'They will, because there *are* no others,' Kit said defensively. 'This product doesn't exist—that's the whole point!'

A smile spread over her friend's face. 'Good. Just checking you were legit.'

Kit sighed. 'But you're right. It could fail. I have to be okay with that.'

'Look,' Maggie said, 'even if it *does* fail, you'll learn so much—'

A small wail came from the baby monitor. Then another, louder and longer. Then a third. Angrier. More indignant.

'You're *kidding* me.' Maggie had finally got Beau to sleep twenty minutes ago; this was supposed to be his big two-hour nap.

Kit put down the sample she was holding. 'Why don't I take him for a walk in the pram? That used to work with Dyl, remember?'

'He won't like it,' Maggie said, sniffing. 'He's a little arsehole.'

'He's gorgeous and perfect, he's just not asleep. Let me try.'

'He will smell you're not me. You don't have the right tits,' Maggie said, with exhausted resignation.

Kit raised her eyebrows as the baby's screams amped up.

'He *does* like movement,' Maggie conceded.

'I'm taking him,' Kit insisted. 'And *you're* taking a nap. Pram by the door?'

Maggie got up, resigned. 'Fine.' She walked off down the hallway, and Kit heard clanging and clicking as she prepared the pram. When she returned, Kit propelled her gently to her bedroom. 'I'll get him. When are Sam and Dyl due back?'

'Not till tonight,' Maggie replied, allowing herself to be pushed.

'Okay: phone on silent, blinds shut, *no Instagram*. Do I need to take your phone?'

'Stop yelling, Jesus . . .' Maggie walked into her bedroom, chucked her phone on the rug and flopped on the bed.

Kit returned to the lounge room and quickly gathered up her samples. She chucked them in her tote bag and left it by the front door, grabbed her phone and Maggie's house keys and popped them in the pram's underbelly, then went into the dark nursery to retrieve a pudgy, cranky, red-faced little six-month-old and force him into a pleasant ride around the city.

As Kit walked around the local park in the midday heat she listened carefully for any cries, but after twenty minutes Beau had gone back to sleep. Kit found a bench in the shade and parked the pram. As she sat there, she went back through her emails to Grant, checking she had been clear about what she wanted. He was a lovely guy, but he had taken eight weeks—twice as long as he'd promised—and none of the samples he'd created were right, or even good enough to explore and evolve and make better. It was as if he wasn't listening, as if they weren't on the same page. She'd worked hard on her brief, she'd researched the ingredients she wanted to include as well as those she definitely did not, and she'd sent him examples of what she would and would not accept in terms of texture and weight. It wasn't like she was asking him to reinvent the wheel; all she had requested was a lightweight cream that was low on silicones (or better yet, devoid of them altogether so it could be used even on the finest of hair), that was moisturising and frizz-taming, for either wet or dry hair, and would give soft, piece-y separation without any heat styling . . . Although it should be possible to use it for heat styling, too, so she should chuck some thermal protectant in there. No shine, she definitely wanted a matt texture; that would be a key point of difference. No greasiness. And *certainly* no heaviness . . .

Okay the brief *was* extremely specific, she realised. But Grant had shown no signs of genius so far, and that was clearly the level of formulating needed. Plus, this was costing Kit precious time and money. It had been kind of Ramona's boyfriend to connect her with Grant, but Kit needed to try someone else. How, though? she wondered. Or, more accurately, *who?* Where did you find a cosmetic formulator? They were like bloody wizards. You couldn't exactly google them, and the only hairdressers she knew who manufactured their own products—Ben and Ant from Royal—were famously territorial, so the chances of them helping were zero.

Negative neural pathways now blazing, Kit was forced to acknowledge that thick, dead-straight hair was not enough of a sampling testing ground. It was too obedient, too pliable. She needed a bunch of different hair types to try it: bleached, curly, coarse . . . How did people starting a brand or making a product get good and true feedback and data? Were you supposed to hire market research people or models?

Her phone chimed loudly. Kit swore, praying it hadn't woken the baby.

Hi kid its dad can you talk?

Kit took a fortifying breath and replied: *Hi dad, what's going on?*

A message came back: *Wondering when are you coming to visit??*

Followed almost immediately by: *Dawn thinks you don't like her*

Dawn was Ron's latest experiment in companionship, a spiritual fangirl living in Maleny, spending money she didn't have on enlightenment she didn't use. She was barking up the wrong tree with her father, who had no interest in being saved, healed or changed; despite all that, they had been together for two years, a long time for Ron, and things seemed to be going well.

What? Silly. Tell her I said hi. How's your health? Kit wrote.

Ron was always low on money, but now he was low on health, too. He'd been diagnosed with stomach cancer last year, and though he'd had surgery and the tumour was removed, he refused to have any further treatment (Dawn's meditation and chanting notwithstanding).

I have a check-up scan next week but my cheque won't be through by then

And here it was.

Wondering if you can help out

Once, just *once*, Kit would like to have an exchange with her father without him asking for money. Last time they needed a new fridge. Before that the car needed a service. Her father refused to get a job because he'd retired on a worker's comp pay-out and lived in fear of being caught and asked to pay it back, something Kit wasn't even sure was possible. Kit suspected some of the money she sent went on the horses; Ron was forever sure that one of his booze-fuelled bets would come through for him.

Just need 200 I will pay you back kid

Kit sighed. This had been the extent of their relationship for such a long time. When Kit's beautiful, funny, rose-scented mother, Jeannie, died in a car accident, she effectively lost her father, too. Kit was eight when it happened, and she was completely grief-stricken. Ron had nothing to offer when it came to helping Kit grieve or process the pain; he didn't know how to do those things, and either chose not to try or wasn't capable of it. Six months later he had invited the nosey divorcee from down the street to move in. Ron was a good-looking man, but even Kit knew he was no prize: he was lazy, quiet and gruff. Tracey brought her teenage daughter Carly with her, which Kit was excited about until she began wearing Jeannie's clothes and make-up, which made Kit cry and scream and strike the walls with her fists. Ron saw everything, but he didn't advocate for Kit or his dead wife: Kit never recovered from that. Ron's increased drinking meant he couldn't hold on to a job and money started to dry up. The memory of having to wear her school uniform and sneakers long after she'd grown out of them still burned hot in Kit; she'd never forget the teasing and bullying about being 'povvo'. Tracey and Carly left a year later, along with all of Jeannie's jewellery.

Ron, who had never had to look after himself, quickly hooked up with Mindy, the deli manager from Coles. They were married within a year. Mindy was kind to Kit at a time when she was desperate for affection and care. She bought Kit her first trainer bra, showed her how to clean her body and face properly, and taught her how to cook a few basic meals. She was a gift from the gods, in other words. But that all changed when baby Rat arrived. She was an extremely demanding baby, and Mindy struggled; there was nothing left for Kit. No longer feeling welcome at home, she was determined to move out as soon as she could. She got a job washing dishes at the local cafe after school and from then on she never stopped working. Ron did his absolute best to keep them poor, but Kit wasn't having it. She babysat, walked dogs, fed pets for people on holidays, was cashier at the pool over summer and delivered mailers, saving every dollar until she left high school at the end of year ten, aged sixteen. She found a room in a share house in Brisbane for ninety dollars a week, and caught the 9.47 am bus out of Toowoomba the very next day.

Kit would never forget arriving in the city. She sat on the mattress in her strange, bare little room, and cried. She cried because she didn't have sheets or bedding, and no one had told her she would need them. She felt intensely alone and homesick. The next morning, she went straight to Kmart and bought the cheapest bed linen she could find, then a week's supply of two-minute noodles. She resolved not to cry anymore. She would push down how much she missed Rat and Mindy, just like she'd pushed down how much she missed her mother. She began a hairdresser's apprenticeship at Best Tressed in Indooroopilly, and that was that. Not long after, Mindy—who'd had enough of Ron's addictions and self-sabotaging ways—moved back to her rural home town with six-year-old Rat, by then a wild, funny, intense little girl who worshipped Kit, and whom Kit deeply adored. If Kit's moving out in any way inspired Mindy, she'd feel forever proud.

Okay, I will transfer today, she typed to her father now.

thank you, he replied, then repeated: *visit soon*

Let me speak to Rat—maybe we can come over Easter.

Was it urgent? she wondered. Her mind always went to the worst-case scenario, which in Ron's case was the cancer returning. She quickly punched out a text to Rat. She hadn't seen her half-sister in a couple of weeks; Rat was probably in need of a decent meal.

Hey sugartits, you round tonight, wanna come over? X

Rat's WhatsApp stayed on one tick.

Kit tried a text message instead. *Are you around tonight? X*

Nothing.

Trying to keep tabs on Rat was a full-time job. She had the focus of a mosquito and was like one of those perpetual-motion toys: she could not stay still. Rat was always moving into yet another house, or getting another intricate tattoo, or quitting her job and blaming the world for her inability to find her One True Purpose, which might mean taking a vow of silence on a hill somewhere one month, or trying her hand at DJ-ing on Mykonos the next. Rat was currently nannying for a very rich family so she could 'subvert the upper class from the inside out'—but as they let her drive a brand-new BMW, took her on fabulous holidays and the mum kept giving her beautiful clothes 'she was throwing out anyway', her anarchy appeared to be on hiatus.

Even though Rat was Gen Z and therefore phone calls were as welcome as chlamydia, Kit bravely called her. A strange tone, then a few minutes later a WhatsApp.

js landed in Paris with the Symons oui oui oui trey bien

Kit shook her head. Of course, she was in Paris.

She wrote: *Our beloved father wants us to visit. Could be serious or could just be an initiation into Dawn's latest cult. When you home?*

Rat fired back: *U go, gonna stay in London few months. I got ringworm from their feral cat last time anyway so hard pass*

If he is dying you will regret this, Kit replied, sighing.

Will I tho? Rat responded with a series of blowing-kiss emojis, nail-painting emojis and cherry emojis.

Neither Kit nor Rat felt much for Ron, but Kit had spent ten more years with him; there was so much more to unpack. Only now, at thirty, was she beginning to comprehend how her childhood had shaped her, how living with an unstable and unpredictable alcoholic, absent in every way, had impacted

33

her. She tried to think of the positives. Ron being such a mess had forced her to become extremely self-sufficient, given her a strong work ethic and seen her amass an impressive pile of rainy-day savings: that could only help her in life, right? Rat, on the other hand, couldn't remember living with him and gave no shits. After they'd moved to the country, Mindy had traded up for a wealthy and industrious one-armed shearer improbably named John Joe Jackson, and Rat's life had become stable and predictable. When Mindy went on to have twins, Rat was largely left to own devices, history repeating itself. Rat had always been a wind-up toy on full tension, which Mindy found tough. Rat would simply leave school if she found it boring, dated naughty boys much older than her, and was regularly returned home by the local police. The fighting ramped up and, in a move right out of Kit's playbook, Rat departed for the city at age sixteen. It broke Kit's heart that Rat and Mindy were essentially estranged. Rat lived a frenzied, untethered life, and now Kit was the only one she could call on to help clean up her various messes. Given how alone she'd felt without her mother, Kit promised to always be there for Rat, even if the girl completely did her head in.

Have fun BE SAFE OR I WILL KILL YOU love you xo

Kit stood up to begin the walk back to Maggie's house. Glancing down at a serenely sleeping Beau, she smiled and murmured gently, 'Don't *you* go and worry your older sister like that, will you?'

4

GRANT SAW HIMSELF OUT. He had emailed Kit to say he'd accepted a position in-house at a global personal care company and could no longer produce her samples. Panicked, relieved and emboldened in equal measure, she asked him if he could refer her on to any other cosmetic formulators, which, like forest fairies and g-spots, were proving impossible to find, and *he actually did*: emailing her the details of an old university colleague. Simon had already produced loads of white-label hair and skin products, Grant said; he would do a great job. Kit had no idea what white label meant, but she didn't care at this point. She had a new start.

That was six weeks ago. Kit had emailed Simon that very day, and the two had struck up an instant rapport. He was incredibly fond of emojis and gifs and had an unusually passionate interest in hair styling and fashion for a scientist living in the outer suburbs of Sydney with his wife and two kids. (His proudest achievement in the field, he'd told her, was a straightening balm he'd created for the Brazilian market.) She forwarded him her updated and extremely detailed brief for the hair cream. Grant getting it so wrong had shown her what she *didn't* want, which had allowed her to understand what she *did* want.

Simon thought her idea was 'freakin' genius' and said he 'could see exactly what she was after', which produced bubbles of excitement in Kit's stomach—but just small, cautious ones, ready to pop in disappointment if his samples arrived and they were terrible.

After a week of emailing back and forth, Simon asking all the right questions to clarify what Kit wanted, he asked for her stance on 'nasties'. Kit had been so focused on nailing the texture that she hadn't given any thought to the ethics or otherwise of the ingredients used to achieve it. Fortunately, Simon had:

> Worth spending some time on it as hair products can cause contact dermatitis . . . Can result in hair loss in extreme cases! Styling products are less likely to irritate than wash and care, but it's good to lay down a brand ingredient philosophy from the outset, one you feel comfortable and secure in, as your product range expands to things like aerosols etc.

It dawned on Kit that in her efforts to give people a good texture, she could make them bald. *What was she getting herself into?* Who was she to think she could make things for people to put on their actual living, breathing bodies? What if someone got really sick? Was she going to get sued if someone had a reaction? Her mind zipped back to a story she'd heard about a well-established brand going bankrupt because a customer went blind. She could *not* be responsible for people going blind. Even a rash was too much! She emailed Simon:

Can we be a natural/clean brand? Safe, a trustworthy short cut for consumers? So people can use it without fear of reaction?

He was immediately on board with the idea, with a few provisos:

The issue is that the definition of 'natural' or 'clean' beauty is not regulated; some ingredients are permitted in one brand but not another. It doesn't, in my humble opinion, mean a great deal. And natural can be very irritating, trust me!

I think what you want is for the customer to feel the products are safe? Not going to irritate? If we prioritise efficacy and safety in equal measure, we'll be dynamite. I'll formulate with proven, high-quality, low-irritant ingredients with a strong safety record—there are great ingredients available out there if you know where to look; I will steer clear of usual suspects!

You were clear on wanting a fragrance, though, and when it comes to reactions that can often be the culprit for people with sensitive skin. The danger is always in the dosage, as we all know. But if it's at a very low level, it should be fine!!

Should be? Kit's anxiety was not helped by Simon's extremely spirited punctuation.

Fragrance is important for me cos it bonds the user to the product—I have my favourites in my kit, and honestly not all of them are because of efficacy, but because the smell is nicer.

Simon replied:

Understood.

Hey, have you thought about calling the brand 'kit?' Actually you probably don't want to call it your name—big headache when you sell the company!!

Signing off and heading to the lab. I will send updated ingredient listing by EOW and once we've agreed samples can be with you early next week.

Who is doing your fragrance?

Kit read the message in confusion.

Not you??

Simon replied with a smiley face, then added:

No, I just create the goo for it to go in. Do you have a nose?

Kit was still trying to interpret this when another message arrived:

LOL sorry, I should've said: a nose is someone who composes fragrances. They are tricky to find, but I do know one. Let me see if she is available.

A shiver of excitement ran down Kit's spine. A perfumer . . . to compose a fragrance . . . for *her product*! That was so fucking cool—and probably *really* expensive, she realised. Simon wasn't exactly cheap either. He charged an hourly rate, and every time she changed her mind or wanted a new version it was costing her. She'd budgeted a maximum of fifty thousand, almost all her savings, to get this product up, and she was *not* going to let it blow out. Kit understood you couldn't make money without spending it, but could she handle a scenario where her savings vanished, the product tanked, and she had to start again? She would have to. She'd never succeed at something unless she was also willing to fail at it, right? Plus, she was just doing a small run, and she would still be making her usual income, because there was no way in hell she'd be stopping work to throw everything at this. Second Day was basically a more sophisticated, expensive version of having a stall at the Saturday markets, she reminded herself.

Earlier in the week Simon had assailed Kit with a million packaging questions: who was doing it, which supplier, which delivery system, when would there be samples available for him to test? How the cream came out of the packaging would inform the texture and viscosity, he said. Of course, Kit said, feigning a level of experience and knowledge she didn't possess. The truth was she had no idea about packaging and had not even made a start. She was already asking so much of Simon, she felt too embarrassed to ask him if he might be able to point her in the direction of a packaging supplier. It couldn't be that hard, she told herself. She'd watched a ton of social media influencers launch fake tan and false lash brands; she just had to figure out where *they* went . . .

She poured some cereal into a mug, added milk, dug a spoon in, then typed 'buy hair cream tube packaging' into a search engine as she ate. Instant results! She began scrolling . . . They *all* looked great. She'd be happy with *any* of them! Green, yellow, long and thin, short and squat . . . It was all there, just waiting to be selected and shipped. All she had to do was go shopping. What fun! She clicked on one that caught her eye: an elegant flat tube that was unlike anything she'd seen in the space. It was garish pink, but she'd get it in a soft lilac colour. So many hair products were either white, or black, or lurid green . . . she wanted to create the feeling of calm, of *confident* calm, and a soft lavender felt right. And it would be matt, not glossy; glossy could look cheap. This brand would *not* look cheap. She was going up against Oribe and Kérastase, after all.

She looked at the information on screen: the product was customisable with artwork done pre-shipping. Great! She scanned the colours available: *they had lilac!* This was too easy: why didn't everyone start a brand?! It was all laid out for her; all she had to do was hire a graphic designer and send the files over. BOOM. She decided to email the supplier about getting a sample. First, though, she clicked back to the product information to check the lid. She hated screw-tops; they always fell off and got lost. Hers had to be flip-top. Functionality was key; she'd given or thrown away full products because of their shitty lids, or frustrating dispensing mechanism. She was scanning the copy when she noticed a bold underlined term: *MOQ.* What was MOQ? A quick google revealed that it stood for minimum order quantity, which was ten thousand. *She had to order ten thousand tubes?!* She'd *never* sell that many products! That was ridiculous! She checked some of the other tubes she liked; *they all had the same MOQ.* Kit realised she had no idea how many products she would need to manufacture; all her focus had been on the formulation. But this was a *business*, not a science project. She had to start thinking about it like a business and treating it like a business, doing proper planning and working out how much it was all going to cost and what she could possibly hope to make back, if anything. One of her big fears, so big that she had chosen to repress it, was that Kit was terrible at all of that. She was good at saving money and sticking to her weekly budget, but she had left school in year ten, and she paid cheap accountants do her tax because it was simply not how her brain worked. Toni said creatives should be sheltered from the world of numbers, because that's when things went bad. Of course, this benefited Toni tremendously, since she now had a stable of right-brain idiots to reign over numerically and financially. From day one Toni had handled all of Kit's work, permits, insurances and income; Kit was blissfully ignorant.

As if thinking of her manager had summoned her, Kit's phone beeped with a text.

darling the cherry shoot is now 7-9th instead of 8-10th, that ok? Let me know. They want to put you on hold!! Big $$$ so make sure its in your cal. Also we need chat re September shows call me xoxo

Kit pushed her phone aside. How could she think about a bloody swimwear campaign when she was trying to find a twenty-cent matt lilac tube that didn't come with so many friggen siblings? *Surely* it was possible to buy packaging in smaller quantities . . .

Two hours and three cups of tea later, Kit found that packaging, and it was awful. She couldn't have lilac, she couldn't have matt: it was a standard glossy off-the-shelf white with a screw-on lid. All her deal-breakers desecrated in one cheap, convenient option. *But* she could order nine thousand fewer of them. *And* it said they could print the label before sending them to Australia, which was something.

She mentally fast-forwarded to the tubes arriving in Sydney. Where would they go? There was no room here, she confirmed, looking around her tiny flat. She didn't have a garage. Would she need to hire a storage unit? Was she supposed to rent an office? Some kind of warehouse space? That didn't really fit into Kit's 'side project' framework. *That* felt very like an 'all-in' plan, something she swore she wasn't doing, and the reason she was still booking all her usual gigs at the usual rate. No, this was a test and learn. An expensive one. But if it showed signs of working, if it demanded more from her, then she would relinquish some freelance work. *Could* the boxes fit here? Maybe she just had to surrender her apartment for now. *Earn* the space for her company before committing too much. Otherwise, she would be paying for storage fees on top of labour and product costs, and potentially end up with no need for *any* of it . . .

Shit, Kit thought. *I need a business plan. What kind of dope starts a business without a plan?* But if she was self-funding, who was the business plan for? She wasn't presenting the idea to anyone; there were no investors. She would just chuck a one-pager together to get it clear in her own mind, she decided.

She googled 'how to write a business plan' and scribbled down some notes:

WHY IT EXISTS
WHAT IS ITS PURPOSE
WHO IT'S FOR

POINT OF DIFF
WHY IT WILL WORK
WHY IT WON'T WORK??

She read an article in *Forbes* that said founders needed to create a 'mission statement' and 'a brand vision statement' plus their 'company values' when starting a business . . . which was the exact moment she quit that task, escaping to the thrill and zing of . . . *cash flow.*

The one thousand tubes she had found—the awful, basic, dull tubes—were only nine cents each, plus shipping. That was fine. Simon had warned Kit that at the rate she was going, selecting gold-standard ingredients and the most exotic botanicals he'd ever worked with, this cream was not going to be cheap. Add in Simon's labour costs. The graphic designer to create a logo and design all the packaging. Plus she would need to send the products out, which meant postage. And oh god, she needed someone to build the website! She had no idea which tasks would be quick and which were slow. The formula was slow—make that *glacial*, thanks to the tube samples that would take three weeks minimum to arrive.

It was a relief to be distracted by a text from Ari, who was in Japan working on a film.

morning pussycat, how's my girl? just ran 10k, had a sauna and am drinking a fancy smoothie are you impressed???

She smiled. *You are the AM king*, she wrote.

He replied, *i miss you, i miss you, why can't you fly in and surprise me? Don't you love me anymore?*

I'm currently working on business cash flow . . . she replied. *I would MUCH rather be in Tokyo with you.*

He sent back a vomit emoji.

Exactly, she replied. *Us creatives aren't cut out for this stuff.*

you've got this, he wrote. *keep at it. i will FT you tonight, around 10 your time. dress code: nudity.*

She smiled and put her phone down. Thank god for Ari and the little glimmers of joy he brought throughout the day. And night. She sighed and returned to her task.

She needed an ABN. And she had to register the brand name. Hang on, was Second Day the *brand* name or the *product* name? Brand, it was the brand. All the products would speak to this kind of unfussy, undone hair. She would stay strictly in her lane and focus on soft, lived-in texture. A simple range, a tight edit. That would be her point of difference. *Shit*, she thought, she'd need to pay someone to help with PR. She couldn't launch a product without publicity! The media and influencers would need an amazing press kit, and that would cost, too. She wrote notes furiously as new jobs and costs sprouted up like bacteria.

TOTAL COST PRODUCT??
SHIPPING?
POST OFFICE A/C??
NEW BANK A/C
FIND COOL BOXES—LOGO TAPE???
TM BRAND!!!
PR—WHO?

Maggie had asked Kit which shops Second Day would be in, and Kit had laughed: why would *any* shop take some random stylist's product? Kit had no contacts in the retail world, and salons were a territorial, political hellscape: she would just sell it online. Less scary, less risky. She could control how people shopped for and received the product, and make sure that the moment when you opened the box was special. She'd include a luxe step-by-step card on how to use the product to cement the education piece and, if budget allowed, some lilac hairclips.

Kit felt she had an above average chance at getting customers. She had one hundred and seventy thousand Instagram followers, a Q&A column on the *Vogue* website, and she'd been posting tutorials to a decent subscriber base on YouTube for years. *The brand would need its own YouTube channel*, she thought . . . Or would *her* account act as the brand's? As the founder, she *was* the brand, right? How did you separate the brand from the founder?

HOW-TO CARDS—MODEL SHOT? PRODUCT SHOT??
GET DOMAIN NAME INSTAGRAM YOUTUBE ETC.
BRAND OR KIT YOUTUBE A/C? BOTH??

She'd need help for the launch, to help her pack and post the product. She'd make Maggie and Rat and Ari help, that should do it. But what if orders blew up and she couldn't manage? How did you even hire someone like that?

STAFF? WHO? TEMP AGENCY??

Kit inhaled deeply, then exhaled. She was completely over-whelmed. She was not only out of her depth, but also sinking fast. She stood up and stretched her arms up over her head. She was sore, her back and pelvis were achy because she was pre-menstrual, she was tired, and hungry, and she *really* needed to get off this mental roundabout. She collected a tin of salmon, mayo and some rice to begin making her Sad Salad, a lunch she turned to when she was already hangry and had no creativity or energy for anything other than pure fuel.

Kit's phone rang shrilly on the counter just as she sat down to eat: Toni again. Kit yielded; she'd have to speak to her eventually.

'Poppet, it's me.'

'Sorry, saw your text, been working, but yep, all good for Queensland.'

'But you're not booked today?' Toni said with puzzlement. Toni's ears were always pricked in case Kit slipped up and admitted she took on secret side jobs that Toni hadn't orchestrated and should be getting commission on.

'It's not a styling job,' Kit said quickly.

'Oh! What is it?' Kit was one of the most lucrative talents in her agency, Toni must always know what was taking up her attention and time, lest it took Kit from her. Maybe it was Kit's fatigue, maybe she was feeling so overwhelmed she needed someone to tell her she was on the right track, or maybe she still nursed a vestigial respect for the famous Toni Masterson-Jones, even after all these years of working with her and knowing she was a ridiculous human, but Kit did the thing she had sworn she would not, and told Toni about her business idea.

'Well, actually . . .' Even as the words began to tumble out, Kit knew instinctively the idea was too fragile and new to be shared just yet, especially with someone as brash as Toni. But she was sick of holding it all in her head alone. She had always been more of a taxi for secrets, rather than a final destination.

'So that's it—that's what I've been working on,' Kit concluded.

She heard the crinkle of foil being unwrapped: Toni was trying to quit smoking and now existed exclusively on coffee, Tic Tacs and nicotine gum.

'You're *priceless*!' Toni said. 'I *love* it, so cute. You know, I hear there's big money in influencers making their own stuff . . .' As always, her brain had immediately moved into money mode.

'I'm a professional hair stylist who also creates content,' Kit said. '*Not* an influencer.'

'Oh, darling, you know as well as I do it's two heads of the same beast,' Toni said. 'Anyway, no shame in being an influencer; they're killing it from what I can see! Ha!'

'Yes, but I've earned trust by working in the industry for years.' That Kit had to point this out to the woman paid to represent her was unbelievable.

'Okay, okay, relax,' Toni said. 'And what about your real job? Not ditching me, are you?' She laughed, but Kit could hear a tinge of concern in it.

'No, no. It's just a side hustle.'

'Good girl. Only a dummy would quit the kind of coin you're pulling in. How long until you launch your little cream?'

'I'm doing my business plan, the packaging has been ordered, and I'm close to perfecting the samples.' Not *entirely* lies, Kit told herself.

'You know, if you do this, all your other hair endorsements will fall away,' Toni warned. 'That's a lot of cash. A lot of risk. I could reel off millions of brands that have launched and failed.'

'I'm not assuming it will be easy,' Kit said. 'But I do think it has a chance of working. That's why I'm doing it.'

'Look at you go!' Toni cried. 'And to think creatives are usually so terrible at business. So who are you doing it with?

Who else knows?' Toni could think of nothing worse than being The Last To Know. She pinned her entire worth on her conversational starting position.

'No one,' Kit said.

'Well,' Toni said conclusively, 'who *cares* if nine out of ten businesses fail, sweetheart; I think it's a *great* idea.'

Kit's instinct was to defend herself, but she didn't have the confidence yet. There was nothing to defend, anyway. Just an idea and a fierce to-do list. But even in the face of Toni's negging, Kit had still felt a rush of glee and excitement when she spoke about Second Day. It was probably just enthusiasm and ego, but whatever it took to propel her through was fine at this stage. She could do all the deep self-work later.

'Darling, I have to ask'—Toni sounded sombre now—'are you doing this because I'm not making you enough money?'

I make you *money*, Kit objected silently.

'I *told* you that you should have taken that contract with—'

'No,' Kit broke in, keeping her tone airy. 'It's time for a change is all, a new challenge. I don't want to be a stylist forever.'

'So, what's it called?'

Kit hesitated. 'Second Day Hair. That's my favourite hair to create, always has been. It's trend-proof and it suits every—'

'Oof, not *me*: mine is a *complete* oil slick if I don't wash it every morning!' Toni cackled. She was renowned for two things: her stubbornness, and her conversational kicks and nips. This, coupled with her thick caramel hair and short stature, was why people referred to her behind her back as Shetland Toni.

'Well, *I* love it,' Kit said resolutely. If she could defend her idea to Toni, she realised, then she could defend it to anyone.

This was all helpful. 'It's the holy grail of hair texture. Soft, lived-in, separated, sexy . . . And weirdly hard to get, genetics aside.' She was on a roll now.

'*SKYLAR LULU MASTERSON-JONES, PUT THAT NUTELLA DOWN RIGHT NOW!*' Toni shrieked abruptly at her three-year-old daughter, one of the miracle twins born when Toni was forty-three.

'For the *love* of god,' Toni said, irritation in her tone. 'She's home sick with the flu and the little creature won't let me do a *scratch* of work.'

'Oh, I'm sorry to hear that,' Kit said.

'She's going to day care tomorrow even if she's a human volcano; I can't take another day of this. Anyway, this is fun, Kit—good on you for having a crack. And when it all falls over I'll still be here for you, getting you those awful twenty-thousand-dollar contracts. What's it called again?'

'Second Day Hair.'

'*Is* it a bit confusing, sweetheart? Do you think people will understand? Not too *editorial*, is it?'

Kit rolled her eyes at Toni's aural air quotes. Despite managing a stable of professional tastemakers paid to create 'editorial' looks for the best brands, magazines and campaigns in the country, Toni still spoke the word with distaste.

'I don't think so,' Kit said, protective of her business seedling. 'It says what it is and does, and that's what I want. Simple and easy to understand.' Why was she justifying herself to Toni? She knew it was a good name!

'Well, it goes right over *my* head—I must be way out of the target demo.'

'No, no,' Kit said. 'It's for everyone. I want to be able to use it on every type of hair, every set, every time. It's like the denim jeans of hair styl—'

'Oooh, see *that's* good, darling . . . the jeans of styling,' Toni said. 'That makes sense, you should call it that. *That's* a name right there.'

'Well, I—'

'And where will you sell it?' Toni interrupted.

'Online,' Kit said firmly, liking the way that sounded.

'Not at the shops?' Toni was aghast. 'How on earth will people find it?!'

'Word-of-mouth, social media . . . I'll hire a PR, of course.' Kit laughed awkwardly. As well as being a talent manager, Toni's agency did PR for select brands. She was breathtakingly expensive; Kit would never be able to afford her.

'Oh, you'll *definitely* need help in that area. No offence, honey. But you should sell it in hair salons. That's where I buy *my* hair products. Doesn't everyone?'

'No, actually,' Kit said.

Toni sighed. 'If you *do* decide to go ahead, we'll need a publicity and launch plan, I suppose. I'll need to make sure everything is perfect: I can't let some junior burger PR ruin a reputation I've worked so hard to create. What date are you working to did you say?'

Toni's lightning-fast pivot from 'inevitable fail' to 'when is the launch' told Kit she saw something of value in Second Day, which was both reassuring and terrifying, because Toni had a way of weaselling into and controlling everything she turned her attention to. This was fantastic when she was your manager and first line of defence, but did Kit want her bulldozing her way into her company?

'You know,' Toni went on, 'after I brokered the deal for you with L'Oréal two years ago—still the highest-paid deal for *any* of my hair stylists, mind you—I kept in touch with Jean-Marc, the marketing director. I'll give him a buzz and get his take on it.'

'Oh no, no,' Kit pleaded. 'Please don't do that yet; I'm still just—'

'Relax, sweetheart; no names or details. This is what I do! I was born with the get-it-done, gene. He will be invaluable to us. Also, have you consid— SKYLAR! NO, SKYLAR! Do NOT touch those flowers! *SKYLAR, COME HERE AT ONCE!*'

A loud crash, a child's scream: she'd gone.

5

SEPTEMBER

KIT STARED AT HERSELF IN the bathroom mirror, hair wet, towel wrapped around her body. There was a message written in eyeliner on the mirror—since his first sleepover, Ari had written little notes on the mirrors around Kit's home for her to find once he'd left. This time he'd written, *AH 4 KC 4 EVA*, and signed off with a row of kisses.

She took a breath in and opened the flip-top of a small white tube. This was one of three new samples from Simon. There had been eight boxes of samples prior to this. She felt they were *extremely* close last round, version thirty-nine, but it was just a *bit* too light. She didn't want it to weigh the hair down, but it *did* need to tame frizzy bits and create texture. She worried she was too close to it now, too deep in the weeds; she was starting to distrust her own judgement. Maybe she'd found the perfect version already without realising; maybe she'd never find it!

She was losing confidence, but Simon was calm, and certain they'd get there.

She removed the towel from her head and squeezed a small amount of the cream onto the palm of her left hand. She sniffed it out of habit, even though Simon's nose—a mysterious, slightly terrifying German perfumer named Albertyne, who had worked at Guerlain before moving to Melbourne for love, and who had blown Kit's budget out substantially—had *nailed* the fragrance, a heady neroli-vanilla blend that smelled like the kind of candle a rich bohemian might burn for a dinner party.

Kit had flown to Melbourne to meet Albertyne in her city apartment—which reminded Kit of the *Beetlejuice* house: stark, shiny, with bizarre primary-coloured sculptures—for a crash course in perfumery.

'What do you wish for it to smell like?' asked Albertyne, a diminutive brunette wearing a Marimekko smock and a chunky wooden necklace. Her accent was thick, and she spoke so quietly Kit had to constantly ask her to repeat things, which Kit worried had put her offside.

'Well, I've always loved oud,' Kit said nervously. 'I know it can be strong, but done subtly and softly, I think it could be really unique. It's a very premium—'

Without looking up from her notepad, and with no intonation whatsoever, Albertyne asked, 'What colour is your packaging?'

'Oh, um, lilac.'

'No oud.'

'Oh,' said Kit, taken aback. 'Why is that?'

'It doesn't match,' Albertyne said, going through some of the tiny vessels in front of her, looking for something. Her dining table was covered in small vials, glass jars and paper testing sticks.

'I'm sorry?'

'It doesn't match for the brain,' Albertyne said, finally looking at Kit. 'If the colour seen does not match the smell, it will not trust. The brain trusts that something lilac will smell a certain way; soft, maybe fruity or floral. If the brain smells something exotic, dark like oud, it won't align, and it won't like it. It's a human survival skill.'

'Oh, wow,' said Kit, genuinely amazed. 'I had no idea. What colour should oud be in?'

'Black, brown, maybe a dark purple.'

Kit knew the smartest thing she could do when commissioning the services of a perfume genius was follow her advice. And so it would be a floral.

Warming Simon's new sample between her hands, Kit applied it, starting at the ends and mid-lengths, applying more and more lightly as she went up, just skimming the roots. She knew her consumer would not be as careful as her; she would do the 'control' application—dumped in on the scalp, too much product, not enough strategy—next time; first *she* had to fall in love with it. Kit gently blow-dried and, as she saw how the hair fell, felt a flash of excitement. *Fucking hell.* This could be it! This could be the one!

When her hair was about eighty percent dry, she set down the brush and hairdryer to look at the result in the mirror. She lifted some sections up and flicked the hair around to inspect the underlayers. She let it fall and watched how it sat. She scrunched some up and let it go; she swished the front sections across and back again. *It looked fucking great.* Even though she was due for a cut and her hair had lost shape, *it looked great.* Lightly textured, no visible product, the perfect amount of volume, weight and hold . . . She knew this was the one. She *knew* it. She grinned at her reflection and looked at her hands, which were shaking. This was really happening. She grabbed the sample and the bright pink Sharpie she kept in the bathroom drawer to mark them and drew a giant heart on the sample before taking a photo, making sure the version number was clearly visible.

She attached the photo to a text to Simon.

She's here. She's HERE!!!! Sdhjsaal cjdsjdkasljdkl!!!!

She took her precious sample and walked back to the bedroom, where she placed it in her handbag before furiously texting Maggie.

I think we have it. THE ONE. I need your hair. And Dylan's too. Where are you?

Kit pulled on some baggy jeans, the cobalt blue Onitsuka sneakers Ari had brought her back from Japan, a white crop top and a cropped lime-green cardigan. She added two neck-laces—one thick and gold, the other made of multicoloured glass baubles—and raced back into the bathroom for skin care and make-up. She heard her phone ping and tore back into her bedroom. It was from Simon.

DIDN'T WANT TO JUMP THE GUN BUT I FELT WE HAD FOUND SUCCESS! CONGRATULATIONS!!!

Congratulate yourself! Kit wrote back. *You did this! You really listened and did everything I asked, no matter how ridiculous and badly explained. Going to do some wider testing now to make sure I'm not imagining things. But I feel so good about this!*

He was a genius in Kit's eyes. She'd begun to feel a fierce attachment to Simon, like he must never leave her, like she couldn't do this without him. She must ensure he stayed working with her forever.

Another message from him came through: *I will make another small batch and fill the tubes once they arrive.*

Kit groaned. The fucking *tubes*. Bane of her life, and probably her afterlife, too, at this rate. She had never been more frustrated and baffled by a process—or lack thereof—in her life, and she'd worked with toddlers *and* their stage mothers. When she had finally worked out how to deal with the supplier direct, Kit had asked for incredibly specific samples, and eventually incredibly specific Pantone colours. Then, realising she had not been specific about the material of the lids, she had chewed up eight weeks of back-and-forth-ing with inappropriate samples—some laughably wrong (lip balm size).

The latest round was due next week; she hoped they would be right but feared they'd be horribly wrong. Toni had 'let' her use her agency designer, Lee, who had zero packaging experience but was bang up for a challenge and had done a pretty great job. The eventual logo—a lowercase, double-spaced typeface with a minimalist bold font—looked modern and clean, but still had energy; it felt to Kit like something that wasn't so trendy it would date and would appeal to a range of ages and tastes. Lee had also created a little 'SD' mini logo, and a suite of fonts and styles for the packaging and website, which was being created by a web designer she'd found on Airtasker. Kit knew it was no Chanel, but the branding was definitely cute. She felt positive the lilac would stand out, and when Lee had suggested a mad fire engine red for all the copy, it *really* popped. As reluctant as she was to feel grateful to Toni, she had to be in this instance.

Don't hold your breath 🙁, she wrote to Simon.

He replied with his characteristic certainty: *They will arrive, don't worry.*

Maggie's reply came in next.

MY LOVE!!! This is EVERYTHING!! Am at playground with local coven. Home at 11 for the frog's nap, will give you our hair in exchange for falafel rolls from Pita House. No hummus for Dyl or you will hear about it.

Kit was buzzing as she bounced into the kitchen and made the first of what would be several hundred cups of tea before sitting down at the bench and opening her laptop. Her notepad—a graveyard of ideas, slogans and tasks to get to—sat to her left, and she scanned it to see what she needed to do today. She'd been struggling with the tedious tasks, especially the trademark lodgement process (surely a test created by the government to flush out people who didn't have the stamina for business), but today she felt renewed passion and excitement. The star had arrived; the backup singers had to lift their game. As Kit flitted manically from email to spreadsheet to texting, she felt impatient to get out there with her sample and start trying it on people. At least she was shooting Friday: three models, all with very different hair—she would use her precious sample on them. She texted Simon asking for more samples for this crucial testing phase: she had back-to-back campaign and editorial shoots for the next month, which was not ideal for getting a brand going but pretty perfect for market research. She wrote more tasks down, hands shaking as though she'd had five coffees.

ASK LEE FOR TIFF FILES AND LO-RES FOR WEBSITE AND IG

*CAMPAIGN SHOOT FIRST WEEK OCT??? WOULD
    RAMONA DO??*
TAX AND ABN SHIT
*CALL GEMMA AT PACKETTE RE: CUSTOM BOXES
    FOR PRESS KIT*
PRESS LIST FROM TONI
FIJI SHOOT CANCEL
CHASE TUBE IDIOTS

Kit was struggling to prioritise her tasks. She wasn't used to having one ongoing project, or being in charge of something that required daily attention and upkeep. Since she'd moved to Sydney at twenty-three and gone freelance, she'd been chosen and requested and told where to go and what to do. Now she was directing and commissioning people to make websites and formulas and shipping boxes and pamphlets and completely incorrect tubes. It was not her natural state: managing, overseeing. She had inexhaustible output and determination when it came to her career, no one worked harder than her on set or creating content, but that was solo stuff. *She* was the only one she needed to think about. The diversity of work and skills required for starting a company felt completely out of her wheelhouse. Many, many times she was tempted to give up. *What the hell was she doing?* But the more time and effort she put in, the more money she spent, the more real it felt, the more determined she became. Failure no longer felt like something she could just accept and be cool with. So, even if she had to push back the launch, even if she had to reject lucrative styling work, Kit was gonna do everything she could to make this work. If her father had taught her anything it was that being poor sucked, and you must avoid it at—literally in this case—all costs. She could still remember the Emilys, two girls in the year above who terrorised her for the grade-one crime of being poor, physically putting her in a bin when she was in year seven. They made her life absolute hell, those two. She wondered what they were doing now. She made a mental note to look them up on Facebook. Bets on them living less than thirty k from the school, and at least one of them having married Darren 'Robbo' Robinson.

Her phone chimed with a text from Toni.

darling did you get my email? The SHA? Thoughts?? Xxx

Kit scanned her inbox and saw the email Toni sent last night with a draft shareholders' agreement. Toni said it was part of setting up a business, a legal requirement along with all the other boring stuff. Kit had ignored it last night because she wanted to look at it with caffeine and a clear head. Now she opened the document and began reading. She'd seen a few contracts in her time, she reasoned; surely she could get the gist. But no. This may as well have been written in Latin. Not for the first time, Kit wished there was such a thing as Google Business Translate, where you fed in a horribly confusing legal document or contract and it would spit out a version written in simple language. How was a hair stylist supposed to understand what a deed of access meant, or pre-emptive rights or capital expenditure? What the hell was a majority parcel? She bit her lip and frowned. Who did she know who could help her understand it? No one. If Toni had not had her lawyer put this together, Kit one hundred percent would not have done it . . . Why did she need a shareholders' agreement anyway? She was the only shareholder! Over dinner last night, Maggie had floated the idea that Kit might want to get a business partner, someone who could do everything she sucked at, someone who could handle all the admin and logistics stuff and let Kit do the creative work. 'You are so shit at that stuff,' Maggie had said. 'No offence.' Was it Toni? Kit wondered. Was she the obvious fit? Toni *had* been in business a long time . . .

Ari thought Toni was trying to muscle in on Kit's idea and take ownership of it, like she did with everything in Kit's career. Wasn't this the one thing Kit wanted to have for herself? Kit agreed in principle, but Toni *had* been helpful. She'd got the admin kicked off, introduced Kit to Lee, handed over her media list, helped sort the press kit materials . . . It may not have seemed like much, but what Ari couldn't see was that Kit needed all the help she could get. She never directly *asked* Toni to do anything, she reminded Ari, and she had even offered to pay her, but Toni said she was happy to help. Yes, Ari countered, but was Toni really the kind of person to help without reciprocity? There would be a fee, he'd predicted, warning Kit to be careful.

Kit sighed and tried to read the document again. *Affiliate . . . Drag-along/tag-along rights . . . Special resolution . . . Debt funding . . . Review of the agreed multiple . . .* She had no chance of understanding this. She'd ask the lawyer who'd drafted it. His name was Gary and he was very blunt and scary in his comms. Terrific.

Can I have Gary's number please? she texted Toni.

Hi darling why? xo

Need help with all the gobbledegook in that doc.

You're so funny!! I can help hon, which part??

Um, all of it?

Meet me at Bill's at 2 and we'll go thru it xox

Should Gary be there??

If you're paying!!! xxx

I think I can splurge for a few coffees.

Gary charges $650 an hour darling!! If u call or email him you will be charged, trying to save you $$ xx

Kit gasped. She really did know nothing.

OK. See you at 2.

That evening Ari sat across from Kit at their favourite Thai restaurant in Surry Hills. It was cheap, pure chaos and, in a move that made no sense, offered some of the best margaritas in town. Ari was wearing a thin black bomber jacket onto which his grandfather had painstakingly sewn all his motorbike club and ride patches in the sixties. He had grown his hair out into a short, choppy mullet and had a new tattoo on his neck: a vibrant pink flamingo. Everything he wore and did was undertaken with such genuine delight and humility; it was impossible not to be charmed.

Kit was clumsily trying to explain the shareholders' agreement, as per her conversation with Toni earlier that day.

'Hang on, why do you need a shareholders' agreement if you're the sole shareholder?' Ari asked, frowning. 'Don't tell me . . . she's not asking for equity?'

'Well . . .' Kit said.

Ari covered his face with his hands. 'Noooooo!'

Kit felt a mixture of emotions. Annoyance that Ari was judging her, fatigue at the topic and a strange protectiveness of Toni. After all, Toni had been her manager for six years. They worked well together. And she was being very helpful, as Kit kept telling herself and anyone who would listen.

'She does contribute. She has done heaps of the groundwork, and she's going to handle all the publicity and manage the press, plus waive her fees for all the shoot talent . . . And she's offered to ship the product from her office, because I have nowhere to keep it.'

'Nice, helpful, but none of that is worth shares in the company,' Ari said. 'She's manipulating you.'

'How? She's giving me a free HQ!'

'Yes—in *her* office, that she owns, so you are indebted to her.' He wore a look of loving frustration. 'I see the short-term benefits, baby, I do. Especially when you're out of your depth in start-up mode. But it's all part of it, right? Learning as you go, all the penny-pinching and chaos you'll look back on when you're minted.' He paused. 'Do you reckon you can suffer an apartment full of boxes for a few months so that you don't have Toni all over everything?'

'Why are you so against me having some help?' Kit asked, trying not to sound irritable.

Ari took a sip of his drink, then tilted his head thoughtfully and narrowed his eyes. 'But her help is never just help, baby. There are always strings.'

'But if she has skin in the game, she'll try harder,' Kit countered. 'I mean, this *is* Toni Masterson-Jones, the top creative manager and publicist in Sydney. She knows everyone in magazines, models, advertising, fashion . . . the leverage is big.'

'How much is she asking for?' Ari asked, face blank.

'Fifty percent,' Kit said quietly.

Ari's eyes flew open, his brows shot up. '*What?* She wants *fifty percent* of *your* company?'

'Ari, you're making me feel stupid.' Kit felt herself getting defensive.

'Hey, hey, hey,' he said gently, covering her hands with his across the table. 'I love you, baby, and I care about you. If I don't challenge you on it now, this will be locked in forever. This is a *forever* contract. It deserves a conversation, don't you think?'

Kit looked up at him, trying to keep it together even though both tears and anger were rising within her. 'I know Toni is a lot. But I need her help right now. I can't do this alone, Ari. It's hard.'

'Of course, it is!' he cried, smiling. 'If it were easy, everyone would do it! All the good stuff in life is hard! Let me put it like this: did she come in with fifty percent of the idea? Did she work her arse off doing hair for fifteen years to collect all the expertise and genius and integrity to start this company? Is she the one people trust for product recommendations or to show them how to do their hair?'

'Okay, okay, I see your point,' Kit said. She was flattered by how much he cared.

'When someone wants to buy the brand for a hundred mill, how will you feel about giving her fifty of them?'

Kit snorted. 'Don't be ridiculous. That'll never happen. I'm one step up from having a table at the Bondi markets.'

'Of course, it's possible. That's what happens to businesses built on good ideas.'

Kit shook her head dismissively.

'So you're in the start-up phase, right?' he went on. Tequila always made him chatty, she remembered. *More* chatty. 'Where you need funds to literally . . . start.' He paused and cocked his head. 'Do you need money?'

'No!' she said, a lifetime of fiscal independence coming through.

'So, if you don't need Toni's cash,' he said, 'she isn't really investing, is she? Can't you just pay her for her time? Pay rent for the office space? Can the transaction be money rather than equity?'

How did Ari know so much about this stuff? Kit wondered. His mum did own a removals business, she remembered; maybe she'd taught him along the way.

'Otherwise,' he pointed out, 'every dollar you make, you give half to her.'

Kit hadn't thought of it that way.

Ari, sensing a breakthrough, changed tack. 'Toni is a good businesswoman, right? So why do you think she wants half of your idea?'

'Because she feels territorial about anything I do?'

'Because it seems like a sure thing,' he said definitively.

'But that's *good*!' Kit said. 'She's *loaded*, she's successful, she's a hotshot businesswoman—all things that I could really use!'

'You can!' he replied. 'And should! Just don't hand over half of your business!'

Kit sighed loudly. Why was she going into battle for Toni? Ari was right.

'I know you're on my side,' she said, 'and that you're looking out for me. Thank you.'

'If you're carving up your business, make sure the people getting pieces of the pie are people you want to work with for a long time—and who bring the skills. Jeff Bezos, for example.'

Kit smiled wryly, pressing her index finger onto a tiny morsel of spring roll left on her plate, then eating it.

'Shall we go?' he said, tipping the last of his drink into his mouth and patting his pockets to check he had his phone. He refused to place it on the table; he believed that was terrible manners. Full attention, always.

'Yep,' Kit said, grabbing her bag off the back of her chair. 'Just going to send a pic of the bill to Toni—we chatted business, so she can pay half.'

Ari winked. 'You jest, baby. But you'll thank me for this chat one day.'

6

OCTOBER

ARI HAD FLOWN TO LA to meet with a Big Deal agency. They wanted to assess whether he would fit in their elite stable of dynamic, cool creatives, and he was ecstatic; this had been his dream for many years. They repped Pharrell, for god's sake! Kit was excited for him and had spent many hours she could not afford to spare making a collection of little love notes to sprinkle through his suitcase. But in truth, Kit was deeply *un*-thrilled by this turn of events. She wanted Ari's career to soar, and for him to get the respect and work he craved, but she did *not* want him to settle permanently anywhere other than Sydney, a city he already treated as a halfway house, and signing with these guys would almost certainly mean he'd move to LA. Also, if she was honest—ugly, selfish honest—not having his support as she launched this business would destroy her. She was disgusted at her self-interest, but his perspective, his confidence and his creativity at a time when she was desperate for validation and reassurance meant the world to her. How could she do this alone?

The two of them had spent so many nights discussing the business, from the press kit gift for media—Kit thought a lilac hair turban would be cool, Ari thought she should offer each influencer and journalist her services for their next event (Ari won)—to the tone of the brand (friendly, confident, a big sister vibe). As well as having an innate business instinct, Ari had an infallible visual sense; he knew what looked great, what read well and had a keen understanding of what people liked. His direction on Kit's graphic design and website and even the aesthetic of the Instagram account had helped Kit shape it into something cool but also beautiful. She had reached the stage where she allowed herself to feel proud: Second Day looked like it belonged on the bathroom shelf among its legacy peers, and in the kits and social media posts of top hair and make-up artists. Without Kit realising it, Ari had evolved from the Good Time/ Short Time lover she had forbidden herself from falling in love with to her Absolute Rock. She knew this was dangerous, given his unpredictability, age and nomadic lifestyle, but she was too far gone; it was done.

Maggie, high priestess of colour and design, had encouraged Kit to go with a slightly less-angry red and a slightly warmer lilac, and challenged Kit's dedication to a wide squat tube, convincing her a long thin version would be much more gorgeous. She was right, of course, and even though the price had almost doubled, Kit backed it. The packaging had to look *majestic*. She had no patience for good enough; there was too much at stake. She was close to a perfect sample (the lid wasn't flush with the tube, of course, so there would be another month's wait for the final

final *final* finished sample) to use in her first-ever photoshoot, for her very own brand, and the battle of Excitement versus Impostor Syndrome was heating up.

Ari badly wanted to come to the shoot (though not as badly as Kit wanted him there), but the LA hotshots needed him in the US yesterday and the shoot *had* to happen tomorrow because Kit was adamant that Joshua Honey, the best photographer in Australia, had to shoot it, and this was his only available day until January. Because Kit and Josh had worked together previously and were both repped by Toni, Josh had not only agreed to the shoot but also charged her mate's rates, which she *really* needed because he was basically at Mario Testino prices now, and she was already dangerously close to exhausting her entire budget.

The quick turnaround meant Kit had to get her shit together fast. Despite having no experience at producing a shoot, Kit had jumped straight in and cast three models, booked the studio and set the creative direction, which was inspired by the fresh, energetic fashion campaigns she loved from the nineties. Glowing skin and make-up, knowing smiles, white shirts and glorious, natural, soft hair. Not too serious, not too intimidating. She wanted the shots to appeal to young and old, novice and aficionado—to feel fun and light, like candid photos of friends that just happened to be taken in superb studio lighting. Ari had strenuously recommended she hire a videographer, just for an hour, which Kit had not budgeted for but agreed to. It was his friend Shari, and she had *not* given Kit mate's rates.

Kit's hastily thrown together creative direction was a Pinterest board full of streetstyle photos of girls with soft, tousled hair that appeared to Always Be Like That: no obvious products or styling, just great hair. Aspirational in its simplicity and style, but relatable and achievable, too. The whole, you-but-better thing. Lots of French girls, obviously. She felt so proud emailing it to everyone the day before the shoot.

Josh had instantly come back asking for lighting and studio references. Shari needed a shot list. Eliza the make-up artist wanted specific skin and face references. The casting agent had shot back with sizes for the models, who would need styling and clothing, and all their dietaries for the catering. Kit almost had a heart attack. She cancelled her job that day, something she never, ever did, and set about finding references, a local sandwich shop that she could pre-order lunch from, and racing to Uniqlo and Zara to buy t-shirts for the models. *And this was only the lifestyle shoot!* She still had to get the product shots done. She'd stupidly thought Josh would do those, too, but he had gently explained that this was an entirely different lighting set-up and skill set, and it would take a day at least to do it well. Kit wanted it done well. She was waiting to hear back from Maggie about a woman her interior design firm used to photograph furniture and objects, and given she had no plan B was putting everything on her being available and less than a billion dollars to hire.

Kit went to bed at eleven thirty the night before the shoot. She woke at two am and could *not* get back to sleep. She texted Ari, who, being in LA, was wide awake. He said there was nothing more she could do, everyone there was a pro, and that nervousness was just excitement wearing a fake moustache. Kit tried to go with that. She *was* excited, except she had spent so much money and time already on this shoot, and had so much riding on it, and was so far out of her depth directing a shoot rather than just doing the hair, that anxiety easily trumped it. It had to be *perfect*. She *had* asked the models to come with clean hair, washed last night and slept on, right? She was pretty sure she had . . . Had she double-checked the gluten-free lunch options? Where was her Bluetooth speaker? An hour later, she was still unable to sleep. Ari once said when he woke in the early hours he thought of the bakers. They were awake, working, and making nice warm pastries for him. That always got *him* back to sleep. Kit tried baker mode for a few minutes, before scoffing at its stupidity and turning on a sleep playlist on Spotify. But the adrenaline was flowing; she was as likely to drift off as a toddler after sinking a Red Bull. You *have* to sleep, she cursed herself. If you *don't* sleep, you won't be any good tomorrow, so you *have to sleep.* Of course, Kit's anger that she couldn't sleep only further riled her up. At four thirty she opened Instagram to find a guru she followed, so she could do a meditation and calm her mind. As soon as she opened her feed she saw a post by a hair stylist from Melbourne who had followed almost the exact same trajectory as Kit, just further down the Australian coastline.

Libby Jones was holding a hot-pink bottle and smiling excitedly in full glam with studio lighting.

So excited to introduce you to my new baby: LJ Hair! I've been working on this for so long and can't believe it's finally ready to share with you all!! There are 3 products (for now!! ;)): Blessed blow-dry balm, Transcendent texture spray and Higher Power volume powder.

Are you ready for hair so good it's a religious experience??? Available at all pharmacies and online at LJhair.com.au. follow @LJhair for how-to's and inspo!! Thank you to everyone who

helped along this crazy mad journey—you know who you are!!!
Let me know what you think and be sure to tag #LJhair xxx

Kit shot up in bed. *Libby had launched a range?* Kit followed
Libby's profile link to the brand page and was assaulted by hot
pink. There were so many posts and so many different models
and product shots and videos and it had only just launched . . .
Kit felt like she had swallowed lead. Libby had absolutely crushed
it. Everything looked incredible. It wasn't Kit's vibe, but it was
cute and it was pink, and pink always sold. At least there was no
texture cream, she consoled herself . . . Succumbing to the fact
that she was awake, she turned on her bedside lamp and went
back to Libby's feed to scrutinise the launch post. Kit had not
thought to do founder shots. Was that essential? It did seem
logical. Should she be doing that tomorrow with Josh? They
wouldn't have time. Also, her hair needed a cut and she had a
stress breakout on her chin. What about the fact that she was only
launching with one product while Libby had three . . . Should
she have waited and launched more? Libby mentioned 'everyone
who had helped her' along the way. Did she have a team? Had
she started, like, a full *company*? Kit knew of celebs who had put
their name on pre-made products: had Libby done that? If so,
how, and why had Kit taken the very long and hard path instead?
Argh! Kit groaned and flopped back down onto her pillow.

At five forty-five am, eyes heavy, brain foggy, heart sad,
Kit gave up and got out of bed. Her lower back was aching, so
she chucked on a crop and some shorts and began stretching
on her bedroom rug, taking deep, calming breaths as she did.
Today can still be perfect, she told herself. *Today can still be perfect*.

Libby is allowed to have a range, I am allowed to have a range, there is enough hair for everyone, today can still be perfect.

She felt nauseous as she showered and dressed in wide-legged red Adidas tracksuit pants with a baby-pink tee and trainers. She put it down to a lack of sleep and nerves, skipping her usual eggs and toast in favour of a cup of sweet milky tea, before heading to the studio to get everything ready before anyone else arrived. Rat was back in town and working as the receptionist at an extremely wanky gym, but although Kit had texted her a few days ago to come help at the shoot, she hadn't even responded. *Hi, it's me, your SISTER,* she'd written last night. *Not one of your dating app dicks. Text me!*

Fucking Rat, Kit thought to herself now, shaking her head.

Arriving at the warehouse-cum-studio perched at the back of a very confusing industrial complex, Kit walked in the open door to find Josh and his assistant already setting up lighting against a white cyclorama. Kit felt a rush of excitement knowing this was all set up for *her*, her brand.

'*YO!*' she yelled, smiling widely, bringing as much hype as she could muster, a charade she would need to keep up until they were wrapped. As she dumped her two suitcases by the make-up and hair station, Josh turned and gave her a broad grin. 'Here she is: Australia's newest tycoon.'

Nine hours later, exhausted to the point of tears, lower back throbbing, Kit dragged her suitcases up the two floors to her apartment, unlocked her door, walked in, dumped her bag on the hallway floor, and flopped onto her sofa. She had one hell of a shoot tucked under her belt; she deserved a rest. The models had been absolute diamonds, despite being zygotes in terms of age and experience, because that was all Kit could afford. They had arrived with excellent energy and decent hair, determined to do a great job and collect some good shots for their fledgling folios. Josh was a maestro; the shots looked like something out of a late nineties Esprit campaign. Kit had oohed and aahed over raws on set millions of times, but these were shots for her *own brand*. She felt enormously proud, relieved and very, very excited. That she had used her Second Day Hair sample to get the looks was the real prize. Kit had started to believe this whole venture might just work when the models flipped out over the cream. They wanted to take some home, they wanted to use it tomorrow, they wanted to use it *every* day. She gave them each a lab sample, made a big deal about how lucky they were because it wasn't out yet, knowing this would add social currency and hopefully they would brag about it to their friends. She took photos of Josh's laptop as the shots came through and texted them to Maggie and Ari, who were aggressively caps-locky and sweary in their approval.

The strange nausea had lingered all day—a vaguely hungover feeling that she attributed to lack of sleep—so she settled for cereal and more tea in lieu of dinner.

Her phone dinged.

Saw the piccies Josh is a GOD hate to think what we'd have done without him well done you xox

Toni had said she would be there to help, which had transpired as her popping in for twenty minutes, enough time to let everyone on set know she was so grateful and thrilled they were working on *her* brand. That had really got under Kit's skin.

She hadn't looked at the shareholders' agreement since their last chat, despite Toni's insistence that Kit hurry up and finalise it. What Toni hadn't banked on was that as time passed, Kit felt more and more protective of her business—protective enough to push back. She felt strangely reckless in her fatigue and decided to do it now. It was *her* business, not Toni's.

As she waited for Toni to answer the phone, Kit began to regret her impulse. What was she going to say? She needed a script! Toni was an Olympic-level manipulator!

'Sweetheart!' Toni said. 'Pop some fizz! Those shots—can you believe Josh? Did I tell you he booked Vuitton? Huge. You are *so* lucky to get him, you know.'

'He is the very best,' Kit agreed. 'It was perfect. I'm so proud. So happy.'

'You always get so anxious, you big silly! There's no need. We are far too blessed to be stressed.'

'Hey, listen, have you got five?' Kit said. 'I want to chat about the shareholders' agreement.'

'Of course, darling. *SKYLAR!* Come back here and eat your cookies or you will make Mummy cross.'

'I can call back?' Kit didn't want to compete with a three-year-old for Toni's already patchy attention span.

'No, no, go on. If I stopped working every time they distracted me, I'd be on the poverty line!'

'Right, okay, well.' Kit took a deep breath. 'I've been thinking, and I've had some advice, and I'm a lot clearer on how I want my company to be set up.' She made sure to call it her company.

'Go on,' Toni said perkily.

'So, yeah, I'm actually going to keep seventy percent because, well, it's . . . it's my idea, and I am the founder, so . . .'

Toni didn't say anything so Kit leaped in to fill the space.

'I just . . . I think that's what I should have, and where I should be . . . I am offering ten percent to Simon because he is super critical and I need him to stick around. I really want him to have skin in the game so he works fast and at his best.'

'*Simon?* You're giving *him* equity? What on earth for, darling?' Toni was aghast.

Kit had expected this: that Toni would think he had stolen 'her' shares.

'He has so much experience and knowledge, he adds a lot of IP and value,' she said pointedly.

'Yes, but you could *pay* him, silly. You don't need to give him some of your company!'

Or you! Kit thought.

'It's what I've decided,' Kit said firmly.

'Look,' Toni said, softening her tone, '*no* offence to this guy, I'm sure he's fabulous, but what can he offer long term as an investor versus you hiring him as a chemist?'

'It's what I've decided,' Kit repeated, not knowing what else to say.

'I'm just asking the hard questions, darling,' Toni said, her tone dangerously close to condescension. 'I've been in business a long time. I sit on two boards outside of my own company; I know what I'm talking about. The last thing I want is for you to make mistakes now you will regret later.'

Every part of Kit wanted to ask what *Toni* offered long term, but she didn't have the guts.

Kit took a deep breath; she was shaking. 'You're welcome to purchase the final twenty percent. The price I need for that is fourteen thousand, because it's going to come out at around seventy K all up. Actually, I'll need more if by some good fortune we have to reorder quickly, but that's where I've landed for now.' Kit had been banking on her first round of sales to buy the next round of product, but would feel much better having some cash on hand to do so.

'We'll jump on a call with Gary,' Toni said decisively. 'He'll figure it all out.'

'There's no need; he's too expensive and, besides, I've already figured it out. So, are you in for twenty percent?'

'Oh, Kit, so impatient. It's adorable. In any case, we *all* pay for Gary's advice now, because we're *all* shareholders! You have *partners* now. And lucky for you, one of us actually knows what's what!' She laughed. 'Darling, did you set up the company bank account and credit card yet? We could be earning squillions of points if you use it to buy all the boxes and tubes you know . . .'

Kit closed her eyes and inhaled. Toni wasn't listening—or, rather, she was choosing to ignore Kit. And, of course, Kit hadn't set up the company credit card! There were so, *so* many things still to do. Kit was flying to Bali for a five-day shoot tomorrow, which meant another week down the drain . . . She was supposed to be launching mid-November, but that was never going to happen at this rate. There were new complications every day. Her first order of five hundred mailers had to be pulped because they were completely the wrong colour—thankfully a printer error, not Kit's artwork error, so it was 'only' an environmental and time issue, not a financial one. Her finished tube and lid were being held at customs for reasons unknown to Kit and—it transpired after several painful phone calls—reasons also unknown to customs. Simon was having second thoughts about the preservative system he used after identifying a strange smell in the latest lab batch, and Ramona had signed a contract with a department store that meant she couldn't post about or promote Second Day at all. Ari kept reminding Kit that her launch date was arbitrary. No one was expecting or waiting for this; it was up to Kit when she went live, and it was far, far better to wait and do it right.

'I'm on it,' Kit said, feeling utterly defeated. 'Hey, Toni, I'm cooked. I'm going to take a nap before I pack for Bali.'

'Remember your gastro tablets—it's a great way to lose weight, but sometimes it can go too far, you know?' she said.

''Kay, bye.'

Kit put her phone on silent and lay back on the couch. She used her toes to push her sneakers off, grabbed her patchwork throw from the arm of the sofa—beloved, battered, it was one of the few items she had from her mother—and snuggled in for a nap. Closing her eyes, she felt the strong pull of sleep. Maybe she would just put it all on hold. Maybe she should just chill on the timeline. Maybe she would just wait and launch in January . . .

Kit woke hours later to a bewilderingly dark room, her phone flashing on the ground. She picked it up: 8.24. She'd slept for almost three hours! It was Ari calling; she answered.

'*There* she is! I thought you might have gone out and got tipsy with that dreamboat photographer and forgotten all about me,' he said, his voice far too loud for Kit's tender state.

'No, no . . .' she croaked.

'Whoa, you okay?' His tone instantly flicked to concerned.

'Yep, just woke up from a too-long nap, I'm fine . . . Man, I was really out of it . . .'

'How did it go? The pics you sent were *breathtaking*. I kinda hate how talented he is.'

'Yeah, really good,' Kit said, smiling. 'I messed up direction a bit but it's impossible for pros like him to do a bad job. I'm so pumped to see the finals; Honey said he'd have them to me over the next few days.' She rubbed her eyes with her free hand.

'Don't call him Honey! Call him Josh, please, for the sake of my heart. Shari do good work?'

'An angel on earth. Thank you so much for that; we definitely needed video.'

'We *should* be having cocktails to toast all this, and instead I'm jet-lagged in my hotel room, sweating bullets about my meeting in the morning.'

'You'll dazzle them,' Kit said, and she meant it. 'They paid for you to come to a meeting from *Australia*. They definitely want you.'

'That makes sense theoretically, but my wired, tired little brain doesn't get it right now.'

'Have a gummy?' she said.

'Way ahead of you.'

'Hey, I had the shareholder talk with Toni . . .'

'Oooh,' he said. 'Did she quit?'

Kit smiled. 'Nah. But she didn't agree to anything. She just said we should have a meeting with Gary. She was *not* into Simon coming on board . . .'

'You're giving them too mu-uch . . .' Ari said in a singsong voice.

Kit ignored him and went on. If Ari had his way, she wouldn't give away *any* equity. 'I told her the percentage, and told her the price, so that's as good as done to me.' Kit tried to sound confident and sure of herself, like a resolute, decisive businesswoman. 'I plan to make them work for it, trust me. Hey, I should clean my kit and pack for Bali. I'm so behind . . .'

He sighed. 'Can *we* go to Bali? Can I meet you there? Can we stay in a massive villa and live on fruit and tequila and sex for days and days?'

Kit and Ari had been to Melbourne for a wedding but were yet to go further afield. They'd go somewhere together once she had launched the brand, she'd promised. A reward for all the hard work. If she could afford it.

'You'll be in New York next week, remember? And I have a brand to launch, apparently.'

'Okay. Dream of my beautiful face. I love you, baby.'

'I think this meeting will change your life in the best possible way. Good luck.' She blew a kiss into the phone and hung up, missing him deeply.

Kit sat there in the dark, feeling the quiet insistence of nausea. She decided to fast, get her stomach right. *Entering* Bali with rough guts was a new one. She stood up and grabbed her suitcases from where she had dumped them in the entryway near the front door, dragged them into the living room and unzipped them. She really could not be fucked with this trip. She'd always enjoyed the travel, but lately things felt different. It was as though a switch had been flicked now that she had another option, one where she wasn't told where to go and what to do, where she didn't have to stand for ten hours, one where *she* had the creative control, where *her* ideas were actualised. *I should do a dry shampoo next*, she thought, as she began the process of pruning her giant local kit for a smaller travel kit.

A dry shampoo that cleans up dirty hair and greasy roots, but you can also apply it on wet hair, to create secret volume and air . . . Secret Volume! She'd write up a brief for Simon while she was away; she needed to get started on more products.

Her phone lit up with an Instagram DM. She opened the message. It was a photo of Aria, the youngest and greenest of the models from the shoot, with three other girls, all long limbs and sharp jawlines and big hair, smiling at the camera, pointing to their hair.

I made them use ur creme and they all want some!! Thx for today ur brand is beautiful xx

Kit looked at the girls. Holy shit. The tall one was Billie Jones! She was a young Aussie who had just appeared in a Prada campaign and was Insta-famous.

Kit wrote back, hands shaking:

Hair looks UNREAL. I can def send to girls, if you chuck me an address? And thank you so much for today. You were magic!

Kit felt giddy. Was this the start of word-of-mouth?! Was this how brands kicked off? She didn't know, but it definitely felt like the start of something.

7

DECEMBER

KIT COUNTED THE ADDRESS LABELS in front of her . . . thirty-six, thirty-seven, thirty-eight. Fuck! There were supposed to be *forty*. There were forty media and influencers and bloggers on the list—well, she actually had almost ninety but could only *afford* to send out forty of the 'good' kits. She'd considered doing A- and B-tier send-outs, then realised if one person posted an A send-out on Instagram and any of the B's saw it, she'd make more enemies than friends. Toni had repeatedly called her crazy for offering her styling services for free to all of these people (the Sydney-based ones, at least), but Kit was dying to do it. She would drive to their home at seven on a Saturday morning and create an updo for the races, she would style their hair for a red-carpet event on a rainy Tuesday night: whatever it took. It would give her a chance to engage one on one and actually use Second Day Hair on them. Connect. Create memories. Climb to the top of their mental heap. Way better than a bloody hair towel, and much more personal than an event, which she couldn't afford anyway, and which she knew these people secretly hated.

Her phone buzzed. She looked at it with an irritated frown, but it was Maggie.

'So Dylan has gone back to napping. Is that weird?' Maggie always started a call as if they were already midway through one.

'She might just be really tired?' Kit responded.

'She should try being me. Anyway, it's about *you* today. I love you and I am so fucking proud of you. How are you?'

'Up and not crying?'

'Oh, my love,' Maggie said with sympathy. 'I know you hated life and everything in it to get here. But you *did it*. How are you feeling? Do Mr and Mrs Redken know you're coming for them?'

Maggie's hyperbole and excitement were contagious; Kit laughed.

'Not super confident, in all honesty,' Kit said, taking a deep breath for what felt like the eight hundredth time that morning.

'You're a marvel, nothing less,' Maggie said matter-of-factly. 'Everything is perfect. It's going to be amazing.'

'I love you, do you know that?' Kit said. She wished she had Maggie's confidence.

'I do. Now, who's helping you? How much coffee have you had? What can I do to help even though I'm in Melbourne?'

'This phone call.'

'I'm back tomorrow and I'm taking you for a drink,' Maggie said. 'Obviously.'

'Yes, good, now leave me alone, I'm busy being a *founder*,' Kit said.

'I love you,' Maggie repeated. 'You're my Kimmy K. Knock 'em dead.'

Kit put her phone back in her pocket and looked around, wondering which task was most urgent. Toni's contribution was her smallest boardroom, her most uninterested intern and her absence. Not even a box of shitty cupcakes, Kit mused. Toni ordered cupcakes for her *dog's* birthday; that's how low on the rung Second Day was. The tiny meeting room was dominated by an oversized oval table and six cumbersome black office chairs that rolled around and blocked all available thoroughfares if you dared touch them. There was no air-conditioning, and a heavy blanket of humidity had settled over the city, giving an already stressful day a pent-up, fidgety energy. Kit tore up and down the stairs, lugging all the boxes, packing beans and cumbersome printer folders to the second floor, making her sweaty and irritable—a fun bonus for someone who had been up until one thirty am posting tile after tile on Instagram before setting the Second Day account to live. With her lower back already aching and no help from Ella the Intern—whose perfect manicure, glossy blow-dried hair and Gucci loafers immediately told Kit she was the kid of a friend of Toni's rather than a uni student desperate for some work experience—Kit dumped all the items on the table and put her hands on her hips. Was that everything? She was still in shock that the finished product, put on earth to send Kit into early cardiac arrest, was actually here. It had finally arrived from Melbourne last night, a week late—launch day was pushed back at the last minute—and it hadn't so much 'arrived' as Kit had driven forty kilometres to the courier company's head office to pick it up, since the fucking idiot fucking driver had decided Kit wasn't home when he fucking knocked earlier that day—she absolutely *was*; she didn't even nip to the corner store for a coffee for fear of missing him. Instead of calling, he had just decided to pop the very critical boxes back in his truck and return to the depot in woopty-woo. Kit had sworn more yesterday than in the entire year before that, and the panic and cortisol she'd been operating on all day, all week, all year, had cumulated in a dramatic and ugly car park cry once she finally had the boxes in her boot. She considered filming it, to look back on if she was successful one day, but she was too upset even to do that. The rest of the shipment, the product for paying customers, was due at Toni's office today but Kit held subterranean hopes of that happening. She was so disheartened by things not arriving on time, or not arriving as she'd hoped, that she didn't for an instant believe five thousand fully filled and finished products even existed, let alone were sitting in a truck en route to her. Well, two and a half thousand of them anyway; the second half of the shipment had been misplaced; they *might* arrive by Christmas, the indifferent monster from customer service had told her.

'Okay,' she whispered to herself. 'Get a grip. This is a product launch, not cancer. *It's supposed to be fun. This is what you have worked so hard for!*'

'Right,' she said loudly to Ella, who was busy scrolling on her phone. She pointed at the two boxes. 'Ella, would you start making the cartons please? They end up in a rectangle, like this . . .' Kit quickly folded one to demonstrate. 'We need forty. Thank you.'

Ella raised one brow at Kit then slowly pulled one of the boxes towards her across the table.

'*Dad* said I'd be on shoots,' she muttered.

Kit smiled, ignoring Ella's negative gravitational pull. 'Just yell if you have any questions,' she said.

'Yah, I think I've got it.' Ella was clearly fluent in the language of *duh*.

Kit surveyed the elements before her. While the quality of the print and thickness of the card going in the press kit was disappointing, the boxes were magnificent: a perfect colour match to the tube and made of thick, glossy stock. *CLEAN HAIR SUCKS* was written in giant letters across the top. Kit's heart swelled with something she had not allowed herself to feel thus far: pride. The press kits looked expensive and glamorous, like a *real* brand. Kit had gone way over budget for them, but the press kit was her best chance at creating a momentum she could ride for sales.

Kit had decided to add three or four mini lab samples into every box so the recipient could pass them on to their friends. Toni said it looked cheap—that they should be full size or don't bother—but Kit was adamant that full size cheapened the product, as though they meant so little they just handed them around like candy, while the mini lab samples were lo-fi and cool. Also, it allowed the recipient to feel generous and in-the-know about a new thing; that was important.

The samples were just one of many micro-battles Kit and Toni had fought during the last few weeks. Kit was in a uniquely moti-vated, creative, untainted headspace (when she wasn't vibrating with stress and anxiety), but Toni was blocking, hindering and dismissive at every opportunity. Kit realised she'd need Toni out of the day-to-day business as soon as possible. She wasn't sure how to do that, especially given Toni had persuaded Kit to sell her thirty percent of the business; Kit had ceded the extra ten percent just so the pressuring and passive aggression would stop. Whether the product sold or not, the first thing Kit would do was move everything out of Toni's office and create some geographic distance and physical space.

The misted-glass door swung open and Toni's PA, Fatima, walked in holding an *enormous* bunch of purple and red flowers wrapped in folds and folds of gold paper. 'Delivery for you, Kit. Someone *really* likes you . . .'

Kit gasped; she'd *never* been sent flowers this beautiful.

Ella glanced up at the flowers. 'Poetry. Only florist worth bothering with.'

Kit took the flowers from Fatima, who retreated. There was nowhere to put the bouquet, so she balanced it on the boxes of product and pulled the card out of the small envelope tucked into the golden folds.

You've done the thing, baby. No matter what happens from here, you were disciplined and determined enough to have an idea and follow through. I love you like crazy! This is really happening! Congrats! Your boy xxx

Kit started crying, even though Ella would definitely feel embarrassed and/or disgusted. She couldn't help it; this was already such an emotional day, and Kit cried at anything at the moment. She wiped her eyes, reached for her phone and tried to call Ari. To her dismay, his phone went straight to voicemail.

Kit took a restorative deep breath and got to work. She slid open the first box, pulled out the bubble wrap and opened the secondary internal box holding her product. She'd wanted matching lilac outer cartons, but after six rounds of samples they could not get a colour match, so she went with red outer cartons, which was much easier, and created a nice contrast against the lilac tubes inside. She smiled seeing them nestled inside—her little red soldiers—ready to head out into the world and, hopefully, right into an influencer's tonal flat-lay. She opened one of the cartons and pulled out the tube, turning it over to read the clever how-to-use instructions Ari had helped her write. ('Why does it have to be serious?' he said. 'Have fun with the copy; there's no law saying it has to be boring.') Kit's stomach turned to ice: halfway down the tube, where the ingredients and legal company info should be, the copy turned into a repeat of '*lorem ipsum*', the placeholder copy designers use to fill the space before the copy comes in.

'No,' she whispered, heartbeat fluttering at hummingbird pace. 'No, no, no, no.' She quickly snatched up another carton and opened it: *lorem ipsum*. A third: *lorem ipsum*. How had this happened? The final sample had been perfect! Why would the printer *do* this? She would KILL THEM!

Breathless with panic, she called Simon.

'Happy launch day!' he said cheerfully.

'The tubes, Si!' Kit was panicking and did nothing to mask it. 'The copy on the back is wrong! Oh god, we're fucked, we're so fucking fucked! This is a disaster!' She was speaking at a million miles an hour, on the verge of crying, or screaming, or both. Kit glanced at Ella, her face the most literal expression of 'what the fuck' Kit had ever seen.

'Take a breath, Kit,' Simon said calmly. 'It's going to be okay. It's a printer error on a very stressful day, but no one has lost a limb. We will work this out.'

He was saying all the right things, but Kit was hurtling rapidly towards hysterical. For weeks—months—she'd managed to keep cool and calm and Taken A Breath when the manufacturer, supplier, printer or lab hadn't followed instructions, or lied about costings, or doubled costings, or sent the wrong thing . . . She had done *everything* in her power and bank account to make sure everything was perfect, and just when she needed it the most, when she finally had her chance to impress the perpetually unimpressed, the drivers of taste, the people who had the power to make or sink this thing, it had fallen apart.

'*How can I send these to the media?*' she cried. 'They look handmade! Like I printed them with a label maker in my bedroom! Like I didn't even proof my product! Oh my god, I can't believe this . . .'

'It's just the back, right?' Simon said, far too composed given the situation.

Kit flipped the tube over to inspect, nausea rising within her.

'Yeah, seems to be,' she said, inspecting the front. *Why* had she not done this last night?

'Is the product coming out properly? Are the tubes functional?'

'Hang a sec.'

She held the phone between ear and shoulder and pulled the small foil tab off the orifice. She squeezed some cream out into her hand and sniffed it. 'Smells good . . .' She rubbed some between her hands and applied it to her ponytail. 'Feels good.'

Ella was folding boxes at the rate of hair growth, watching Kit lose her mind.

'Okay,' Simon said with the confidence of a parent used to dealing with tantrums. 'The goo is good; the front is fine. It's a printing error, but this happens. People will understand. No one photographs the back, right?'

'Shit,' Kit said. 'Do you think the whole shipment is like this? All five thousand?'

Simon went quiet. 'Well,' he said at last. 'Possibly. They are from the same production run. But we did order this batch separately as they were supposed to arrive four weeks early for media. So it's possible—but unlikely—that they made this batch of tubes first and are planning to produce the other, bigger run later. In any case, we need to send a photo to the manufacturer right away, because someone will need to pay for this and the redo . . . Unless it happened at our end—but why would Lee have dumped dummy copy in at this stage?'

A wave of heat shot up the back of Kit's neck. *Redo.* At the last moment, she had asked Lee to hold off on company details because she didn't want to use Toni's office address, and she'd wanted to de-science some of the tricky ingredients for the consumer. *And she had never supplied the new copy.* Neither of them had caught it, and that file must have been sent to the printer.

'Oh, Si. Oh my god. I feel sick. This was me. *This was all me!*' Tears sprang to her eyes. 'I was making edits at the last minute.'

'Aw, Kit,' Simon said kindly. 'That's going to happen some-times. You're only human.'

'I knew I'd mess this up. I *knew* it.' A raft of long-dormant emotions bubbled up in Kit: feelings of inadequacy, of being stupid for even trying. She knew deep down she'd fail. She crumpled onto a seat and covered her wet face with her free hand, sobbing openly now.

'Kit, are you okay?' Simon asked worriedly. 'Is anyone there with you?'

At that moment Ella accidentally knocked over the small column of boxes she had assembled. Kit looked over, daring the intern to make one of her bitchy faces. But she looked chastened as she mouthed, 'Sorry,' and kept working quietly.

'I'm . . . I'll be okay,' she said, recovering her composure. 'I just need to think about what to do.' She sniffed. 'Do I have to bin the whole lot?'

'Oh god, no!' Simon said emphatically. 'This happens all the time. I had a big pharma company misprint a run of five hundred thousand one time. They just printed new labels, stuck them on and got on with it.'

'Should we do that?' Kit asked.

'Well,' he mused, 'we can't sell these as is. Legally the ingredients and company details must be on there. We can *give* them away . . . but we're probably not in a financial position to be quite so philanthropic at this stage.'

Kit took a steadying breath. 'How long until we can get a sticker on there?' Kit wanted to hide from the answer; she knew it would be bad.

'Oh gosh, Kit—not till well after Christmas if we have it done locally. And if we send the tubes back to China, then they need to be in and out before Chinese New Year, since printers shut their factories for February, so I would say . . .'

Kit zoned out, feeling tears rise again. How could everything have gone upside down so quickly? She looked at the flowers, the press kits, Ella: all for nothing.

'Si, can I call you back? I just need to get my head around this.'

'Of course, Kit,' he said. 'I'm so sorry. This must be very disheartening on your big day. But you're not alone. We will find a solution. I'll get on to my contacts now and come back to you with a plan.'

See, Toni? This *is why you want your chemist to be a shareholder. Because this is his company and his problem too. He's not just a contractor who shrugs and gets back to his other clients. He cares.*

'You're the best. Thanks, Si.' She meant it.

Kit hung up and sighed. 'Wow,' she said. 'Just wow.'

Ella looked at her, head tilted. 'Why not just own it?' she said, as if it were the most obvious solution on earth. 'Be honest about the mistake. Turn it into publicity. It makes it, like, relatable.'

Kit frowned. 'What?'

'I don't know,' Ella said, folding a box as if a launch was still going ahead. 'Like, just let everyone know you're a hair stylist, not a business expert, and you made this dumb mistake, but it's what's inside that counts. People don't want to be tricked or see the cover-up. They want to feel part of the realness, you know?'

'Huh,' said Kit, taking in the Gospel of Ella. 'Spin this into a positive. That's quite a reach.'

'And you could say you were going to have to dump them all but that was shitty for the planet, so you decided to just sell them a bit imperfect.'

'Ella, do you want a job?' Kit asked, laughing.

'No, thank you,' she said with absolute sincerity.

'Noted. But you have an amazing brain for this stuff.'

Ella was made of teenage hardware, but she was running middle-aged software. She smiled as if it were no big deal.

Toni walked in at that moment. She was wearing a light tan blazer over a tight white cardigan, and a brown miniskirt. Her caramel shoulder-length hair, the recipient of a salon blow-dry at one stage, was now hanging limply around her face, the ends curling up in rebellion.

'Lord, what a mess! Bella, darling, don't you look gorgeous today. Kit—have you seen Ramona's Instagram page?'

Panic gripped Kit. 'No, why? Is she okay?'

'Oh, she's fine. *Incredibly* silly, but fine. Look.'

Kit glanced at Toni's phone. There was a gorgeous selfie of Ramona in a hotel bathroom, with not a speck of make-up on, holding up one of the first-round 'finished' samples Kit had sent her.

Clean hair is THE WORST. I have been using this Second Day styling cream when I wash my hair and I get instantly cool hair, like I had it done for a party then slept on it. My beloved long-time stylist Kit created it and she knows her sh%t! I was one of her guinea pigs and can confirm it's awesome. Congrats Kitty, love you mean it!!

'Oh my god,' Kit said. 'She could lose her new contract over this!'

'Good for us, though,' Toni said, shrugging.

'She's such an angel, she didn't need to do that . . .' Kit murmured. She was trying to comprehend what the impact of Ramona posting about Second Day to her two million followers might mean. She had tested and tested the website to ensure it was functional, but *how could they sell products that were not legal to sell?*

'Hang on a sec.' Toni clicked the button on her ever-present Bluetooth headphone—'Oh, Louise, darling, I'm so sorry, I'm on the tarmac, just about to fly. Sorry, hon, call you when

I land!'—then clicked it again before carrying on her conversation with Kit. 'On the plus side, if they fire her, then she can be *our* ambassador, right?' Toni said this as if Second Day could possibly afford Ramona's lucrative fee.

Kit's phone rang: Simon was calling. Kit held a finger up to show she needed a minute and turned her back to Toni and Ella.

'Kit,' he said, slightly breathless. 'Are the company name and ingredients on the carton?'

'I think so.' She picked up a carton. 'Let me check . . . yep.'

'*Oh, thank the stars!* We're okay! The Australian cosmetic regulatory laws say that either but preferably both the primary and secondary packaging must clearly display the address of the company and the full and accurate ingredient list.'

'So we can still sell them?' Kit's body was suddenly so light she could have levitated.

'Stickering would still be the best option—and I'm working on that—but okay to sell these as is.'

What would Kit do without Simon? Who could she have asked these questions? What hair stylist on earth had a clue about cosmetic packaging regulations and laws?

'I could kiss you. Thank you, thank you!' She ended the call and closed her eyes, absorbing the enormity of what had just nearly happened.

'Kiss *who*?'

Kit thought she must be hearing things, but no, it was Ari's voice behind her. She turned to see him in place of Toni, leaning against the doorframe and smiling.

'*Oh my god!* What are you doing here?' she exclaimed as fresh tears began to flow. Today was *preposterous*.

Ari manoeuvred his way over to her and hugged her with the intensity of a returning soldier. He smelled so good. He felt so good. *God*, she needed Ari right now. It felt surreal that he was actually here in front of her, after weeks and weeks of being away. And this day—of course, he came on *this* day.

'There's no way I was going to miss the fun! I wanna do boxes and bubble wrap *and* I borrowed a friend's van so I can do the courier run as well.' He looked over at Ella. 'Hi, sorry to barge in. I'm Mr Kit—Ari.'

The intern smiled and blushed as she whispered, 'Ella.' Ari had that effect on women. Men. Dogs.

'You won't believe . . .' Kit began. 'I can't . . . You won't believe what's happened . . . oh my fucking god . . .'

He held her close again. 'Baby, you're shaking!' He turned to Ella. 'Hey, could you give us just a sec?'

She rocketed up, grabbed her phone, and shot out the door.

'I've missed you so much,' Ari said when they were alone. 'Too much. Criminal amounts.' He kissed her again and again on the mouth.

'I . . . I really needed to see you,' she said, looking into his eyes.

'What happened? Did something go wrong?'

Kit laughed despite her tears. 'Understatement of the year. Yes. I'll get to that.' She felt light-headed, nervous and extraordinarily emotional. 'Ari, I've got to tell you something,' she said seriously. 'It's important.'

'Oh.' His smile faded. 'What's up?'

She swallowed. She'd spent so many nights thinking about how she'd do this, and how he would react, and none of her scenarios included a stifling, overcrowded meeting room, but Kit was so ragged from emotion and adrenaline that she needed to get it over with. She had primed herself for a disappointing, even distressing response. There might be a terrible fallout. She stood back and took his fingers between her own clammy hands, looking him directly in the eyes.

'Ari, we've accidentally made a baby.'

Part two

SIX YEARS LATER

8

JANUARY

'MUMMY, MUMMY, THAT LADY HAS the same skirt as me!' a small girl cried as Kit walked past on her way into the building housing the Second Day office.

Kit looked at herself under the fluorescent light of the lift on the way up to the fourth floor, trying to imagine how she might appear to outsiders. She wasn't in any danger of looking like a businessperson, but that was a positive in her eyes. She wore a faded vintage Luna Park t-shirt over a long chartreuse silk skirt that stopped at her ankles, chunky black loafers, and her long, dark brown hair was pulled back into a tight low plait with a slick centre part. It might have been a lot, but a lot was the only amount she knew. She wore her usual gold 'Gretel' nameplate necklace, her usual gold hoops and her usual red lipstick, and a smattering of fine-line tattoos peeked out from behind her ears and on her neck. She liked her outfit. The kid had taste.

As she rummaged around in her giant tote for her phone, the lift door opened directly into the office.

'Moooorniiiing,' purred Hyun, the Second Day admin coordinator slash PA slash social media content creator, whose desk was directly in front of the lift and therefore devoid of any natural light. He had bought an enormous 'Inside daylight' lamp from Amazon and two large fig plants on his first day using the company credit card, which Kit found both impressive and disturbing. Kit noticed Hyun had dyed his very short hair platinum blond over the weekend. Against his bronze, glowing skin, and teamed with his leopard-print satin shirt, it looked especially dazzling.

'Piccolo?' he asked.

'Yes, please. Hyun, that colour looks incredible on you,' Kit said admiringly.

His hand flew up to his head. '*Right?* I've never looked better. Are we still doing oat milk? Apparently it's high in cals and will ruin your microbiome.'

'Really?' Kit was shocked. She'd thought she was being a Good Person ordering oat milk. 'Okay then . . . I dunno—skim? Make it a double, please.'

'Got it. Avocado toast? Honey and chilli?' Hyun was already walking.

'Thanks.'

'Always welcome,' he responded as Kit walked past him into the main office. He smelled better than Kit, he looked better than Kit, he was a beautiful, shiny little dolphin exploding with talent and ambition. Kit was so pleased with herself for headhunting him two years ago when he assisted her on a shoot. He had been training as a hair stylist but hungered for his own 'Ky-J empire', so Kit offered him a job in the office, where he could learn the ins and outs of the business and style hair for content. He doubled Second Day Hair's social media followers in three months and had become a star within the brand in six, because he was outrageous, ferociously honest, the camera loved him, and he knew his shit due to industrial-level YouTube inhalation from age eleven. He came fully loaded, in other words. Kit knew this would drive some founders batshit crazy—only *they* were allowed to front the brand—but it suited Kit fine. She was busy, and the older she got the less inclination she had to create content for whatever new social media platform crawled out from the depths of hell; Hyun was welcome to it. She had not one speck of doubt he would trump her profile and success within a few years; he had more direction, gumption and self-assurance at twenty-three than she had at thirty-seven. If Kit didn't already have offspring, she'd leave everything to him.

Kit dumped her bag on her desk and pulled out her laptop, which Gretel had covered with unicorns and cherries and stars. An improvement, in Kit's eyes. Her purple desk—Hyun had it painted when she was on a work trip, as a surprise—was jammed into a small nook that used to house the printer and copier. She sat with her back to giant windows looking over the city—one of the uglier areas, admittedly, but before this she'd crammed three staff *and* stock into the spare room and garage of the Bondi home she, Gretel and Ari had rented, which was not only a health-and-safety issue but also a life-enjoyment issue. Gretel had been a baby back then, and while Ari was away a lot, when he was home it was absolute chaos. Such was her desperation to compartmentalise work and home life she had taken this overpriced, underwhelming space after a four-minute tour, while breastfeeding Gretel. The real estate agent hadn't known where to look, and she harnessed his awkwardness to lock in a three-year lease and new carpet. They'd been there five.

Kit looked out onto the small open-plan office and sighed in disappointment. There were four hubs of four desks, a small break room and kitchen, plus one shit meeting room they'd long outgrown. The decor urgently needed attention, as did the furniture, and Kit's fundamental need for aesthetic perfection died a small death every time she saw the sun-faded campaign posters propped against the wall because they were forbidden from nailing anything into these pathetic walls, lest they deflate. Kit was looking for a new office, so she prohibited herself from caring, or noticing, or complaining. She told everyone to say they were 'renovating' and that all meetings were to be held off site so no one would see their little cave of mess, samples, work and the thirty boxes of unusable Second Day merch spelled 'Secod Day'. That's what she got for buying in bulk for a discount. Never take the short cut, she reminded herself. *Never take the fucking short cut.*

Camille, Second Day's GM, marketing director Jordan and product manager Delilah emerged from the meeting room.

'Hello, hi, bonjour,' Kit called as she fired up her laptop.

'Did you see the email from Alexa?' Camille asked, walking over to Kit. Small talk was not in her repertoire. She wore a white silk shirt, open-necked with the sleeves rolled up just so, and slim-belted white trousers; her layered brown hair fell into a perfect centre part around her face, and her kohl-lined eyes were framed by thin gold aviator frames. She smelled of honey and tobacco, a fragrance Kit adored but which Camille refused to name. Her vibe could be summed up as insouciant, effortless, *expensive*.

'Yeah, what's *that* about?' Kit asked, frowning. Their contact at Sun, the Australian health and beauty retailer they'd gone into twelve months ago, had sent a very confusing email late last night.

'From what I can understand, they want to give us more shelf space in some stores but halve it in others. Why would we agree to this?'

'What does our contract say?'

Camille sighed. 'It doesn't. It's at their discretion.'

'Shit.' Kit pondered this for a moment. 'Sidenote, did they agree to windows for the smoothing balm?'

'Ten stores only,' Camille replied.

'Good stores?'

'Good enough. I'll call Alexa now, sort it out.' Camille walked away, and Kit turned her attention to Jordan and Delilah.

'She did it,' Jordan sang, tipping her head towards Delilah and smiling.

'Did what?' asked Kit.

'Found a paddle brush made completely from recycled plastic that doesn't suck,' Delilah replied. Kit was used to Delilah's manner now, but it had taken some time. Hyun was convinced she was on the spectrum; he honoured everyone with a complimentary disorder diagnosis and said it was his way of helping people be true to themselves. His flavour was ADHD, he said, and he loved it because it gave him 'one hundred and twenty minutes for every sixty'.

'Unreal,' Kit said. 'Can we get it in our colours?'

'I'm trying.'

If 'no' was a religion, Delilah was a devout atheist. Camille had knocked her back when she first applied for a job—a job that didn't exist—but Delilah wouldn't accept that. She did a six-month online course on industrial design, sustainability and packaging in half the time, and applied again. Camille knew Delilah was far too smart for a hair care company, but she wasn't about to tell *her* that: Delilah was future-proofing Second Day. She kept a team prone to frivolity and trends practical, realistic and grounded, ideally on a planet that wasn't going to end in environmental catastrophe in a hundred years. Delilah cared about more than her products and her job; she cared about Doing the Right Thing. Kit was grateful to have an impassioned activist on the team, even if having the ambassador for Being Woke on staff was tiring at times.

'You got time,' Kit said. 'We don't need it till March.'

'Feb ten, or it won't be on shelf when we launch,' Delilah said, as she jabbed her glasses back up her nose. Despite being assaulted by colour and novelty at every turn, Delilah was one TED Talk away from being a Silicon Valley founder: black skivvy, black jeans, black ankle boots and heavy, black, square frames.

Kit nodded slowly. They had been strictly online for so many years she kept forgetting that Sun, being bricks and mortar, needed an extra four weeks to get stock in and on shelf. She was used to flying by the seat of her pants, getting the product filled, approved and into the warehouse with only a day or two to spare for launch. It was wild, stressful, intense Indiana Jones shit! Lots of bonding and even more swearing. All this pre-planning and six-weeks-before-launch-in-the-retailer's-dock was a real buzzkill.

Thankfully, after many fails, numerous time-wasters and far too many factory visits, Camille and Kit had secured the manufacturers and suppliers they wanted. The security and efficiency of this freed Kit up to get creative again; product and marketing ideas were pouring out of her. This had ultimately led to their decision to move from direct to consumer into retail in Australia: they now had the bandwidth to focus on customers in store, and Kit was willing to invest in additional hires and marketing to support this new direction. Then, three months ago, after a year of negotiations and trips to Seattle, they went into Catalyst, an upmarket department store across the US. This was a huge deal, and they were all on a steep learning curve. Even though they had a distributor in the US helping them, Kit deeply felt the additional pressure. Their small but mighty team of twenty-one had to do everything *really* far in advance, with much planning and spreadsheety tedium. She found herself wondering why on earth she'd agreed to it; why take on the US *now*? It had always been part of the plan, and Kit was ready and eager to grow the brand, but they were still getting their heads around domestic retail!

Camille said it *had* to be now. They had momentum, the brand was hot, and given her years of wholesale experience she was confident she could handle both Sun and Catalyst.

Toni told anyone who would listen it was well overdue. Said Kit was mad for staying DTC—direct to consumer—for so long, that Second Day was losing out to competitors, that staying small when you're selling well was business suicide. Her acting like she had already done all this before annoyed the shit out of Kit. Despite maintaining a civil relationship, the two women had ongoing conflicts, the principal one being Toni trying to grow profits to pay Toni rather than to grow the business. She had insisted on a director's salary of one hundred and fifty K after year two, even though she did nothing apart from attend quarterly board meetings and try to make the products cheaper and the customer experience worse, which would happen only over Kit's dead body. Toni's favourite hobby was to send Kit articles about extremely high-growth businesses doing enormous Sephora takeovers or influencer trips to Iceland, businesses from the US that had been around for fifteen years already or were recipients of enormous capital injections, and say: *Why aren't we doing this?!*

'How're you feeling about launch?' Jordan asked as she clicked away on her keyboard with long French-tipped nails. She was referring to the de-frizzing smoothing balm, Calm Down, that Kit had finally signed off on after thirty-five iterations and was now ready to send out into the world. 'We've got to film your how-to videos next Tuesday, but otherwise we're all set.'

'Don't jinx us,' Kit said in earnest. 'Nothing is set till it's set, you know that.'

'We've got this,' Jordan replied confidently, taking a sip from her giant pink water bottle. 'Not our first rodeo.'

Jordan was Kit's work wife, a brilliant and extremely efficient one. Like Kit she was small-town alumni, she moved to the city for uni from Marulan and never looked back. She ate up life, Second Day and Sydney with absolute rapaciousness; there wasn't an exhibition, concert, Instagram-famous bakery or harbour walk she hadn't done. She was very small and favoured very tight clothing, obsessive about the gym and white wine in equal measure. She wore her shoulder-length black hair in a tight ponytail every single day, which emphasised her toned shoulders and tanned skin that had enjoyed a hot summer or thirty.

'What the fu—' Kit took a breath. 'What is this headshot of me in today's EDM?' She stared at the Second Day marketing email in horror: there was a huge founder photo from her first shoot, done on the cheap, with Maggie's shit camera and overhead fluorescent lighting. She was puffy from pregnancy, wearing an ill-fitting blazer and posing next to a window. Her hair looked greasy and limp. It was, objectively, awful. And fifty thousand customers now had it in their inbox.

'Is there a problem?' Jordan asked.

Kit turned to look at her. 'Are you serious? Jordan, that photo is from a time when dinosaurs roamed.'

'What's wrong with it?' Delilah asked with genuine curiosity. Delilah, who had last year, without anyone's approval, sent an all-staff email declaring a no-retouch policy for all future campaigns.

Jordan looked at Kit with a half-smile, daring her to say.

'It's just . . . really off brand is all,' Kit replied. 'And super out of date. Also, I mean, founder stands next to window in a blazer. Groundbreaking. We have new ones—me on the factory floor in a tutu surrounded by all our products? Margot Park shot them.'

'But you look the same,' Delilah said, going back to her work.

Jordan clamped her lips together, repressing a smile.

'Founder headshots may seem narcissistic, but they are representational of the brand,' Kit argued to no one. 'Never mind.' She told herself no one would open the EDM anyway because it didn't feature *FREEBIE* or *40% OFF* in the subject line.

She had moved on to scan a dense email from Simon about raw ingredient shortages when her phone chimed. It was Shona, one of the kindergarten mums, using the class WhatsApp as her personal Siri: *where can we park for the swim carnival?*

Kit slumped back in her chair. She wasn't going to be at Gretel's first swimming carnival today, and it made her feel guilty in a very specific way. Ari was away as usual, and Kit had even asked Rat to step in, but Aunty Rat was being annoyingly conscientious about her job for once and said she couldn't. *How would Gretel get changed back into her school clothes with her wet little body making her undies roll?* Kit wondered. She didn't know how to dress herself at home, let alone in a change room at a public swimming pool! Would anyone help her? She didn't know how to do up her shoes either . . . Kit closed her eyes, inhaled slowly, and told herself Ms Kellan would help her, of course. She wished she'd put more effort into making some mum friends in Gretel's class, so they could spot each other at times like this. She had Caro, Remy's mum, but Caro was a partner at KPMG and even less on top of school admin than Kit.

Hyun floated over and popped Kit's coffee and toast on her desk. As always, he was clutching his emotional water bottle, iPad and phone in case an influencer urgently needed hairspray. How he never dropped anything was an office mystery.

'Any update on the twins?'

'Who?' Kit asked.

Hyun and Jordan exchanged a look. Jordan gave a micro shake of her head. Hyun widened his eyes in reply. Jordan repeated her head shake but added her own eye widening. Hyun crossed his arms and sighed dramatically.

'It's nothing,' Jordan said. 'Seriously.'

'What's nothing?' said Kit warningly.

Hyun raised his brows respectfully at Jordan as if to say, go on.

'What's the company rule on trolls, Hyun?' Jordan said. '*We don't feed them.*'

'I'm not gonna watch my boss get semi-cancelled cos I didn't warn her,' Hyun said loyally.

Kit felt a familiar light-headedness set in; her heart quickened. 'Please, guys, what are you talking about?' Kit was still wounded from her most recent troll experience—last year she'd been accused of copying a smaller brand, a brand she had never heard of, a fact she stupidly explained until she realised facts are like unicorns to trolls: they don't exist. The brand's founders had amassed a small but potent band of people to attack Second Day in every conceivable forum: Reddit, Facebook, Twitter, TikTok, Instagram posts . . . even the posts of Second Day's suppliers. It had then got a spin in the Daily News, which is when other trolls, feral, hungry, international trolls who didn't at all under-stand the situation began piling on. Kit had done her best to be calm for the team while internalising tremendous anxiety.

'Hyun is both vigilant and protective, which is adorable but not always helpful,' Jordan observed.

'I love you all dearly, but I will kill you if you don't talk right now.'

'Don't look at me,' said Delilah, hands in the air. 'I know as nothing as you.'

Hyun chirpily jumped in. '*So*, Kari and Isla, the twins from our Sunday Nights campaign? Turns out they are *super* problem-atic. There is a giant Reddit about them, which has now moved on to *you*, and how *you* are pro-racist for hiring them, and—'

Kit's hand flew to her heart. 'Have we checked in with the twins?'

'You wanna make sure their KKK uniform is ironed and ready for the weekend?' Delilah piped up as she tapped away on her laptop.

'Delilah, they're still human beings even if we don't agree with their—'

Hyun showed Kit his iPad.

'Fuck me,' she said. 'Are you *serious*?'

The screenshot showed the heavily pierced young sisters with their noses scrunched up holding takeaway containers. The caption was: *When the delivery driver leaves his Eau De Indian on your butter chickchick.*

'There's worse,' Hyun said, taking his iPad back to find it. Hyun was positively *buzzing* playing Cancel Detective. In the next screenshot he showed Kit, the twins were applying eyeliner, pulling their eyelids up and towards their ears. The caption: *Chinky wings.*

'*Jesus*,' whispered Kit. 'How did we not see this when we were vetting them!?'

'These posts were on Tumblr,' Hyun explained. 'We didn't have access to that as it was a private account, but in truth we didn't think to check it cos Tumblr is basically pre-Internet.'

'Are there more? How recent are these?' Kit asked.

'Racism has no expiry date,' Delilah piped up. 'Just a reminder.'

'Judging by their hair colour, six to seven years ago,' estimated Hyun.

'Can I see the Reddit?' Kit asked.

'Don't do it,' Jordan warned.

Hyun tapped his iPad a few times then offered it to Kit, brows raised.

She took it.

'*Wow*. That escalated. I didn't realise my eyebrows, voice and child's name were so disgusting.' She felt light-headed and floaty, a primal response to bullying taking over her body. Breathing deeply, she tried to keep it together, tried to find some calm. 'Okay, we'll have to remove all campaign imagery.'

'Really?' asked Jordan. 'You think?'

'We're as much ambassadors for them as they are for us.'

'Perfect. Trolls won't quit until they see action,' Hyun said knowingly.

'First day on the internet?' Delilah said. 'Trolls go *harder* if you take action. They're provocative to get a response because they thrive on attention. Then when they get one, they go for another. I could explain the whole troll ecosystem to you, but I don't have the time or the crayons.'

'Hang on,' Jordan interjected. 'But we didn't post those things. *They* should remove their posts, but do we really need to remove ours? It *was* years ago . . .'

'We do,' Kit said calmly. 'You've never seen an athlete get dropped by a sponsor cos they did something to bring that brand into disrepute?'

'We spent so much on that campaign,' Jordan muttered.

'Hyun, have the twins said anything publicly about this yet?'

'They're posting,' Hyun interrupted, scrolling TikTok as he spoke. 'Protein powder spon con and a new puppy.'

Kit was completely unsure of what to do, while projecting the appearance of innate confidence. She'd handled a lot of unknowns as a founder, but the public accountability and trolls never got any less complex or weird. It was akin to guessing which direction an angry swarm of wasps was going to go; there was no handbook, no rules and no obvious choices.

'For now, do nothing. I know troll time is ten times faster than real time, but just sit tight while I think on it. And *do not reply. Anywhere.*'

Kit took her bag and phone and walked to the lift, pressing up.

Once she got to the rooftop, she walked out of the lift and around the corner, dumping her bag on an air-conditioning unit and rummaging around inside for her vape. She found the small pink cylinder and took a few puffs in quick succession. She knew she should quit. She *would* quit. But not today. Because today she had trolls. Her treacherous phone lit up with another ray of sunshine—Toni.

Sighing, Kit answered the incoming call. 'Hey, Toni,' she said, with as much enthusiasm as she could muster.

'Sweetheart'—Toni's patronising affection was immediately grating—'Jenny from JLM just told me you've booked two of her models for our US campaign?'

'I told you we'd be doing that,' Kit said, her tone intentionally breezy. 'They need lifestyle creative for in-store and we don't have global rights for our domestic creative.'

'But, darling, why not use *my* talent? I have some stunning creatures, like Victoria, a lovely little ballerina sprite from Russ—'

'You don't have any diversity,' Kit said bluntly. 'We've talked about this. Quinn is a beautiful trans model and that visibility is important. And beyond being exquisite, Jessa is First Nations, and, of *course*, I want to showcase Indigenous models in the US if I can.'

'Yes, yes to all that, but you said we would always use my girls, remember? That's what we decided in the beginning, darling, to keep costs down. What about Brooke? She's a big girl—size sixteen, at least.'

'Toni, can we . . .' Kit paused. 'The shoot is booked. It's happening. We are a tiny Aussie brand in a zoo of established brands over there: we *have* to invest. You know what Baby Romeo spends a year in marketing there? Three million dollars, just in the US! Do you know what we allocated? Two hundred and fifty K. It's laughable!'

'Oh, darling, brighten up! We're in Catalyst; the job is done. Remember how we celebrated? The champagne, the lunch at Icebergs? *They* will do all the heavy lifting; it's in their best interest!'

'How so?' Kit said, deliberately setting a trap for Toni.

'Retailers need the stock to move or they lose cash, darling!'

'That's not how it works,' Kit said, coming in for her slam dunk. 'They send it back to us, *we* lose cash—and bear all the freight costs.'

'Well, *that* doesn't make any sense!' Toni said, aghast. 'Why on earth did we agree to that?'

'Toni, *that* is retail, that is the model, there is no other way.' Kit no longer bothered to hide her exasperation. Toni paid no attention to the plan, then came in at the eleventh hour and tried to flip it. Also, she never wanted to spend a cent. Kit was no business Yoda, but she knew you had to spend money to make money, especially in a new market. *No one* knew about Second Day in the US, the most competitive beauty market in the world, so marketing dollars were needed badly. If they didn't do well after twelve months, Catalyst would drop them. Then

113

they'd have a stink on them. Then no other retailer over there would want them. It would be over.

Kit was feeling the weight of it all. Everyone was panting for newness: a new product, a new retailer, a big new ambassador—*new-new-new-bigger-better-more*. She assumed a big deal like Catalyst would buy her some breathing time, but that just led to a much bigger market operating at a much faster pace harassing her for more products, more media, more everything, more often. Kit was okay with two to three launches a year. They got to build up each product then bed it in with strong education and support. She saw other brands drop new products every three months, but while she was envious for a hot second, she reminded herself their model was to do fewer things better. Of *course*, she wanted to grow, but she firmly believed that if they focused on making great products and looked after the customer, the rest would take care of itself. A kind of strategic slowness. She was such a brand protectionist, Toni said, as though that were a bad thing. It would hinder growth, she warned. But Kit was well past caring what Toni thought.

'We all agreed to investing in the US,' Kit said wearily. 'You did, I did, Simon did, Camille did. Please don't—'

'And what about *us*? We spend, spend, spend, but we never pay ourselves, darling! Do you know how rare it is to be in profit? I can think of several companies that are bringing in a million plus a year in sales, but are still in the red.'

'Yes, we're in a good position, and I'm using that position to invest back into the company,' Kit said.

'Yes, but profits are for shareholders, too, sweetheart. That's the whole point of business!'

'It's a bit confusing, Toni. You're always pushing me to grow the brand and do retail; investing in the US is both these things, yet you're not on board.'

'Oh, honey,' Toni said. 'I let you run free with this company and you know it.'

'Toni,' Kit said, in a slow, careful tone, 'we said we would pay dividends provided the company didn't need the cash, but as I am trying to explain, the company *does* need it.'

'I know you've always saved your money, it's something you're very good at, but this is not *your* money, darling, it's the business's money and—'

'And I own most of that business,' Kit reminded her.

'Yet you barely even take a salary for yourself! There is no valour in poverty, sweetheart, I'll tell you that much for free. What's the point of having a successful business if you don't see any of that success in your bank account?' She paused, before saying in a quiet voice, 'I see how much is in the account, you know: there's over *three million dollars* just sitting there! And you are telling me we can't make a payment? That's absurd. Outrageous. *Criminal.*'

Something clicked in Kit: *Toni needed money!* That was what was behind all this.

'Toni, are you . . . Do you need some cash?' Kit asked gently.

Toni laughed forcefully. 'Of course not, don't be silly. I'm just . . . moving some investments around, you know how it is. And I'm keen to get what I am owed so I can tie it all up. Shall I chat to the accountant—what's-her-face . . . Melanie—about how to move on this?'

'It'll have to wait till the board meeting,' Kit said firmly. She could issue some dividends, but she absolutely would not be paying out all their profits. What if something happened? Like when they needed to bin a huge production of leave-in conditioner because the preservative was *too* natural and didn't stop rapidly developing mould from setting in? Kit could only feel secure if there was a substantial pile of cash on hand. It was just who she was.

'This is ridiculous,' Toni said, her voice low. 'I'm entitled to some of the money sitting in there. I'm thinking I might need to seek Gary's advice. I'm an owner, too; you seem to forget that.'

'You're going to use our company lawyer against me?' Kit couldn't hide the amusement in her voice. The days of being intimidated by Toni were well and truly gone. 'Look, relax. We'll chat about it at the board meeting. I have to go now. Bye, Toni.' Kit ended the call. She didn't regret much, but she *really* regretted not listening to Ari when he told her to keep Toni out of her business.

9

AFTER A TRYING DAY PUTTING out micro-fires and guessing which move would manoeuvre Second Day out of cancelled-adjacent, Kit left the office.

As the peak-hour traffic shuffled along at geriatric pace, Kit reluctantly hit play on the American business podcast she'd been interviewed for. Jordan had already listened and was forcing Kit to listen, too. Her notes: *You're fantastic but too self-deprecating. This is for the US not Oz. PLZ ADD EGO!!!*

Kit pressed play, tossed her phone onto the passenger seat and inhaled for strength in the face of forty-three minutes of audio torture. She rarely did podcasts; she hated the sound of her own voice, and the whole thing felt so transactional: the host needed a weekly ep and Kit was simply a tool to help her achieve that. Not once had she listened to an interview with herself and thought, *I am so enlightening. I should do more of these!*

'*Welcome to* How I Did It, *a podcast for founders about founders, and your weekly hit of hashtag career inspo! I'm Maisie Brenner, and this week I spoke with Kit Cooper, an exciting Australian entrepreneur—or should that be, entreprenHER!—who has just launched into Catalyst stores in the US, a huge coup for any brand, let alone an indie brand from down under. She joined me for a chat about how she did it, why raising capital wasn't for her, and what happens to a brand when an A-lister like Selena Gomez Instagrams your product!'*

'Entrepren*her* . . .' Kit muttered. 'Can't I have a vagina and be in business without being assigned a novelty title?'

She'd sensed doing this podcast was a waste of time, and as she listened she knew she'd find proof of this many times over. Jordan had Kit doing as much US press as possible, and Kit understood it was important, but did anyone *really* listen to these things? People creating the illusion that business was something you could plan and predict instead of mostly stress and guesswork . . . There was this expectation that just because you started a business, you could *explain* that business. Kit would always choose more time *doing* the thing over talking about it.

A guy on a Vespa in front of her missed the crucial change to green because he was texting. Kit gave him three courtesy seconds, then tooted. He turned and glared at her. She gave him a thumbs down and he drove off.

'Since coming up with the idea of her hair care line, Second Day, almost seven years ago, Kit has amassed legions of loyal fans—including Selena Gomez and Kylie Jenner, no less.'

'It was Kendall, but I'll take it,' Kit interjected.

'Quality of product really matters,' Kit's voice came through. *'But so does how you communicate with your customer, how you look*

after them. We value our community above all. You can get people in the door with cute packaging and influencers posting about you, but if people don't understand your product, or your product isn't genuinely effective or doesn't change people's habits, they won't come back.'

Maisie went on to ask about the secret to her success. What Kit *wished* she'd said was that she was a working creative who made a thing that didn't exist and then tried every day to explain and sell that thing to people. That was it. There was no magic business map. What she actually said was: *'I saw a gap for something that would make a specific hair texture, what I always referred to as Second Day Hair, that went-out-last-night hair that looks undone and cool. Since I couldn't find it, I decided to make it myself. It's definitely our hero product; we have over twenty thousand five-star reviews.'*

Jordan had drilled it into her that a listener would only retain one, maybe two things, and not for long, so make one product the focus, and for the love of god, *use stats.*

Maisie: *'But how did she know what to do? How do you jump from stylist to start-up? Kit is transparent about asking for help to get things up and running.'*

Kit: *'I think it's unhelpful and disingenuous to suggest I did this alone. I needed a lot of help. I was a freelancer with an agent controlling my schedule, then suddenly I was trying to find a temperature-controlled warehouse and learn the safety profile of preservatives!'*

Maisie: *'Kit admits she made a lot of mistakes along the way. But one thing she feels she did right was hiring a GM just ten months in. Hiring a senior role so early is an unusual step—founders usually hire down and do the heavy lifting themselves—but Kit maintains she made the right call.'*

Kit: *'The company had no chance if I oversaw logistics and inventory. I hired Camille, who came with two decades of beauty and retail experience. She was an expensive hire, but aside from having a newborn and desperately needing help, I knew if I had someone running the operations, I could do what I do best as founder. I know my strengths and my weaknesses: I am not good at business!'*

So you're a confident genius *and* an impostor?! Choose your team, woman!

Maisie: *'This sounds like some trademark Aussie self-deprecation. After all, could the founder of a company turning over millions of dollars really be "not good at business"? Kit bootstrapped the company— Second Day hasn't raised any capital so far—but would she ever take investment?'*

Kit: *'We're lucky enough that we don't need to just now: we have enough profit to invest back into our growth.'*

Ah, there it was: 'lucky'—a critical signifier to offset even the slightest hint of hubris. Australians were hypersensitive to both complaining *and* bragging, and women were never allowed to be proud of themselves lest they seemed up themselves, so Kit made sure to always express surprise about her (breezy! accidental! lucky!) success and downplay her own part in it. Her self-deprecation *was* authentic—she was making hair products, not saving lives—but she couldn't help thinking it would be more helpful for people to know it *was* possible for someone to be unskilled and out of their depth at finance and business, and still succeed. That the learning was in the doing. Hard things were hard. Building a business was hard. Making ideas stick, maintaining momentum was hard. Sometimes, rarely, an idea and passion were enough, but most of the time you needed more: financial leeway to make some mistakes, a hell of a good team, and true fans who buoyed you up and cheered you on no matter what. Spreading the idea that she was just #blessed and #grateful and #excitedaboutwhatsnext felt both deceitful and wicked. She wanted anyone out there struggling to feel seen, and those who had worked hard and guessed their way along to feel validated. Everyone was just putting one foot in front of the other, doing the next thing on the list. Kit had a job, like everyone else. Everyone needed to calm down. But she never said any of this, for fear of being branded a whinger, or ungrateful or, worst of all, unlikeable.

A text came through, and Siri paused the podcast to announce it.

'Message from Magdog: I'm here three cocktail emoji zero rush my love I repeat you are safe to be late five turtle emoji love you two unicorn emoji poo emoji.'

Maisie: *'Initially a direct-to-consumer brand, the overheads were low. And because Kit came into the game with credibility and celebrity advocates, Second Day was immediately profitable.'*

Kit recognised her privilege and how it had helped with her brand. She was a white woman with a decent profile and celebrity clients swimming in a small pond. Had she cheated the system? Or had she seized the opportunity, like anyone else would have?

Maisie: *'Does she have advice for any founders starting out?'*

Kit: *'I'm going to steal from my hero here, Seth Godin, who says if you try to be everything to everyone, then by default you become average. Instead, be really specific about what you're making or doing. I made a really specific cream for a really specific look, but I believed it would find its audience.'*

'Got your Seth mention in, phew,' Kit scolded herself, as she parked the car.

Kit: '*Oh, and hire people who have the skills you lack and always trust your gut.*'

'Groundbreaking! Never heard that before! Give that woman a trophy!' she yelled as she turned off her car, grabbed her handbag from the passenger seat and opened the door.

Kit walked down the hazardously steep Darlinghurst street, looking for the wine bar Maggie had suggested they meet. She had exactly one hour and five minutes before her nanny Lily finished, so this would be one hell of a hasty catch-up, but time with Maggie was always worth it. It was a critical line break for each of them before they returned home to the chaos and children and mental load.

Finally spotting the ratty, graffiti-covered door she'd been told to look for, Kit pushed it and walked in. She blinked a few times to adjust to the dimly lit room. To her right was a row of jewel-toned upholstered booths with colourful marble tables, and on her left a long bar covered in bulbous lamps, wild vases and, even though it was only just after five, lots of people. She felt like she'd stumbled into a bar during the Prohibition. Kit *loved* it. She felt like she should be ordering a negroni, lighting up an ultra-thin menthol and making eyes at handsome young waiters.

She saw Maggie waving at her from the last booth, her red curls bouncing madly, her thick fringe accentuating her feline green eyes, her low-cut black top serving up some truly glorious cleavage. Maggie was not a trend tryer or a fashion lover. She had her signature look, she loved it, and she didn't deviate. She had applied the same black kohl before bed since she was sixteen because it lined her eyes perfectly for the next morning. 'It's my version of your Second Day Hair,' she claimed.

Kit walked down to meet her, scanning the crowd as she did. Lots of complicated haircuts, sneakers and t-shirts: these were her kind of people.

'Oooh, this place is *goood*,' Kit said as she slid into a seat across from her friend.

'It's the tits,' Maggie agreed. 'Cow Studio did the interiors. They're so good. I'm livid.'

'So do a bar that's better,' Kit said as she reached for the drinks menu.

'I *would* if I had their budgets. They do *all* the Brewster venues, which is why they can smear Gaetano Pesce and Murano all over the place . . . I mean, would you *look* at those sconces? Fucking stunning.'

'It actually reminds me of your home a little bit,' Kit said truthfully.

'Shh, I love you, stop trying to make me feel better. It's okay; I will twist my rage into admiration with the help of this.' She tipped her martini—double olives, always gin—towards Kit.

'You'd never jump ship, would you?' Kit asked, turning towards the bar to try to get someone's attention for her express happy hour.

No one looked over. She might need to walk over and order, a crime on par with manslaughter in a bar like this.

Maggie exhaled and rested her chin on one hand. 'I've considered it. But Henry is so good to me, and I have so much freedom. I know the guys over there are all whipped by the creative lead, Kasumi: it's all just whatever she wants. I'd hate that. I mean, she's a knockout, absolute gun, but . . .'

'You need to be the creative lead. So do I. We're ogres.'

Kit finally got a young waitress's attention. She had a short shaggy mullet, full lips and the kind of enormous brown Pixar eyes that ensured she pulled in three times the tips of everyone else.

'What are you having, babe?' she asked, leaning on the table with both hands as though they were old friends.

'Negroni, please,' Kit said. 'And olives. And fries. Please tell me you have fries.' Kit pulled her phone out and placed it in front of her in case Lily or Hyun or Camille or any number of people needed her.

'I gotcha, babe,' the waitress said. She winked and strolled off.

'Can you even *imagine* what having that kind of self-confidence must be like?' Kit asked, incredulous. 'She's phenomenal. That face. I want to shoot her for a campaign.'

'Whoa, slow down—I can see your boner from here,' Maggie joked.

'I'd *love* to see a boner, just quietly.' Kit sighed. Since she and Ari had separated three years ago—Kit finally concluding that having no partner was better than an unreliable, hectic partner who was away ninety percent of the time—she hadn't given much energy to finding a replacement. Between Gretel and Second Day, she had no time left. Certainly none for guys who turned out to be either flakes or weirdos. One guy she slept with had 'do not resuscitate' tattooed across his collarbones; the next listened exclusively to sob folk and made his own kombucha. When he asked if she wanted to go to bush church with him and his family, she realised she needed to get off the apps. Personal introductions only from now on.

'Did Moustache ever message?' Maggie asked. Moustache was a friend of a friend of Camille's, a private chef who catered to the whims of the very rich or very busy. He and Kit had slept together after a fun dinner and then drinks at a whisky bar, and he'd said he wanted to cook for her the following week. That was three weeks ago.

'He did not. And I wanted him to, which is the annoying part.' Kit grimaced. 'He's been eliminated.'

'What a muppet. He had promise, too.' Maggie loved hearing about Kit's sex life, on the rare occasions she had one.

'The sex was good,' Kit said thoughtfully, 'but he was full of shit. Did I tell you his ick is if a girl sends him a link to a song? That's basically my love language. He was the one who suggested dinner, by the way, but I knew he wouldn't follow through.'

'But you *did* get laid, that's the important thing.'

'It kind of is at this point.'

'You deserve to be in dick paradise. Speaking of dicks, is Ari back?'

'Next week.' Kit looked around anxiously for her drink: time was a-wasting.

'The full set coming?' Maggie took a deep sip of her almost-finished martini—she didn't drive to work, so she could have two, unlike Kit—and raised her brows.

'Yeah, I presume so.' Ari had been dating both a man and a woman for the past year, they all lived together in LA in a fully committed throuple.

'Tell me again which type they are? I was trying to explain to Sam but couldn't remember.'

'They're a triangle, meaning they're all in a relationship with each other. A V is when only one person is in a relationship with two people, but those two are not in a relationship with each other.'

'It's a bit sexy, isn't it?' Maggie said lasciviously.

'Hard work, if you ask me. *Two* people's moods and routines to accommodate? No thanks.'

'Gretel like them?' Maggie asked.

'Of course, she does: the three of them spoil her rotten.'

'Can you imagine your dad coming home with a boyfriend *and* a girlfriend? Like, in the eighties, can you imagine?'

'Ronny is *definitely* the type,' Kit said, laughing. Maggie's dad—also named Ron, though their fathers could not be more different—was the most white-bread-and-margarine father on this green earth. He thought Maggie having three ear piercings was outrageous.

'Here you go, babe.' The waitress was back with Kit's drink and a bowl of olives. 'Jai makes them nice and strong—just how we like it, right?' Another wink and she was off.

'The winking is too much,' observed Maggie. 'She doesn't need it.'

Kit smiled and took a deep sip of her drink, feeling the warmth move down her throat. *Hoo* boy, did she need this today.

Maggie's phone buzzed. She looked at it and slammed it down, rolling her eyes. 'If the school sends me one more email about head lice this term, I will scream. They should send one saying year two *doesn't* have head lice—*that* would be news.'

'I got a foot-and-mouth missive last week. And gastro is ripping through Gretel's class.'

'NO!' Maggie said, her face deadly serious. 'You must take her out. Now. Before it's too late. The shit . . . the vom . . . don't risk it.'

'I can't take her out,' Kit said. 'I don't have anyone to look after her. Lily has uni, and work is mental right now. I know, shut up, it kills me—I fully expect diarrhoea to kick off any moment.'

'They don't tell you all this before you have kids,' Maggie said, licking her lips. 'That your whole life becomes school admin and sickness avoidance. I need a PA just to handle school comms.'

'At least you have Sam,' Kit said. Maggie had two kids and worked full-time, but she also had a husband. Single parenting was a whole other level.

'Yeah, well, Sam is doing his best to win the Guy Who Attends The Most Conferences award, but I know I'm lucky to have him. Has Ari been *any* better lately?'

Kit shook her head and took a sip. Ari had not been fulfilling his half of their co-parenting deal, not even close. He never had. Kit was at the point where she'd finally had enough.

'The custody situation could not have been simpler,' she said. 'It was half-half, that was the agreement. We kept it flexible so that it could be whatever worked best with our schedules, but the split had to be even over the year, you know?'

Maggie snorted. 'Even my arse.'

'I am the primary carer, though, so wherever I am he has to work around that—meaning no stealing her away to live in New Zealand or bloody Stockholm or Narnia or wherever he bases himself for a job.'

Maggie frowned. 'You are far too good to him—always have been.'

'Well, not anymore,' Kit said. 'Gretel being in school has added so much more to my plate, Second Day really needs me, and I just fucking need him to do his half. This drop-in-for-a-minute-between-projects thing is bullshit.'

'It *really* is,' Maggie agreed.

'He needs a proper base here in Sydney; somewhere that isn't a hotel or Airbnb. How is this stable for Gretel? Any of it?' Kit could feel her anger rising.

'Is it affecting her?' Maggie asked with concern.

Kit thought about that and had to admit that it wasn't—yet. Gretel actually loved getting away from boring Mummy with her boring bedtime rules and boring dinners. But she was young; things would change.

'What shits me,' Kit said, 'aside from his schedule and inconsistency and unreliability and lots of other things, is that he is a total Hollywood dad. The fun guy with the exciting life who swoops in and lets her stay up late and watch Netflix on her iPad before school and eat pizza for breakfast. Or he takes her to set and everyone spoils and panders to her. I'm the Stasi by comparison, because I'm trying my best to give Gretel routine and stability. It's so fucking frustrating.'

'Oh, my love, I don't doubt it,' Maggie said. 'If it's any comfort, I have a *lot* of notes on Sam's parenting. I realised he's'—she did air quotes—'"weaponising his incompetence". Last week I was stuck on a job and I texted him: *you're on dinner.* He goes, *sure.* Then ten minutes later: *which sausages do they like, beef or pork?* Then, the next text: *how many potatoes should I cook?* Then, and this is when I lost my shit, a photo of the potatoes on two trays in the oven, asking if that was enough. Like, *make a fucking decision!* All I do is make decisions; can't he make one about fucking potatoes? It shits me to tears, I can't tell you.' Maggie shook her head and reached for an olive.

'Maybe he's scared of getting it wrong because you'll eat him alive, so it's easier for him just to check?' Kit offered, brows raised, lips pursed. She really liked Sam. She could see how Maggie could be scary.

'He *should* be scared.' She sighed. 'At least we are aligned on the kids having routine,' she conceded. Then, in a kinder tone: 'He dresses them appallingly, but he's a great dad.' She looked deep into Kit's eyes. 'You handle single mum life so fucking well. But we bitches need help to rule the world. Call your lawyer and make Ari get a place here and do his bit, or *you* will start getting spicy with custody. Like, *Enough, Ari. You're someone's dad. Act like it.*'

'Yeah,' Kit agreed. 'I know I should. I think I put it off because legal drama on top of everything else might tip me over the edge . . . Did I tell you our manufacturer just put their fill prices up by a *third*? For no reason? How is that legal?! We're already haemorrhaging cash over in the US—and look, Catalyst have been really good, I *dreamed* of this, but we're still such a small team, and my guy on the ground over there is a pathological liar; I've caught him out, like, four times already, but he—'

'Hey.' Maggie reached over with both hands and grabbed Kit's. 'I don't understand what you're saying, it's all word salad to me, but I get that it's a lot. You always get through, though; I've seen you do it again and again. You are so fucking capable. Do you need to fly over there and kick some heads or kiss some rings while Ari is with Gretel? Can you do that?'

Kit felt tears spring to her eyes. All it took was the smallest amount of kindness, of care, and she crumbled. She was so tired of holding it all together, all the time. She looked after Gretel, her team, her brand, her profile, but who looked after her? Maggie. Maggie did. And had done since Kit was twenty-three, friendless and fresh to Sydney. They had met at a soulless housewarming hosted by a hairdresser named Julian; Maggie complimented Kit on her platform shoes and offered her a Vogue Menthol, and they became instant friends. Having a friend that spanned decades was a unique and special thing: Maggie knew all Kit's secrets, spirals, successes. She was her person.

'Listen to me,' Maggie said, squeezing her friend's hands. 'You're doing such . . . a . . . good . . . *job*. We see it. We love you: you're our number one.' Maggie's enormous eyes, outlined with lashings of clumpy mascara, bore into Kit's. Kit saw them glimmer with tears, even in the low light. Maggie felt things deep.

'Something a li'l hot for my ladies,' the waitress interrupted, placing a bowl spilling over with fries on the table. 'Another martini?' she asked, looking at Maggie.

'Fast as you can,' Maggie responded, without breaking eye contact with Kit. 'Please.'

The waitress spun off and Kit quickly wiped away a tear. She tapped her phone to check the time. She had nineteen minutes before she'd need to leave, and even that was pushing it. She grabbed a pincer full of fries and popped them in her mouth, piping hot, salty as the sea and absolutely perfect.

'Thank you for that pep talk. I needed that, I needed you, and I needed these,' she said, grabbing more fries.

'Hey,' Maggie said conspiratorially, as she plucked a fry from the bowl. 'What if we *both* went to the US? Henry's been pestering me to do a buying trip. Well, in LA, in truth, but New York is basically LA.' Henry was a bookish, avuncular man in his sixties who essentially let Maggie run his design firm, as long as she kept the big clients happy and the big contracts coming in.

Kit smiled. 'Remember last time we were there—what was it, ten, twelve years ago?—and I went home with that guy whose pick-up line was: "You look like my sister"?!'

They burst into laughter.

When Kit recovered, she said, 'I can't go just now, but I'll need to soon, I reckon . . .'

'When was the last time we went away together?' Maggie asked, wiping her salty fingers on her velvet pants. 'And *don't say the Hunter Valley*. That wasn't a holiday; that was a hellscape. I haven't had merlot since. Disgusting.'

'I think I've reached the stage of life where I understand why women go to health retreats,' Kit remarked. 'They always sounded so boring, but *I get it now*. They serve fries and martinis, yeah?'

Maggie screwed up her face in disgust. 'Can we not? All that five am tai chi and all those depressing vegan salads. The last time I went to one of those I was five weeks pregnant. The morning sickness kicked in and all I wanted to do was vomit and cry and eat hash browns, but they keep serving me raw milk and alfalfa and I hated it SO MUCH . . .'

'Okay, maybe I wouldn't love it,' Kit said.

'Meh, if you're not pregnant, it might be okay.'

'Think that ship has sailed,' Kit said, wolfing down as many fries as she could as fast as she could.

Maggie cocked her head and narrowed her eyes. 'Really? No more?'

Kit looked at Maggie as though she had just offered her some heroin. 'I'm thirty-seven and single, and all I do is work. How am I going to do all the things it takes to have another kid—meet someone, like them enough to breed, get hitched in Vegas—while I'm running Second Day?'

'But in your heart, your heart of *heart* of hearts, are you done?'

'I am,' Kit said. 'Gretel and I are a good team. I have my baby girl. I'm good.'

'Dreamiest of teams.'

'Speaking of, I've got to go—Lily has a lecture tonight.'

Kit looked at her phone, seeing two texts from Jordan, a trail of Slack messages from her staff, a WhatsApp from Shona asking if anyone has seen Jamie's lunchbox and multiple Instagram DMs from Hyun. She swallowed the remainder of her drink, cursing the fact that she had already used up her weekly fry quota and it was only Tuesday.

'Never hire a nanny who has a life,' Maggie advised.

'Oh, Lily has no life. She just studies. She's such a sweetie, so book smart and gentle,' Kit said, standing up. 'Gretel is learning all kinds of shit I could never teach her. Plus, she loves doing all the puzzles and painting and I really, *really* don't.'

'Outsource it all, I say. Let's get that chef happening! Where's your masseuse, darling?' Maggie cried.

Kit scoffed as she leaned over to give Maggie a kiss. '*Past* me froze a batch of Mexican chilli for future me,' Kit said smugly, 'so I don't need a chef tonight. I love past me, so thoughtful. You staying?'

'These drinks are twenty-two dollars; I'm not going anywhere till this glass is empty. Plus, it means Sam does dinner and bath, an hour of the day I will avoid at all costs. I'm going to do some emails and perv on the youth.'

'Smart. I love you—see you at Pilates.'

Kit picked up her vintage Fendi handbag, a late-night purchase from her favourite online vintage store, and walked out of the bar and into the street. The bright summer sunshine hit her in the eyes, a confusing contrast to the dark, glamorous interior of the bar, and she had a crazy idea to take Gretel for a quick swim when she got home. *Why waste a perfectly warm evening?* she asked herself, the negroni successfully dulling her anxious work thoughts and reminding her, if only for an hour of the buzz, that there was more to life than Second Day.

10

MARCH

KIT AWOKE AT SIX AND immediately sat up like a possessed doll. Launch day. Their new smoothing balm, Calm Down, was out today. Her brain had been cycling furiously from two to four am, and she was shattered. Historically, trying to launch a new product and mumming had always been a disaster; she hoped today might be different. She'd done most of Gretel's lunchbox last night, that would help, and with a bit of luck she could knock off some work now.

Kit grabbed her phone and fired off a text to Lily, considering neither time, boundaries nor professionalism, asking if she could possibly do a few hours this morning. For the thousandth time Kit considered a live-in au pair before shutting the idea down. There was only one kid, and she was at school most of the time—and even though Kit and Gretel were together before and after school, it mostly ended up with the TV on and Kit on her laptop, rather than the meaningful eye-gazing and rolling in crisp autumn leaves she'd assumed would happen. What was really *missing* from this picture was not an au pair or nanny, it was Gretel's father. In these moments, she wanted to stab Ari in the eye with a fork. This man never hesitated to accept gigs in other countries for months at a time, as though Gretel, as though *Kit*, didn't matter. It was appalling to Kit that he could leave his little girl for such lengths of time; Kit felt unfinished, incomplete, when she was away from Gretel for even one night.

Sensing she had just minutes before Gretel came in, Kit picked up her laptop from the floor, where she had left it around midnight, and navigated to the staging website to see if her designer had somehow read her eleven pm email and implemented the changes needed to the body copy and font size.

Of course he had not, and nor should he have, given that was only seven overnight hours ago. Kit stopped and took a box breath: four in, four hold, four out, just like that podcast had said to do when she felt her stress hormones take over. It did nothing; what she needed was coffee. Cortisol was always gonna win today, why not give it some goddamn petrol.

She shot off an overly polite, *no-big-deal!!* message to the designer and started to get up, before cursing and sitting back down to write a thankyou email to her team. Why did she always leave these things till launch morning? She *knew* this morning would be crazy, yet she always left things like the team email and even her Instagram posts to the day-of. She never learned her lessons. This idea that all founders had ideas and then also knew how to *execute* those ideas was complete horseshit to Kit. The team were prepared, but as usual Kit had not allowed enough time for her approvals and final checks and inevitable tweaks. She needed to do better by them and for them.

Suddenly, there was an almighty crash in Gretel's room next door. Kit pushed her laptop aside and bolted to her daughter's bedroom.

With immense relief, she saw that her daughter was *not* pinned underneath her dresser gasping for life. She had simply pushed a pile of books onto the floor in her effort to get to the one at the very bottom.

'Oh, baby, that noise scared me!' She scooped up her little girl and gave her a tight squeeze, kissing her multiple times on the top of her head. Gretel, being Gretel, immediately wriggled to be let free.

As Kit got to work tidying the books and Gretel thoughtfully arranged a selection of soft toys on her bed, Gretel said, 'Can I stay with you today, Mummy?'

Kit felt her heart take a hit. It was bad enough she got Gretel to school just as the gates opened most days, as well as putting her into after-school care, but knowing she didn't want to be there at all was the kicker. She grabbed her daughter's pudgy little hand and kissed it, looking into her eyes.

'Imagine how sad Reya and Ava and Frankie would be if you didn't go? They would cry so much the whole school would flood.'

Gretel didn't smile, but nor did she become upset and indignant, which was a win.

'Ready for breakfast? I might even let you watch some *Bluey* this morning . . .'

Gretel snapped her head around. TV in the morning was not allowed. This was highly unusual.

'But it's not the weekend . . .' she said suspiciously.

'No, it's not, but Mummy has to be on her computer this morning because today her new product comes—'

'I'll choose. You always choose the bad *Blueys*.'

Kit nodded. Gretel's job was to teach her patience and keep her grounded, she knew that.

'Sure. But first I'm going to go make some yummy porridge.' She kissed Gretel on the forehead and walked back to her room to get her robe.

'No hot fruit!' Gretel yelled.

'No hot fruit,' Kit confirmed. Kit had once dared to put banana and blueberries into the porridge and in doing so had scarred her daughter permanently.

As she walked to the kitchen, Kit checked her phone; nothing from Lily yet. Shit, she still had to finish the team email. She darted back to her room for her laptop and carried it back to the kitchen. Her phone chimed as she added secret chia seeds and LSA to the porridge. Gretel was yet to notice them, but since the rest of her diet consisted of crackers, jam sandwiches and squeezy yoghurts, they might be the only nutrition she was getting.

Good morning happy launch day

It was Camille, brilliant at running a company; wildly allergic to punctuation.

Happy launch day! Kit replied. *I've been told backend is working w review at 7.30 as slated. Customers expecting to buy right on 8.30 so let's stay on it*

Camille came back with: *noted social and EDM will be staggered to avoid a blowout and keep order flow reasonable*

Thank you. Here's to another million-dollar day!!!

Kit was joking. Well, *half*-joking. They had done a million-dollar day for their invisible texture spray last year, which absolutely floored them. Kit thought it was a strong product, maybe even as strong as the original texture cream, and their pre-launch campaign was incredible, but they *had* spent a lot of cash on influencers in the lead-up. They had not done the same for this product; the budget wouldn't allow it, given the inventory and logistics costs required for the US. Kit was afraid they would learn the true reach of the brand today, which added to her already bulging anxiety sack. Also, did people understand what a smoothing cream did? That it wasn't just for straight hair or blow-dries? How magic and multipurpose it was? No matter their hair type? She was always like this when a new product came out—desperate for everyone to *really* get it, and *really* understand it, and use it *properly* so they got all the benefits. Camille was focused on sales; Kit panicked about the education.

Camille sent back a string of emojis just as the porridge began to boil over and spill down the saucepan sides and into the grooves of the stovetop.

'No, no, NO!' yelled Kit as she quickly tried to stop the boil and clean the mess. But nothing had the determination of spilt porridge; it got into every crevice and dripped down onto three separate surfaces.

'Are you okay, Mum?' Gretel asked, entering the room with her toy cockatoo in a shoe box nest, surrounded by small plastic figurines, scrunchies and some ribbons from her beloved pile.

'Yep, just a spill. Would you like to be my helper and get the frozen strawberries from the freezer?'

'No, thank you,' Gretel said sweetly, leaving the room again.

Kit's phone pinged again: a Slack notification from her IT manager.

We have a problem with the loyalty customer checkout, may not be able to go live 8.30, he wrote.

Okay, thanks for heads-up . . . what would happen if we launched without that? Kit asked.

Thousands of our most loyal customers would not get their points and hate us?

'Fuck,' whispered Kit.

Understood. So launch would be when? Kit wasn't sure she wanted the answer.

Working as fast as possible. Hopefully by 9.

Oh! That's fine, heart attack averted. Thank you!

Kit slammed her phone on the counter and rubbed her eyes. She quickly served up two bowls of porridge—adding frozen strawberries and sprinkles to Gretel's; yoghurt, walnuts and honey to her own—and hollered for Gretel to come and eat. She juiced a sad old orange she hoped wouldn't taste rank and poured it into a plastic cup adorned with unicorns for her daughter because: vitamins.

Gretel finally stomped in, a ratty, tight mermaid costume twisted around the upper half of her body, face brewing a storm.

'Honey, what's wrong?' Kit asked.

'This dress is so so stupid—it won't even BE ON!'

Kit was careful not to laugh. Gretel's hanger was intense in the mornings; she was to be treated with extreme caution.

'Okay,' said Kit, repressing her smile with everything she had. 'I think it's because you've outgrown it; that was from when you were really little. Here, let me help you.'

She tried to rearrange the tight mess of polyester and sequins, but it was a dress for a much smaller, younger Gretel. Gretel wriggled and fought against every move, grunting with annoyance. Finally, as Kit got it the right way and tugged the 'tail' down over Gretel's legs, she lost it.

'WHY IS THERE MY FEET? IT'S SUPPOSED TO BE A TAIL!'

Kit looked down and coughed to stifle her laugh.

'Honey, this is a costume to *pretend* to be a mermaid. If you had a tail, how could you walk?'

'I DON'T WALK—I *SWIM*!'

'Hey,' said Kit, 'why don't we have some porridge and fix this after, okay? I put extra sprinkles on . . .'

'Mum, mermaids eat *WATER*!' Gretel cried, her face crumpled in exasperation at her stupid non-mermaid mother.

Kit's phone pinged three times in succession in the background.

The freezer door, left open, beeped.

The fan from the stove was still on, whirring into Kit's brain.

Kit wanted to scream. She took a deep breath and focused on her daughter. She held her, despite her resistance, and patted her back.

'Hey, this is fixable. It totally is. I will make sure you can't see any feet. But first, let's have some breakfast.'

'I'm not hungry,' Gretel said sullenly.

Kit changed tack. 'Okay, know what? Special mermaid treat. I'm going to put some Nutella on top, okay? Will that be tasty?'

Nutella was Kit's red button, for emergency use only. The Queen of Don't Want To begrudgingly allowed herself to be plonked at the breakfast bar.

'Have some juice, little girl.'

'I'm not hungry for that.'

Kit's phone pinged twice more. There was less than an hour till launch and Kit had no team email, no nanny, no social media copy written and a daughter several kilometres off being ready for school.

She gave Gretel a spoon and sat down to eat with her. *Please let one of those texts be good news*, she begged silently.

'You *love* orange juice!' Kit enthused, as if a reminder would change Gretel's mind.

'My tummy hurts,' Gretel countered.

'Gretel, come on, breakfast is happening and you know it,' said Kit, kindness finally paving the way for frustration. 'We need to give our body batteries for the day. Eat, *now*.'

Gretel folded her arms, gave her mother a nuclear stink eye and a deep, lowered chin. 'You're a *mean* mummy and you always will be.'

Kit's patience reserves had dried up. She wanted to check her texts but had set a rule of no phones while eating with Gretel. She wanted her daughter to eat her goddamn breakfast so her personality would return. She wanted her website to be functional *and* beautiful. She wanted to be better at forward planning, so she didn't try to launch products and parent simultaneously. And she wanted her fucking ex to *start being Gretel's fucking father*. She was done enabling his Peter Pan lifestyle. As Maggie said, he was a *father* and he needed to *act like it*. Furious, Kit picked up her phone to text him.

We need a discussion about the amount of time you spend with G. This is not working.

She hit send and felt her pulse race. It would be a jarring text to receive out of the blue, but she didn't care. He needed to step up.

'Mum, no *phones*!' Gretel was not one to let a rule break slip past.

A text pinged. *That was fast for Ari*, she thought.

'Sorry, sorry,' she said. 'You're right. It's just, this morning I have a new product out and . . .' Why bother? Gretel was five. She didn't understand or care, and nor should she.

Kit glanced at her screen and saw a Slack notification: *We will have it live by 8.30.*

Oh thank god. *One* thing was working.

Buoyed by the small win, Kit was able to source some patience and calm for Gretel. *Emotions give the opportunity to connect*, she reminded herself. *Emotions give the opportunity to connect.*

'Hey,' she said, sitting down and looking directly at Gretel. One shoulder of the costume was almost cutting off circulation to her chubby little forearm.

'You're frustrated, aren't you? Because your costume isn't how you thought.'

Gretel said nothing.

'It can be tricky when you imagine something and it doesn't work the way you hoped,' Kit said. 'I see that. It happens to me, too.' Gentle parenting 101.

Nothing.

'Was it the mermaid tail that was important? Or did you just want to look fabulous? Because if it's *fabulous* you want, I have something amazing you can wear.' Kit smiled enigmatically.

Sure enough, Gretel's curiosity was piqued. She looked up at her mother. 'A new costume?'

'Even better. Let's eat our porridge, then I can show it to you.' Kit was creating a dangerous level of allure and intrigue based on absolutely nothing, but she had no choice.

'Is it mine to keep?' Gretel asked.

'Just wait till you see it,' Kit said. 'Oh, look at that big glob of Nutella—it looks like it's that little strawberry's beanie! Ha ha ha!'

Gretel reluctantly began eating, which satisfied Kit enough that she could set about finishing off her lunchbox. The change in mood was instant once Gretel's blood sugar went up: pure magic.

A WhatsApp chimed from the kindy group.

Reminder the tickets for Alice in Wonderland go on sale today 9 am sharp!!

Last year they sold out in an hour so get in fast guys ☺

Who is going the wed night??

I can't find the shoes they need for the production, where is everyone buying them pls

Lewis Carroll was a grown man obsessed with a little girl, I can't believe they chose this for the production, it's so problematic

Where are the tickets on sale???

Olivier has lost his bucket hat has anyone taken it home by mistake I checked lost prop already

Gretel's school production. Of *course*, the tickets were on sale this morning. Kit added an alarm at eight fifty-five am to remind her. She *could not* miss out on these tickets.

'Mum, I have a new funny face, do you want to see it?' Gretel said suddenly.

'Of course,' Kit said, turning to see Gretel attempt to cross her eyes. 'I love it! Very funny. Hey, once you're done there, you can pop on your uniform then maybe you can watch *Bluey* . . .'

'But what about my new costume you said about?!' Gretel asked.

'You know, I think that's an after-school one,' Kit said. 'It's so delicate and precious and we have to do your hair and you can wear Mummy's glitter shoes . . . Let's *really* dress up after school. I will, too, okay?'

'But you said *after porridge*!'

Kit forgot that bit. A lie would be required.

'Well, the thing is, it *is* a new costume for you. I have to go collect it. So it'll be here after school. How *exciting*! Now, let's get dressed. I think we should do space buns in your hair today, what do you think?'

Gretel allowed herself to be walked out of the kitchen to her room. Kit hated how often she relied on smokescreens and lies and tricks for her daughter. How often she was rushing her and distracting her. But what choice did she have? Today of all days, Kit just needed things to keep moving.

As she brushed off Gretel's school skirt from yesterday, Kit's phone pinged. It was Jordan.

Happy launch day! Let's hope it kills it. HMU setting up and Hyun getting coffee. There is parking for you in the Deer Studios spot. x

'Oh my god,' Kit whispered. 'Oh my fucking god.' *How did she forget?* Kit was supposed to be at her founder's shoot in four minutes' time. At a studio thirty minutes away. In the opposite direction to Gretel's school.

I have a bit of a situation with G, she typed, hands shaking. *I am so sorry. I will be there as soon as possible but likely not for 45!!*

Lies fell from her mouth with such ease now. She didn't even notice she was doing it. This treading water wouldn't work forever. When would she sink? *Oh, sinking seemed like such a wonderful notion*, she thought. Peaceful, calm, quiet . . .

Another ping. This one from Rat.

Soooooo turns out Xanthe IS running a semi-brothel from the house which I thought she might be cos even she doesn't use enough apps for the amount of D walking through the door ANYWAY we had a fight and the energy is off so I need to come stay a few nites ok??

Before Kit could even respond she sent a follow on.

Dont have a menty b I can cook dinner and look after G xxxxxxx

Kit sighed. Rat's version of looking after Gretel was making a cake at eight pm, followed by zero cleaning up, and three giant spoonsful of red icing at bedtime. She was a pure liability.

Yes yes you have your key xxxx

Kit was impressed Rat had warned her; usually she just showed up.

As Kit quickly rifled through her daughter's drawers looking for underpants and socks, she heard Gretel make a strange whimpering noise. Kit turned around to look at her daughter, who was looking back with fear and panic in her eyes. Before Kit could ask her what was wrong, she began vomiting all over the carpet.

11

MAY

KIT HEARD A KNOCK ON her hotel room door. She looked at her watch: 9.55. She'd agreed to be ready to go ten minutes ago. She was speaking on a panel with two other founders on the topic of 'What Creates a Successful Business' and she was all hot nervous cucumber, rather than the cool calm one she'd been envisioning. She had spent too long trying to navigate Gretel's school's ludicrous canteen app and doing her winged liner. Plus, she'd gone to sleep far too late. *Be better*, she reprimanded herself as she tried to balance on one foot while sliding the other into a dainty heel.

'One sec!' she called to Jordan, who was waiting on the other side of the door.

Jordan saw everything as marketing, so she always accompanied Kit, even though Kit had told her repeatedly she was fine to do these things solo. In truth, Kit was glad Jordan ignored her; it was nice to have one of your people in a room full of strangers.

Kit jammed her room card, phone, mints and lip gloss into a preposterously small handbag, and did a final check of herself in the full-length mirror. What stared back at her, she hoped, was what people thought a beauty founder looked like. She'd spent extra time styling her new shaggy bob—cut in a feverish blitz of PMS, but as yet to be regretted—because if you're the founder of a styling range, you must always have perfect hair. She wore an oversized blue suit over one of her favourite vintage tees to show she was definitely still a creative and not a business bot, three necklaces around her neck and her sleeves pushed up. She had added new Gucci heels for psychological edge. She felt the look was considered and polished but still fun; consciously selected armour against Kit's aversion to public speaking, and also against the other founders, who always seemed to look more put together and shinier than her, with their elegant shirt dresses and complicated blouses.

Kit opened the hotel door to Jordan, who looked Kit up and down quickly then said, 'You look cute. Come on.'

She strode off so fast Kit had to rush to keep up. 'I'm not on till ten fifteen, right?'

'I texted you! It starts at ten. You're on *now*.'

'But I need coffee,' Kit said plaintively. 'My brain won't brain without coffee, you know that.'

They arrived at the lifts and Jordan stabbed the button impatiently.

'Can I be honest?' she said, both women knowing full well Jordan knew no alternative. 'I think you're actually better *not* on coffee. You speak kinda fast and get a bit too . . . candid.'

'Oh.' Kit was taken aback. *She* thought coffee made her very engaging and clever.

'It's only forty-five minutes,' Jordan said reassuringly, her hand on Kit's shoulder. 'You'll be great.'

They walked quickly past the double doors to the conference room, which buzzed with the sound of five hundred women who had paid eighty dollars to spend a day listening to founders and entrepreneurs 'reveal the habits, routines and secrets to their success'.

'Who am I on with again?' Kit asked.

'Piper Beaty from Red Carpet, and Storm Lyon-Frederick from some tea brand. The interviewer is Carly Kingsman.'

'From the news?' Kit asked.

'From the news,' Jordan confirmed.

'Weird,' Kit said.

A middle-aged guy wearing a *Rick and Morty* t-shirt and jeans so ripped that a full knee was on show was waiting next to the stage door, holding a mic pack.

'Ms Cooper?' he said, his eyes flitting between Kit and Jordan.

'Present and accounted for!' Kit said brightly, assuming the persona of someone who'd recently had coffee.

'Turn, please,' he said brusquely.

He clipped the mic pack onto the waistband of her pants and thrust the mic at her, gesturing for her to feed the wire through to her lapel. As she did so, Kit's mind went completely, terrifyingly blank. Everything smart she wanted to say onstage, stuff that might genuinely help the people who'd paid to be here, vanished, and she could barely swallow for nervousness. It never got easier for her. As she kept telling Jordan, she was a *backstage* person. Events like this killed her.

'You good?' Jordan asked.

'Yep, yep, it's just the usual me stuff . . .' Kit closed her eyes, put her hand on her heart and took a deep breath. She tried to imagine herself onstage, laughing and confident. It didn't work at all.

She opened her eyes to see *Rick and Morty* motioning for her to join the others onstage. Kit placed her bag on a table with a couple of others and strode towards the stage with a big fake smile.

Behind her, Jordan whispered, 'Bingo on "journey", "self-belief" and "purpose". See you at twelve.'

'And what advice would you give to yourself back when you were just starting out? What do you wish you'd known then that you know now?'

Carly asked the question then sat back in her soft pink armchair; the entire stage, even the flowers and the guests' water glasses, were various shades of pink.

Piper went first. Kit had met her before; they were among only a handful of young female founders in the hair space in Australia. Piper had been in the game for longer than Kit; she had already built up and sold a business—a vodka drink in a can, from memory. Her hot tool brand, Red Carpet, was huge in the US, where she based herself now. She wore her long, buttery blonde hair like a crown, and had long ago locked in her work uniform: bright minidresses and a blazer. Piper was friendly and warm with a permanently upbeat vibe, everyone's favourite hype girl. She loved panels and podcasts and was extremely confident on both. *She's so good at being a founder,* Kit thought. *How can I be more . . .* that?

'I know it's a cliché'—Piper paused for effect, crossing one bare leg over the other—'but you have to believe in what you're making and doing, and don't let *anyone* derail you. Because there are people who will try, believe you me, whether it's investors, the media, even your customers. But a strong sense of purpose will keep you steady. Don't let anyone eff with your dream, in other words!' She looked down at the audience, eyebrows higher than Kit thought was physically possible, a gleaming mouth of brilliant white teeth on full display as she smiled knowingly, connecting with the audience as though they were her friends—which, given her prolific engagement on social media, they probably were. Piper was known to reply to almost every comment, and always had. She credited much of her success to that one small thing.

'For me,' said Storm earnestly, 'it comes down to knowing your *why* from day one. The why should be what drives everything you do, for your customer and your company. With my teas, I wanted to bring that ritual and ceremony into modern life, to give people space to just *be* for a few minutes a day. It all grew from that.' She nodded sagely, causing her silver earrings to swing. She wore a smocked olive-green dress and brown strappy sandals, and her long brown hair was pulled up into a soft, high bun. It was all spectacularly on brand.

'Really salient point, thank you both,' Carly said. 'And what about you, Kit? What would you tell start-up you?'

'Well,' she said, looking at Carly, trying to pretend it was just the two of them, not a massive public event, 'I guess my advice is to think about who you do business with. Sometimes, founders rush into a business because they are excited . . . They're so focused on this idea they want to bring to life that they don't spend enough time thinking about who they will take with them on that journey. Because it becomes like a marriage, you know? But you spend a *lot* more time scrutinising a potential spouse before committing.'

The crowd laughed but Kit suddenly tensed up, wondering if this was being recorded, if there was any way Toni might see or hear that answer.

'Oh my god, I *totally* agree,' cried Piper. 'That is *so* important, and no one talks about it! You make these huge decisions that will really impact you later, at a time when you have *no* idea what you're doing. Like, think about all the due diligence you do with investors down the track, but when you start out it can be like, oh, we started some random cocktail blog together, so that means we should be in business together, am I right?' She winked at this reference to her now ex-business partner and ex-BFF, and the audience clapped. Piper was on another level.

'Completely,' added Storm, nodding. 'And if I could just add one thing: try not to go into business with friends or family. It creates complications you could really do without.'

The audience murmured and chattered at this.

'To close it out today, ladies, what does success mean for you? Kit, why don't you lead?' Carly looked at her, smiling.

'Okay, sure,' Kit said, stalling for time. 'Well, honestly, success to me is . . . I just feel lucky being able to make great products, useful products . . .' She had managed to minimise herself and everything she'd achieved in one sentence. *No*, she thought. *No*. She took a beat and thought carefully about what she wanted to say. 'Look, at the heart of it, once I have made something

I really care about, and it's something I feel proud enough to share, that is success. Getting to do more of that cos it worked? *That* is success.'

'I like that, Kit,' Carly said, nodding.

'I want to grow my brand,' Kit went on, finding her flow, 'because I want to help as many people as I can have hair they love and feel good about. That may sound superficial, but I know how much confidence good hair can bring. I have an incredible team, and we all really believe in that purpose, which I think—I hope—comes through to the customer. Because it *all* comes down to the customer.'

Kit reached for her glass of water and had a sip.

'Exit at the highest possible value,' said Piper decisively. 'If I can build my company up to the point where someone acquires it—at a super-high multiple, please!—*that* is success, because it means I've done the best possible job as a founder and mother to my brand. Good companies are *bought*, not sold, know what I mean? If people want to buy my company, if they really see what I have done, *that's* success.' She beamed at the audience.

What? thought Kit. She felt like she was running a completely different race from Piper—or, even worse, the same race, she was just several hundred kilometres behind.

'You used the term "mother", Piper,' Carly observed. 'I find it interesting how often founders refer to their business as their baby, or use other parenting-style language. Is there a strong emotional attachment? Will it be tough to step away?'

'I prefer to see it as, like, graduating, you know?' Piper said. 'Like, you raise this business into a high-performance enterprise that will be super appealing to a buyer who can then take it on to bigger things . . . and then it's time to sell.' Kit found her self-assurance and clarity utterly captivating. 'You have to know *when*, though. That is the hard bit. Lots of founders miss their moment because they didn't *know* it was their moment, or they thought it was too early. But your valuation reflects tomorrow's best-case scenario. Sell on the way up when you're hot. Don't wait till you're losing your cool factor, or things have slowed. High valuations come because of potential, not saturation or tapering off.' She smiled and crossed her legs, as if everything she'd said was common sense.

'So exiting is always the goal?' Carly asked.

Piper nodded. 'I have plenty of other business ideas . . . serial entrepreneur over here!' She raised her hand. 'Can't help myself.'

'Would you say having an exit plan is essential as a founder?' Carly probed.

'Absolutely,' Piper said, nodding. 'It gives shape and a trajectory to your business plans. Also, I have investors; they expect their returns, and if you want to be seen as an investable entrepreneur, you've got to have a solid exit strategy. It shows you're serious, you know? Like, you have thought about where the business is heading, not just where it is *today*.'

Kit was frantically trying to absorb everything Piper was saying. She had been pedalling so furiously for so long on Second Day, she'd never even thought about an end goal. She didn't even know businesses *had* an end goal, she realised. Certainly she'd never formed an exit plan. Maggie had riffed about her selling the business for millions one day and buying a mansion, but that was all just a funny fantasy; Kit genuinely had no idea what would become of Second Day. She'd just assumed it would keep going until she was bored by it, or it no longer worked, and then she would, well, *stop* . . . Had she done Second Day a disservice by not imagining its future clearly? But how could she? She didn't know what she wanted to do next week, let alone in five years' time!

'I have no doubt someone amazing will acquire your beautiful brand, Piper,' Storm said, smiling dreamily and patting Piper on the knee. 'For me,' she continued, 'it's about building a legacy brand, a brand of trusted tea that Australians still use and love in ten, twenty years' time. But more than that, I am building a social enterprise with my tea fields that provides not only jobs and livelihoods, but also a bio-positive enriched soil to help reduce carbon for decades to come.'

'That's really admirable, Storm,' said Carly. 'Did I read correctly that you recently did a four-million-dollar raise?'

Storm smiled. 'Yes, a beautiful investor from California who is really on the same wavelength. That money is going to help us bring in the tech we need to be able to break new ground, as it were, for truly sustainable tea-growing.'

Hang on, Storm was in on this shit, too? *How did everyone else know all this stuff?* Kit wondered. She felt sick to the stomach, like she was back at school, left out because she couldn't afford the cool new schoolbag or shoes. She'd thought she was doing okay; she was making money, they were growing, she'd expanded into new retailers and new markets, but not once had she thought seriously about investors or an exit. She adored Second Day; it seemed mean to plan a break-up when you were still happy.

As Storm spoke about soil being the key to unlocking climate stability, Kit felt herself plunge rapidly into a mid-career crisis. Did she want to do this forever? Was this her life's work? Was this what she was put on earth to do? Make hair masks? She wasn't curing cancer. She was just selling stuff. But if not Second

Day, then what? Back to styling? Open a salon? Surely not; she'd go nuts. Kit had become accustomed to the chaos and mania of running a business . . . that must be why founders just created business after business. It was addictive. Listening to Piper and Carly, Kit felt so rudderless. She had started Second Day spontaneously, making it up as she went along, and she realised with a shock that she was still operating in the same fashion.

'Well, that sounds like a really noble plan; they all do,' said Carly, wrapping things up. 'Ladies, thank you for sharing your secrets, your stories and your success with us all here today. I'm sure the audience agrees, we have learned so much and have so many great takeaways. Very inspiring stuff.'

The audience went wild clapping and hooting, and the three founders smiled and clapped each other. *How did* they *know what to do?* Kit wondered as she clapped. Who helped them? Could she ask them these things over a coffee, or would they guard their secrets closely, every founder for herself?

The women walked offstage, back down to the small waiting area. Piper unplugged her mic from its battery expertly and placed it in the Louis Vuitton handbag sitting next to Kit's on the bag table. 'Oh yeah,' she said, noticing Kit watching curiously. 'I always bring my own; sharing mics is so icky.'

'You're so good up there,' Kit said.

Piper beamed. 'I'm my best self onstage. Wish that was my whole job!'

'You're both such incredible women, I loved sharing some space with you today,' said Storm as she floated over, giving Piper a kiss on the cheek. 'I have a flight to catch; soooo divine to meet you, Kit.' She leaned over to kiss Kit's cheek, too. 'I'm going to check out your stuff asap. And I'll have my team send you one of my SOS rituals; you look after you, okay?'

'Thanks, Storm, that's really kind,' Kit said, smiling warmly.

Sensing her opportunity, now that they were alone, Kit decided to strike.

'Hey, Piper,' she started, her voice catching in a very uncool way. She cleared her throat. 'This sounds like such a dumb thing to say but, like, how did you learn so much about business? All that exit stuff. You are light years ahead of where I'm at . . .'

'Oh, I was a *total* dumdum till I had Priya,' she said. Piper reached out and touched Kit's Gretel necklace. '*Dying* for your necklace by the way, I need one for my son.'

'Priya? Is that an app?' Kit asked.

'No, silly!' Piper laughed. 'Priya is a *person*. She's the chair of my board. Do you have a good chairperson? They are *so* important. Priya keeps all the shareholders in line and blah blah but she is also like an *awesome* brain in the room, you know? I wish I had her for my first exit. She also completely sorted out our tax structure; it was *really* dodgy, if you get my drift. Anyway, she just makes me see stuff so clearly—oh my GOD, how are you?!' Piper was looking over Kit's shoulder now.

Kit turned to see a woman in her forties in a chic beige suit walking up the stairs, wearing the 'here goes' expression.

'You look *beyond*,' Piper declared. 'Oh my god, have so much fun out there, that audience is *electric*.'

'Wow, okay,' said Kit, trying to comprehend what Piper had said. They had board meetings, but they were mostly just her, Simon, Toni and Camille catching up four times a year to go over the trading for that quarter and complain about packaging issues.

'Outsource *everything* that is not your superpower,' Piper said. 'I'm not kidding. I have a guy who just does our sustainability and inclusivity posts, cos I don't trust my social team to do it. Like, why would you risk the fate of your company to some twenty-four-year-old who films herself doing her hair for a living?' Piper looked at Kit as though they agreed on this but that was literally Hyun she was describing. 'I can't afford to be cancelled; it will ruin any potential deals,' she said offhandedly. 'Are you CEO?'

'No,' Kit said. 'I've always thought founder and CEO are such different roles. I have a great GM, though, Camille.'

'Is she a flight risk?' Piper asked. 'I made my GM our CEO and gave him a pay rise so he didn't jump ship. They say it takes half their wage and a full year to effectively replace a CEO, so you might want to think about that.'

'Whoa, okay,' said Kit. A world without Camille by her side was a world she didn't want to live in.

'How old is Second Day?' Piper peered at Kit as if seeing her properly for the first time.

'Almost seven.'

'What are you doing in sales a year—five, ten?' Piper asked this as casually as if she were asking what size shoe Kit wore.

'Um . . .' Kit wondered if she should be sharing such sensitive information with someone she'd just met, but Piper stared at her so hard she gave it up. 'I think we did around nineteen last year.'

'Are you in profit?'

Kit felt uncomfortable answering, but knew she had to give to get back. 'Yep, I'm investing it all back in.'

'Oh yeah, it's time,' Piper said authoritatively. 'Props, by the way—that is *amazing.*'

'Time for what?' Kit asked.

'To get serious, babe! Structure your exit. Since you don't need to raise to grow, you could even sell down, clear some cash off the table. Trust me, you do *not* want to leave it much longer. Otherwise, you risk the plateau. *Yergh.*' She made a disgusted face, then mimicked sticking her finger down her throat. 'Let's walk 'n' talk.'

'What's the plateau?' Kit asked, picking up her bag. She could not recall a single moment in her life when she'd needed coffee more.

The two women stepped out into the hallway.

'If brands are proven *and* trendy, they're worth more,' Piper explained. 'When they're cool everyone wants in, so the valuation is higher and you get more money and have more bargaining power to find the right buyer. But you can't stay hot forever, unless you're, like, *Apple*. You flatten out, sales dip, and then you drop off. Think of Freya. *Such* a moment five years ago, right? She and her brand were everywhere, total market saturation, right? And now . . .'

'You don't see Freya much anymore, do you?' Kit reflected.

Piper shrugged. 'She should've sold when she was everywhere; she missed the window. You need to strike while you're looking good. Who'd buy Freya now?'

'Maybe she didn't want to sell then,' Kit said, thinking of poor Freya.

'Babe, *everyone* wants to sell,' Piper said as they entered the lift together.

Kit laughed. 'I have genuinely never thought about selling. If you're making a profit and you love the work and your brand is bubbling along, do you *have* to sell?'

'No, no, you can stay the course, some people do—but life is long: if you're lucky enough to have a business that people want in on, you kinda owe it to yourself to explore that, no?' Piper winked. 'Don't feel bad,' she added, sensing correctly that Kit was. 'Founders are expected to just work it all out for themselves, but it's tough. That's why I always pay it forward. I learned so much in my first deal, did *such* a hack job—I don't want anyone else going through that shit show!'

'That's really generous of you,' Kit said as they exited the lift into the lobby. 'I really appreciate the insights . . . even if I am kind of having a heart attack.' She laughed nervously.

Piper checked her phone.

'So what will you do after you sell?' Kit asked quickly, sensing the chat was nearing its end.

'Depends how long I have to stay on. Buyers always want the founder around for a few years. Do you have investors? Did you tell me that already?'

'When I started the company, I gave equity to my business partners.'

'Too much?' Piper asked, wincing.

Kit nodded sheepishly.

Piper smiled knowingly. 'Common *as*. Also, no one tells you that your shareholders' agreement is a business pre-nup. You're *supposed* to plan for a scenario where you hate all your shareholders and they're trying to screw you over. Not because it will happen, but so that you're protected if it does.'

'Business pre-nup . . . that's *exactly* what it should be called.' Kit thought about her shareholders' agreement, a document she had barely understood when she signed it.

'Hey, so, want me to connect you to Priya?'

'*Really?*' Kit asked, thrilled. 'That would be amazing. Is she in the US?'

'She's here. My company and board are all in Sydney; it's just me and the fam in the US.'

'Thanks, Piper. I feel like I have so much work to do.'

'You do,' Piper said matter-of-factly. 'But listen, those numbers? You're killing it. You know what you're doing. Stop negging yourself. Celebrate your success! Take up space! Do what you need to do! This is *fun*. My brother is a tradie and works eighteen hours a day for a total pig and no money, and look what *we* get to do!'

'So true,' Kit agreed.

Piper came in for a hug. 'Message me anytime. This is a crazy ride; you gotta have your peeps, you know?'

'Thank you so much,' Kit said as Piper pranced off, hair flying, handbag swinging.

Kit blinked a few times, her head spinning. Things had just changed. She had been activated. Something had been put into motion that was inevitable; she could feel the shift. She didn't want Second Day to plateau! She needed a plan. She didn't want to fall behind, or mess it up, or undo all the time and love she had poured into this business, all the happy, loyal customers, her team . . . The exit didn't need to be tomorrow, Kit told herself. But what would it look like, in an ideal world? Piper's words rang in her ear: *You need to strike while you're looking good.*

Kit checked her phone. She had an interview in the lobby cafe with *Start Up* magazine in ten minutes; she'd go there now and caffeinate. She walked through the breezy, open-plan hotel foyer, which had been designed to evoke California or Fiji or Florida, with yellow and aqua chairs and mini palm trees and gold mirrors. *Gretel would love it here*, she thought, looking out through the glass doors to the huge island-style pool. She should take her on more holidays, even just short ones. Maggie said they were the only memories she really had from when her kids were young: the day to day was all one big blur. Kit felt a pang of love for Gretel; she missed her.

Kit found a table for two underneath a sign saying SURF's UP! and sat down.

She ordered a double piccolo, and while she waited the kindy WhatsApp began to blow up about the athletics carnival: what the kids were meant to wear, were parents meant to go, did anyone know if they were running the four-hundred-metre race, what would happen to canteen orders. Shona was yet to chime in with a question about where the toilets would be situated and if they would have hot and cold water.

Her phone rang. It was Toni. Kit's heart jumped into her throat; she hadn't heard what she'd said onstage, had she?

Kit let it ring out.

A few seconds later the phone chimed with an incoming text.

Darling please call me its urgent we talk Toni

Frowning, Kit called her back.

'Oh, thank god this is *not* a text conversation, I don't understand why your generation are so terrified of actually *speaking*,' Toni said in lieu of hello.

'What's going on?' Kit asked. 'I only have a minute.'

'I'll cut straight to the chase. It's not pretty. It concerns the business, my shares. It's—oh, it's not pretty, I'll tell you that much.' She was sounding even more unhinged and frantic than usual.

'Go on,' Kit said.

'I want to make it *incredibly* clear that Ricky did this without my knowledge and I would never have allowed it . . .'

Ricky was Toni's husband. He owned a discount appliance superstore and did his own terrible TV ads.

'Toni, what's going on?' Kit was sitting very still now, even as her pulse started to race.

'Well, from what I can understand, it's that my shares have been'—she paused and clicked her tongue as if trying to recall—'mortgaged. No, no, that's not right, I can't remember the word *exactly*, but Ricky needed money, and to get a loan approved the bank took hold of all his assets, *including* the Second Day shares which were in both our names, and so now the *bank* owns my shares in Second Day.'

Kit's left hand flew to cover her mouth as she inhaled sharply.

'Oh, I *know* it sounds bad, sweetheart, but Ricky assured me everything is fine, there are ways around it, and it will all work out provided . . .' She tapered off.

'Provided what?' Kit asked.

'I have to sell my shares,' Toni blurted. 'If I do that, we can pay off this loan and get everything straightened out. Now, I figure *you're* the obvious buyer, since you were all uppity about selling me shares in the beginning, so we just need to work out the price and then we can put all this behind us. See? No big deal.'

'Hang on, back up,' Kit said, trying to make sense of it all. 'The bank has taken ownership of your shares because you owe *them* money, and the way to get them back is for *me* to buy them? Is that what you're saying?' Kit felt her body tense up, alert and ready for danger, as though a sabre-toothed tiger was about to chase her.

'We can't pay the loan *back* until we have the cash, so yes, darling, selling the shares is the best way. Ricky said they'll be worth a heck of a lot more than when I bought them, given how well the company is doing!'

'But you're asking *me* to buy them, right?' Kit said, puzzled.

'You want them, don't you?'

'Toni, this is a lot to process, and I have to go. But just so I'm crystal clear: you need to sell your thirty percent.'

'Yes. Do you have enough cash to buy it?'

It seemed Toni couldn't decide if she was utterly desperate or trying to get a good price, forgetting the two positions cancelled each other out.

'Toni, I don't think you can just sell shares, like, friend to friend; I think there is a process . . .' Kit very much *did* want those shares, but she wasn't going to get stiffed on the price. And since they shared Gary, the whole 'run it past my lawyer' thing wasn't going to fly.

Toni sighed impatiently. 'Well how long will that take? Ricky wants it sorted asap. Though lord knows it's *his* fault we are in this situation, I should never have—'

'Toni,' Kit broke in, 'I can't give you an answer now. I have to get my head around it. Can you please speak to Gary and find out the next steps?'

Kit hung up and folded her arms. Well, shit. She hadn't seen this coming. Could Toni really be leaving the business? Could Kit buy back the shares she wished she'd never sold? This was *good*, Kit realised. *Really* good.

'Excuse me, Kit?'

Kit swivelled around to see where the voice had come from. Sitting behind her was a woman in her sixties, smiling kindly.

She was dressed simply in a maroon blouse and grey pants, bare faced but for a swipe of pink lipstick. She had straight grey hair that just touched her shoulders and, save for a vintage-looking watch, was completely unadorned.

'Yes, hi, I'm Kit.'

'I caught some of the panel just now,' the woman said. 'I liked what you said. Do you enjoy this kind of thing?'

Kit was caught off guard by her bluntness. 'Oh, it's, um, it's okay, I guess. The other two are much more suited to it than me, I think.' She laughed good-naturedly.

'I liked what you said about making something and being proud of it,' the woman said thoughtfully. 'Lots of founders get caught up in the cult of exit; they think that unless they have investors involved and are grinding their guts out for the big sale, they're not doing it right. But that's not true. It's completely individual.'

'Yeah, for sure,' Kit agreed earnestly, even though she had just ten minutes ago decided to make a path to exit her chief focus.

'I think the best founders focus on solving a problem and building a deep connection with their customers,' the woman mused. 'They are intentional about what they offer and how it differs from the others . . . they strive to be the *only*, not the best, you know? Buyers will always find you out if you stay that path.'

Who was *this woman?* Kit wondered.

As if reading her thoughts, the woman smiled and said, 'Sorry, how rude of me—my name is Susan Catteridge. Good to meet you, Kit.'

She stuck out a hand, and the two women shook awkwardly, laughing a little. Kit liked Susan's broad Australian accent; it made her feel calm somehow.

'So what brings you here, Susan?' Kit asked. 'Are you hoping to start a business?'

Susan smiled enigmatically. 'I'm visiting a friend, just flew up from Melbourne. Well, Geelong, to be exact. Anyway, I'll let you go. I just thought you were refreshing and wanted to wish you the best. Keep doing what you're doing.' She smiled and nodded as a kind of full stop to their conversation.

'That's very kind of you. Thank you.'

Kit turned back to her table. *What a nice lady*, she thought. *I hope she succeeds in whatever she's doing.*

Her coffee arrived, and she took a long, comforting sip, a much-needed breather before being asked eighty-five questions about how to business, a form of witchcraft she had just been reminded she was wildly unqualified to advise on.

Her WhatsApp pinged—Shona.

Has anyone seen Jamie's ballet shoe she is missing one

12

JUNE

KIT SAT ACROSS FROM MAGGIE, watching in disgust as she loaded up a thick slice of sourdough with jam and avocado then topped it with poached eggs.

'Not even Gretel could devise a more revolting breakfast.'

'Don't yuck my yum,' Maggie said, sprinkling salt all over as a finishing touch. 'And don't knock it till you've tried it. Want some?'

'I'm good,' said Kit, sipping her coffee. She and Maggie often met at this cafe for a post-Pilates or pre-work breakfast: the service was fast, the staff were friendly, the view of Bondi Beach was glorious and the people-watching was phenomenal. It was like they were *in* Instagram.

'What's happening with Dyl and those awful girls? Have things settled down?'

Maggie sighed. Dylan, who was in a year five/six composite class, was being ruthlessly bullied by a clique of year six mean girls. She was anxious and reluctant to go to school. Maggie was desperate to help her, to fix the situation, but it was delicate.

'Not really. I've spoken to her teacher and the principal, and I know they have spoken with the girls and their parents, but not much has changed . . . They're so clever about it, is the problem. Even her best friend Charlie has undertones of enemy . . . I'd be impressed by their sophistication if my baby girl wasn't their target.'

Kit looked at Maggie. 'Why do you think they've made her their target?'

Maggie pursed her lips. 'Why do *you* think?'

Kit grimaced. Dylan had been 'blessed' with early puberty and the body of a thirteen-year-old at age ten. The poor kid was being hammered for something utterly out of her control.

'I'm so sorry,' Kit said. 'I can't give any advice, because honestly my instinct would be to go nuclear. Completely nuclear.' She knew there was bullying ahead of Gretel, but despite her own long history of being shamed and teased, Kit had no idea how to protect Gretel from it or, more accurately, support her through it.

'Very hard not to. You know me, I'll give anyone a serve. They're *such* little creatures. It's really triggering, you know?' Maggie said. 'I got my period at nine, boobs at ten, just like Dyl. I remember the boys in year seven writing "*fat tits*" and "*virgin slut*" all over my locker at school. This takes me *sssss*straight back.'

Kit got it. Every time she was trolled or yelled at on social media her core memories of being bullied at school were awoken. That pain ran deep.

'I'm so sorry, my love.' Kit's phone was pinging nonstop, so she checked to see what on earth was happening. ''Scuse me.'

Reminder to wear orange tomorrow!! Gold coin donation for Cystic Fibrosis foundation.

We don't have any orange will red be ok?

I had to go to Kmart we didn't have any either ☺

I'm sending Lulu in pink close enough lol

Does anyone know if swimming is still on tomorrow?

It is, the email went out last night please be sure to label all towels, bathers and goggles as several items were unlabelled and unclaimed last week

Thanks Marie sorry didn't see the email while I am here does anyone want 2 go 2 The Wiggles this weekend we have tix and can't go now

Oh what time is the show?? We might!!

Love the wiggles so cute

Reminder that this forum is not for personal messaging, thanks all.

We don't have any orange clothes ☹

Does anyone know if the gymnastics holiday camp spots are open yet??

'Everything okay?' Maggie asked as Kit jammed her phone into her bag.

'Yep, yep, sorry. Did you think any more about changing schools next year?'

Maggie nodded, finished chewing and said, 'The advice is moving a kid in year six is a terrible idea. They've finally earned their big-fish-little-pond status, and uprooting them is a real blow. Plus, the coven will have moved on to high school.'

'Of course,' Kit said. 'That makes sense.'

Maggie wiped the crumbs from her lips. 'Sam's solution is a lap around Australia till it's time for her to start high school.'

Kit stared at her friend, slack-jawed. 'You're not . . . are you serious?'

Maggie smiled. 'It's always been on the cards. We just had to wait till Beau was bigger, but he's six now. He's good to go.'

'Wow. That would be amazing,' Kit said. 'Hang on, are we talking caravans and camping?' She could not picture her extremely urban best friend doing any such thing. Sam, yes.

Maggie laughed. 'I know what you're thinking; don't worry, I'll pack a La Marzocco. I think it will be worth it. Let the kids go bush! See more than the Westfield and the park, you know? I'm dying to go to the Kimberley . . .'

'I can just see you in a communal shower block in forty-degree heat putting on your Dior foundation while a giant huntsman watches,' Kit ribbed.

Maggie shuddered. 'Oh, I will be facing some demons. But I'd do it for the sprog.'

Kit checked her phone; she really needed to get going.

'I've got to head,' she said. 'Board meeting. You know how it is when you're building an empire.'

'What's the update on Toni's shares?' Maggie asked.

Kit was impressed that she'd remembered. She felt like she was always unloading on Maggie but that was just venting; she didn't expect her to actually *retain* any of it.

'It's a whole thing,' Kit said, which was an enormous understatement. Between Toni's haranguing and Gary's glacial pace, Kit was not much further along than when Toni first dumped the mess on her. 'I'm going through it all with the lawyer, but it's not going to be a simple she-sells-it-I-buy-it scenario.'

'And you definitely want to do that?' Maggie asked.

Kit nodded. 'Whatever gets her out fastest,' Kit said.

Maggie sipped her coffee and nodded. 'Respect. Okay, love you, you look like a fierce business tiger—go get 'em.'

Forty minutes later Kit walked up the marble staircase to the mezzanine level of the Sheraton, taking in the people around her: on holidays or celebrating big life moments or having sexy affairs; fun stuff, unlike her. As she waited for the lift, she watched a young couple with a curly-haired toddler. Kit could barely remember Gretel at that age; it was a blur of running the business, holding down the fort at home and trying to make her and Ari's relationship work. She had been sprinting for so long, she realised. But if she stopped, she might never get going again. Better to keep moving.

She exited the lift on the third floor and walked along the tan-and-gold hallways, looking for their room. Hyun had rented them a tiny, 1980s relic of a boardroom, which made Kit scoff. It was just the five of them, Kit insisted; could they not just do it in the office? It would save them nearly a grand. But Priya had insisted they start behaving like a proper board, just as Piper said she would.

Camille was all for the new direction. She had come from a global cosmetics house, and Kit knew the small-time-ness of Second Day frustrated her. She had big ambitions for the company—bigger than Kit even. '*Finally!* A grown-up!' she'd said when Kit had told her she was bringing Priya in. Camille, who was not so much no-nonsense as nonsense-intolerant, immediately liked Priya, and was excited that she was pouring a hot jug of governance all over everything. At Priya's insistence, they would now have monthly board meetings, with proper minutes and expensive new board software to capture it all, as well as an agreed-upon agenda. Even though there had only been two meetings so far, Camille was thriving. Her ideas, her formalisation of those ideas and her planning had ramped up immensely, which made Kit wonder both what might be possible and what *might* have been possible if these systems had been put in place earlier.

Today Kit was going to tell the board she was promoting Camille to CEO, with a swollen new salary to match. She dared them to push back. Everyone knew Camille was critical in the journey of Second Day. As Piper had pointed out, she needed to look after her and keep her happy. Next on the list was promoting Jordan from marketing director to CMO, which meant Michaela, her brand manager, was also taking a step up. Kit felt like a salary Santa: she loved being able to reward her team for their hard work and loyalty and also provide a genuine career path. Baby steps, baby steps, Kit reminded herself. Just because she'd had an electric business shock, it didn't mean everyone else had. She couldn't spook them with too much change too fast.

Kit walked into the 'Darwin' conference room and was unsurprised to be the first of the shareholders to arrive. Camille came later, once the top-level shareholder stuff had been discussed. Priya was already seated, tapping away at her chunky black laptop. She wore the classic corporate uniform: navy suit, simple silver chain around her neck and small pearl earrings. Her dark brown hair was in a deep side part with a ponytail, and her bright red nails popped against her brown skin. Kit wore an ankle-length lime-and-yellow-chequered shirtdress with an oversized collar and pointy white booties. Her hair was in a centre part, soft and wavy, and she wore a stack of pearls and intricate studs in her ears. She'd done bronzer, a baby liner wing and a pink lip stain today; she'd had no time for anything tricky.

'Good morning, Kit.'

'Morning, Priya,' Kit replied. 'I like your nails.'

'You don't think they're a bit much?' She was still tapping away, eyes on her screen.

'You're asking *me*?' Kit asked, brows high.

Priya looked up and smiled, taking in Kit's colourful outfit. 'How are you? Did you get a chance to look over the board pack last night?'

Kit's hand flew up to slap her forehead. 'I'm so sorry, Priya, I just didn't have the time.' She *did* have the time; she'd just chosen to see Maggie for breakfast instead. 'You're shaping an opinion of me right now, I can see it—and I deserve it, I do.'

This was the third time Kit had not read the material before the meeting. She recognised it was no longer cute.

Priya's expression was neutral, eyes back on her screen. 'The other two are running late so you can read it now. It's fairly light on this month anyway.'

'Okay, got it.' Kit dumped her tote on the floor and pulled out her laptop. She was a bit scared of Priya. Even though she had hired her and was technically her boss, Priya was in her fifties and had fifteen years of experience as a mergers and acquisitions lawyer before turning her hand to board work. Her calmness and her experience read as don't-fuck-with-me, which Kit liked and respected. Piper had said her superpower was helping founders and creatives be better at business, especially the financial and strategy side; Kit was all ears.

As Kit quickly connected to the hotel wi-fi, she felt emboldened.

'Hey, um, Priya, am I allowed to speak about the other shareholders, or is that talking out of school?'

'Was there something you needed to table for the meeting? That has to be done five days prior, I'm afraid.'

'Oh. Well, actually, this isn't something I'd want to bring up in front of those guys,' Kit said.

'Is it about Toni?' Priya continued to tap away, face to her screen.

'It is,' Kit said. 'Nothing's happening.' Priya had been brought up to speed on Toni's situation.

'Can I ask how you two happen to be in business together?' Priya studied Kit, resting her hands on the table in front of her keyboard.

Kit glanced at the doors. They were glass; she'd be able to see when Toni arrived.

'Well, she kind of forced herself in, to be honest,' Kit answered. 'I had the idea for Second Day while she was still my manager—she no longer is. I mean, she *was* helpful in those early days, but I definitely didn't need to give her equity for that stuff. Or that *much* equity at least . . .' Kit leaned back in her chair and folded her arms.

'It's not uncommon for first-time founders to undervalue their equity. Eventually they learn to treat it as though it were gold.' Priya smiled wryly. 'Selling shares is rarely a fast process, even if it's to an existing shareholder, so in the meantime, what is the plan for Toni? Do you still want her as a director, or can she fall back to just being a shareholder?'

Kit frowned. 'There's a difference?'

'Shareholders *own* the company,' Priya explained. 'They have the right to bring in or remove directors, or wind down or sell the company, but directors control the running of the business and wear all the ethical and financial duties, from appropriate governance and risk-taking measures to budgets, investments and staffing or marketing decisions. Perhaps she is less useful in that role now.'

'She was *never* useful in that role. Genuinely! I'm not being snarky. It's just not her skill set or interest.'

'I see,' said Priya. 'Kit, do you mind telling me why you want to buy her shares?'

'I regret ever selling them to her,' Kit replied. 'Toni keeps saying that since the company is doing so well they will be worth a lot . . .'

'So she wants you to buy back the shares at market value?' Priya asked.

'Sorry, what does that mean?' Kit asked.

'The value the market would attribute the shares. *That* requires an independent third-party valuation, and they are not cheap. We're talking two hundred, two hundred and fifty K.'

'Oh, she has no money so that won't be happening,' Kit said shaking her head.

'Unfortunately, the company pays for valuations.'

'*What*?' Kit spluttered.

'It depends on what is outlined in the shareholders' agreement,' Priya said. She paused. 'But, Kit, the bigger question is *why* do you want to buy the shares back? To what end?'

'It's *my* company.'

'So it's a principle thing?' Priya probed.

'I guess so,' Kit conceded.

'And that's worth spending an enormous premium, one that exists because of the value *you* created in this company?' Priya asked. 'Even if it costs you everything you have made, and even more? I mean, we could be talking millions of dollars, Kit. You would do that?'

Kit was quiet, chewing her thumbnail as she thought about what Priya was saying. She hadn't considered the fact that it could cost her millions.

'*Everything* in business comes back to the value created,' Priya went on. 'Value for the company, shareholders and customers. Your brand has a wide community of loyal fans, for example—that is hugely valuable to a buyer. But *you* are the reason they're there, Kit. Why should you be paying for yourself?'

It clicked. The premium Toni was charging for was value *Kit herself* had created.

'Kit,' Priya said gently, 'sometimes there is more power in letting go than holding on too tight.'

Kit nodded slowly. 'So should I make an offer at what I think the shares are worth if I extract what I have added in terms of value . . . Wait, does that even make sense?'

'It's more complicated than that I'm afraid,' Priya said. 'Look, Kit, only you can make this decision. But consider all the possibilities. For example, what if you didn't buy the shares, and instead a new partner bought them, someone who could add new and different value and experience to the company and help you grow in a meaningful way?'

'Do you mean like raising capital?' Kit asked, frowning.

'I'm talking about selling down. Raising capital is bringing funds into the company, usually with equity but not always, to scale. To pay for hires, or tech, or inventory, or keep a business afloat in some cases. What *I'm* referring to is moving shares from an old shareholder to a new one.'

'Right,' Kit said, too confused to play smart. 'But if no money goes into the company, why would we do it? How would that help us grow?'

'With expertise, Kit. With connections, reach, experience. Toni could be replaced by someone with industry experience, insight and contacts to accelerate Second Day's expansion and visibility.'

'*Ohhh*,' said Kit, mulling it over. The company was doing well, but it did have some big gaps. The biggest being that *Kit didn't have a plan*. She was still cruising on gut and instinct and the talent of her team. She would love someone to bring new, exciting ideas to the table! If she wanted to make Second Day bigger and take it further, Kit needed a board she respected, that challenged and inspired her. Kit knew her limits, and she'd just about reached them.

'We could really use some experience,' Kit admitted. 'I mean, you've seen our board . . .'

'Bringing in new directors will certainly add experience,' Priya said. 'Of course, that can also come through paid advisory board members, like me. But the difference with an *invested* partner is they have skin in the game. They answer the eleven pm email. They solve the tough problems with you. More to gain, more to lose.'

Kit nodded, thinking affectionately of Simon in those early days.

'I like this,' said Kit, feeling excitement fizz through her. 'I think we really need it. I've always had this fear that I'm going to mess it all up. I have no business training, no experience. Give me a model and forty-five minutes and I can make hair magic, but this stuff . . .' She shook her head. 'It's beyond me.'

Priya leaned forward and locked eyes with Kit. 'Hey. Your company is in a great position, and that's because of what you have done. Also, you have Camille, and she is formidable.'

'Oh, she's terrifying,' Kit said with a laugh. 'I love her.'

'What does your shareholders' agreement say about pre-emptive rights for shares?' asked Priya.

'I couldn't understand a word of that document then and wouldn't now,' Kit admitted.

Priya gave her a look that flirted with exasperation but stopped just short. 'For all intents and purposes this is your company, Kit; I assumed you put that SHA together, or at least read over and fully understood it.'

Kit felt like she was back in year one, being reprimanded by a mothball-scented Ms Van Hepel. She felt embarrassed, stupid. She knew her defence was pathetic.

'Well, I read it, of course, but all that crazy legal jargon—it may as well be written in Swahili.'

'Send it to me and I'll read over it this afternoon.'

'I'm sorry, Priya. I'm just not good at business,' Kit said, chastened.

'Can I offer some advice?' Priya fixed her with a stern look. 'Never say that. It is diminishing to your success, and your point. Stick to facts.'

'Right, okay.'

Priya switched her focus to her laptop screen. 'Let's get back to today's business. I noticed your agenda item regarding dividends, and Toni requesting early payment. Is this going to impact the capital you need for the US?'

'I guess it depends on how much the dividends pay, but almost certainly, yes.' Kit'd need Camille to answer that one. She was the colourful, creative one—not the numbers one.

'Her request isn't unreasonable, Kit. Shareholders have a right to dividends. And from what I can see, you could afford to pay dividends *and* invest. But it's not my call.' Priya looked up at Kit. 'I wonder if you realise how rare it is to be so profitable so quickly in business. I have worked with a lot of companies, small, medium and large, and what you and your team have done is something to feel very proud of, Kit. Eight out of every ten start-ups fail, as I'm sure you know, but only one really thrives. It's fair to suggest you are that one.'

Kit felt her neck and face grow warm with embarrassment. 'Thank you, Priya, I—'

The door opened and Simon entered, bringing the cold air in on his coat. He was, as usual, working hard to fight the stereotype of scientists being wiry-haired and out of touch in his dark blue jeans, high tops and a black long-sleeved tee. But then, this was Simon 2.0. When Kit met him, Simon was married with kids and living in suburbia. Then he met and fell in love with Ben at a conference, and everything turned upside down and inside out.

Kit smiled and stood up to hug him. 'Hi, Si. How's the new house? Settled in?'

'Oh, you know us scientists: we don't welcome a lot of vari-ation in life, generally speaking, but it's going well.' He set down his laptop bag and pulled his glasses out, cleaning them on his shirt as he spoke.

The door swung open and Toni collapsed into the room in a haze of cloying, chocolatey fragrance.

She carried a tan Coach handbag on one arm, and her laptop and charger under the other. From the knee-high boots to the tote, she had been swallowed in various shades of brown and tan, her lip liner and eye shadow forming the perfect crescendo.

'Always late but worth the wait!' she announced in a singsong voice.

When Kit gave her a hug, Toni pulled her in tight, like a clamp. It felt very symbolic. They were like family, Si, Toni and Kit—and as in so many families, there was dysfunction and hidden resentment.

'You did well on *The Today Show*,' she said to Kit. 'Ugh, that lighting was *ghastly*, though. Why do they insist on making everyone look like cadavers? It was like you had no make-up on at all!' One compliment, two criticisms—the Toni special.

'We always sell a stack afterwards, otherwise I'd give them a wide berth,' replied Kit. A tremendous minimisation: Kit almost had a heart attack before going on live TV.

'At least your hair was good,' Toni said. 'You know, I used to manage Larissa, the host, back when she was just a badly dressed kid with buck teeth. Oh, she had reams of talent, anyone could see that, but she had *no* self-confidence . . .'

As Toni went on and on, Kit thought back to the days when Toni was *her* manager, not her business partner, and how all her Too Muchness and braggadocio just seemed funny. They'd never been able to iron out the creases of that power dynamic, Kit realised. Toni still felt like she had 'made' Kit.

'Okay,' said Toni, dumping her bag and coat on a side table. 'I have a hard out at twelve—that going to be okay, chickens?'

Kit looked at her with barely contained contempt. She could not get Toni out of this business fast enough.

13

JULY

RAT WAS BACK LIVING WITH Kit and Gretel after another relation-
ship/job/attempt at Doing Life failed, and Gretel was as thrilled
about it as Kit was not. She was sleeping on the pull-out trundle
bed in Gretel's room, which meant that instead of being woken
by Gretel's warm body and hot little kitten breath demanding
jammy toast in the morning, Kit was woken by Rat doing loud
impersonations, songs or stories for her teeny roommate. Rat
might be a hopeless adult, but she was a *really* fun aunty, Kit
conceded, as she heard the two whooping and howling next
door. Kit looked at her phone: 6.12 am. No. This was too, too
early. Why could they not stay quiet until Gretel's little cloud
light turned from red to yellow, like they'd discussed a million
times? Why was her twenty-six-year-old sister as disobedient
as her five-year-old daughter? Why did Kit always have to be
the boring one enforcing rules?

Kit pulled her silk eye mask off her head and rubbed her eyes. Was her hair clean or dirty? This was always her first thought, as it would inform how much time she needed to get ready. She counted it out: three days in. Still good. She lay quietly for a moment, thinking about the day ahead. She, Camille, Jordan, Simon and their senior chemist had locked in a half-day for a new product planning session. Kit usually loved planning new products and categories—SPF oil? Wax stick? A collaboration with a designer for Christmas?—but she wasn't feeling her usual excitement and zing. She was just so tired. She wanted to call in sick and stay in bed all day, but she couldn't. It never quit: there was an issue with the nozzle on their texture spray, which they were trying to fix as fast as possible, but customers were commenting about it on every Instagram post, so the customer service team were flat out emailing them and issuing replacements or refunds . . . their primary manufacturer had put their prices up *again* . . . and their senior designer had quit to work for a competitor, the biggest insult possible. Plus Gretel's sixth birthday was looming. She knew she was supposed to invite the whole class to a petting zoo or an arcade, but she was going to try to get away with a few friends and cake at the house. She really didn't have the bandwidth to organise a party for twenty-five six-year-olds right now . . . Kit took a deep breath and rose, wrapped a robe around her, jammed her slippers on, and headed to Gretel's room.

Rat was sitting cross-legged on the floor wearing a cropped singlet and undies, her long box-bleached hair pulled up and secured in one of her g-strings. Her stomach and limbs were soft and tanned, her face scattered with the kind of tiny, non-offensive pimples that kept her relatable despite her beauty. Rat had amassed a decent following on social media because she genuinely gave no fucks. She wore, said and did what she wanted, and the more outrageous her videos, the more followers she scooped up. She was the personification of giving your boss the bird and walking out; people loved watching Rat do things they never could. Watching her bounce around with Gretel, eyes smudged with yesterday's mascara, her plump, full lips exactly the kind Toni sought through injection, Kit realised she was just innately sexy. Even in this silly room at this silly hour when she was absolutely not trying. It was in her DNA. Rat was a chaotic manic dream girl, who sailed through life with the assuredness and confidence of a celebrity, yet still ate cereal for dinner and couldn't use an iron. Who would she become? What was her future? Kit needed stability, control, a clear path; Rat thrived on the opposite.

'I hope that one is clean,' Kit said, tipping her head at Rat's makeshift hair tie. 'Good morning, angel, may I have a cuddle?'

Kit walked over to Gretel, who was busy drawing with the textas she absolutely was not allowed to have on her carpeted bedroom floor.

Without looking up, Gretel said, 'Mum, Rat turned the night-light off cos she said monsters can see you better if there is a night-light.'

Kit glared at her sister.

'And she said there was unicorns on the world, and we can see them if we wear special glasses. Can you get me some?'

Kit kneeled behind her to hug her; Gretel instantly wriggled her way out. 'Mum, I am *drawing*!'

'Ooh, it's so colourful,' Kit said, looking over her daughter's shoulder, trying to remember what the Instagram therapists said about not giving general 'nice job' praise. 'Do I spy a unicorn?'

'Yes, and this is his house and his pet cat. Rat said unicorns all have pets, but not from the pet shop cos they torture animals.'

Kit shot her sister another frown. 'We talked about getting a pet, didn't we, G? A black-and-white cat?'

Gretel looked up at her mother with excitement. '*Can we? I want to call it Muffin . . . Muff . . . No: Muff Puss!*'

Rat burst into laughter. 'Oh my god, *yes*—that name is perfect.'

'Muff Puss . . . cute,' Kit said, trying to keep a straight face.

Gretel looked at her mother and then Rat. Her nostrils flared, her eyes flashed. '*Why are you laughing?*' She hated feeling like a fool. 'You are the *worst girls ever* and *I wish I'd never had you*,' she said through gritted teeth, before standing up and storming out.

Kit looked sternly at Rat, who covered her mouth but was unable to stop laughing.

'Sorry, but *Muff Puss* . . . come on,' Rat managed to get out. 'Just call it Vag Snatch and be done with it.'

Kit went out to the living room and found Gretel curled up in a ball on the sofa, the indignity of being laughed at coupled with her hunger combusting in her young brain. Kit sat next to her and pulled her daughter onto her lap for a cuddle.

She covered her head in kisses. 'I love you so much. We are not laughing at you, my darling; we love that name. Rat is in a silly mood is all.' Kit turned her daughter on her lap to face her, her sweet morning breath and little upturned nose and long lashes and sleepy eyes Kit's favourite things in the entire world. 'Hey. Why don't we sneak some banana into Rat's smoothie to get her back? What do you reckon?' Rat hated banana; this kind of joke was right up Gretel's alley.

'And fish,' Gretel whispered gleefully. 'She *hates* fish.'

'Okay,' Kit said. 'Let's make our secret smoothie!'

Rat walked into the kitchen a few minutes later and turned the coffee machine on.

'We made you a *very special* smoothie!' Gretel said, giving everything away.

'I don't eat brea—' Rat paused as Kit frowned and shook her head behind Gretel. 'Actually, you know what?' she said. 'I *do* feel like a smoothie.'

Gretel clapped her hands as Kit turned on the blender, and then poured the mix into three glasses for them all.

'*Madame,*' Gretel said in a fancy high-pitched voice, as she climbed up to sit on the bench next to Rat and pushed Rat's drink towards her. 'Your smoothie.'

'Almond milk?' Rat asked suspiciously.

'Of *course!*' said Gretel.

'No banana?'

'*Absolutely not!*' said Gretel. 'This is *not* a banana cafe!'

Kit braced herself then took a sip and moaned in appreciation. 'It's like there's a tropical party in my mouth and everyone's invited!'

'Everyone is!' said Gretel in delight. 'Even Aunty Rat!'

Rat read the play, and took a big, excited sip. As she swallowed, her face crumpled in disgust.

Gretel dissolved into hysterical giggles.

'We got you! It's got *soooo much banana in it!*' Gretel was bouncing up and down.

'Gretel Buttface Cooper, I am gonna eat *you* for breakfast. Come here!'

Gretel jumped off the bench and tore off up the hallway, Rat in hot pursuit.

Kit set about assembling fruit, a cheese sandwich and cucumbers for Gretel's lunchbox, figuring Rat could earn her keep by taking Gretel to school today. That would give Kit the chance to go for an endorphin-fuelling run before heading into the office. She needed to walk in with energy and vision. She was the founder, for god's sake! The captain!

Her phone beeped.

just got your email, was out of range . . . can we chat please please please there is so much to say before we go down that nasty path pls let me know when is a good time??

So Ari *had* received her email. She'd been starting to wonder if it had bounced or he had a new email address, the overthinking division of her brain delighted to have something meaty to chew on. Kit had carefully crafted the email with the help of Maggie and her new bare-minimum family lawyer. It said he needed to honour their custody agreement, or find a permanent residence near Gretel's school, or he risked losing custody altogether. After years of making it work, Kit was done. Ari didn't respect friendly arrangements, so he was being given a formal one. This issue had been at the heart of their separation three years ago, and very little had changed. After a particularly trying night with a sick three-year-old Gretel, Kit had realised that living with Ari was just living with his clothes. He was a completely absent father. So why keep up the facade? Kit had called it that very day, deciding to single parent for real, instead of pretend. Kit needed clear lines, not some nebulous fantasy life where he swung in and out of their home and life between high points in his fabulous and exciting career. Kit's main association with Ari was disappointment and resentment, and Ari felt it, so it was a civilised split. Ari helped devise the commitment; a minimum of four days a fortnight pro rata. And yet, here they were again, weeks with no Ari. Sensing the exact brand of artful persuasion about to come, Kit reminded herself that she was within her rights, legally, mentally, financially, to ask for this.

I can talk after 2, she wrote. Clear terms, no wriggle room for his weaselling. *This is not 'nasty', this is a reminder of what we agreed on. You have not upheld your side of this deal for years, Ari. I can't*—she deleted the word 'can't'—*won't do this anymore.*

lawyers??? we dont need those monsters we can work this out we always do

Then another text: *I hear u I have a plan xxx*

Will call you at 2, she repeated.

ok but thats 3 am here maybe we can do later?

Then 5 pm our time. Maybe you can speak to your daughter too.

Gretel was 'your daughter' when she was pissed.

i will do better

i am so sorry

i love u both your my forever girls xxx

He reminded Kit of a junkie, the way he communicated. Full of false promises and make-goods and anchored in meaningless emotional assurances. How had she ever found that attractive? Kit shook her head ruefully. Of all the people in the world she could have made a human with, she'd ended up with *this fucking guy*.

'Gretel, can you come back and have your smoothie?' Kit yelled towards Gretel's room, which had gone dangerously quiet. 'Hello?'

Kit finished up her daughter's lunchbox and popped it into her schoolbag. Looking inside, she saw a note from the school: *DON'T FORGET THURSDAY IS PRESENTATION DAY* ☺

Today was Thursday: what was Presentation Day? What did they need to do? Why was she always the mum who didn't know the thing that was on?!

'Gretel?' she called, as she scrolled through the seven million messages in the class WhatsApp. She couldn't ask; she was *always* the parent asking. She felt so horribly incompetent.

Trying to keep the rising anxiety out of her voice she yelled, 'Honey? What is Presentation Day? What do you need to do for that?'

No response. Still way too quiet in her room. Kit walked down the hallway and opened the door. She found Rat drawing a series of tattoos around Gretel's upper arm.

'Rat, are you SERIOUS?! What are you *doing*? They're permanent markers, for shit's sake!'

'Mummy said the f-word,' Gretel carolled, admiring her arm.

'They look cool, don't they, G?' Rat said, ignoring Kit.

'RAT, STOP!' Kit was furious. 'Jesus, I just—I can't with you sometimes.'

'Mum said the Jesus word,' Gretel singsonged.

'Oh, relax,' Rat said. 'Stop being such a narc.'

'Don't tell me what to do in my own home as you graffiti my daughter. For *once* in your life can you be a goddamn adult?'

Rat looked up at Kit with a look of pure loathing. It was very unsettling.

Kit grabbed Gretel's hand. 'Honey, you need to get dressed for school, come on . . .'

'Why are you so mad at Aunty Rat, Mum?' she asked. 'The pictures are pretty.'

Kit took a breath and tried to calm herself. 'They're just not allowed,' she said. Then, changing the topic so she wouldn't explode: 'Hey, what's Presentation Day? There was a note in your bag.'

'Dunno,' said Gretel, tracing her finger over the flowers and birds Rat had drawn on her arms. She did look like a very small, very cute bikie, Kit had to admit.

'Did Ms Kellan say anything about it yesterday? Is it show-and-tell?'

'*That's* public speaking—we talked about bats,' Gretel said earnestly. 'And Remy fell off the monkey bars so we talked about S A F T Y.'

'You ever seen a bat in real life?' Rat asked, ignoring Kit. 'I know the cave in the city where they all sleep. We should go! We can take a picnic and torches . . .'

'Now?' Gretel said excitedly.

'NOT now,' Kit interjected. 'Rat, once Gretel is fed and dressed, walk her to school, okay? You'll need to get moving; she has to be there by eight forty-five.'

As her sister stalked off to the bathroom, Kit realised she'd better find out what Presentation Day was before she dressed Gretel, in case it required a costume. Pulling her phone from the pocket of her robe, she typed: *Morning! . . . What do the kids need to do for presentation day today please? Gretel doesn't know. Thank you, sorry!!*

A few seconds later, there was a reply from Marie—the class parent slash angel always there to remind them if the canteen was going to be closed, or if there was (another) mufti day, or if school photo money was due.

Hi Kit, that was last Thursday, when the kids presented their family tree ☺

Kit felt sick, stupid, heartbroken. Letting down her daughter, missing an important school thing, putting her in a position where she would feel left out and embarrassed at school brought on deep shame. Kit's childhood was spent worrying about money, bullies and her dad's moods. She'd had no one solid to depend on after her mum died, so she had sworn she would be reliable for Gretel. She would be her daughter's rock. She picked up Gretel's school skirt from where it had been thrown on the floor last night and unzipped it.

'Honey, did you talk about your family last week at school?' she asked casually.

Gretel, wearing nothing but My Little Pony undies, her gorgeous little tummy with its carrot-shaped birthmark jutting out, said innocently, 'I don't have a family.'

'Baby girl!' Kit scooped her into her arms. 'Yes, you do: you have me, and Daddy, and Aunty Rat . . . *We* are your family, and we adore you. You are the shining sparkly heart of our family.'

Gretel, uninterested in Kit's projections and fears, pulled away, grabbing the clean polo Kit had placed on the bed for her to wear.

'But it's not a *real* family,' she said as she pulled the top over her head.

Kit felt that like a kick in the guts. Tears pooled in her eyes as she watched her daughter step into her skirt. It took all her willpower to stop herself from her usual gaslighting, telling Gretel she was being silly and, of course, it was. She recognised it was a core moment in Gretel understanding the make-up of her family, and the people who loved and cared for her.

'What do you mean by that?' she asked gently.

She could hear Rat slamming and banging things in the bathroom, using all Kit's cosmetics no doubt—Kit wanted to stab her.

'I don't have a daddy or a dog or a grandma,' Gretel said, tugging at her polo in frustration. 'I don't want to wear this top! I want to show Reya my drawings.'

'You have a daddy, honey.' Kit looked her daughter in the eyes. 'And he loves you so, so much,' she said, obeying the number one rule, which was never shit on your co-parent, even if they deserved it.

'Then why doesn't he live in my house?' Gretel asked, a perfectly rational question.

'Well,' Kit said carefully, 'because Mummy and Daddy don't make each other happy if we live together. Like you and Cory at school—you know how you fight all the time? But that doesn't mean we don't both want to live with *you* . . . Just not at the same time. And as for grandparents, what about Pam and Colleen?' Ari's parents lived in New Zealand, so weren't exactly a constant presence in their granddaughter's life, but they were loving, from afar. 'And Poppy!' Kit tried to muster up some warmth as she mentioned her father.

Gretel frowned. 'The old boy who lives in the forest?'

'Yes, that boy,' Kit confirmed, mentally rolling her eyes.

'Last time his lady friend gave me a magic crystal to keep me safe.' Gretel scanned the piles of books, stickers, toys and dolls scattered over the floor, looking for it.

'You are always safe,' Kit said, pulling her in again for a hug. 'You are the safest, most loved human on the whole planet. You don't need a big family for that.'

Gretel wriggled away and plonked on the edge of Rat's trundle to pull on her socks.

'But the magic of families,' Kit went on, 'is that you can always add on new members. So Maggie and Sam and Dylan and Beau are our family, for instance. And what about Lily, and Sian?' Sian was Gretel's nanny for the first few years of her life, and Gretel would have swapped Kit for her in a heartbeat.

Gretel looked at Kit, thinking hard. 'Mum, when I grow up I want to be the letter Y cos *everyone* knows the alphabet so that means I will be famous.' And with that, she walked past her mother and out into the hallway.

'Also,' she added over shoulder, 'I want a nose earring like Aunty Rat.'

Kit pulled her hair into a high ponytail, tapped go on her Apple Watch and set off down the street. Her lower back had been aching lately, but Kit thought the mental benefits of a run far outweighed the risk of a flare-up. She always had good ideas when she ran, and today she very much needed some of those. She'd been considering making a cleansing conditioner, but she'd not fleshed it out yet, and it would show. Also, she had an idea for coloured hair powder for root touch-ups that you applied with a little powder puff, so it was precise.

She headed down the street towards Centennial Park under a brilliant, sparkling blue sky, the kind Sydney did best. Her time management was awful, and she almost certainly should not be doing this, but it didn't matter if she was a bit late. She was the boss, she reminded herself; they weren't going to start without her!

Kit found a good pace, and turned her mind to her exchange with Gretel. She knew kids often spoke without fully under-standing what they were saying, but they were also bare-faced truth tellers. Maybe if she told Ari what Gretel had said *that* would finally make him understand that he needed to be around more. But in her heart of hearts, her lowest basement heart, Kit felt hopelessly to blame. She simply couldn't offer Gretel a large, loving family. All she had was an unhinged aunty, geographically removed grandparents, a sometimes-dad and paid help. Kit ran faster, trying to outpace the sadness and shame. She had felt so alone as a kid, and now she was unwittingly replicating that for Gretel.

Suddenly her phone pinged, interrupting the extremely loud Fred Again in her headphones. She stopped to read the message.

Good morning, Kit, I wondered if you had time for a call today?

It was Priya. She had *never* texted to chat. Kit immediately assumed this meant bad news. (*Was it normal to always default to the worst-case scenario?* she wondered. *Or was she just wired badly?*)

She texted back: *Hi! I am in a strategy meeting all day but can chat now??*

Kit did not want to spend the whole day worrying about what Priya wanted to discuss. Thankfully, Priya's name flashed up on the screen immediately.

'Hi, Priya!' she said cheerfully. 'Sorry, just out for a run, don't mind my panting.'

'Good for you, Kit. Sorry to call before nine, but I'm heading to San Francisco this morning and wanted to chat before I went. I'll cut to the chase: I spoke with Camille yesterday—are you aware she is constantly fighting off inbounds from private equity?'

'She is?' Kit had no idea.

'Yes. She told me you weren't interested in investors, so she just issues a blanket no to all meetings.'

'Yeah, I did.' Kit recollected. 'We don't need cash.'

'Understood,' Priya said. 'But remember when we were chatting about the Toni situation, and we spoke about the option of you moving her shares over to a partner to help you scale? Well, inbound interest is a pretty good indicator of timing. Second Day is bursting with potential, you've moved into the US, there is a buzz around the brand. That's generally a good time to transact.'

'Huh,' said Kit.

'As you know, I've been working with Piper on her deal,' Priya went on. 'Since she is also in hair care, this has given me a real-time insight into the valuations coming through for beauty, and quite frankly, they are astonishing—and plentiful. I questioned whether it was my place, but I felt I had to raise it with you.'

Kit frowned, trying to take it all in. 'Why would anyone buy when the price is high? That makes no sense.'

'Because of the promise of more money later, because of the growth trajectory, because of the *potential*. What you're actually selling is tomorrow, not today.'

Kit's brain was speeding at Shinkansen pace. 'So if I was buying Toni out, that price would be high for me, too?'

'I'm afraid so,' Priya confirmed. 'Toni has the right to sell at market value.'

'*Shit*,' cursed Kit. 'That's right.' Priya had been through the shareholders' agreement thoroughly and discovered Toni was in an annoyingly strong position. What Kit *did* have was control over whom Toni sold her shares to: a right she fully intended to exercise.

'What I see here,' Priya went on, 'is a mutually beneficial situation, where you can replace Toni with someone who can help you supercharge your growth, who has the experience you spoke about wanting, at exactly the time you need it. Toni gets her cash, and you get a partner and board who can evolve Second Day alongside you. You might even like to sell down some of your shares, too, if the price is right.'

Kit could only manage deep thinking if she was completely still. She took a seat on a low brick wall abutting the footpath.

'Think it over,' said Priya. 'No rush.'

'I can't imagine I'll be thinking about anything else, to be honest,' said Kit.

'Bringing on experienced partners can make a big difference, especially when it comes to a clear path to exit,' Priya said.

Kit exhaled. 'Of course.'

'Put it this way,' Priya said. 'It's crude, but you'll get the idea. Do you want to still be running this business with Simon and possibly Toni in ten to twenty years? Or do you want to create a fantastic company valued at tens of millions of dollars, even *hundreds* of millions, and sell it?'

Kit snorted. 'I can't see *that* happening . . .'

'Anything is possible,' Priya replied. 'This is a timely discussion to be having—most companies have these chats in the first year or two of business. Look, I understand if this line of thinking doesn't come naturally, Kit. Founders are expected to be both creative visionaries *and* business tycoons, which is ludicrous if you ask me.'

As Priya spoke, Kit was privy to an unfortunate scene involving a dog with diarrhoea and a very embarrassed teenage boy watching in horror, holding a limp doggy bag.

'I think I'm a leave-the-party-while-it's-still-good person,' Kit said finally. 'The last thing I want is for Second Day to peter out on my watch. She's beautiful and she's my responsibility; I owe it to her to give her the best chance of success.' She thought about all the brands she had known and loved that had disappeared; the retail universe was scattered with their corpses. She could not let Second Day be one of them.

'Honourable, but it doesn't really answer the question,' Priya said.

'How much will Toni's shares be worth, do you reckon?' Kit asked.

'You don't put a price sticker on a company, I'm afraid,' Priya said. 'The enterprise value, or EV, will be whatever the market thinks it's worth, whatever people offer to pay for it.'

'So no independent valuation?' Kit said.

'No, that's only if you, an existing shareholder, wants to buy the shares. The movies would have you believe someone barrels in with a briefcase full of cash and won't take no for an answer, when in fact it's a long, arduous process.'

'Count me in!' Kit replied facetiously.

Priya chuckled. 'Mergers and acquisitions can certainly test the limits of sanity. Bidders will want to know every detail about your business yesterday, today and for years to come before they put in an offer. You will not love it. But it can lead to wonderful things. Give it some thought. Okay, I'll see you Tuesday.'

'One last thing before you go,' Kit said. 'What would I do without you?' She meant it.

Priya chuckled. 'Probably lead a much simpler life.'

Kit stood up and began jogging home, her head spinning. This was *really real*; this could actually happen.

Her phone chimed with a text. It was from Priya, a link to an article in *The Business Review* about a period-underpants company that had just sold for one hundred and forty million dollars to a big legacy clothing company. Her phone chimed again. This time an article about how the beauty industry was the fastest-growing industry in retail, and company valuations were double, even triple what they were a year ago. Kit read between the lines.

Another ding—this time an email from Gretel's teacher.

Hi Kit,
Gretel tells me you are making mermaid cupcakes for her birthday next week—cute!
    Can I remind you that we have egg, dairy and nut allergies and to exclude all of those please. There are 24 students.
Thank you,
Eliza

14

SEPTEMBER

KIT WAS STANDING IN THE kitchen, trying to stay calm despite the wildly emotional conversation she knew lay ahead. Gretel was finally in bed, despite Ari obliterating her entire evening routine, pushing out bedtime by nearly an hour by giving her a pile of extravagant absent-parent compensatory gifts just as she settled into bed for her stories. Kit took a deep sip of her red wine as she waited for Ari to emerge from Gretel's room. It was her second glass for the night, a habit that had become all too regular. She told herself she needed it to unwind from the stress and extra work of trying to sell Toni's shares, on top of her already huge work-and-life load.

The deal was already very distracting, and it had only just begun. Priya had connected Kit to a friend of hers, Rupert J. Ferguson, a corporate adviser from Linley Advisory who specialised in financial and strategic advice for founders looking to sell, raise capital or exit. He *should* have been dull, working in that field, but Kit liked him the moment she met him. He was a friendly, effervescent and extremely personable man in his late fifties. He wore a great deal of colour, despite being in the corporate army, and cared about making Kit feel comfortable and in control. He reminded her of the fun, wise teacher at school, the one you actually tried for. Rupert would be Kit's person through the deal, Priya explained. Her go-to, her first line of defence, her translator, her guide and her protector. His job was to ensure she—and Simon and Toni—got the exact deal they wanted, and nothing less. To her enormous relief, Rupert would be the one who dealt with bidders and their circus of lawyers and advisers, not Kit. 'We treat founders like a rare bird,' Rupert said to Kit. 'We keep you hidden, save for a smattering of presentations and meetings with vetted, serious buyers. Private equity people think founders are magical creatures—human idea fountains—and we don't want to do anything to dispel the mystique.'

For the past month, Rupert and his associate Hugo, an ambitious young guy lacking all of Rupert's charm and warmth, had been working alongside Kit, Camille, Jordan and Second Day's new finance guy, Ben, as they documented the company's entire history—financials included—and then forecast its future for the information memorandum. The IM, which would be sent out to potential investors, outlined the problem the company was solving, introduced Kit, and described the customer, what the brand stood for, how it was doing so far, how and where it would grow, how much it would grow and so on and so forth. Its job was to sell the dream, Rupert explained: convincingly but honestly. The team were working hard on collating all of

Second Day's new product development, promotions, retail plays, marketing investment and Cost Of Goods Sold (COGS) into one clear outlook to show the company's growth projection—which, Rupert warned, bidders would do their aggressive best to refute in order to get a lower price. It was a daunting task, and it was putting a lot of strain on Second Day's executive team. Plus, Gretel had been off school sick most of the week, and that always threw things out. Gretel's body seemed to instinctively know when Kit absolutely could not miss work and immediately latched on to the nearest virus.

Ari finally appeared in the kitchen. He spilled himself over one of the stools and rested both arms on the bench, one hand propping up his chin. He looked fantastic, to Kit's annoyance. Gas station cap with his fringe peeping out under the lip, a tight black singlet tucked into vintage-wash Levi's, chocolate-brown leather fisherman sandals and a raft of tattoos snaking up his toned arms. He was a beautiful, stylish man more suited to the lens of a New York streetstyle photographer than this messy suburban kitchen.

'Where's Rat?' Ari asked. He was in two minds about his daughter being around Aunty Rat. He was as fast and loose as they came, but even he thought Rat was too much.

Kit sighed. The truth was she didn't know. 'She took off a couple of weeks ago.'

Rat and Kit had had a big, nasty fight. Kit had told her sister to get her shit together, get a job and find a place to live, or start paying rent and doing more around the house. Rat, being Rat, chose to storm out. She always ran away as soon as things got hard, Kit realised. She never stuck it out, she never tried, she just left, and picked up a new thread somewhere else.

'She really has mastered Little Sister Energy, hasn't she?' Ari mused, eating grapes from the fruit bowl on the bench. 'Where did she go?'

'Yamba, according to her latest video.'

'What's there?'

'Oh, Rat is living the van life now. She bought a second-hand Sprinter, put up fairy lights and curtains and plants, and set off for the north coast. Filming it all for TikTok, of course.' Rat wasn't replying to Kit's texts, so she was forced to watch her sister's life unfold on the socials, like everyone else.

'Respect,' Ari said, brows raised. 'Alone?'

'Yep. It's just so *her*, you know?' Kit said, unable to conceal her frustration. 'No direction, no responsibility . . . just drifting.'

'You worried?' Ari asked. It was a question that didn't need asking. Kit's default mode was worry. Rat's was a lack thereof. Kit worried double to make up for it.

'Of course! She's out there alone in a bloody yellow bikini, filming all her unhinged, unfiltered rants, smoking a ton of weed, telling everyone where she is . . . Someone slashed her tyres as she slept last week, and she got stuck on the side of the highway overnight with a flat battery the week before . . .' Kit shivered.

'There's no telling Rat what to do,' Ari said.

'I feel like I'm the only one who cares. Why doesn't she have any real friends?'

'Um, she's undiagnosed but certified?' Ari said.

'Not her fault.' Kit immediately switched to defence. Only *she* was allowed to pour shit on Rat.

'Oh, come on. You telling me some treatment or meds wouldn't help?'

Kit raised one eyebrow, or hoped she did: she'd been to visit Maggie's injector for her biannual botox, and 'Dr Rina' had been extremely liberal. 'I only do the angry lines,' she'd said cheerfully in her Russian accent, as she'd pricked Kit's forehead. 'We keep the happy ones.'

'Sure, okay, *you* try getting her to see a doctor,' Kit said.

Ari sighed and looked around, aware that the conversation about Rat had reached its standard conclusion.

'Could a drifter trouble you for a splash of that wine?' Ari asked.

Kit poured Ari a glass, before pouring the rest of the bottle into hers. He looked at her as he drank, brown eyes wide, lashes long. When he was out of sight, Kit forgot how exquisite he was. She preferred it that way; his appearance was distracting and made her want to be nice to him.

'Okay, let's do this,' he said, after taking another sip. 'I'm here to listen, I'm present. Tell me what's in your heart and on your mind.' He made a show of putting his phone in his back pocket. 'Before you start, I want to say I will do whatever Gretel needs, and I will do whatever it takes to support you.' He stopped for a second, looking down at the bench, shaking his head slightly. 'She's so funny, and so smart, just so unreal in every way. You are building one hell of a human, baby . . . and it *is* you doing it, I know that. I miss her so much. I know you think I'm living my best life overseas, but it kills me being away, you know?'

Kit closed her eyes and breathed very slowly, trying to rein in the tirade that was scrambling down from her brain to her mouth. She'd gone over this moment so many times in her head: while she was in the shower, while she was running, in traffic. She'd planned to be firm, kind and neutral, *not* let Ari trigger her.

'I understand it must be hard to be away from your daughter so much. But, Ari, you have *chosen* to be away from your daughter.'

'Baby, it's my *job*. I *can't* do my job in Sydney; it doesn't exist here. You know that, you know I've tried, but travel is part of who I am, it always was.'

'Who you *are*?' She made air quotes around the word. 'Who you *are* is a father. Not just a guy with a career. You centre your whole life around your needs and dreams, and whatever scraps are left, Gretel gets.'

'Ouch,' he said. 'That's mean. Come on—don't do that.'

Don't do that? Hot lava flowed out of Kit's mouth now.

'Don't tell me what to do,' she hissed. 'Don't you fucking dare. The only reason we're still in each other's lives is because of Gretel. You are a selfish, ridiculous man who thinks he's still eighteen. You bring nothing but frustration and disappointment into our lives.'

'But you want me to move to Sydney? Even though I am a ridiculous, disappointing man?' He laughed good-naturedly, further inflaming Kit's rage. Arguments and accusations did not scare Ari; he'd grown up in an open, all-emotions-on-the-table household with two mums who were more like friends or workmates to their kids, forever sharing whatever thought or emotion popped into their brains.

'*No*,' she said in frustration. 'I don't *want* you around, I *need* you around, and so does your daughter. Do you know she told her teacher she doesn't have a daddy?'

Ari looked as though he'd been punched. He went quiet, and Kit could see he was blinking back tears. Kit rubbed her eyes with her hands, trying to calm herself down. She hadn't wanted to say that. Not while she was angry, anyway.

'It's not good enough, Ari,' she said softly. 'You think it's fine now, but this is all imprinting. She will lock in her experience of her father, and you will have missed the boat forever. And don't get me started on how critical a father is for a girl's self-esteem . . .'

'*What?* I can't tell her enough how incredible she is!' he argued.

'Yeah, except words don't count if you're not around, Ari,' Kit countered. 'She needs you to be present; to be consistent, reliable, a trusted source of love and safety. You're none of those things.'

Kit saw something change in Ari's eyes. He rearranged himself on the stool and then looked at her with an expression that was not quite indignation, but maybe a second cousin of it.

'Well,' he said, 'did you ever consider . . . I mean, there *are* ways for her to have a male presence around. Like, what happened to that Lucas guy? He was good . . . Don't look at me like that, why is that weird to say? You *should* have someone to love you and help you. Don't you deserve love?'

Kit was so floored her mouth dropped open. 'Are you fucking serious right now? *That's* your solution? I ask you to play a bigger part in Gretel's life and you suggest I outsource it to some rando guy I found on an app?'

'It's about what *you* need, too,' he said. 'It's not all about her.' His volume was not even close to meeting the level of Kit's. 'You're at max capass; it's clear you need help.'

'Of *course*, I need help!' she yelled. 'From *you*, because we are CO-PARENTS, Ari. She's *our* child. *We* are supposed to share the job. Do you know how many weeks you've done so far this year? Do you? *Six*. Six in thirty-seven. That's *disgusting*.' She paused for a moment to catch her breath, then continued,

'The lawyer said we're at the stage where if we legalised our custody arrangement you could end up with none. Do you see how serious this is?' Kit was furious, her whole body burning hot with emotion.

'Is that what you want—to cut me off?' He looked at her in shock.

'Don't play the victim,' she warned. 'I cannot *believe* how much you are missing the point here. First you shame me for not finding a new dad for Gretel—which is just . . . I can't even wrap my head around how messed up that is—then you paint me as unreasonable. I'm not having it, Ari. Fix your shit.' She began noisily piling dishes into the sink, fighting the urge to storm out.

Ari folded his arms, his brows knitted together. 'Kit, I'm sorry. I knew from the start I would never be a good dad. I always said that, didn't I? That I would love the kid with everything I had, but I wasn't made for—'

'Don't say it,' she cautioned. 'Don't say something you'll regret.'

He looked at her, defeat in his eyes. 'I don't know how to fix this. You're so good at balancing work and Gretel—'

'What choice do I have?' she said flatly.

'I'm letting you both down so badly.' He stopped to swallow back tears. 'And the worst bit is, I can *feel* myself doing it, you know? I'm *aware* it's happening.' He exhaled and looked at Kit.

Kit said nothing.

'I don't know how to be a dad, I don't know how to be stable and settled and normal. I didn't have a dad to be a role model, so—'

Kit interrupted, 'I *did* have a dad and he was an atrocious role model. That's no excuse.'

Ari looked at Kit, acknowledging the hit. 'I worry that if I'm made to sit and stay, I will be so . . . so *resentful*, and feel so trapped, that I won't be someone you would want to have around anyway.'

'Ari,' Kit said, as gently as she could, 'we all find ourselves in situations we wouldn't have chosen for ourselves. But let's be real. You don't have a disease; you have a *daughter*. Yes, you have shit you want to do, and no, you can't sit still. But there's a little girl who loves you and needs you down that hallway. That is not a curse; it's a *gift*. She is beautiful. Amazing. Hilarious. And she is half you. So for fuck's sake, *sort it out*.' Kit felt a tear fall down her cheek.

Ari got up and walked around to where Kit stood and pulled her into a deep hug. She resisted at first, but then allowed herself to soften, leaning her head on his shoulder, the softness of his skin under her cheek. His smell, always Comme des Garçons, was unhelpfully nostalgic.

'I am so sorry,' he said, his words slightly muffled in Kit's hair. 'I see your pain, I do. I have to make this better. I will work it out.'

Kit drew away. 'So, you'll pick her up from school tomorrow, and I'll collect her from you on Sunday?' she said, trying to normalise things.

'Well, I wanted to talk to you about that, actually . . .'

Kit stared at him in disbelief. 'Really? After what we just discussed?'

'Hey, just listen,' he said, hands in the air. 'I was *going* to ask if I could take her next week as well and, if it's all right with you, visit Pam and Colleen in New Zealand.'

Kit frowned. Gretel was only in kindy—a few days off colouring in and counting was fine—but the idea of Ari taking her so far away . . . She shuddered, thinking about what Gretel would be eating every day and wondering who would ensure she was dressed warmly enough. But she knew she had to allow it. She couldn't ask for help then reject it.

'Staying on the farm?' she asked.

'Yep. They said it's pretty cold still, but Gretel could get some good riding in on the rail trail.'

'You know she's still on training wheels, right? Bikes are a dad thing. That's on you.'

'By the end of the week she'll be ready for the Tour de France,' he said, grinning.

Kit sighed. 'Okay, sure. *Any* grandparent interaction is welcome.'

Ari's face lit up, and he grabbed her for another quick hug. '*Yes!* Thank you, thank you. I know you think she will live on red snakes and Coke, but I promise I'll take good care of her.'

'Wren going to be there?' Wren was Ari's new partner. They were a huge Twitch star from LA, and Ari seemed genuinely smitten. Wren could game from anywhere, which suited Ari and his nomadic lifestyle perfectly.

'Nah. Not really their scene. Plus, they're competing in Vegas next week,' he said. 'So what will you do with all your free time?'

'Free time?' she scoffed bitterly. 'As in, what you have your whole life while I raise Gretel and run a business?'

'Whoa, I didn't mean it like that,' he said.

'No, no, you never *mean* it . . .' She took a swig of her wine. She hated how vicious she'd become.

'Can I buy you a self-care party?' he said, eyes shining. 'Every massage and spa treatment in town? Come on, let me. It's the least I can do.'

'I can't,' she said, shutting him down. She needed him to know he couldn't just waltz in and band-aid everything. 'I have a big week of presentations and meetings . . . I'm selling some of the company. It's a whole thing.'

Ari leaned forward, as if to hear better. 'I'm sorry: *what?*'

Kit straightened up. 'Yeah. Toni needs to cash out, so we're selling her shares to a new partner.'

'Wow,' he said. 'That's big. But hang on, didn't *you* want to buy Toni out one day?'

'I did, but buying back my shares would cost me millions of dollars I don't have, and the reason they would cost that much is because of all the work I have done. So: hard pass.'

'Hang on—did you just say *millions?*' He beamed. 'Can we just hold up for a sec and acknowledge that? Your company is worth *millions of dollars*! I'm so proud of you . . .' He shook his head, looking at her with genuine affection. 'So, who's helping you with all this?'

'Linley Advisory. Acquaintances of Priya, our non-executive chair. They're nice guys. Treat me like a legitimate business owner, not a girl who needs everything overexplained. Even though I am.'

'What's the company being valued at?' he asked.

'Don't know yet. The market, the buyers, determine the value.'

Kit got back to cleaning up, wiping the dinner debris off the bench into the bin. Gretel had barely touched her chicken skewers and rice, even though that was what she had asked for. She'd eaten all the apple pie Ari had brought, though. Her daughter existed on garnishes, dessert and cups of milk.

'You ever fast-forward twenty years and imagine what your life will be?' he asked.

Kit sighed. 'Ari, I'm not in the mood.'

'Okay, specifics then. Do you want to still be doing Second Day when you're fifty? When Gretel leaves for uni?'

'I don't know.' All she knew was that right now, she needed to go to bed.

'If it is, that's great . . . but, like: *is it*? I know you love the business, but you *are* pretty stressed most of the time.'

Trigger officially pulled.

'Yes, weirdly,' she said. 'And you know what else I am? I'm *exhausted*. I'm a single mother—*don't even*, Ari; for all intents and purposes I may as well be—and I have Rat to look after, Toni to manage, this deal to nut out, I am the "mum" of the team and company . . .' She trailed off.

He nodded, giving her space to go on. When she didn't, he said, 'Your biggest curse and greatest blessing is that you make really tricky shit look effortless, so no one ever thinks you need help,' he said. 'You're a total productivity beast. You never, ever take your foot off the gas.'

She shook her head. 'I have to, because *no one else does it right*!' Hearing herself, she knew how dysfunctional a statement that was. How could he be so curious and caring, yet be completely oblivious to the fact that he had contributed to her burnout?

'What if I bring in a new partner and they ruin everything?' she said, obsessively cleaning every last bit of debris from the sink hole.

'You're far too good a judge of character for that to ever happ—'

'I chose Toni, didn't I?' she said. 'And you.'

'Ouch.' He looked genuinely hurt.

Kit wasn't sure she cared.

'So what's the exit plan?' he asked. 'Hotshot investors now, then in a few years the multinational overlords take over?'

'I don't know,' she said honestly.

'This is the dream, baby. Why work so hard and not take the prize? You could have never-work-again money, live-your-best-life money, buy-a-fucking-*yacht* money.'

'I don't need a yacht; I'm happy just not to be poor . . . All right,' she said, changing tone. She was desperate for a shower and sleep. 'Gretel has been coming in at all hours of the night and I have a huge day tomorrow.' *How wonderful it must be for Ari*, she thought, *getting a full night's sleep every night. How perfectly delightful.*

Ari stood up, collecting his keys off the bench. '*Muy bueno.* Toni's out, new partner's in, you get a meaty cash pile in a few years . . . sensational. Life's too short to waste your best years all tired and stressed.'

'Oh, fuck off,' she said softly, turning her back to him to close the dishwasher. *Was* she always tired and stressed? Probably, but who was this unreliable, infuriating Peter Pan coming in and telling her how she should live her life and run her company after a ten-minute catch-up?

'See you tomorrow,' she heard Ari say as he walked to the front door.

Then he stopped and walked back to the kitchen.

'I think you're amazing,' he said. 'And you're doing an incredible job. You have created something really cool that heaps of people really love. I'm your biggest fan.'

Kit kept facing the sink, tears welling in her eyes as he finally left.

15

OCTOBER

'WHO WE MEETING FIRST?' JORDAN asked, as she scrambled into
the back of the taxi with Kit, wrestling with her unwieldy,
oversized handbag. *That skirt is too short*, Kit thought, glancing
at Jordan's tanned thighs as she scooched across the back seat
before reprimanding herself for being so judgey. But no, actually,
it *was* too short: they were off to meet serious people who wore
serious clothes and used serious acronyms. They needed to look
professional.

'Big boys. Top of the town. Small fries after lunch.' Kit spoke
confidently, as though she wasn't quietly shitting herself about
all of this. The Second Day information memorandum had gone
out to dozens of parties after six weeks of collating and analysing
from both Rupert's and Kit's teams, and these were the first presentations with interested investors: two private equity firms,
both vetted and both keen. Reassuring self-talk swirled in Kit's

head as they drove along: *They're potential partners, not monsters.*
They're just friendly people who want to help Second Day be bigger,
better and do more. But her palms were clammy; she was very, very
nervous. Kit could barely manage speaking in front of people
from her own industry, she got nervous giving a speech at the
work Christmas party! Kit wanted to be impressive, intelligent,
knowledgeable. This was *her company*; if she couldn't sell it, who
could? She had practised her speaking bits in the shower and in
the car this morning, but she knew in the moment she'd panic.

'Quality pastries, then—thank Baby Jesus for that,' said
Jordan, who, as an incredibly assured presenter, had the luxury
of contemplating croissants rather than death by public speaking.

Camille, riding up front, was directing the driver through
the maze of one-way streets in the CBD.

'Never waste calories on cold pastries,' she said over her
shoulder. 'Eat them warm or don't bother.'

Kit took a deep breath and went for it. 'Jordan,' she said,
voice low but friendly, 'I hate saying this—I know it makes me
sound like a 1950s schoolteacher—but do you think you could
wear pants or a longer skirt or dress next time we present? Your
legs are spectacular, but we're in corporate land now; we've got
to dress the part.'

Camille snorted. 'Says the half-woman, half-beach umbrella.'

Kit was so stunned by this, she burst into laughter. She
looked down at her outfit: a dopamine-green silk shirt dress
with statement gold buttons done up all the way, with a pair of
blocky orange Jil Sander heels. She wore lashings of mascara
and red lipstick and had styled her hair—made to look slick and
wet—into a deep side part tucked behind the ears. She felt

polished, and colour always made her feel confident; she *very* much needed to feel both of those things today.

Camille answered a call and began talking animatedly in French.

'Okay, fair point,' Kit said. 'Just try not to flash anyone, yeah?'

Jordan grinned. 'Might get you a better price.'

'It's not *my* price,' Kit shot back. 'I wish.'

Kit might not be taking any money away from this deal, but that didn't stop her from obsessing over the value of the company. Their EBITDA—which she now knew meant earnings before interest, tax, depreciation and amortisation, a way for investors to measure company profitability—was strong. Their sales this past year were even stronger. But Rupert had made it clear to Kit that even though their numbers were impressive for a company of its size, bidders wouldn't let on. They would try to dismantle Second Day's projections, make them as low as possible, to bring the price down. They would also hammer the team, he warned. Which products were coming next? Why was the margin for retail so high? Which global market would they target next? How much should the US arm be bringing in? What was the founder's long-term plan? What would the ecommerce team be eating for breakfast next May? At one point Rupert had casually suggested seventy million dollars as a possible total EV, and Kit had gasped audibly. *Seventy! Million! Dollars!* For her little hair care company! Started at her kitchen bench! It seemed unthinkable. It also meant that Toni would walk away with more than twenty million dollars, a fact that Kit struggled with. Camille barely bothered to disguise her annoyance at the fact that, in order to achieve Toni's windfall, the whole senior team at Second Day had to step out of the running of the business to spend weeks creating document after document. But despite that, and her general distrust of private equity, Camille had thrown herself into the process with gusto, and Kit had the impression she was genuinely excited about finding a good partner. Provided Kit still retained control, of course.

'What's our contact's name in here?' Camille called from the front passenger seat.

'I think Rupert said his name was Clay,' Kit replied, as she scrolled through a wasteland of emails from fashion brands on sale or newsletters she'd signed up to in the hope of leading a more contemplative, present life full of breathing techniques and inspiring quotes and five am journalling.

The class WhatsApp pinged.

Numerous lice cases discovered this week. Check your child's head and ONLY send them back to school once all nits are removed.

Perfect: just as Gretel returned from NZ. She'd come home with various scrapes and cuts and far too many new freckles for Kit's liking, but she said she'd had 'the best holiday of my life'. Once Kit swallowed the sting of that, she sent a text to Ari thanking him. Positive reinforcement, et cetera, et cetera.

'Did you see Gotham sold?' Jordan asked Kit.

'Crazy, huh?' Kit said, shaking her head. 'No investors, cash straight into the founder's hands. Unbelievable. No stock either. Pure cash.'

'Oh my god, you *fully* have the lingo down,' Jordan said, amazed.

Rupert had sent Kit a link about the Gotham deal given it was vaguely in the same world as Second Day; they were an

Australian self-tanning brand with a ludicrously viral product range and huge Gen Z following that had sold to Unilever for one hundred and fifty million dollars. Rupert had told her this deal was a rarity—hence why it made the press—and not to get hung up on it, or any other deal, even if they *seemed* like they were comparable: every deal was entirely unique and dependent on not only the numbers and forecast, but also the current market and industry landscape and what each bidder was prepared to pay.

Kit wondered if one day people would read about *her* deal and be impressed. She imagined the Kylies from school, those witches, seeing her face next to a figure in the millions one day, and something deep inside her, a strange blend of pain and motivation, was activated.

'I heard he's a dirty ol' dog,' Jordan said.

'Who? What?' Kit asked, checking her lipstick in her compact.

'Jermaine, the founder. Apparently cheated on his wife, who is the *co-founder*, by the way, with some half-goth he fell in love with online. Same age as their daughter. *So* grubby.'

'How do you know all this stuff?' Kit asked, annoyed to see another two grey hairs had settled in around her hairline.

'*Back of the Shelf*,' Jordan said, as if it were common knowledge. 'The Facebook group? Who's moved roles, who's selling up, who's toxic to work for. Have you not been on there? I thought Hyun would've shown you . . .' She frowned.

'What?' Kit snapped her head to look at Jordan. 'Am *I* on there?' She already had zero chill today; this was going to send any scraps of it spiralling deep into the negative.

'It's nothing, seriously,' Jordan assured her. 'Just that the IM went out. People have thoughts.'

'Of course, they do.' Kit sighed. 'People have thoughts on *everything*. Someone DMed me last night saying I was green-washing because we use post-consumer recycled plastic. How is that something to be angry about?'

'Don't take criticism from people you'd never take advice from,' Camille interjected, tapping away on her phone. 'Every judgement is actually a deep confession.'

'Whatever it is,' Kit said, 'it's not fun.'

'You can handle it,' Camille said indifferently.

Kit loved this woman.

The driver slowed the car to a stop and they climbed out. Kit's phone pinged as they walked towards the building's intimidating entrance. There was no sun here in the dark, shady CBD, and she felt both cold and silly in her party-coloured clothes compared to everyone else. *They all looked so rushed and angry*, she thought to herself as she pulled her phone out.

It was Toni.

darling we need to have a little chat about a few things can you please call NOT text me today? Xoxox

Toni had an uncanny ability to destabilise Kit right when she needed to feel rock-solid. Kit put her phone away and shook her head as she inhaled, filling herself with calm and confident thoughts. The sooner Toni was out, the better.

As they waited at the security desk for their photo visitor passes to be created, Camille looked around at the foyer full of bustling suits. 'Corporate slaves,' she muttered, shaking her head.

'Didn't you used to work in a building around here?' Jordan asked.

'Yes, and *that* is how I know they're all miserable.' Camille flicked some fluff off her black leather skirt. She'd paired it with a thin caramel knit and black heels, her only jewellery a thin gold chain and her vintage Cartier watch. She looked chic, a bit superior. The essential antidote to Kit's colour and Jordan's thighs.

A young woman wearing a fitted red midi dress and an enormous smile walked up to the three women. 'Camille Barreau?'

Camille nodded.

'Hi, I'm Alicia, I'm going to take you up to level forty-eight.' She beckoned them to follow her through the glass security gates towards the lifts.

As they stood waiting for one of the twelve whispering and whoosing elevators, Alicia smiled at Kit and tipped her head conspiratorially. 'Can I just say, I *love* seeing three ladies in here. It's so rare. And colour! Even rarer. I don't really belong here obviously, I'm a temp; I feel like a caged bird.'

'We don't actually know how to dress for this place,' Kit said, laughing politely.

'So what brings you here?' Alicia asked.

One of the lift doors opened, and the four women stepped in, six or so men stepping in behind.

'We make hair products,' Kit whispered, the silence of the lift unnerving her.

Alicia smiled excitedly and pointed at her hair, which was tightly coiled and pulled back into a high bun. 'Will they work for me?'

'For sure,' Kit said, smiling.

'What's it called?'

'Um, Second Day?' Kit said hesitantly.

'No, *way*! I *love* your curl cream!' Alicia's eyes were wide, face alight. 'No word of a lie, it has changed my life. I can get past day four with ease now. I tell *all* my curly girlies to buy it.'

'Thank you, Alicia! I *love* hearing that.' Kit beamed at her. It was as though Alicia had been sent to remind her why she did what she did. It was easy to write off hair care as frivolous, but it *did* matter to people; it changed their hair habits and routines for the better. Kit straightened up, pulled her shoulders back and held her head high.

'Here we are!' Alicia stepped out of the lift and the others followed. The all-glass interiors gave them a stunning view of the glittering harbour stretched out before them, tiny ferries chugging around looking like toys in a huge bath.

'*Whoa!* If we go with these guys, can we move in?' Jordan whispered to Kit.

They were led into an enormous conference room, bathed in muted sunlight care of delicate sheer blinds, set up with glasses, printed decks and pens for—Kit did a quick count—fifteen people. Her heart began to pound in her chest. *Fifteen?*

'If you've ever wondered who has all the money,' Camille said, as she perused the giant double-door fridges stocked with VOSS, Sanpellegrino and FIJI Water, 'it's these guys.'

Alicia returned, this time with Rupert. Kit could not be more relieved: more support, more known entities, more safety blankets. Rupert was wearing a dark grey checked suit over a pink shirt, an amiable seen-it-all-before expression on his face.

'Rupert,' Kit hissed, once Alicia had left, 'why are there eleventy chairs in here?'

Rupert smiled. 'Good morning, Kit.' His English accent and jaunty attitude were usually enough to put Kit at ease, but it would take more than that today. 'Four of those chairs are for *us*,' he reminded her. 'Clay will bring one or two decision-makers with him, the rest will just be lackeys and onlookers. It's to impress you!'

'*Intimidate* more likely. Aren't they trying to woo us? This is *not* a woo move.'

'Speak for yourself,' said Jordan, her back to them as she gazed at the view, hands clasped behind her like she was inspecting to buy.

Alicia returned again, this time with a line of men shuffling behind her, chatting amiably.

'Still no danger of any women in private equity, I see,' Camille said quietly.

'Good morning, everyone,' said the only guy not in a suit. The casual master, a smiling silver fox in dark blue jeans and a black shirt, with twinkling blue eyes and the kind of tan that spoke of long days on boats or playing golf, said, 'I'm Clay Morrison, partner here at Blue Tree.' He then introduced navy blue suit, light blue shirt and some form of boot, one, two and three.

Kit smiled her most dazzling smile and began shaking hands and introducing herself. Jordan and Camille did the same.

'Please,' said Clay, gesturing to the table, 'sit wherever you'd like. Alicia will grab your coffee order and we can begin. We know your time is precious.'

Jordan started setting up the presentation. Kit, who had exhausted her repertoire of idle chat once she'd covered weather and upcoming holidays, looked to Rupert in desperation, but he was deep in loud, blokey conversation with one of the suits about Formula One. She had forged on alone, trying to pretend she knew something, *anything*, about skiing in Niseko, when yet another man entered. She glanced at him discreetly. His dark gold hair was full and wavy, pushed back with his fingers, and he wore grey suit pants and a navy knit, unzipped just so. As he removed AirPods from his ears and placed them in his case, Kit took him in. He didn't match the other men, who were wiry and lean, the kind who cycled at six am. He looked like he'd enjoyed a career as a rugby player before finding himself in a glass tower, the kind of man who knew how to fix an engine or deliver a calf. Kit looked away, just in time to see Jordan widen her eyes meaningfully and tip her head in his direction. Jordan was back on the market after a decade with a CrossFit-obsessed robot named Dean, so handsome wedding-band-less men did not escape her attention. Kit ignored her and continued to *mm-hmm* as the guy in front of her waxed rhapsodic about Kyoto in April.

'Last but not least,' Clay said to the room, 'this is Max Darling. Forgive him, he is in a bit of a beast of a deal currently and completely at its mercy, hence his late arrival. Max is the lead on all our lifestyle investments, even if he looks like he'd be more suited to bouncing at nightclubs.'

The men laughed heartily, save for Max, who gave a curt smile. *Max Darling*, Kit repeated to herself. *For real?*

He glanced at Kit and caught her curious look. She quickly blinked and plastered a smile on her face. He kept looking at her, his expression unreadable, and began moving towards her. Once he reached her, hands in pockets, fat watch jutting out between fabrics, he continued to stare at her intently, like he couldn't make out if she was animal, mineral or gas.

'Hi,' she said, realising he may never speak. 'I'm Kit.'

'Max.'

She waited for him to go on. He didn't.

Who doesn't shake hands? she thought. *Rude!*

'Thanks for having us in,' she said, stepping into the awkward silence. 'Incredible office . . .'

'You've made something pretty impressive yourself, Kit,' he responded. 'Solid profit, your COGS are low, infrastructure has potential, visibility is rising . . .' She noticed his lashes, which were long and fluttery, and clumped together in small sections, like a baby's. It was unsettling how pretty his eyes were. It didn't seem right on such a large man.

'Oh, thanks,' she said goofily.

'I mean, brand awareness is *well* below where it could be in such a small market, your retention rates are slipping badly and your active customers have stalled, but your marketing investment is vigorous and you're sitting on decent cash reserves, so that's something.'

Rupert had warned her they'd neg her on the business, but surely there should be some polite foreplay first?

'The August EBITDA adjustment—how do you qualify that?' he asked, as Kit wondered why she was thinking about foreplay.

'All in the presentation,' Camille interjected, sensing an adversarial conversation, her favourite kind. 'We'll take you through it step by step.'

'I see Max is charming you with his effervescent small talk,' Clay said loudly from across the table, smiling broadly. 'Really he should be locked up in a finance cubicle, but he offers such intriguing market insights we have to let him out occasionally.'

Kit, still smarting from Max's brusque manner, sat down between Camille and Rupert.

'Shall we begin then?' Clay said. 'Ah, look, here's our talking juice.' Alicia had entered with the coffee. 'Thank you Alicia, perfect timing.'

Kit liked Clay. He was good-humoured and welcoming, unlike *some* people.

'So,' said Clay, taking the lid off his coffee, 'let me begin by telling you a little about Blue Tree. We're not your average private equity firm. I started the company with my partners Leon and John a little over five years ago to do things *differently*. We've all worked in big firms—I was over in Chicago, John was in London, Leon was in Melbourne—but we felt there was *another* way to operate. To really *push back* on this idea of private equity being an oppressive, impatient, bottom-line-only machine. It can be so much more. A real *partner*, in the true sense of the word. *Shared* dreams, *shared* challenges, *shared success*.' (If the world ever ran out of italics, Kit would know who'd hogged them all.) Clay smiled at Kit as though this must be deeply reassuring, when in fact she had come in with no preconceived notions, because she had never met anyone in private equity before.

'We work *intimately* with founders to create the growth and reach they seek, to realise their dreams. We are *always* on, offering full support, but we *never* interfere, and since we don't have a roof on any of our investments, you can rest assured there's no three-year churn and burn here, ha ha ha.'

Kit didn't get the joke but smiled knowingly all the same.

'To begin, Kit, what we'd *really* love is to hear the Second Day story,' he said.

'Yes, of course,' said Kit, shifting her weight in her seat, nerves asserting themselves in her shaking hands and rapidly beating heart. She knew this, it was her life and story. 'So,' she said, psychosomatic frog catching in her throat. 'Ahem, sorry,' she giggled. 'So, I created Second Day seven years ago, after fifteen years working as a professional hairdresser and stylist . . .'

She went through the origin story, only faltering when she glanced over at Max to see his eyes boring holes into her.

'Um . . . where was I? Oh yes . . . I think a big USP for us is our educational slant: I worked as an educator with L'Oréal for years and have created reams of how-to content for brands and social media, so I felt like I was in a really strong position to launch products that customers could understand instantly. Hair products are super confusing and hard to master, never mind expensive, so I wanted to be in the customer's corner, teaching her how to use these products so she felt competent and, ultimately, confident.'

Jordan had gone too fast on the slides, which threw Kit. Panicked, she decided to ad lib.

'We were lucky enough to have early success—cue my first manufacturing and inventory woes, ha ha!—thanks to some of my high-profile clients spreading the word, and we have maintained strong sales ever since.'

Camille jumped in. 'We are up thirty percent year on year.'

'Remarkable, really,' Rupert said, nodding.

Kit went on. 'We currently make and sell fifteen SKUs and have a very strong new-product rollout in the next thirty-six months, with a minimum of three products a year. Since March we have been sold in over three hundred Catalyst doors in the US, which has—'

'Boots on the ground?' Max interrupted.

'I'm sorry?' Kit said politely to the pig who had thrown her flow.

'You got boots on the ground over there?' He looked not so much at her as through her.

'We have a distributor who works exclusively with Catalyst; *they* act as our boots on the ground,' Camille said.

'And we use a local creative agency for all our press and influencer and marketing,' Jordan added.

'Almost impossible to make a dent in the US without your own people there,' Max said. 'As I'm sure you know, the ground is littered with Australian brands that have failed in the US of A.'

'Yes, mainly because their investors made rash, damaging and uninformed decisions,' Camille shot back.

A half-smile spread across Max's lips, but he remained quiet.

'We outsold their initial forecast,' Camille went on, a cheerful clip in her tone, 'and are using a local manufacturing plant to remove freight costs and bring down COGS. Sales are fifteen percent up on projections, which isn't too bad for a company with not a single boot on the ground.' She smiled with closed lips as a full stop.

'Back home,' Kit jumped in, 'we have a really strong online business. That's where we started and where our strength lies—'

'The consumer has tired of shopping online, though, hasn't she,' Max chimed in, more of a statement than a question. 'I see here your DTC sales have dropped by twenty percent in the past eighteen months.'

'Yes, but as I mentioned earlier, we're up thirty percent overall year on year,' Camille replied. 'If you take wholesale into account. Which you should.'

'We're stocked in Sun, Australia's oldest and most loved pharmacy and beauty retailer,' Kit went on bravely, unsure of how to handle Max's constant hits. 'We're in all seventy stores, and we sit at number three in hair in there, which is huge given all the legacy and value brands we're up against. So, yeah, we feel confident our omnichannel approach is working, and our international plans are really just kicking off . . .' Kit stopped there;

she'd forgotten *all* her talking points. Fucking Max Darling, interrupting all the time.

'Wonderful, terrific,' said Rupert enthusiastically, just shy of clapping. 'Thank you, Kit. I think we can all agree it really is a unique success story in such a noisy, competitive and saturated category. In the interest of efficiency, since we're all familiar with the IM, current trading and forecasting, et cetera, we'll hold all of that for Q&A, but Kit perhaps you could detail your vision for a partner?'

'Yes, of course,' she said, nodding vigorously; she'd hoped to project calm. 'Well, essentially,' she said, trying to recall what she'd practised in the shower, 'we feel ready to cross the chasm from small- to medium-sized business, and bringing in a strategic partner with experience and a skill set we don't currently have will help power our growth and global reach.'

Good one, Kit! she cheered herself. *Jargon touchdown! More of that!*

'My team and brand deserve to realise their full potential,' she went on. 'We have got to where we are with luck, hard work and gut instinct, but I know big things are possible if we bring in people who can share their wisdom, capability and network.'

'Who are the other shareholders?' Max asked as he flicked through the printout of the IM, without looking up.

'They were instrumental in the early days,' Rupert jumped in, 'but their contribution is . . . less valuable at this stage.'

'And are you selling down?' Max asked, looking directly at Kit.

'The exact split of the shareholder selldown remains proprietary at this stage,' Rupert said quickly.

'Noted,' said Max. 'But why would we invest if the founder is cashing out?'

'I'm not going anywhere,' Kit blurted out, instantly regretting it. Rupert had made it clear he would handle any questions around her involvement.

'Kit will remain with Second Day in her capacity as founder, board member and creative director,' Rupert added smoothly. 'She is simply looking to strengthen and scale the business with a partner who has proven hits on the board and the ability to supercharge growth.'

Clay removed his ankle from his knee and pulled his chair in to the table. 'Wonderful to hear.'

'Perhaps you could tell us why you believe Blue Tree would be a good partner as Second Day scale?' Rupert asked Clay. No one could outdo Rupert when it came to firm but charming conversational pivots.

'Seth, can you pull up our deck?' Clay asked.

One of the suits tapped a few buttons on his laptop, and a giant Blue Tree logo filled the screen.

'I'll kick off with our lifestyle brands,' Clay began. 'And I urge you to contact *any* of the founders mentioned here; it's *really* important you get a sense of who we are from people who work with us in the same capacity you potentially would—or who *have* done, before exiting with millions of dollars in their pockets.'

He smiled roguishly and Kit, remembering her role as a compatible, friendly woman, immediately smiled back.

'First up is Sola, a sunscreen company developed by a married couple who are both cancer research scientists. Incredible story and, as I'm sure you've seen, a very successful range . . .' As Clay listed all their investments, Kit nodded sagely in all the correct spots, raising her brows at Rupert when Clay got to Slick, a huge

UK make-up brand with a very aspirational founder story. Kit began to imagine what might be possible . . .

'Can I jump in here?' Camille asked.

'Of course, Camille,' Clay said—a man clearly proud of his ability to retain people's names.

'Sorry if you were about to ask this, Kit, but what *exactly* would you offer us as a partner day to day? What would it look like practically, who would we be dealing with, who would be on our board, what sort of touch time would you expect?'

Oh yes, thought Kit. *Took the words right out of my mouth.*

'It will be whatever you want it to be, whatever is useful,' said Clay, smiling. 'I know Seth here chats to Adam from Sola weekly, for instance.'

'Channels,' Camille said. 'These are very important to Second Day. What if you came in and tried to put us in discount retailers and supermarkets? How can we be assured you won't mess with—'

'The special sauce?' Clay cut in. 'Because *that's* what we're investing in: what you do so well. The last thing we'd want to do is waltz in and pretend to know how to run Second Day; *you* are the experts at that. What we *can* do is offer you insights and investment when you want to crack China or need an in at Ulta or Sephora. We are at your disposal.'

Camille nodded and sat back in her chair, seemingly satisfied.

'Hit us with *any* queries you have,' Clay urged. 'We want you to feel safe to explore even your worst fears with us: challenging the status quo is what we do best.'

He seemed so nice, so safe, like the handsome dad in a home insurance ad, Kit thought.

'I have a question,' Max said, leaning back in his chair, crossing his arms. 'I'd like to know how you arrived at those projected earnings given what you've been capable of historically, with a pipeline of new product that is potentially cannibalising due to a lot of category depth but very little in the way of genuine newness. I can't see any universe where your EBITDA will be double what it is now in three years.'

Not for the first time, Kit wished she had subtitles.

Rupert quickly leaped in with a logical and elegant defence, before Camille, with a dangerous edge to her tone, took Max through the rationale. This combative back and forth continued until Clay tactfully turned the taps off.

'Thank you, Camille, we have a far better understanding now.' He turned to Kit, smiling. 'Kit, you mentioned you're not going anywhere, and your passion for the brand and its growth is evident. But one thing we would need to understand, as it really informs how best we can support you, is your eventual plan for Second Day.' He sat back in his chair, left ankle perched casually on his right knee. 'In other words, are you looking for an exit in three years, or is this more of a ten-year journey?'

Kit looked at him, deer in the headlights. She had no idea.

16

THE MEETING RAN OVERTIME. As the trio quickly raced across town for the next one—Camille madly texting and Jordan delivering a stream-of-consciousness monologue about the meeting (Max was super-hot but up himself, Rupert didn't let her present her slides, Clay was married but was he *happily* married, do we think)—Kit was thinking about working with Blue Tree. And it felt exciting. They were so . . . *impressive.* How different their board meetings would be with some of those guys—not Max, never Max—in them. How different their whole business could be, how much *bigger* and *better.* Kit had always dreamed of a stand-alone store in Sydney (she could so clearly visualise the purple wallpaper and red shelves); maybe these guys would be the path to that . . .

Kit checked her phone and noticed a series of missed calls from Maggie on her lock screen. That was weird; for one thing, Maggie hated phone calls as much as Kit did, and for another, she was in Paris on a sourcing trip. Why would she be calling?

'Hey, Siri, what time is it in Paris?' Kit asked.

'*It is currently three-oh-two am in Paris, France,*' her phone answered.

This is not right, Kit thought.

She called; no answer. She texted her friend.

My love are you ok? Are kids ok?

In a few minutes' time she'd be bustled into the next meeting; she needed Maggie to write back.

WHAT IS GOING ON U R KILLING ME, Kit wrote.

all safe just did a really dumb dumb thing, Maggie replied, finally.

In taxi with team then straight into meeting, Kit mashed out, *Text me what happened???*

Three dots, then nothing.

The car slowed to a stop in front of a pretty, leafy terrace in the back streets of Paddington. If Maggie didn't put her out of her misery before she went into this presentation, there was no way she could focus. Kit would have to remember to kill her when she saw her next.

'Thank you so much, Jeb,' Kit said warmly to the driver, since it was her Uber account and she wanted to maintain her 4.9 rating. The three of them clambered out with their handbags, and after fumbling around for her lipstick, Kit expertly ran a lap around her lips sans mirror to freshen up.

'This looks like my house,' Camille remarked, as they walked through a small gate and up to the terrace door with a small sign reading CANDLE INVESTMENTS. 'Strange place for an office.'

She knocked and the three of them waited.

'Wonder if Rupert beat us,' Jordan mused, looking back out to the street.

The door opened, and a woman in her fifties smiled at them. 'Hi, come in—don't worry, you're at the right place, this *is* an office despite outer appearances.' She'd clearly had to greet people this way many times.

'Thank you,' Camille said, as the women walked into a crowded hallway that looked and felt very much like they were in someone's home.

'Hold the door!' came Rupert's voice from behind, and Kit turned to see him trotting up the path towards them.

As she followed the woman towards a narrow spiral stair-case apparently built at a time when humans didn't exceed one hundred centimetres in height, Kit felt her phone buzz in her bag. She pulled it out: Maggie, thank god.

OK. I was drunk and horny last night so watched some porn BUT instead of closing the tab I hit SHARE, cos I do that a million X a day for work, and the first person in my contacts was Henry, cos we'd been work texting, and I HIT SEND.

She continued in a new text. *So my boss now has link and pic to amelia gets rammed by a big black cock . . . from me. I'm DYINGGG*

And the final text: *he hasn't replied. Not even a laughing emoji. Nothing.*

Kit was so immersed in Maggie's texts she wobbled in her heels and began to tip dangerously backwards. As she grasped the railing to save herself she heard the sickening smash of her phone meeting the hard tiles below.

'Oof, Kit, are you okay?' Rupert asked from behind her.

'My phone went to heaven, didn't it?' she asked, already knowing the answer.

'I imagine so. I'm just glad it wasn't us,' he said with a relieved smile.

'I'm sorry,' she said. 'I was in an urgent text conversation.'

Rupert tilted his head. 'Is Gretel okay?'

'Gretel? She's fine. Why?' She looked at him quizzically.

He smiled. 'Then it's not urgent.'

'I've got it!' the friendly woman who'd let them in hollered from below. 'Be here waiting for you after the meeting.'

'Thank you!' Kit yelled down. 'Sorry for the mess.'

Once they were all seated in the boardroom, which was one-third the size of Blue Tree's and entirely unburdened by sweeping city views, Kit's adrenaline made way for deep, whole-body tiredness. No phone and a presentation would normally have her buzzing with anxiety, but she didn't even have the energy to wig out. Camille had queried why they were doing two presentations in a row, said no good ever came from going back to back, but Rupert insisted on keeping to the timeline. 'I've seen these things bloat out to twenty-four, even thirty-six months; I don't wish that pain, nor those fees, on anyone.'

Kit took what she hoped was an inaudible breath to freshen up and assumed the expression of a dynamic, passionate founder anyone would simply *love* to invest with.

'Welcome, Second Day,' said a smiling man in his early fifties with a broad, regional accent, the kind that was usually accompanied by R.M. Williams, a ute and a blue heeler. He wore a white shirt, black jeans and a giant Rolex, and had an enormous scar across one hand and up the arm.

'It's great to have you in so we can get to know a bit about Second Day, and we can let you in on what we do here at Candle. I'm Luke Collins, investment director, and this is Nigel Bradbury, our founder and chair.'

A grey-haired man in his seventies nodded and pretended to tip an invisible hat. He had a banana in front of him and was the only one at the table with their phone face up rather than face down.

'And over there you've got Adnan, he's one of our investment managers.'

Adnan smiled warmly at everyone around the table in turn, which was a welcome distraction from the obvious hair transplant line marching across his upper forehead.

Luke went on. 'Everything we do here is real targeted, real specialised; we're very selective about our investments. We want to make sure we can give every founder in our portfolio the time and attention they need to grow. We've been around for over twenty years, with offices in Melbourne and Auckland. We're not slick, like some of your city PE firms, and we like it that way. We think small to grow big. And it felt to us as if you think the same way. We can see your passion, your care. We like your story and see the potential.'

'Thank you, Luke,' Rupert said. 'Now, you all know me, of course, but it gives me great pleasure to introduce you to Kit Cooper, the founder of Second Day, Jordan Edgar, CMO, and Camille Barreau, CEO. Three more formidable women you will not meet.

'Now, as no one has a *whisper* of time to spare, I think we should get right into it. Kit, would you like to give Candle an overview of the brand and what inspired you to run a process for a partner?'

'I'll just get the presentation up . . .' Jordan murmured, opening her laptop and scanning the table for the input console.

'No need,' Luke said. 'We prefer more of a fireside chat.'

'Of course,' said Kit, nodding. She rattled off a slightly waffly, low-energy summary and then Candle kicked off with their questions.

Luke went first. 'Can I just ask, right off the bat, why is it you have never sold your products in Chemshop? We know the fellas in there and their turnover is astonishing. Their leading hair care brand does around sixty mill at the register every year.' Luke had the same tone and character as the boys she grew up with, in a place with more Gavins than shops.

Kit opened her mouth to answer, but Jordan beat her to it. 'Because it is not the right channel for us,' she said. This was her area and she felt passionately about it. 'Their merchandising and constant discounting would be irreversibly damaging to our brand and the margin would destroy our profit line. We are trying to take our products to the rest of the world, to best-in-class retailers, and they look to where we are sold in our home country. Sun is the best channel for us, both as a signifier and also as a retail partner. Their emphasis on customer experience and education is as strong as ours.'

Luke raised his eyebrows and nodded thoughtfully.

'I suppose it's a case of quality versus quantity,' Nigel said. 'You could be in the fanciest stores, right in the front window, but sell very little. Or you could be in the cheaper stores, make a big volume play, and shoot the lights out.'

'I hear you,' Jordan replied. 'For us brand placement is a higher priority. You can always *end up* in Chemshop, but if you start there, no one else will touch you. It means something to Second Day customers where we sit on shelf. It's status. We didn't *need* to do wholesale, we chose to. So it had to be right.'

'I see,' Nigel said quietly, as if he really did.

Maybe it was the softening that came with adrenal comedown, but Kit felt a strange affection for this man. She'd never had a grandfather figure; Ron's father had died of cancer, and her mother's dad had taken off when she was a kid. She'd always envisaged the cookie-advertisement version, the kind who sat by the fire in a chequered shirt and asked mildly probing life questions before imparting deep wisdom with a smile and a tousle of the hair.

'Why don't we walk you through some of our current investments to give you an insight into how we operate as founder-first investors,' Luke suggested, interrupting Kit's warm and fuzzies. 'Adnan, can you talk a little around Goal?'

'Certainly,' he said, sitting up straight and rubbing his hands together. 'So, Goal is actually something we invested in just over eighteen months ago, an innovative and exciting Australian business from the Gold Coast that has, like Second Day, cornered their market beautifully. Since we've come on board, they have grown their workforce by forty percent and their distribution has doubled. They are getting ready to launch into Brazil, which will be an enormous market for them, and—'

'Sorry,' Camille interrupted. 'What do Goal make or sell?'

'Oh, goals. Sport goals. Children's football and soccer goals. But not only that; they also make cones, flags, markers, dishes, domes—anything you need on the field.'

Camille was unfamiliar with the idea of camouflaging opinions; her face said it all.

'Similar size company to yours,' Adnan went on. 'Relatively similar sales and EBITDA, wanting to scale up, get that proof point of success in another market for exit.'

'I wonder if there might be something in your portfolio in the lifestyle arena?' Rupert asked hopefully. Kit knew Rupert liked these boys; he'd worked with them several times and had made her promise to hear them out before casting judgement.

'Are you familiar with Skin Science?' Adnan asked.

'The skincare brand?' Kit snapped to attention. They were amazing, with a huge presence in the US. *That* was the kind of sibling brand she wanted!

'Yes,' Adnan said proudly. 'We were *very* close to becoming a majority stakeholder with them actually, but were pipped at the final post. Perhaps you know Brilliant White, the on-the-go tooth-whitening brand?'

'Yeah, they're all over TikTok,' Kit said, nodding. Not bad.

'Fantastic marketing, isn't it?' he said. 'Yes, we were very keen to invest, got right to the pointy end, but they went with another party. So while it's fair to say we don't *presently* invest in any beauty brands, we have been *looking* to invest in the beauty sector for some time.'

Kit slumped back in her seat, nodding. These guys were not it.

'We also have Supermulch,' Adnan said, barrelling on in sweet ignorance. 'One of our most successful investments And confidentially'—he lowered his tone and head—'close to acquisition by one of the largest nursery chains in the southern hemisphere.'

Camille pulled back her shirt sleeve to check the time. She'd been very clear about only partnering with someone already in the beauty category.

'There's also Mats All,' Adnan went on. 'Our biggest investment, actually, and one we're most proud of given that their recent valuation is six times what it was when we bought in two years ago. We are looking to exit in the next twelve months.'

'And they make . . .?' Camille inquired.

'Beer mats for pubs,' Adnan said cheerfully. 'You know the ones that are bouncy with the nice smooth edges?'

'If I may,' Rupert intervened, sensing the audience had been well and truly lost. 'What's important here is that the growth Adnan has described is no joke! Candle are experts at meaningfully scaling small- and medium-sized companies and, if appropriate, taking them through to a material exit.'

'May I ask,' Nigel said, his light blue eyes resting on Kit's, 'what is *your* exit plan?'

'Oh,' said Kit, yanked from thoughts of Maggie, her smashed phone and where the nearest Apple store was. 'Well, that's not what this process is about, really.'

'But you must have some idea,' he pushed gently. 'Even if it is *not* to exit.'

Kit looked to Rupert and widened her eyes for him to take over.

'Fair question, Nige,' Rupert said. 'But this is a shareholder transition for a minority stake, not a capital raise or pathway to rapid exit.'

'I understand,' the older man said. 'But how can anyone possibly invest without knowing the long-term plan? As you well know, Rupert, it will factor strongly in the term sheet.'

'Divestment is something we will address in stage two,' Rupert confirmed. 'Our intention now is to test for synergies between Candle and Second Day, to assess if there is a viable partnership.'

'How would you help us grow?' Camille interrupted suddenly, looking at Luke. 'Without any beauty experience, what can you offer in real-world terms?'

'We can provide you with whatever is needed,' Luke said. 'If you need a CFO, we will help you find the best one. If you need a distributor in the UK, we will use our connections to get that happening. If you need capital for a big advertising play, we can supply a cash injection. It's reactive, in that sense. A good investor offers more than just money.'

'And if you inject cash . . . is that a loan? Or are you talking equity dilution?'

'To be determined by the board at that time,' Luke said.

'With Mats All,' Adnan piped up, 'we actually loaned capital so they could invest in a new waterproofing spray for all of their mats, which actually—'

'Thanks, Adnan,' Luke said, cutting him off. 'We will be a partner in the true sense,' he continued to Camille. 'I am on the phone to my founders at least once a week. Sometimes it's a manufacturing issue, or a retailer problem, or even just staffing. Sometimes you just need an ear, someone at arm's length.'

Camille issued a polite smile. Kit smiled widely to compensate.

'Well, thank you everyone for your time,' Rupert said.

As they all stood, Kit made sure to say goodbye to Nigel. 'Thank you for meeting with us today,' she said sincerely as they shook hands.

He looked at her with the exact expression she was hoping for: a mixture of fondness and pride, the perfect Grandfather Simulation. She could die happy.

'Good luck,' he said. 'You should feel very proud. To be in profit, a healthy profit, is nothing to be sneezed at. You're doing a good job, which is far more important than just having a good idea.'

'Thank you,' Kit said, blushing.

'You know,' he said, picking up his banana, 'I don't like to judge—everyone is on their own journey—but we meet a lot of founders who just build and sell, build and sell. There's no heart. You have heart. And I'm pleased to see you're not selling a majority stake. That's when you run into trouble.'

A lump formed in Kit's throat. Was she *that* deprived of validation and kindness that a stranger saying a nice thing could make her crumble?

'It can be overwhelming, the transaction. But you only need enough courage for the next step. Do you have a family? Children?'

She nodded.

'Always make time for family. Companies and deals come and go, but your kids, well, they just go.'

Kit looked up at him, this lean little equity Santa Claus, with his white beard and twinkling eyes, and nodded, blinking back her pathetic, embarrassing tears. She had a sudden urge to go collect Gretel from school and hug her for a hundred days straight.

After collecting her phone, now in pieces in a plastic takeaway container, Kit and her team said their farewells and waited out front in the midday sun for their Uber. The air was warm, the sky a terrific blue: a truly glorious day. Kit wondered how she'd come to find herself in boardrooms discussing margins and profits instead of lying on Bondi Beach.

Rupert nodded at the takeaway container.

'RIP?'

'Already reincarnated as an iPad. I'll have to get a new one this afternoon.' She checked behind her to ensure no one was listening and then said, 'So I guess we can rule them out?'

Rupert tipped his head to one side. 'I understand their investments weren't necessarily sexy, but I recommend taking a more wholesale approach to potential partners.'

'I understand, but compared to Blue Tree . . .' She looked at him; surely she was just stating the obvious.

Rupert smiled. 'Remember, Kit, Australia is a small place, with a relatively small pool of beauty companies and an even smaller pool of investment firms who have bought into beauty companies. This is a new world, largely a product of the internet and social media. The type of firm you're imagining, with several beauty runs on the board, simply doesn't exist here. They're international, and unfortunately our cheque size is too small to interest them.'

'What does that mean?' she asked.

'The value of Second Day is too low,' he clarified. 'They need to spend at least a hundred million dollars on their investments for it to be worthwhile.'

Kit laughed. 'So put the price up!'

He chuckled. 'If only it were that simple. They would also expect a majority stake, usually around seventy to eighty percent. Correct me if I'm wrong, but that's not what you're selling here. Also, to be frank, I don't think you would love the terms, or the pressure.'

'Affirmative,' Kit said. No deal was worth making life hell for her and her team.

'On that,' Rupert added, 'several parties, including Blue Tree, have given early indications they want to buy more than Toni's shareholding—well over fifty percent, in fact.'

'But that's not what's on offer,' she reminded him.

'Deals do have a funny way of evolving,' he said cryptically.

'I need to stay majority shareholder, keep control,' Kit insisted.

'All I ask is you remain open-minded. Dismissing a genuinely good partner to retain so much personal equity may not make the most sense for the future of the company and your eventual exit . . . Ask yourself *why* you need control, and in which areas. The things you care about—your retailers, brand and marketing—can be retained through the shareholders' agreement rather than a larger shareholding. There's also drag-along rights, depending on the quantum of equity being sold.'

'What's that again?' Not every financey term trying to get into her brain was successful.

'Means you can sell one hundred percent of the company whenever *you* want to and drag the other shareholders along with you, even if they don't want to sell at that time. It's non-negotiable in the current deal, obviously, and anyone coming in at thirty percent wouldn't expect anything different. But if you were to sell anything beyond fifty percent, it gets trickier.'

Rupert caught the puzzled expression on Kit's face and hastened to reassure her. 'Kit, whatever happens, there is no outcome here that won't be entirely in your best interest.'

'Or yours and that healthy commission,' she said cheekily. Rupert stood to clip two percent off the final price of the shares.

A white Camry was inching up the street towards them. Camille, who'd ordered the car, was waving her arms madly to get the driver's attention. Jordan was eating a protein bar and texting simultaneously as though one controlled the other.

'Why does everyone need to know my exit plans *now*?' Kit asked, frowning.

'There are key terms bidders assess before accepting a deal. One is how involved the founder will be and how much equity they own. At your current level of sixty percent, they will feel very comfortable. Another consideration is the sunset date, or when they expect their investment will be returned, when the company is sold in full. You can make it five years, even seven. And there's that drag-along if you want to go sooner. But we will need to put something in writing eventually, so I do need you to have a think about it.'

Even when things were intensely complicated and confusing, Rupert had a way of making Kit feel like it was easy breezy, nothing to worry about. It was quite the skill.

The driver had finally worked out what Camille's dancing meant and zoomed up to them.

'Let's go, ladies,' Camille hollered as she elegantly folded herself into the front seat.

Rupert smiled at Kit fondly. 'You were fantastic today, Kit. I know this is all new for you, but so was running a business at one stage, and look at how you've mastered that.'

Kit was grateful for Rupert's kind words, but she was very much bluffing and smiling her way through all of this. The question was, could she bluff and smile long enough to find the right partner for her business?

17

'CLARISSA IS LOOKING FOR YOU,' Hyun said, when Kit finally shuffled into the office, tired and hangry. 'She said she needs to talk to you about the pump in the frizz serum?'

Clarissa was a freelance chemist who worked for Second Day two days a week. Simon was desperate to bring her on as head of formulations so he could step back, but Clarissa wasn't ready to leave her lucrative role at a pharmaceutical company, so for now Simon was it. This suited Kit just fine.

'You okay, girl?' Hyun asked. His face was doing a terrible job of hiding how he thought she looked.

'I formally identify as exhausted,' she said, walking through to her desk. She collapsed into her chair, firing up her laptop to reply to poor Maggie, who would have turned herself inside out by now with no reassuring response from her bestie.

'Me too,' said Hyun, who had followed her. 'I look hideous.' He knew full well he did not. He had been using retinol since he was seventeen and his skin had forgotten how to do anything but glow. '*Probably* cos I broke up with Davey last night . . .'

'Oh, Hyun, I'm sorry. What happened?'

'Did a keyword search on my name in his phone,' he said matter-of-factly. 'He was talking shit about me to other boys. I screenshotted everything, of course. Going to make them into a collage and use it as the invite to my Single Reveal party this Friday night.'

Kit smiled. 'Keyword search, wow. FBI-level.'

'It's the bare minimum,' he said, as if she were a moron. 'So, how were the meetings? We got our new fairy business mother?'

'They were fine,' she said. 'No, they were good,' she corrected herself. 'We did well, I think. Those people may as well speak in QR code, though . . .'

Kit tapped her touch-pad impatiently as her laptop whirred itself to life. She desperately wanted to goss and hypoth about Blue Tree, but she had made a decision not to discuss the deal with her team. She needed to shield them from it, protect them from all the CAPEX and EBITDA.

'Umm, what is *that* . . .' Hyun nodded at the takeaway box with her phone.

'I dropped my baby—it's a goner.'

'Probably just the screen,' he said confidently. 'Give it to me and I'll get it fixed; there's a place on Crown Street. It'll be less than an hour.'

She looked at him with a pretend-cry face. 'Really? Thank you.' She handed him the container. 'Godspeed.'

'No one should be without their phone. *No one*.' He clutched the box to his chest solemnly and turned to go before whipping his head back. 'Have you eaten today? Big oily laksa? Extra veggies, no shallots? Coke Zero?'

'Yes. One million times yes. Thank you.' She made praying hands, and he winked in response before swanning away.

Her MacBook finally came to life and Kit hammered her password in, desperate to get into iMessage and put Maggie out of her misery. Also: what if Gretel's school had called? What if any number of disasters had occurred in the past two hours?

An onslaught of unread texts appeared. *If I didn't know the context, I might very well worry for these people's sanity*, Kit thought.

Toni was the first cab off the rank.

how did the meetings go any good options?? xxx we need to speak are you confident this deal will happen?? We really need to know the date funds will be through xx

Kit scoffed. Toni could not have less of a clue.

Should I be in them do you think?? she wrote in a follow-up text. *when is the next one? Really I think I should be there. I'll tell Rupert. Or will you?? I should be there. xxx*

'You *really* shouldn't,' Kit said under her breath, cringing at the thought of Toni seated next to her in the boardroom this morning at Blue Tree, all cloying perfume and conversational hijacking.

Maggie had unloaded, as expected.

WHERE R U

And then: *TALK ME OFF THE LEDGE*

Three missed calls and then: *Do I text and apologise?? Send a LOL emoji and say hahaha big woops message for my husband do NOT open?? Will this get me fired?? Is it sexl hssment??*

Followed by: *I sent this for him to see when he wakes up I couldn't do nothing*

Then: *Henry DELETE the last message I sent. Do not open it. It was a joke meant for Sam. You can't unsee it once you see it. Just DELETE. Okay? See you at breakfast. Mx*

Followed by one just for Kit: *FYI you are dead to me xx*

Kit quickly shot back a response even though Maggie would be asleep.

My love! I dropped my phone and it smashed. I am SO SORRY. Just got back to office and on laptop replying. Forgive me forgive me xxxxx

And then, because Kit could only text in thought bubbles, one at a time: *That was a perfect text. Everything will be so okay. Henry is a gent, and he is familiar with the concept of porn, I assure you. I love you! We will laugh about this one day! Xxxxx*

Feeling like she had confidently put a bow on that, and that Maggie would live to see another day, Kit opened the next message. It was from Ron.

Give me a call please

The most underwhelming invitation on earth.

Hi dad, can only text for now—everything ok?

He replied immediately. *Just call when you can kid*

Okay, my phone is at shop being fixed, will call later. X

Next was a message from a number she didn't know.

Hi Kit! It's Flora's mum from kindy. Flo has been asking for a play date with Gretel and I thought that was a lovely idea, how are you placed this Friday after school? We could take them swimming??

Gretel had never mentioned anyone named Flora. Kit could barely make time for play dates with Reya and Frankie, let alone *new* friends! And spending a whole afternoon with a mum she didn't know? Kit didn't have the social battery for that right now. She'd reply later, when she was less grumpy.

Up next was Ari.

*ahem **as per my last email**... sorry sorry chasing up emails is super pathetic but worried you didn't get? or did you just hate it? Axx*

Kit closed her eyes, took a deep breath, plonked her elbows on her desk and rubbed her temples with her fingers. She had completely forgotten about the email Ari had sent earlier this week. Perhaps by design. Perhaps because they always came in during the middle of the night so they didn't exist in her framework of 'new emails that need attention' like those that came in daylight hours. It had pissed her off, though, she remembered that much. She had stupidly believed he'd taken their conversation back in September seriously. He'd made genuine efforts to find a home in Sydney and was looking for gigs here. Kit didn't want to applaud him for doing the bare minimum, but it was all relative. Whether he was expertly distracting and procrastinating Kit couldn't be sure, but he had flown home twice in the past month to meet his parenting quota and, while that was still a lot less than he should be doing, Kit had seen the positive effect it had on their daughter. And that counted.

Seizing the moment, even though the moment was one influenced by intense hunger, she hammered out a reply on her keyboard:

Saw it, yes. It kinda feels like you have already made up your mind, tbh.

His email had said that if he sacrificed his allocated Christmas holiday with Gretel to do a job in Thailand, he could take a job here in Sydney that would last three months from the start of February. *Three whole months!* he'd written, as if Kit should pop champagne. What annoyed Kit was that it wasn't so much an ask as a 'flagging it with you'. He was still prioritising his career, his schedule, and the exciting, sexy lifestyle he had created for himself. Gaslighting felt too strong a word, but Ari had a real talent for rearranging Kit's boundaries and requests to suit his needs, and then convincing her it was totally going to be great. So, nope.

She fired off another text. *You know Gretel has 7 weeks school holidays, right? And you're saying that you cannot see her for any of that? Also I booked a week in Bali with Maggie in January during the fortnight you were supposed to be with her: what do you suggest I do about that?*

She paused. *So, actually, no, I don't think this works for us.*

Earlier that week, during a hectic five thirty pm dual-family dinner at a local pizza restaurant, Maggie had asked Kit about her endgame with Ari. After all, where was the punishment in telling a man he couldn't see a child he already didn't see? How would having sole custody help Kit? It would just strip her of the few co-parenting crumbs she *did* have. Kit had hoped the threat would be enough to spook Ari into action, but she was starting to wonder if anything could penetrate Ari's self-centredness. Kit pulled her hands back from the keyboard and folded her arms across her chest as she considered this.

Movement caught her eye. She looked over to see that Jaz, the adorable new head of community and content (and Hyun's first underling), was forcing the staff to perform some kind of social media dance, one at a time. She could make anyone do anything; it was a form of witchcraft.

Kit gazed at them absently, deep in thought. She was just so disappointed in how Ari had chosen to do fatherhood. How low a bar he had set for himself. Her parenting, her work ethic, her company, her friendships, how she presented herself and lived her life: *it had to be the best.* It had to be *perfect.* She expended so much energy making sure she never let anyone down—the idea of it made her sick—yet Ari was completely comfortable doing it again and again. Kit delighted in her wins, be that reaching a nice round number in her savings account, or a successful product launch, or remembering to buy Gretel's Book Week costume on Amazon in time. That was just who she was. But Ari only cared about Ari. Was she an intolerant perfectionist, though? Could she really hold other people to her own extreme standards? Maggie said perfectionism was a coping mechanism to mask feelings of inadequacy. Kit could see how that might be true: what was a more powerful driver than feeling you were not good enough?

Kit judged herself harder than she would ever judge anyone else. All the Instagram therapists she followed said that having an unreliable, unpredictable parent and a fragile household led to hyper-independence and a need for control, ie it was a bad thing. But Kit struggled to see her childhood as a negative, especially given it had led to so much success.

Clarissa was marching across the other side of the office and happened to see Kit at her desk.

Kit quickly threw the words 'pump, frizz, serum' into the Google search bar of her brain, but nothing came up.

'I spoke with Simon about this before bothering you,' Clarissa said, her expression apologetic, 'but the serum pumps cannot be made from recycled plastic because the manufacturers believe it's too risky, that it may compromise the dispense mechanism, so they will not entertain the idea. They don't think this serum is safe in recycled plastic either.'

'Safe?' Kit asked, wincing.

'Because of the hyaluronic acid, it should be an airtight pump.'

'Right, got it,' Kit said. Achieving the holy trinity of gorgeous, functioning and sustainable packaging was now the most complicated challenge at Second Day. 'Would we go back to that small bottle with the nozzle? I loved that one. And we know it can be PCR.'

'I liked it, too,' Clarissa said. 'But Kit, we have already done stability on this vessel; it would cost us another three months to do it with that variety.'

Seeing Kit's frown, Clarissa went on. 'Back when we began stability, we all agreed this vessel was the right choice. You liked it because no one else had that exact ball shape?'

Kit remembered now. She exhaled noisily through her lips as though whistling. 'Would you consider the pump being virgin plastic in order to make the production deadline?' Clarissa asked.

'I can suck that up. Thanks, Clarissa,' Kit said. 'I know this stuff makes your job harder, but I really appreciate all you're doing to get this one up.'

A text came through from Priya: *How did the presentations go this morning?*

Kit was just typing out a reply when Jaz walked over. She was wearing a short denim apron dress over a pink baby tee and chunky loafers with little white socks. All of this was capped off with a pixie chop, tucked behind her ears. She looked like the lead in a 2001 high school movie, which was absolute fashion catnip to Kit.

'Um, Kit, would you have a minute?' Jaz said, raising her perfectly bushy brows up and down playfully. 'Actually, I only need thirty seconds. And you will be so great at this, you'll love it, trust me. So, it's called the *I'd Never Okay Maybe* and you just have to do this quick set of questions and—'

'Jaz,' Kit interrupted, 'I'll do whatever you ask, but tell me honestly: would it matter if I did it or not? Will anyone notice? Serious question.'

Jaz twisted her mouth to one side, thinking. She actually tapped her foot, like a cartoon character.

'Well, the Nuclear Shine founder did it, and so did Jamie and Krissy from White Nights, and the *whole* team at ghd did it, so yeah . . .'

'Okay, next question,' Kit said. 'What do you think when you see a founder do these kinds of things? Like, you as Jaz the person, with your Second Day hat off.'

Jaz put one hand on her hip, the other holding her phone under her chin as she thought. Kit noticed she had a tattoo of a little steam train on tracks going up the entire underside of her arm. She loved it, and was dying to ask its significance, but Delilah had told her that was inappropriate.

'Well,' Jaz began, 'first off, I think you're *amazing* at this stuff, you *never* look silly. Second, I think we *know* you don't wanna be doing it? Like, shaking your butt for content is *not* what you set out to do when you started a hair brand? But that you do it *anyway*, cos you wanna be there for your customers, and show up for the fun stuff, not just the salesy stuff? Yeah, I think people respect that.'

Kit pushed her chair out with her bum and stood up. 'Good point, and well made. Okay, Jaz, let's do this.'

As Kit walked around the desk to Jaz, she tried to shake off her cranky old man vibe. She absolutely didn't have the energy or appetite to be dancing around like a goose for social media, but being the founder was no longer just creating products then making, marketing and selling them; it was about being a performing, smiling lunatic who was always fighting to be top of mind—not to mention an ethical, political role model who was completely up to date on all matters of sustainable packaging, innovative ingredients and problematic influencer behaviour. It was a lot. A life of four am starts and shoots in Bali no longer seemed so bad by comparison.

Jaz waved Kit over into position next to the giant fiddle-leaf plants that acted as a loose privacy shield for Camille, Kit and Jordan in the most open of open-plan offices. Kit went along with the video, smiling, playing, abashed and adorable, to the delight of Jaz, whose level of encouragement was so over the top it came close to being patronising, but that was just who she was. Out of the corner of her eye, Kit saw Hyun enter the office and she quietly thanked god. She needed that phone, and she needed to go home. She wanted to pick up Gretel from school, take her to her favourite playground with a bag of short-bread and some frozen grapes, and forget about Second Day for a few hours.

Shit, she realised, looking at her chipped gels. Forget the playground; she'd have to get a manicure because she was shooting first thing tomorrow morning, and her hands would be on show. Of all the things she wanted to do with her time, getting a manicure sat somewhere near having her haemorrhoids removed (Maggie said this was the most painful thing she had ever done in her life, and she'd given birth to Dylan drug-free in the back of a car). Kit was tired of having to be on show all the time, whether it was an investor meeting or filming content. *Oh well*, she sighed. Gretel could get a manicure, too; she'd be down for that.

Hyun placed an Apple bag on Kit's desk. 'It went to heaven. I had to get you a new one.'

'*What?*' Kit gasped. 'But they're, like, two grand!' She hadn't upgraded for three years; she was too stingy and, besides, her phone still worked perfectly well.

Hyun stared at her as if she was speaking another language.

'It's a *work* tool! That's an expense, so I paid on the company CC. Anyway, it was only fourteen hundred dollars. And I got you a cute glitter cover. *Very* you.'

'Work pays for phones?' Jaz asked, delighted. 'That's *amazing*— this one's battery life is kaput.' She waved hers in the air.

'No, just Kit's,' Hyun said—a bit too snippily, Kit thought.

'Sorry, Jaz,' Kit said anxiously. She lived in perpetual fear of one of her employees turning sour and telling the world what a horrible place Second Day was to work. She needed them to all be happy at all times.

'No prob!' Jaz smiled and skipped back to her desk.

'Gen Z, am I right?' Hyun said, rolling his eyes as he placed Kit's lunch on her desk.

'*You* are Gen Z,' Kit said. 'And she's delightful, I won't hear a bad word about her.'

'I'm *Grandpa* Z. She's Baby Z.'

'Be nice,' Kit warned. 'You're her manager, remember—she looks up to you.'

Hyun shrugged. 'She's only human.'

A laksa was far too messy to eat on the go, so Kit sat back down at her desk to eat and jam her SIM into the new phone. She placed a Second Day tote bag over her neck like a bib to protect her clothes from the inevitable laksa splash (something Jordan ridiculed her about no end), and as her phone came to life carefully ate her soup. Just as her new phone's home screen finally appeared, her phone rang. She flinched, spooked. It was her father.

'Dad?' she answered.

'Hi, kid,' he said, voice gruff.

'What's up?' she asked brightly, assuming this would be a bigger than usual financial request if it necessitated a call.

'You at work then?' he asked, not answering her question. He was a total monosyllabic drainer on the phone, which was why she generally kept it to texts.

'Um, yeah. Lot going on here actually, really busy time.' She paused. To her disappointment, but not surprise, he'd never shown any interest in Second Day.

'Dawn uses your hairspray, you know.' *Well, this was a first*, Kit thought. Positive feedback!

'Oh, that's nice to hear. It's doing really well. I'm'—she hesitated, feeling strangely nervous and proud—'I'm actually in the process of selling some of the company.'

'And Rat? Seeing her much?' he said, ignoring her big reveal.

Kit rolled her eyes. Why did she even bother?

'She *was* living with me and Gretel, but she went off on a solo road trip up north. Wait, so she hasn't dropped in yet? That's weird, I know she was near you guys . . .' Kit felt wicked for dumping Rat in it, but she deserved it.

'She never calls,' he said. 'Neither of you do.' But there was less resentment, less bite than usual. If anything, he sounded sad.

'So,' she said again, trying to move things along, 'everything good with you? Do you . . . Can I . . .' She paused, aware of how blatant she was being. 'Can I help you with anything?'

'I just wanted to have a chat. Can't I call my daughter for a hello?' he said.

Yeah, she thought, *but that is something you literally* never *do.*

'Of course,' she said, then stopped. She wasn't going to help him out; if he wanted to chat, he would need to start chatting.

'So it's your mother's birthday tomorrow,' he said quietly. 'Would have been. Her sixtieth.'

Kit inhaled quickly; her body stiffened.

'Shit, so it is. I didn't realise . . .' Kit always used to honour both her mother's birthday and the day she died, but in the past few years she had become sloppy. She felt shame wash over her. She'd had a ritual on these days when she was little: she'd put a load of sheets in the dryer, and when they were hot and toasty she'd pull them out and hug them, something she and her mum used to do.

'October twenty-one,' he reminded her.

'Yes, of course,' she agreed quietly. She sat frozen, trying to understand what was happening. Ron *never* spoke about Jeannie. As she'd grown older, Kit realised this was more likely down to pain than forgetfulness or wanting to move on. That's what she told herself anyway.

'Have you been thinking about her lately?' she asked, encouraging him to keep going.

'Yeah, a bit,' he said. A pregnant pause. 'I wish you'd known her like I did—as a grown lady, I mean. She always knew what to say, what to do. She loved you, kid.'

Kit's eyes filled with tears. She had waited a long, long time for her father to say something like this. The longest and loneliest time. Of course, it had to happen on a random weekday while she was wearing a bag for a bib. She swallowed back a sob and gave him space to go on.

'Anyway,' he said, reverting to his usual self, 'just thought that was worth saying.'

Kit sniffed and wiped a tear from her left cheek. 'Thanks, Dad. That means the world to me. I love hearing about her.'

'All right then, won't keep you, know you're busy.'

'You're not keep—'

But he'd gone.

18

DECEMBER

'SOOOO, WHAT'S THE LATEST? Blue Tree still got your heart?'
Maggie asked as a pack of young men ran past, full of pre-workout
drink, all loud talking and *Top Gun* moustaches and calf tattoos.
'You know I don't understand the words but tell me the feelings.'
Maggie was panting slightly from the brisk pace of their walk.
She always asked about the deal, even though it was complicated
both to explain and to understand. Kit kept her up to date
partly because it was such a foreign, fascinating world to them
both, and partly because if she didn't keep Maggie in the loop
it was impossible to get her back up to speed, such were the
twists and turns.

'Yeah,' Kit said. 'But Rupert needs me to keep at *least* three
bidders in the mix. I honestly feel like I'm on *The Business
Bachelorette*, and the casting this season was terrible. Even the
good parties, like Blue Tree, have big cons.'

'Oh, my love . . .' Maggie gave her friend's hand a quick squeeze. 'Hang in there. Sam's your biggest financial fanboy; he keeps asking for updates. His Count Dracula biohacking freakboss has decided to sell Veat, so he's going to be in the same boat as you now, I guess.'

'Oh, poor Sam—it's not fun. Hey, speaking of bosses, has Henry *still* not said anything about your Parisian porno?' Kit grinned.

'Not a word,' Maggie said, shaking her head. 'He'll probably say something after too many whiskies at the Christmas party.'

'A-plus, no notes. What a guy. *I'd* have given you endless shit about it,' Kit said.

'You do,' Maggie reminded her.

'Hey,' said Kit, changing the subject, 'when this deal is finally over, we're going to get a fancy hotel room and eat gummies and drink champagne and order room service and watch movies, okay?'

'Will you buy me a Terrazza sofa? *Please?*' Maggie whined.

Kit laughed. 'I keep telling you: *I'm* not making any money from this.'

Maggie stopped walking and turned to face her friend. She took Kit by the shoulders and looked her directly in the eyes. 'Listen. I love you to death, and you know I don't really understand any of it, but even I can see it's crazy you're not taking any cash from this deal, if there's a chance you can . . . You work *so* hard. You never, ever turn off. It's *your* business, your baby. Don't you *want* some money? Haven't you *always* wanted money? Financial security is your religion; why not take the money now so you never have to worry about it again?'

'Jesus,' Kit said, as Maggie released her grip. 'Calm down.'

Kit began walking again, indicating Maggie should do the same. 'My money will come later,' she assured herself as much as Maggie. 'Right now I've just got to solve this problem. I've got to choose the right partner, someone who won't ruin the company or the fun of working there. Camille says private equity almost always rips the heart out of a business, but selling them a majority stake *ensures* it.' She sighed. 'I don't know who to trust. I'm terrified I'm going to mess it all up . . . They say what I want to hear in the meetings, then the next day they send through terms no one in their right mind would accept.'

'What you're doing is *really hard*,' Maggie said. 'Do you know that? You used to be a hairdresser and now you're negotiating shit with MBA people! Do you even see how clever you are? You are Elon Musk in my eyes.'

'Ew,' Kit said.

'You know what I was thinking last night?' Maggie said. 'You need to get laid. Take your mind off things.'

'That's why vibrators were invented,' Kit replied.

Kit saw her car up ahead, spliced between numerous others, sparkling in the warm morning sun. The air snapped with excitement; Sydney had transitioned into Christmas season: people were buzzing, in full party and socialising mode, holiday heads already firmly on. Kit wanted to go another lap, but there wasn't enough time: she had what Rupert assured her was the very last presentation to potential investors this morning.

'That's not to say getting laid wouldn't be welcome,' she conceded, 'but it's not like I have a ton of options: everyone in my industry is either female or a gay man.'

'What about all those finance boys? Surely one of them could get the job done.' Maggie moving her tongue over her lips lasciviously.

'First of all, no,' Kit said definitively. 'Second of all, banging potential shareholders doesn't strike me as a super good biz move. And third, *no*. They are not my people.'

'Not asking you to *marry* them,' Maggie scoffed. 'Just bang one.' She frowned at her fingernails—they were neat, short and always painted glossy black—then looked up. 'Are you still on the apps?' she asked. 'Actually,' she said, getting excited, 'fuck the apps! Let's go to a bar for its hotties not its food reviews for once. Come on: it's summer, you're single, it's sexy out there, I've lost three kilos being semi-vegan and I want to show it off in some new Zara. Let's go!'

They'd reached their cars by now. Maggie leaned one arm on the bonnet of her electric four-wheel drive and took a swig from her water bottle. She wore black bike shorts and an oversized Rolling Stones tee with tube socks and chunky sneakers. Her red curls were pulled up into a high bun, a few curls having slipped out to frame her face, and her ears were decorated with numerous earrings—hoops, pearls, diamonds, dinosaurs, all the things.

'Okay, okay. When's Sam back?'

Sam had popped over to Denmark to visit the HQ of some genius start-up that claimed to have invented lab-grown salmon which tasted as good as the real thing.

'Not for another week, but the mother-in-bore can babysit. I wish I'd gone,' she said wistfully. 'I *so* want to snoop round Copenhagen's vintage and antique stores . . . Meanwhile, Dyl reckons she doesn't need a babysitter anymore; apparently the fact that she has a phone means *she* is a fully responsible adult and can do it.'

'Can she?' Kit asked, genuinely curious. Dylan was only twelve.

'Yet to test her theory. Oh my god, she has a boyfriend, did I tell you? His name is Noah and his look is one hundred percent Bieber circa 2012—it's *incredible*. Her friends are all so cool and mean, I'm scared to talk to them.'

'Her boyfriend comes over?' Kit said with raised brows. The idea of Gretel having a boy over one day was mind-boggling.

'Oh, don't worry, it's *always* a group hang,' Maggie said. 'I get, like, five of them at a time, and they all sit downstairs watching YouTube on their phones and drinking nine-dollar Frappuccinos from Starbucks. It's a whole thing.' Maggie rolled her eyes.

Kit unlocked her driver's door. 'You're the fun house. That's good; at least when they start drinking you'll be able to keep an eye on them.'

'*Don't*,' Maggie said heatedly. 'It's all happening too fast. She's stealing my fucking Dior lip gloss already . . .'

'Dyl being a teen makes me feel prehistoric,' Kit said. 'Do you know what Gretel said to me last night? I was drying off after our shower and she pointed to my chest and said, "Do I have to have boobs like *that* when I'm a lady? Cos I don't want 'em."'

Maggie laughed. 'Better not show her mine then. What you got on now?'

'I have to film a tutorial on big nineties hair, then race to a meeting in the city to meet a late-entry investor.'

'Wait, are the nineties back *again*?' Maggie moaned. 'Not the Rachel-from-*Friends*, please no.'

'Think more Claudia Schiffer in Versace.'

'Sexy. Well, *I* have a painful client coming in to shit on everything I've designed for her.'

'What? Why did she even hire you then?'

'You know,' Maggie reflected, doing her usual goodbye-extending, 'I wish I could see you in those meetings. Doesn't it suck that you never get to see your best friend kill it in their workplace? I want to see you be the big boss.'

'I'm better at it now,' Kit said. 'I used to shit my pants before these presentations, all impostor syndrome and no sleep, but now I'm, like, I know my stuff, you'd be lucky to have a piece of this company: *impress me.*' She pretended to smoke a cigar.

Maggie placed her drink bottle on the roof of her car and clapped loudly. '*YEW!* That's my girl. Show them what's *up.*'

'Yeah! Gonna go in there and show them my big *deck*!' Kit yelled.

Laughing, she climbed into the driver's seat. She opened her window and blew Maggie a kiss as she reversed her car out.

'Tell me when we're going out so I can wash my Temu ponytail!' Maggie yelled as she drove off.

Two hours later, Kit sat at yet another enormous shiny table in an enormous, windowless boardroom, waiting for the team from Pinnacle Capital to arrive. Everything was beige: the carpet, wallpaper, desk, chairs . . . Kit felt like she was inside a very elegant padded cell. Pinnacle had apologised for not hosting, but their office was undergoing renovations and so the meeting was set in the bowels of a hotel attached to a shopping centre down at The Rocks. Kit wondered if she'd have a chance to swing next door and grab a quick birthday present for Frankie, a friend of Gretel whose party was tomorrow. Every week, another birthday party, another seventy-five-dollar bundle of unicorn and mermaid paraphernalia. She should buy Frankie a basketball and a slingshot instead, just to see the look on everyone's faces.

WhatsApp lit up her phone screen.

Does anyone know if they still need volunteers for the excursion to zoo on Friday?

I can't sorry guys hv to work xx

Yes they need 2 more, wrote Marie, *from 8:45-2.30, please only reply if you CAN do it*

Sorry guys can't this time x

I thought the botanic garden was it for this term??

Would love to help out next time!! X

I can but not til 9.30?

If they want a zoo they should just come to our place 😂

It supposed to rain Friday what happens then?

Sorry can't help out this time xx

I'll ask Tim, Daddy's turn me thinks ;)

Kit thought about her Friday. She had a meeting with the Linley guys, Priya and Curtis, the M&A lawyer she'd hired for the deal to go over all the non-binding indicative offers submitted by bidders. Pinnacle had come in late to the process but said they could move fast and make the deadline provided today went well. That would be a long-arse meeting, Kit realised. How could she make this work? How could she be That Mum for Gretel? Her daughter was desperate for her to be an excursion mum. Or a canteen mum. Any mum with a presence at school.

Rupert sat beside her, texting away.

'Do you wish you'd done more school stuff when your kids were little? Like, excursion helper and stuff?'

He looked up at her. 'There is honestly nothing on earth I regret more. If you can do it, always do it.'

'Great, then I'll need to move Friday's meeting to Monday. I'm going to be an excursion mum for Gretel.'

Rupert smiled. 'Understood.'

I can do it! she wrote to the group, feeling giddy.

'I think we've saved the best for last here,' Rupert said. 'Pinnacle have a sterling track record for scaling medium-sized companies, including Jolt, the protein drink, Wiffles, the baby organic food brand, also an ingestible collagen supplement called—'

'Inside Out,' Kit finished. 'I *do* read the proposals, if you can believe it.'

'As I said on the phone yesterday, the interesting thing about these guys is that they own a wide-scale manufacturer who makes some of these products and some of their other Therapeutic Goods Administration stuff. That's unusual for a PE firm, but they're non-traditional in that sense. Malcolm, the president, likes doing things his own way—whatever makes sense to him on the day. Could be some *fantastic* savings to be made if you manufactured in-house.'

'Okay,' she said, finding it almost impossible to feign enthusiasm.

Rupert looked at her with paternal concern. 'How are you going, Kit? Handling things okay?'

Kit was exhausted, and clearly it was showing. Between the presentations and meetings with bidders, satisfying all their requests and questions with the exec team, weekly shareholder meetings with Priya, Simon (on Zoom) and Toni (usually via speakerphone from her car), and daily calls and updates and documents from Rupert or Curtis or both, Kit was slipping behind on every other aspect of her life. Her solo parent mental load was heavy; she'd stood at the fridge holding some chicken soup for over a minute last night trying to recall when she'd made it and if it would still be okay. Second Day was falling further and further behind on its next launch, and last week Kit had made a stupid packaging oversight that had cost them fifty K to remedy. Plus, the management team were distracted by the deal and it was showing.

'I'm okay,' she said finally. No point complaining to Rupert; he was energised by deals, like this was a game he had to win.

'You're certainly burning the proverbial candle,' he mused. 'I was thinking this morning, we should talk to Curtis about implementing your licence deed.'

'Once more in Kit?' Kit asked.

'Licence deed,' Rupert said, chuckling. 'It's common for founders with a public profile to have an agreement in place with the company that means the company pays them for use of their persona . . . in marketing, advertisements on social media and so on. A bit like an ambassador royalty.'

'So my own company would pay me to promote Second Day?' Kit frowned. 'That doesn't sound right. It's my job to promote my products.'

'Do you create sales and add value?' he asked.

'Definitely,' she said.

'How much would you pay influencers or celebrities for that?'

'Shitloads,' Kit said, shaking her head. 'And their prices keep going up.'

'So why shouldn't *you* be paid for that? On top of the trust and experience you bring?'

Kit was quiet, thinking.

'The answer is, you should,' he said. 'The company is leasing Kit Cooper, it doesn't *own* Kit Cooper. The company should be paying a royalty for the value you bring with your involvement and public endorsement. You'd be amazed how many founders don't have this in place. But since we are redoing the shareholders' agreement and bringing in a new partner, now is a good time. Any party coming in will need to agree to it; all shareholders will.'

'I don't know,' Kit said. 'It still doesn't seem right . . .'

'If this agreement is not in place,' Rupert explained, 'you won't be remunerated for the value you bring to this brand and company. Everyone will benefit from your association with Second Day, but you will be providing that association for free.'

Rupert sensed she wasn't quite seeing the big picture.

'Fast-forward to someone buying one hundred percent of the company in a few years,' Rupert said. 'Does that mean they are buying *you*? Do they get to attach your face and name to some horrible new product they make just because they own Second Day?'

'Of course not!' Kit said huffily.

'As it stands, they could, because there is nothing distinguishing the person from the company. If you don't draw a clear distinction between personal brand and company brand, you could end up being associated with the brand in perpetuity—for free—even if you don't own it.'

'Right . . .' Kit said, starting to grasp the implications now.

'Curtis will draw up an agreement between your own personal Kit Cooper company and Second Day Pty Ltd. It will list a minimum and maximum amount of publicity days annually, for example, as well as the termination period.'

'What's the fee?' Kit asked.

'It's a percentage of gross sales usually. It adds up to a nice little revenue stream over time.'

'This makes *so* much sense,' Kit said, shaking her head. She'd done so much more for the company than Simon and Toni, but she'd never been remunerated for the value she added as spokesperson, content creator and public face—it was just expected she do that as the founder.

'Do you know Mia Geddes?' Rupert said. 'The Olympian? She sold her yoghurt company years ago but is still pulling in millions each year as the brand face. That was Curtis's doing.'

'I suddenly love Curtis so much,' Kit said dreamily.

'Spending on a decent lawyer is always worth it.'

Rupert cocked an ear, as if he'd heard something outside. 'Here they are.' Rupert adjusted his tie, light grey with polka dots—lovely pairing with his charcoal suit—stood and smiled.

A huddle of middle-aged men entered the room. Kit knew men in this industry were limited in wardrobe choices, but seven blue suits had to be some kind of record. Kit shook hand after hand, before requesting a piccolo from the young woman taking coffee orders.

A guy in his fifties, wearing a frown and the unmistakable swagger of Guy In Charge, walked over to Kit and shook her hand firmly. 'Kat, I'm Malcolm, thanks for coming. My partner Ian is supposed to be here, but he got pulled away at the last minute, apologies.'

Kit smiled confidently, returning the handshake just as firmly. She no longer bothered to correct people if they got her name wrong; they'd figure it out. 'Good to meet you, Malcolm.' She'd stopped saying 'nice to meet you'; 'good' felt more powerful, more . . . masculine? She'd also stopped waffling nervously about the weather and the office space; now she just *stopped*.

'Got everything you need?' he asked.

'I'm all set, thank you.'

He nodded with a closed-mouth smile and took a seat at the head of the table.

'Kit?' A youngish guy stood before her, but all she could see was his glorious hair: thick, full hair and a unique dark, mottled grey, like a thundercloud. Incredible. He'd complemented it with round brown frames and a beard that was edging on Newtown but at the last minute retreated to Surry Hills. He had gone for a woollen polo under his suit and—controversial!—brown loafers, no socks.

'I'm Omari, one of the principals here,' he said, smiling faintly.

Kit spied some small tattoos on his neck. *Good on you, Omari,* she thought. *Look at you breaking the corporate stereotype.*

Once Omari took his seat next to Malcolm, Kit sat down on the *vastly* outnumbered Second Day side of the table. Neither Jordan nor Camille had been able to make it to this eighth and surely last presentation to a new party, because they were attending a beauty trends and insights conference with a non-refundable cost of one thousand dollars per head. This meant Kit was the lone woman, save for the one taking coffee orders.

Kit recognised that, historically, she was supposed to be nervous. She had no right to be in this room, doing these things, yet here she was. She didn't have her teammates, and she wasn't a confident speaker. She *should* be riddled with anxiety; she was a pro at that. But for some reason, today she felt strangely calm. Maybe because she thought Blue Tree were inevitable, and these guys weren't really in the race. Maybe it was seeing Maggie this morning and getting a pep up. Or maybe it was the recognition of what a unique moment in her life—in *any* founder's life—she was living through that made her feel strangely buoyant. It was *her* company these swanky finance men wanted to be part of: *hers*. She had made something of value that they believed in. She wanted to sit with that instead of listening to the cacophony of inane thoughts that usually pinged around her brain. That she was a fraud because she pronounced CAGR wrong and didn't know how to use it in a sentence confidently, that she *really* belonged backstage at fashion week, or in a hair and make-up wagon at sunrise putting KY jelly into a model's hair to make it look like she just came out of the ocean. Kit felt *powerful* for the first time in this whole process. Maybe ever. She had made a good thing, and people wanted to buy that good thing. For a lot of money.

As she waited for them to stop chatting and begin, she reminded herself that she couldn't afford to zone out today: she was the only one present to answer questions, aside from Rupert, and it was up to her to gauge if Pinnacle could be a good partner. She couldn't imagine what would set them apart from the seven million other private equity firms on earth; every one she'd met so far had offered exactly the same 'differences': they were not like the big firms; they were founder-led; they were not here to interfere or put pressure on her. It was hard to pick a winner when every horse ran the same race and wore the same uniform.

Rupert had told her not to overthink it at this stage: the term sheet was when they revealed their true character.

Within fifteen minutes of their presentation—an impressive deep dive into the Australian hair category they had obviously spent a lot of money on—Kit found herself tuning out, inspecting her citron-coloured nails. They played perfectly against Kit's lilac blazer; she knew all her colours and patterns confused and dazzled the suits, which only made her lean into it more. As she straightened in her chair and sipped her coffee, she glanced over the table and noticed the young guy sitting opposite was paying even less attention than she was. He didn't quite match the others; his hair was wild and curly, and his suit was oversized and ill-fitting. He caught her looking at him and immediately looked away, flushing red.

The slide with Pinnacle's health and beauty investments popped up; Kit always liked this bit since it was never on the website. She scanned it: there was a medicated muscle soreness cream, a dandruff brand, an oral care brand, cold sore treatments, heel balms, but no outright beauty brands. They *did*, however, own the majority of the biggest wellness ingestibles brand on the market. That counted. These PE firms were always so keen to get into beauty, but knew so little about it. These guys had the pharmacy landscape covered; hair care wouldn't be too great a leap.

After another ten minutes Kit glanced ever so briefly at Rupert and raised her brows almost imperceptibly. He usually did a micro nod and moved things along when she did that, but instead he did a micro shake of the head and returned his gaze to the screen. Fine, she huffed. She'd listen to Omari go on and on. If Rupert thought there was something in this, it had to be for good reason. He was courteous enough never to waste her time, even if once or twice he'd insisted they take the meeting just so news of it would get back to the other bidders. She decided to get involved, if only to keep herself awake.

'Omari,' Kit interrupted, 'who is your retail partner for Inside Out in the US and Canada?'

'CVS, Walmart and a speciality pharmacy,' Omari said without skipping a beat.

'But you *want* to be in Sephora,' she said with conviction.

'Uh, no, that's not in the current plan . . .' He sounded confused.

'No specialised beauty retailers, no Sephora, Bluemercury or Ulta? Even though it's specifically marketed as a beauty drink?'

'We are in over three thousand doors across the US with our current strategy,' he said. 'The brand sits at number two in Walmart and we believe—'

'Huh. Would've thought a premium play would be more effective for the kind of early adopter seeking out ingestibles, but go on,' she said, nodding.

As he began talking again, Kit smiled to herself discreetly. She'd done that for every woman who'd been cut off in every meeting for all time, herself very much included. Her mind floated to Max Darling, as it had on more than one occasion. She'd had two follow-up meetings with Blue Tree but he had not been in either. Kit's disappointment when he didn't show surprised her.

Curly hair guy suddenly snapped his hand onto his wrist as his Apple Watch began beeping loudly.

'Well,' Malcolm said, 'looks like it's time Marty woke up, everyone.' He laughed unkindly, and the rest of the room joined in obediently. Malcolm was an impatient man, always tapping his finger or switching his leg position. Perhaps he felt this meeting was beneath him.

'It's a calendar reminder, Dad,' Curly Marty mumbled, pushing one hand roughly through his enormous hair. *Ooh, father–son tension*, Kit thought. *Juicy.*

'I have a question—or, rather, a comment for you, Kit,' Marty said suddenly, looking everywhere but at Kit. He spoke with a slight nasal whine, which along with his glasses, wild hair and giant suit had all the unfortunate hallmarks of your classic nerd. 'There is no scalp care in your product pipeline. I see you have wash and care launching next year, which I agree is an obvious way to grow the product line, impact shelf space in store and increase hold on the customer, but—and forgive me for being crude—it's not reinventing the wheel.'

'Hi, Marty, is it?' Kit said, smiling. Negative feedback no longer rattled her. 'My background and experience are anchored in styling. Wash and care is the natural extension of that, since if you use rubbish shampoo and conditioner *no* amount of styling product will work, but scalp and medical stuff? That's not really us.'

He looked down as he replied. 'Dandruff shampoo and conditioner is the biggest seller in hair care in both of the leading grocery chains and pharmacies in Australia,' he said.

'Is that so?' Kit replied, not sure where this was going.

'By adding proven anti-dandruff components into your wash and care, you could create a whole new association with scalp care, a much . . . funkier one. Supermarket-brand scalp care is a proven seller, but it lacks the design and marketing aspects of a brand like yours.'

'I see what you're saying,' Kit said, feeling a twinge of excitement.

'Why don't you follow up this thread with Kit post meeting,' Malcolm said to Marty.

'Pinnacle can offer genuine innovation in your new product development,' Marty said, ignoring his father.

'That's definitely food for thought Marty, thank you,' Kit said, her brain spinning wildly.

'Nine out of ten homes feature an unsightly dandruff bottle in their shower,' Marty went on. 'If we utilise your branding strength with our—'

'Innovation is just one of the many services Pinnacle Capital can offer Second Day,' Omari interrupted, easily wresting the conversation out of Marty's clutches. 'As I said earlier, we offer a fully integrated vertical service, unlike so many of our competitors.'

'May I ask what your standard exit window is?' Kit asked, now au fait with the lingo. But she wasn't asking just for show; she genuinely wanted to know what their plans were for Second Day. Some bidders had been upfront about a three-year term, some said ten years was fine, even longer if Kit was happy to stay on that long. Knowing their MO would help Kit understand whom she was getting into bed with.

'We don't—' Omari said.

'It's completely unique to—' Malcolm said.

The two men laughed like old chums. 'Take it away,' Malcolm said with a warmth lacking when he addressed poor Marty.

'I was going to say it's entirely unique to each investment,' Omari said, speaking directly to Kit. 'We are extremely well-funded and very stable, so we don't have the time pressure many others have. We'd work with you to sell the business when it was right for you, for the company, for the brand. We try to position ourselves as Shadow Founders, so we get into the right mindset, to be led by the same drivers as the actual founders.'

Did Omari know how many times Kit had heard guys like him say things like that?

'How long have we had Protect and Prepare now?' Malcolm said, leaning back in his chair, manspreading aggressively. 'Must be almost eight years.'

'That's right,' Omari confirmed. 'We work closely with the founders, Tim and Tristan, and they're not looking to sell yet— certainly there's no pressure from us.'

'We care about revenue and profitability,' said Malcolm. 'It would be disingenuous to pretend otherwise. But we understand the founder and management team know what's best for the brand. Otherwise we wouldn't be here meeting with you, trying to buy in on what you've created, would we?'

He smiled, and Kit did her best to return serve, even though he had rubbed her the wrong way from the moment he'd walked in.

'Do you think I could have a chat with those guys, and maybe a couple of the other founders in your stable?' Kit asked. She wanted to know what Pinnacle were like as a partner from current founders—or, better yet, founders who had exited. She knew any founder still partnered with them would feel obliged to say nice things, but some of the founders in the Blue Tree stable had been wildly honest, and Kit was encouraged by their transparency.

'Absolutely,' said Omari. 'I'll connect you via email.'

'Terrific, everyone, what a fantastic conversation,' Rupert said cheerfully. 'Unless there are any further questions, we might just wrap it up there!'

Marty had his hand raised to just above his shoulder, almost as though he didn't want to be noticed.

'Yes, Marty?' Kit said, deliberate in her kindness. He was the only one in *any* of these meetings to take the conversation into an area of innovation and specificity. She rated that.

'Something else I was thinking,' he began, pushing his glasses up the bridge of his nose. 'Have you considered hair growth? It could be with supplements—in fact, we make one already for Inside Out—or serums and masks.' He tapped the table rapidly with one index finger as he spoke. 'Or perhaps a line of hair-extension accessories? We own PlayCo, the children's dolls, so we have access to wig-making materials and machinery already.'

Marty was absolutely on another planet, Kit realised. Still, she was picking up what he was putting down.

'Why don't we tee up a call and chat about some of these things?' She smiled broadly, sensing this was not an easy professional environment for Marty and his supersonic brain.

Rupert began packing up his notes and laptop. 'We can certainly get that happening. Thank you for your time today, gents; we hope you got everything you need from us. Omari, we'll send over revised actuals this afternoon.'

After a succession of friendly goodbyes, the Pinnacle Capital team walked out, leaving Kit and Rupert in the room to debrief before parting ways.

'What in the ring of fire was that Marty chap going on about?' Rupert said, sounding baffled.

'I liked him,' Kit said. 'He spoke *product*, not profits. In fact, he's the only person in this whole circus I could spend more time with. They all bang on about we can do this and we can do that, but Marty *actually has ideas.* Okay, the dolls thing was genuinely bonkers, but I like that he's thinking outside the square.'

Rupert looked at Kit with interest. 'So you could entertain Pinnacle as a partner?'

'I dunno.' She shrugged, feeling her usual post-meeting come-down, her body and brain now in Kit Lite mode. 'They're the only ones other than Blue Tree who have piqued my interest, put it that way. Malcolm I didn't get a great vibe from, but the others seem nice enough.'

'I wish Ian had been there; he's a blast, I think you'd like him . . .' He paused. 'Look, Kit, I know Blue Tree are your pick, but you do need backups. This is a merciless and bizarre charter we're on and things can change quickly, even at the very last minute. Pinnacle's original proposal was highly compat-ible, outsized equity requirement notwithstanding. I think they deserve a run.'

'All right,' Kit said. What did she have to lose? The more prospects, the better.

'Terrific stuff, Kit. That's how you do it. Now, we'll need to move quickly, so once we have their indicative offer, we can finalise the pool that will proceed to stage two.'

'How long will that take?'

'Walk with me,' Rupert said, motioning towards the door. 'We should have second-stage parties in the data room and doing due diligence by next week.'

'But no one will work over Christmas,' she said, collecting her bag and walking out of the room with Rupert.

Rupert smiled. 'Oh yes they will, Kit. Might be worth flag-ging that with your team, actually. Anyway, if all goes to plan,

I think it's reasonable to expect you will have a new partner by . . . April?'

Kit groaned. 'That's *ages.*'

'We're talking about tens of millions of dollars here, Kit. Everyone needs to have their ducks in a row.'

'I understand,' she said, trying not to think about those tens of millions flowing directly to Toni.

'I'll send a wrap-up around to the shareholders later this afternoon,' he said. 'Enjoy your day, Kit—always a delight to see you.' He walked out of the lobby doors onto the street.

Kit hoicked her bag over her shoulder and set off to find this birthday present before heading back to the office. She could have asked Hyun to do it, but last time he'd spent one hundred and twenty dollars on a designer tutu, insisting it was a forever piece despite it being a children's size six.

Her phone buzzed: Priya.

How did it go? Rupert had high hopes for this group . . .

Kit replied: *Hi! Same guys saying same things . . . One had some cool ideas for new products, though, which was refreshing.*

Any kind of connection is good. After all, you will be working alongside these people for years. Is Blue Tree still your preference? They won't settle for less than 50% is my understanding, Priya replied.

I'm hoping they come around. They have the most beauty experience and they seem to really get the brand. Even Camille is on board! But Rupert says I need to stay open-minded in case they grow another head at the last moment.

He's right. On another note, the board pack was sent out today. Please find a moment to read it before the board meeting Friday.

More thrilling financial documents to sift through, thought Kit. *Just how I wanted to spend my evening.*

After buying an overpriced unicorn headband, a glittery notebook with a padlock and a book about a princess raised by dragons, Kit took an Uber back to the office. As she sat in traffic, Kit had the strangest compulsion to call her father and let him know what she was doing. For someone to see her, tell her she was doing good. He would have no idea what she was talking about, of course, but some part of her wanted to show him that she was capable, that she was impressive. That even though she had grown up with nothing, a little girl from the country with no leg-up, no advantages, she'd made something of herself.

If only she could go back and tell little eight-year-old Kit that it was all going to be okay, that she would find her people and her thing, and she would be pretty good at it, actually. Kit felt a stab of pain whenever she allowed herself to revisit that time. She still missed her mother, but this many years later, with the memories of her touch, smell and smile long faded, Kit realised what she more likely missed was the *idea* of her mother: someone who would be proud of her, always there for a chat and a hug, someone who would remind Kit she was loved, and she was worthy, a loving grandmother for Gretel . . . Kit wiped a tear from her eye, feeling rarely and tremendously sorry for herself. She allowed herself to indulge for a moment, before telling herself it was just a motley mix of fatigue, stress, hunger and PMS. She never let herself wallow; she was a master at repressing her emotions, especially the deep, painful ones. She would deal with them when things had calmed down, ideally while on ayahuasca under the watchful eye of a shaman in Peru.

Kit took a deep breath as the Uber neared the office and pulled out her concealer to touch up her blotchy cry face. She had to believe she could go on as usual if this whole thing fell over, if no transaction emerged and the Toni situation somehow resolved, but she knew she'd be devastated. At the moment she could only see a future in which she had a new partner, and Second Day went from small and mighty to big and inspiring. She imagined billboards, global celebrity endorsements, new categories, retail stores . . . It was all possible, she knew it was. Kit understood the transaction was delicate—given that it involved ego, and money, and control, how could it not be? So who would best help her to achieve these goals? Who did she want to work alongside for the next however many years? Both Blue Tree and Pinnacle seemed feasible—they had a proven track record and felt new and shiny and . . . *dynamic*—but Rupert had warned her everyone came with caveats, whether it was a controlling stake or ludicrous financial goals or, as one party had proposed, removing Camille and inserting their own CEO.

It was exhausting, all the mental gymnastics. To envision and entertain new parties and get her head around new percentages and goals and endgames, all the while trying to protect the team, the staff, the brand and decide her own future. *Pah*, she thought. She was just tired. Some down time with Gretel over Christmas and everything would be fine.

19

JANUARY

'MUM,' SAID GRETEL, 'IF I say swearwords inside my head, is that allowed? Not in my mouth, just in my brain?' She sat on a cushion on the floor in her nightie, facing the TV—she always put her nightie on after a shower, no matter the time of day—a long scruffy plait snaking down her back.

Kit smiled. 'What you say in your head is entirely up to you. Go nuts.'

'*Yesss*,' Gretel said under her breath. 'Can I have some more frozies?'

'Of course, baby,' Kit said, eyes blissfully closed, the afternoon sun warming her stomach as she lay on the couch under a wide-open window. 'You know where they are. Just grab the bag out of the freezer and pop some more in your bowl.'

She heard Gretel run to the kitchen, open the freezer and wrestle with the bag of frozen mango.

'Mum, *I can't open it!*' She spoke with urgency because *The Little Mermaid* was on and she didn't want to miss a beat.

'Bring it here,' Kit said drowsily, sleep beckoning.

This past week in the Northern Rivers had been perfect, exactly what they both needed. No plans except finding a good place to swim and deciding which ice-cream flavour they wanted in the afternoon and what they would make or buy for dinner. Kit had *almost* rented them a four-bedroom palace with ocean views, but when it came time to pay, she baulked and switched to a much cheaper but still cute two-bedder in town. The constant dialogue around millions, and tens of millions, occasionally tricked Kit into thinking it was *her* money, not Toni's. Toni had gone to Bali with Ricky for January. *It's so cheap here darling, butlers, cooks, massages . . . we live like kings on ten dollars a day!* she'd hollered at Kit via text after telling her she would be unavailable for meetings while she took a well-earned rest. Given Bali was where Kit was supposed to be with Maggie before Ari had decimated their plans, this did not modify Toni's position as Kit's least-favourite person.

Gretel rushed over and dumped the cold bag of fruit on Kit's décolletage.

Kit sat up as if she'd been electrocuted. '*Shit!*' she said, louder than was probably necessary.

Gretel's bottom lip trembled; her eyes were stormy under her furrowed brows.

Kit quickly sat up and reached for her daughter. Gretel was always sensitive to yelling or loud noises, but especially this afternoon. The two of them had spent all day exploring a small lagoon around the corner from a major tourist beach, eating watermelon, racing in and out of the sea, and building a giant sand mermaid with seaweed hair on the beach—one of those fairytale days Kit knew she'd remember forever. She'd heard somewhere you only had twelve summers with your kids before they started to prefer their friends or devices to their parents; she mustn't waste a day of them. Kit couldn't recall much of her mother, certainly no beach holidays came to mind, but she knew she was kind, and inventive, and gave her only child her undivided attention. Kit strived to be like her, or who she imagined she'd been; she wanted Gretel to feel safe, and heard, and for her to process her feelings. Kit apologised and made amends if she snapped at Gretel, explaining her reasoning and taking accountability. This couldn't be more unlike her father, who'd used his size and power to make Kit feel small and inconvenient. Any time she showed big feelings, she was shut down and dismissed. Kit had vowed never to do that to Gretel.

Hugging her tired little girl, Kit said, 'I scared you when I was loud, I'm sorry. I get scared by loud noises, too. Let's watch the movie together. Here, look'—she grabbed the bag and poured a tumble of frozen mango pieces into the bowl—'all for you.'

Gretel swiped some loose hair out of her face with the back of her hand, took the bowl, turned around and plopped on the couch next to Kit. Kit's phone vibrated on the coffee table, she picked it up to hit decline, then saw Rat's name. Rat never called. She was more likely to send a DM on Instagram or hire a sky writer.

'Honey, Aunty Rat is on the phone, and I think it might be important, so I'm gonna answer.'

Kit stood up and walked over to the sliding door then out into the backyard.

'Don't tell me the Pest broke down again,' Kit said, smiling.

After their blow-up, Rat had accused Kit of kicking her out and being 'as bad as everyone else'—but in the past few weeks the sisters had been texting again. She missed Rat, and Gretel was *really* missing Fun Aunty.

'Nah, she's a sturdy little wench,' Rat said, the sound of birds and children squealing in the background. 'You chill? Having fun?'

'I'm hydrated and rested. What about you, where are you?'

'I reckon I might be near you guys,' Rat said.

'What?' Kit said, confused. 'I thought you were up in Cairns . . .'

'You're in Byron, right?' Rat asked.

'Brunswick Heads—the fancy place fell through,' she lied.

'Magic of a van, always got a place to sleep.'

Kit noticed her sister was low energy. Big drops after big highs were not uncommon for Rat, but this sounded different.

'How come you're back down this way?' Kit asked gently.

'No reason, just thought you guys were gonna be around and I—' Rat's voice cracked.

'Rat, what's wrong?' Kit was suddenly wide awake. Rat was never fazed, never rattled.

'I just—I had to get outta Cairns, that's all.'

'What happened?' Kit was losing her cool at a rate that suggested she never had any to begin with.

'Relax,' Rat said, regaining stamina. 'It's just full of weirdos, that's all. Bad juju, you know?' Rat fell silent. Rat *never* fell silent. Kit wanted to dig in but knew she risked being shut down.

'Okay, then . . . It's just, you don't sound like yourself,' Kit observed mildly.

'Just tired, you know? Like, it's a *lot* of driving and it's not like I have a co-driver.' Rat was on the defensive now.

'No doubt—'

'It's not a big deal,' Rat suddenly blurted. 'Some shit went down with this guy and I . . . it just . . . I had to leave, okay?'

'Like a boyfriend guy?' Kit asked.

'Un-fucking-likely.'

'All right.' Kit went quiet, hoping her sister would keep talking.

Rat sighed impatiently. 'This guy and I were making out at the club, him and his dumb friends were buying bottles and doing shots, real frat-boy style, and I got too drunk—I never *drink* anymore, give me shrooms any day—then he did some coke, I think, and he started getting all aggressive and rapey, like grabbing my tits and putting his hand up my skirt, but I *knew* I was gonna vom, I had the spinnies, so I left the club but he *followed* me, all the way out to the Pest, which was parked on the street, and he said I'm coming in, and I told him to fuck off, so then he got angry, saying I was a cockteaser, and he smashed a window and, like, ripped the side mirrors off and—'

'He *what*?!' Kit interrupted.

'And then I just screamed at him, like as loud as I could, to scare him,' Rat went on. 'He pushed me onto the van and was trying to make me unlock it, and then when I pushed back he hit me, like, in the *face*—'

'*Rat!* What the fuck! Are you serious?' Kit couldn't believe what she was hearing.

'Then these guys walking past heard me screaming and they scared him off, and I just fell on the ground, like, in a heap.'

Kit was seconds away from needing a paper bag to help her breathe. 'Ratty, oh my god, I am so, *so* sorry. Oh my god . . .' She took a breath. 'I don't even know what to say. Did you go to the police?'

'Don't know his real name; his friends called him Teabags. And he had a fierce mullet, which could be any guy in Australia right now.'

'Police?' Kit urged.

'Nah. The guys who found me gave me their number if I needed a witness, but what's the point?'

'Because CCTV!' Kit yelled. 'Because he should go to jail! Because he might do it to others!' Kit instantly regretted saying that. The last thing Rat needed was to be shamed. 'Have you been to a doctor?' she asked gently.

'Just ice and Nurofen. Eye looks like stage make-up, it's full on. The Pest came off worse than me, though.'

Kit went into mum mode. 'Where are you? I'm coming to get you.' *Do not lecture her*, she told herself sternly. *Comfort and validation; what she needs is comfort and validation.*

'Wategos. Everyone's filthy on me for parking a van here, even though I'm just stopping for a swim.'

'Stay there, we're coming,' Kit said, grabbing Gretel's Crocs and taking them over to her, signalling that she needed to put them on.

'Jesus, will you relax? Give me the address and I'll come to you. I gotta move the Pest anyway.'

Kit paused.

'No detours,' Kit said. 'Come now. Okay?'

'You'd better make up a story for G; my eye will spook her. I bought some Speed Dealers from the servo but I can't wear them twenty-four seven. Maybe I got thrown off a horse or fell down some—'

'Stairs. Got it.' Kit closed her eyes and took a breath. 'I love you, Rat. We'll look after you.'

Kit stood sipping a wine, watching her sister and Gretel on the verandah. Three days, a lot of pesto pasta, and many, many hours of Rat sleeping in a post-traumatic comedown later, Kit had extended the rental, leaving Camille and Jordan in charge of the office. The three of them needed this time, this rest, this togetherness so much, and Rat needed round-the-clock care: physically, mentally, emotionally. Her bravado and energy had faded now that she felt safe, and she was quiet, withdrawn. Gretel was confused. Why didn't Aunty Rat want to come to the beach, or play unicorn circus, or go out for pizza? Kit explained Rat wasn't feeling well after her accident, and she needed rest. Gretel had drawn a picture of Rat with a purple eye and sad face, crying, with Gretel next to her, handing her love hearts in every colour, and slid it under Rat's door.

In her quiet moments, Kit couldn't help feeling responsible in some way: Rat had only fled because Kit had told her to get her shit together. But Rat wouldn't listen to any of Kit's warnings about safety, about being a woman alone in isolated places, about constantly telegraphing her whereabouts to her followers. She did whatever she wanted, when she wanted. Kit felt deep shame admitting she had half-hoped Rat would have a wake-up call, a bit of a scare even—something to show her that life wasn't all sunshine and sleep-ins—but what eventuated was horrific. She decided that no matter how much Rat fought her, Kit was bringing her home to live with them back in Sydney. She needed time and compassion, not judgement and ultimatums. *You are being a good sister*, Kit assured herself. *You are not perfect, but you take care of your girls*. It was always going to fall to her: Kit was the sensible, serious, straight one, the rule-follower, while Rat and Gretel were bold, carefree, full of curiosity and big ideas. Kit needed routine and certainty to feel safe; her sister and daughter thrived on the lack of it. Was it because they knew Kit would have their back? Did they feel safe to explore and test boundaries because someone was looking out for them? Kit wholeheartedly hoped so.

The sky slowly changed from deep blue to a warm, golden pink. Gretel shuffled up onto Rat's lap as she licked her second ice block for the day, and watching them nuzzle together Kit felt a sense of intense love and affection. *This* was her family, and it was perfect.

'Hey, Rat,' Kit said gently. 'Let's take the Pest to the mechanic tomorrow and fix the side mirrors.'

'Yeah, maybe,' Rat said noncommittally, pointing out to Gretel where her ice block was about to drip.

'I don't think she's roadworthy as she is,' Kit added.

'Yeah,' Rat said vaguely. 'I might just sell her to some backpackers. I heard there's a place in town that sells on consignment.'

Kit couldn't believe what she was hearing. That van was Rat's pride and joy; she'd spent all her savings on it.

'Okay,' said Kit. 'I see why you would want to . . . okay, let's do that.'

'I can buy it!' Gretel said. 'I have twenty dollar-bucks from my birthday. Do you know that can buy a whole bag of stuff at Kmart, Aunty Rat? Even perfume textas?'

Rat ruffled Gretel's hair. 'You big dope. Why wouldn't you just spend it all on lollies?'

Gretel turned to face her mother, her eyes enormous as the thought of that sunk in.

Kit's phone rang inside, a sound that never failed to startle her. Who was calling? She really hoped it wasn't Rupert . . . she wasn't ready to be a deal head again.

She went inside and picked up her phone from the kitchen bench: Ari. Hang on, he was supposed to be offline, off the grid, off the everything in the Thai jungle. Why was *he* calling?

'Hello?' Kit said.

'Hi, hi, it's me!' he yelled happily. 'Did my number not come up?'

'No, I just— You're not supposed to be contactable for weeks. What's going on?' she asked suspiciously.

'Nothin', nothin', I just wanted to chat to baby G,' he said. 'I miss her so *much*. How are you, *where* are you? Is she an all-out roller derby girl yet?' Ari had given Gretel glittery red light-up roller skates for Christmas, but no knee pads or wrist guards, and until Kit had got around to buying those, there would be no skating.

'She loves them,' Kit said. Wasn't a lie.

'So,' he went on, 'I've got some good news: I finished early! The two final contestants quit. Gave up the prize money and everything, never seen anything like it. They cahooted and made this weird co-dependent alliance and decided they were, quote, "better than this". Show can't go on if there's no one to film, so I can come home! See my girls!'

'It was a *reality* show?' she asked, aghast. He'd turned down summer with his daughter for reality TV?

'Kiiiiind of,' he said. 'But not. Super-high production values and a wild budget. Sort of like if James Bond let a bunch of charismatic arseholes stay at his island lair to compete in psychologically messed-up challenges, you know?'

'Right.' Kit was distracted, looking out the window. Gretel was giving Rat a huge hug and Rat appeared to be crying. Kit needed to get out there.

'Sorry, can you make it quick? Got a bit of a situation.'

'What's going on?' he asked seriously. 'Everyone okay?'

'Yeah, yeah, it's . . . hard to explain. I'm up in Brunswick Heads with Gretel, and Rat has joined us.'

'I noticed she hadn't posted for a while,' he said slowly. 'She goes all right on the Tikky Tok doesn't she? Did you see when that seagull shat in her bed and then got stuck in the roof panels? I mean, just magic. You couldn't script it—'

'There was an incident,' Kit broke in. 'Some guy attacked her, gave her a black eye, smashed the van. She's not in a good way.'

'*What?!*' Ari gasped. 'Is she okay?'

'No,' Kit said. 'I'd say she's probably in shock. It was a few days ago, in Cairns . . . It's a long story, she's okay, but I am going to look after her, so we're in no rush to get back to Sydney.'

'I'll come straight there,' he said determinedly. 'I'm pretty sure you can fly straight to the Gold Coast from Bangkok.'

Kit chewed her lip as she thought. She wanted badly for Gretel to spend time with her dad, but this week was tender and sacred, this little beach shack, helping Rat heal . . . Ari hadn't done enough to deserve a spot here. That was the truth of it.

'We'll see you when we get home,' she said. 'At this stage that's next Monday.'

'Oh.' Ari's disappointment was palpable. 'No problem.'

'Okay, so next week,' Kit said, wrapping it up, 'you'll be with Gretel? I won't say anything to her just yet, but she'll wet her pants when she finds out.'

'One million percent,' he said gleefully. 'She is my only plan. I've already got the keys to Zach and Kane's place in Tamarama.'

Kane and Zach were TV producers; the thing they seemed to produce the most was more money.

'Nice,' Kit said, trying to hold back any snark.

'I'm *panging* to see her,' he said. 'And you, too, Kitty. I really, really miss you guys. I've been having all these flashbacks to when G was a toddler, taking her to the playground in Bondi with the little boat, making her pikelets for breakfast, and remember that weird cat that lived with us for a moment? What did she name him?'

Kit smiled. 'Susie.'

Ari laughed. 'Good ol' Susie.' He paused. 'If you change your mind, I'll be there in a heartbeat. No place I'd rather be.'

'Noted,' she said. 'Speak soon.' She ended the call, put the phone on silent, and went back outside to be with her girls. There being no place she'd rather be either.

20

'ARE YOU SURE YOU'RE UP to this?' Kit peered at her sister with concern. Ron had called Kit earlier that morning and Kit had panic-answered so the phone didn't wake Rat, curled up on the couch after having fallen asleep there last night. When Ron learned they were on the north coast, he insisted they visit, even though Maleny was a solid three-hour drive from Brunswick Heads. Kit tried to explain that Rat wasn't feeling well, but Ron wasn't having a bar of it: they were coming for lunch. Dawn would make chicken rolls. *They were coming for lunch.*

Rat shrugged, leaning against the kitchen bench, sipping on the tea Kit had made her.

'I'll have a gummy. I'll be okay.' She somehow had a never-ending supply of CBD and THC gummies. She said she couldn't sleep without them, but right now she couldn't wake without them either.

Kit looked at her sister, her greasy hair up in a top knot, wearing the same Nirvana t-shirt she'd chucked on three days ago. 'Okay. You might want to have a shower before we go . . .'

Past experience had prepared her for pushback whenever she asked Rat to do something, but somehow this was far worse: Rat had gone limp. She didn't care. She said nothing.

Kit walked over to her sister and put her hands on her shoulders.

'We don't have to do this,' Kit told her.

'Just be putting off the inevitable,' Rat replied dispassionately. 'He's been whining for a visit for the past year. Why doesn't *he* ever visit *us*?'

'True,' Kit said. 'But if we're doing it, we're doing it properly. Dressed, arriving with a bottle of wine and a tray of mangoes, and not engaging with Dad's rage bait or if Dawn starts up on her batshit 5G conspiracies. Got it?' She raised her brows at Rat, awaiting confirmation.

'Whatever,' Rat said.

She set off for the bathroom, her Pikachu slippers slapping loudly on the floorboards as she went.

'Little girl?' Kit called out the sliding door as she quickly set about downloading some Netflix shows onto her iPad for Gretel to watch in the car. 'Come and get dressed, we're going to visit Poppy.'

'*Who's Poppy?*' Gretel yelled from the backyard, where she was playing with two of her mermaid Barbies in a giant Tupperware container full of sudsy water: their 'spa'.

Kit wasn't sure whether to laugh or grimace.

'The old boy who lives in the forest,' Kit said. 'Your grandpa.'

Gretel's head whipped towards her mother. 'Will they give me magic rocks?'

Kit smiled. 'Maybe! Anyway, I put a dress and undies on your bed, so can you please get dressed and brush your hair? We've got to get going.'

Fifteen minutes later, as Kit blended cream blush onto her cheeks using the bedroom mirror (Rat was taking forever in the bathroom), Gretel raced into the bedroom.

'Mummy, Rat's hair is *gone!*' she exclaimed, eyes huge with excitement.

'What?' Kit asked, turning to look at her daughter, who'd put not one, not two, but seven clips in her hair.

'She cut it all off! I asked if I could have it cos I want my hair so long like Elsa, but she said it's the wrong colour . . .'

Kit, frowning in confusion, followed her daughter to the bathroom. The door was still closed.

'I just walked in!' Gretel said proudly, grabbing the handle and opening the door. 'See?'

Rat was standing with her back to them, facing the sink, which, like her feet, was covered in wefts of blonde hair. Her head was entirely shaved.

'Whoa . . .' Kit said gently, as if approaching a wild animal.

Rat ran one hand over her scalp. 'Feels amazing.'

'Can I feel?' Gretel squealed excitedly. 'Is it spiky?'

Rat turned around and bent over so Gretel could pat her now-bald scalp.

Gretel giggled. 'It feels like a carpet!'

'Suits you,' Kit said. And it genuinely did. 'What made you decide to do that?'

Rat stood up. 'Saw some clippers in the cupboard and thought, *Why not?* Hey, G, help me clean this up.' Rat gestured at the mess.

'No, thank you,' Gretel said sweetly before skipping out.

Rat began collecting handfuls of hair and putting them in the tiny bin. Once the hair was cleaned up, Kit placed a hand on her sister's back and rubbed it gently.

'Actually there are a few sections that need tidying,' she said. 'Can I?' She reached for the clippers.

Rat closed her eyes and Kit saw her swallow hard. A lone tear rolled down her cheek. Kit felt tears prick her own eyes.

'I wanted to start fresh,' Rat said, her voice catching.

'That makes sense,' Kit said, trying not to cry herself, trying to be a sturdy rock for Rat to lean on.

'I don't know how to explain it,' Rat went on. 'Like, so that it makes sense to someone not in my head. I just'—she took an unsteady breath—'I feel so different. I wake up every day and go, *Okay, be me again, be real, start some shit*, but I can't. I don't feel like the same person as before.' The tears were flowing freely now.

'Oh, Ratty,' Kit said, pulling her sister into her chest, holding her tight. 'It's so fresh. You're still processing. It's big; it will take time.'

Rat began sobbing, her face mushed into Kit's shoulder, her body heaving with the release.

Kit rubbed her back until finally her sister lifted her head and nodded that she was calm now. She was gaunt and sad, but her beauty persisted.

'I say to myself, *Oh, but you got away, you're okay, you are safe now, things are okay*, but it's like I'm tripping and can't get off the trip—my brain just keeps going back there.'

'I can see how that would happen,' Kit said.

Rat stared at the floor. 'I was grinding, you know, slutty club stuff, and he *knew* I was travelling alone—*everyone* fucking knew that, didn't they?' She shook her head. 'I didn't even tell you the times I had, like, full stalkers rock up outside the van. Everyone said—*you* said—that a girl shouldn't travel alone, but fuck that misogynistic shit, *why* can't we? I'm not gonna live my life worrying about boogie monsters and TV backpacker killers. Anyway, I don't want anyone to feel sorry for me, cos it's my fault.'

'Rat, no,' Kit interjected in a firm voice. '*You didn't do anything wrong*. You did not invite that violence. He attacked you. You are a victim, and it's really, *really* important you understand that. Okay?'

Rat shook her head, her bottom lip trembling. 'I feel anger, too, like, *savage* anger. I was having fun and living my dream and he fucked it all up. *And* he fucked up my head.'

Kit was strangely relieved to see Rat furious; anything other than the impassive twenty-five watts she'd been stuck on.

'That makes total sense to me.'

Rat sighed and wiped the tears from her eyes, but Kit could sense she was getting agitated: Doing The Work was not a very Rat thing to do.

'There's this woman,' Kit said, 'Dulcie, who helped Maggie with her postnatal depression. Maggie can't praise her enough. Maybe you could talk to her?'

Rat sighed, looking at her reflection in the bathroom mirror. 'They sent me to a counsellor at school cos I kept getting into fights. Mrs Feltam. She was such a potato.'

Kit smiled and put her arm around her sister. Rat rested her head on Kit's shoulder.

'I think it will help,' Kit said. 'I'll pay. As many sessions as you need.'

Rat nodded slowly, resigned.

'And stay with us in Sydney. Stay forever, we don't mind.'

'You do mind,' Rat said.

'I *did* mind,' Kit conceded. 'But things have changed.'

Three hours later, weary from a long, hot drive in a rental car with the aircon stuck on 'pointless', Kit, Rat and Gretel sat, squinting and sweating, at Ron and Dawn's outside table in the intense midday sun. 'Vitamin D deficiency causes more deaths than skin cancer,' Dawn said, not at all bothered by the lack of shade. Gretel and Kit wore hats, at least, but Rat had wanted to explore people's reactions to her hair and went without.

'What's all this?' Ron had said, when Rat had given him a peck on the cheek as they arrived. 'Get into a fight with a lawnmower?'

Kit noticed how frail he looked in his shorts and old Adidas t-shirt, so much thinner than when she'd last seen him. He looked much older than his sixty-five years.

'It's the new me,' Rat had said serenely, combing her fingers from the front of her head to the back. 'I love it.'

Ron had looked at Kit conspiratorially, as if to say, *what a shocker*, but Kit gave him nothing. She was Team Rat.

'Come on, give your poppy a hug,' he'd said, bending over to talk to Gretel, who was hiding behind Kit's legs.

When she refused to budge, he'd been embarrassed.

'Why's she being rude?' he said, standing back up.

'She's not. She's just not up for a hug right now,' Kit said, defending Gretel and her very understandable choice.

'She's not gonna say hello to her grandad?'

Kit swallowed the urge to go at him. 'Let her warm up,' Kit said. 'She hasn't seen you in a long time.' She rubbed Gretel's shoulder as her daughter face planted the back of her thighs.

'We brought some chardonnay, still your favourite?' Kit said brightly, walking past her father and through the screen door into the house.

True to her word, Dawn served hot chicken rolls, a meal Gretel wouldn't touch until all remnants of hot chicken were removed.

'Fussy, isn't she?' Ron said, as though Gretel didn't have ears. He took a long sip of beer.

'She doesn't like roast chicken,' Kit said. 'Never has.'

'My taste bugs don't like it,' Gretel said quietly.

Ron raised his brows. 'Dawn went to special trouble to go into town and get it.'

Kit ignored him, instead smiling kindly at Dawn, who was sitting across from her and next to Rat, all jangly bangles and ylang-ylang and fluttery silk fabric.

'Thank you, Dawn. I know this was all very last minute.'

Dawn closed her eyes and flapped her hand dismissively. 'Not at all. I needed some more activated charcoal anyway.'

Gretel stared at Dawn, taking in her long grey hair, dangly, turquoise earrings and many silver rings in quiet awe, as though she were a human-sized fairy.

'WHOA!' Rat said suddenly, eyes glued to a spot behind Kit and Gretel. '*Snake*. Big one. Fuck-fuck-fuck, what do we do?!'

'Rat did a swear!' Gretel cried happily, missing the part about the snake.

Ron looked over then back again, taking a bite of his roll. 'That's just Cleopatra. She won't hurt you.'

Rat shot up. 'I can't with the snakes, I can't. I'm out.' She grabbed her plate and edged around the corner of the table furthest from the snake side, then shot into the house, screen door slamming behind her.

'It's just a carpet snake,' Ron said casually. 'Only thing they eat are mice, nothing to worry about.' He looked at Gretel. 'You can get up close to her if you like; she won't move.'

'She has been keeping us mice-free for years,' Dawn added, nodding. 'She also keeps the browns and red-bellies away. She's our protector, our angel.'

Gretel looked over at the snake warily.

'I'll take you over to meet her,' Dawn said, standing up and offering her hand to Gretel.

She *was* very sweet with Gretel, Kit conceded. And it was important for Gretel to mix with people other than those in the Eastern Suburbs of Sydney.

Gretel looked at her mother for reassurance.

'It's okay, honey,' Kit said. 'Cleopatra is basically their pet.'

Reluctantly, Gretel stood up and went with Dawn to the corner of the yard where the python was coiled, sunning herself on a wide, flat rock.

'Natalie's hair,' Ron said, a furrow in his forehead. 'What's that about?'

'She's been through a rough time lately,' Kit said, knowing he wouldn't probe any further.

'Boy problems?' he said knowingly.

'You could say that.'

'Yeah, never really knew how to help you through those,' he said, fiddling with his napkin.

Kit laughed. 'Fair to say I didn't really have too many.' A half-truth; she'd had her heart decimated by Jeremy Logan in year nine, but Ron was the last person she'd have gone to about that.

'I'd do it differently, you know,' he said, rotating his chair around to watch Dawn and Gretel. 'I wasn't the best father. I know I let you down. And your mother. She loved you more than anything, you know that? More than she loved me, I used to say.'

Kit swallowed down the lump that had formed in her throat.

'You did the best you could with what you had,' she said, valiantly pushing through her resentment to find compassion.

'When Jeannie died, I just . . .' He shook his head, his lips pressed together.

She waited, but he didn't go on.

'Same, Dad.' She took a breath. 'I know it was tough on you, but I'—she cleared her throat—'I felt like you forgot about me. Like I'd lost two parents.'

'I tried,' he said in his own defence.

He was wasting the opportunity to comfort and commiserate in favour of protecting his ego, Kit thought.

'Do you honestly believe that?' she challenged him. She felt strangely energised, like there was nothing to lose. She knew he'd never give her the answers or apology or closure she wanted, but she wanted to get some stuff off her chest. She'd had a break-through with Rat this morning; maybe this was the day for it. *New year, new me* and all that jazz. She turned to face him, inhaling for confidence.

'Was leaving an eight-year-old alone all weekend trying? Was drinking till you passed out trying? Could you have tried to deal with your grief in other ways?'

'You had a roof over your head, food on the table,' he nipped back.

She snorted. Food and shelter were literally *the bare fucking minimum*.

'All I wanted was some attention,' she said. 'Just the smallest amount of love and affection.'

No one spoke. Ron continued to gaze at his granddaughter and girlfriend.

'You know what I learned?' he said finally. 'Money isn't everything. Doesn't buy you health, doesn't buy you happiness.'

Oh, here it comes, Kit thought. Pity parties were Ron's favourite kind.

'Yet you *made* it everything,' Kit said. 'Because we had none. You always told me you'd get another job and then everything would change, everything would be perfect. When we lost the house, you told me we'd get a better one, and then life would be great. So *I* learned that money was the fix, money meant we'd never have to worry ever again. I've spent my whole life believing that.'

'Well, don't,' he said bitterly, right in the spot where the word 'sorry' might have fitted.

Kit shook her head. Who did he think he was? Some sage old man imparting wisdom as he looked back on his life? *Give me a break*, she thought cynically.

'My parents did me no favours in that area, let me tell you,' he muttered.

301

'Were they financially insecure, too?' She'd never known, never asked. They were long estranged, both dead.

Ron blinked a few times, still looking at Dawn and Gretel rather than Kit. 'Dunno what that means but they were filthy rich. Farming money. Owned half of Lockyer Valley.'

Kit stared at him in disbelief. '*What?*'

'Lost it all,' he said, sipping from a can of beer in an Ettamogah Pub stubby holder. 'Bad deal with some city shonks. From kings to peasants. Dad spent his whole life trying to get it back.'

Kit leaned back, taking in this information. 'Wow,' she said. 'I wish I knew more about them.'

'Mum was a good stick,' he went on. 'Clever lady, like you. Loved little crystal animals—collected hundreds of them. She didn't care about money; Dad's obsessiveness sent her barmy in the end.'

'Were you ever close?' she asked.

He shook his head. 'Dad just saw me as another pair of hands on the farm. Violent man, too. Couldn't wait to get out of there.'

That's two of us, Kit thought sadly. 'I'm sorry to hear that, Dad.'

He inhaled and shuffled in his chair. 'That's life. I'm all right, aren't I?'

Kit sat for a moment, watching Gretel collect tiny daisies as an offering for Cleopatra, thinking about what Ron had said. They'd both grown up poor, with fathers desperate not to be. *I'm going to break the generational curse*, she thought. Ron needs to know that it ends with me.

'Do you remember how I told you I'm selling some of my company?' she said, changing the tone of the conversation.

'Mm,' he said, permanent frown etched on his face.

'Well, turns out a lot of people want to buy it.' It made her feel light-headed and jittery to be talking about it with someone she knew had the power to make her feel like it was nothing. 'For a lot of money.' She cleared her throat, suddenly nervous. 'The company is being valued between sixty and eighty million dollars at the moment . . .'

His eyes widened, and he turned his head to look at her, blinking in shock. 'You're pullin' my leg.'

'I'm not,' she said, smiling shyly.

'*You're* going to be a millionaire. *My* daughter.'

'Well, it's not—' She started to correct him.

He cut her off. 'Don't mess it up. Whatever you do, kid, do *not* mess this up. If you get the chance to set you and your kid up for life, you bloody well take it.'

She laughed. 'You just said money wasn't important. Health, happiness, et cetera?'

'Yeah, well, that was before you said sixty million bucks,' he said, back to looking out at the yard. 'You'd be a bloody idiot not to take that. Buy you all the health and happiness in the world, that would.'

21

RUPERT NEEDED KIT'S HEAD BACK in the deal the moment she returned to Sydney. She'd been intermittently 'jumping on' video calls and 'circling back' on emails while she was up north, but her physical presence was required again now that things were getting serious. Camille, Ben and Jordan had spent half of January answering the hundreds of bidder questions flowing into the due diligence software, a process designed to expedite the final stages of the deal and ensure potential investors knew every single little thing about Second Day before making a final offer. It had meant a huge amount of time and toil for her team. She felt guilty knowing they were doing all of this on top of their already big workload, which only exacerbated her anxiety about choosing the right partner. A world where they'd done all of this and ended up with a bunch of interfering muppets was unthinkable. She had to constantly remind herself that, should none of them feel right, she could back out altogether. But all this effort, all this time, all those fees . . .

Ari picked up Gretel the night they arrived home, whisking her away for what Kit knew would be a week of unfettered Dad Treats. They'd be back home every second day for something Gretel wanted or had forgotten, but at least a) Kit could wholly, selfishly focus on the deal without feeling like a piece of shit for knocking back Gretel every time she wanted to create a birthday party for her teddies, or play schools, or basically engage in any activity that required Kit's attention and patience, and b) Gretel was spending one-on-one time with her father. Kit had overheard Gretel telling a kid at the playground that her dad only saw her half the time (optimistic) but she knew he loved her all the time because he wrote her notes (he *did* send postcards) and bought her candy even when he wasn't there. This made Kit so sad. She couldn't tell if it was because her daughter didn't have a dad who was more present, or because Ari was forever granted hero status in Gretel's mind, no matter how deficient he was as a father.

Rat's interest in the world and being part of it had increased, but she was still not herself. And historically, she had a lot of self to go around. She spent most of the day going on long walks—which Kit approved of—or watching *Love Island* on her laptop in bed. Any region, any season, any episode. Kit checked in with her every day, and worried about her every night. *This is why you make best friends*, she wanted to say to her sister, who'd never held down a friendship for longer than a few months. Rat's friendships always started with the energy of a fireball—*soul mates finally united!*—then either faded into nothing or exploded. Ditto her boyfriends.

As Kit drove to work through streets still devoid of back-to-school traffic, she decided to call Piper. They'd been missing each other's calls for the past few weeks, but Kit had a few questions for her. She knew Piper was in Sydney with her family and therefore in the same time zone, so she went for it.

Piper picked up almost immediately.

'You were actually on my mind today, swear to god,' Piper said.

Kit laughed. 'Nice to be home over summer?'

'*Love* it for us. We rented a house in Palm Beach and now I'm literally made of Aperol and cheese boards. I need to work out *bad*, but just can't seem to make my legs actually do it, you know what I mean?'

Kit did not know what she meant. She had been running every day since Rat had returned, given there was always someone to watch Gretel for thirty minutes. She did it to clear her head and balance out her nocturnal wine and vape consumption.

'For sure,' Kit lied. 'So, how's your deal coming along?'

'Oh, you know,' Piper replied, sighing. 'Usual surprise salad. Just when I think we're close, BOOM, they pull a move and we're back to square one. How about yours? What's up? How can I help?'

'I won't take much of your time,' Kit promised, 'it's just there are a few, shall we say *interesting* outcomes shaping up, ones I hadn't anticipated, so I wanted to ask: how do you know when it's time to let go? How do you get past the idea of someone other than you in control of something you created that's so tied to you and your name?'

'Comes down to your end goal,' Piper said. '*I* live to grow and sell. That's my MO. I mean, I'm not saving the world with curling tongs, right?' She laughed. 'Why get too attached? It's just business. Think of it like a child: you feed it and look after it and help it grow, but you don't ever really *own* it. It has its own life force, right? You're just its guardian. And eventually it's time for it to leave home.'

'Yeah, right,' Kit said, nodding slowly. That was a new perspective.

'Of *course*, we're bonded to something we create,' Piper said, 'but that doesn't mean it's forever. Like, was making hairspray your childhood dream?'

'Ah, no,' Kit said. It was 'not be poor'.

Second Day was not a *calling*, Kit realised, as she drove out of the Kings Cross Tunnel and the city came into view. It was great, but it was just something that happened; luck intersecting with timing. She didn't need to load it with all this extra emotion. There was a universe where she never started a brand, and none of this happened, and she would have been just as happy. Maybe even happier! *Definitely* less stressed.

'I just had few weeks offline with my daughter and sister, and it gave me the mental real estate and distance to remember there's more to life than business.'

'Right?' Piper said. 'I *adore* my company and my customers, and I've worked super hard on Red Carpet, but it's just what I'm doing, not who I *am*.' She paused a beat. 'You feeling stuck with the deal?'

Kit released a breath she hadn't even known she was holding. Despite bounding through conversations like a small, fast dog, Piper was wildly intuitive.

'I have a preference,' Kit said. 'And a backup. Both are great in some ways but problematic in others. Sometimes it feels like they're full Jekyll and Hyde-ing me. Does that happen to you?'

'One *hundred* percent,' Piper said, and Kit knew there were rolled eyes to accompany it. 'I don't believe a word they say till I see the mark-up. Hang a sec—HUNTER, MUMMY IS ON THE PHONE, BUT I CAN SEE YOU, OKAY? I'M WATCHING, BABY. Sorry, go on.'

'My first choice, for instance, they're asking for a fifty percent stake, but only thirty percent is on offer. They knew that from the start, we were so clear. It's outrageous. We've said no, obviously.'

Piper took a loud sip of something. 'Pretty standard unfortunately,' she said. 'Remember, they do this all day every day, this is rote for them. You're fresh meat, you're young, you're—sorry, babe, but it's true—female: they're gonna try it on.'

'Yeah, I forget that,' Kit said. 'Anyway, I'm not selling more than my defaulting shareholder's thirty percent, so they can suck it.'

'Can I ask why?' Piper probed. 'If you believe these guys can really *do the thing*, really make Second Day fire, then why not sell down, too? *They* buy in at the top of the market, *you* get some cash and de-risk yourself from being this huge shareholder who could lose it all, *they* do everything in their power to grow profits, then you all exit in a few years. Happy days!'

Kit blinked a few times, absorbing Piper's scenario. Making something incredibly complicated sound as easy as one, two, three was a real skill.

'Whatcha hanging on to?' Piper asked, when Kit didn't reply. 'What's your fear?'

Kit had to think for a moment. It *was* a fear, she realised. 'I've heard all these horror stories of investors coming in and destroying the soul of a company,' she said. 'I can't let that happen.'

'Oh, girl,' Piper said dismissively. 'If your adviser is doing his job, you'll get all the protections you need in the shareholders' agreement. Still control all the things that matter to you, like product or retailers. Plus, no one said you had to sell majority; just don't sell more than forty-nine percent, you duffer!'

'Yeah . . .' Kit said, deep in thought.

'What you should be asking yourself is: what are you risking by *not* doing this deal. This is *real money in the bank*. Exit money, later money, is maybe money. I say take the sure thing.' Piper's tone was the equivalent of dusting off her hands.

Kit sighed loudly. 'I wish I had a crystal ball.'

'A good lawyer is far better. Listen, I understand your hesitancy, but the best time to cash out is *always* when it feels a bit too early. Better than when it feels a bit too late, trust me on that one. Just make sure you're protected against the worst possible situations: takeovers, insolvency, you being pushed out, all that nasty stuff.'

Kit's eyes widened. Pushed out? Takeovers? She knew it wasn't going to be all cupcakes and rosé, but *insolvency*?

'Right, will do. Piper, thank—'

'Look. There's no perfect deal,' Piper interjected. 'You gotta take the good and suck up the bad. But the juice can *really* be worth the squeeze.'

'I hope so,' Kit said.

'Well from what I hear you are looking at some pretty crazy numbers, girl! Go you!'

'Thanks, Piper,' Kit said, embarrassed. 'I really appreciate your advice. You can't know how much.'

'Oh, you'll pay it forward. Tons of founders will come at you for advice when you close, you watch.'

'Of course,' Kit said. 'And it will be my honour to pass on your phone number.'

They both laughed and said their goodbyes, making well-intentioned promises to catch up for a drink that they each knew would never actually eventuate.

Half an hour later, Kit sat in the tastefully decorated Linley Advisory boardroom with Rupert and Hugo, sipping her third coffee for the day. Kit felt she had a decent enough perspective on boardrooms now to know that this one, with its art, and beautiful cork wall done in a chequerboard style, and green sheer curtains, was made using a substantial money pot and a professional interior decorator. Hugo had been preoccupied selling a national car dealership to a global auto retailer recently, but with that climaxing in an explosion of cash on Christmas Eve, he was now free to work on the Second Day deal. *This is good for us*, Rupert had said. *Hugo is a closer.*

Rupert took a sip from a tiny espresso cup. He noticed Kit admiring it. 'It's something, isn't it? Client brought them back for us from Ravello. Handmade, apparently.'

Kit smiled. 'Lovely.'

She'd been a good shareholder and read the full summary of both Blue Tree and Pinnacle's proposed terms. Camille was firmly in camp Blue Tree given their track record with beauty brands, while Jordan was firmly in the hands of a handsome Brazilian she'd met at a NYE party on Bondi Beach. She'd tapped out mentally and Kit couldn't blame her. She'd choose wild summer sex over complicated legal jargon, too.

'Can you catch me up briefly?' Hugo said. 'I recall Rupert saying Longitude were looking strong earlier on. They're good operators; why have they fallen out of favour?'

'They tried to dictate how much I could and could not sell down,' Kit said, 'as well as how long I needed to remain in the business, and when the business would be sold in full—all as minority shareholders.'

'I see,' he said, nodding at Kit knowingly. 'That was a bit silly, wasn't it?'

Kit couldn't get a read on Hugo. Was he unfriendly, or was she just used to Rupert's overly florid language and warmth? He looked like Adam Sandler, she realised, and she unfairly expected him to be funnier.

'And Liberty?' he asked.

'Who were they again?' Kit looked at Rupert quizzically.

'They flew up from Melbourne, bullish about return hurdles and a fast exit.'

Kit frowned; that could have been any of them. Her phone flashed with a call on the table in front of her: Ron. She'd call him back later.

'I think—' Kit began.

'Kit's CEO,' Rupert said at the same time, 'asked Finley Roberts why they didn't have a single woman in their investment arm.'

'*Oof*,' Hugo said, raising his brows. 'He would *not* have enjoyed that.'

'Ohhh, *those* guys,' Kit said in recognition.

'Most firms are usually pretty considered with their offers, but female founders tend to throw them a bit,' Hugo remarked. 'Bet you've had a lot of "my wife uses your stuff".'

Kit rolled her eyes. 'How did you know? Or they bring in a single token woman—she doesn't get to say a word, mind you, but they think it will make me—'

'The funny thing is,' Hugo interrupted, 'a lot of women *do* work in mergers and acquisitions, but they're rarely on the deal stuff.'

'Why not?' Kit asked.

'It's a particular mindset. Competitive. A bit of a sport.'

'Women can be competitive!' Kit scoffed.

'What Hugo is trying to politely illuminate, Kit,' Rupert chimed in, 'is that you often have to be a bit of a prick, excuse my French. And generally speaking, us gents are better at that.'

Kit frowned.

'It's just an act,' Rupert said quickly. 'Everyone plays a role in a deal, like characters almost. Once you begin working with them, they revert back to—'

'Decent human beings?' Kit asked.

'Precisely.' He smiled roguishly.

'My sense is Liberty were not right for Second Day anyway,' Hugo acknowledged. 'You're looking for more of an active partner than a silent backer, right?' He paused, peering at her. 'Kit, can I ask why you won't sell anything beyond a minority stake?'

Why did she have to keep explaining this? There were plenty of companies with investors as minority shareholders. 'Because it's my baby—' She stopped herself. 'Because it's my company, my product, my team. I can't let a bunch of finance lizards come in and take control.'

Rupert and Hugo exchanged a look.

'Kit,' Rupert said, 'the reason we asked you to come in is because Blue Tree submitted their final terms yesterday. As we predicted, they have rejected the thirty percent on offer. They need seventy percent to proceed.'

'*Fuck,*' Kit whispered angrily. She was so attached to the idea of Blue Tree; *they* were the ones she wanted to work with! She'd been so sure they'd come around.

'But they *knew* that wasn't on offer! They made out like they were fine being a minor shareholder!'

'I bear witness,' Rupert agreed.

'Fucking time-wasters,' she muttered. 'Unbelievable.' She looked up at Rupert. 'Could we offer them forty-five percent?'

'Oh, we've tried it all,' Rupert said, shaking his head. 'I even— forgive me—went up as far as forty-nine percent. But I'm afraid Clay has drawn a line in the sand. They love the brand, and you, they really believe in it, but their board will not accept anything less than seventy percent. They are also resolute on their preference share structure, baking in disproportionate equity returns. Grubby behaviour, if you ask me.'

'Shit, shit, shit,' said Kit, feeling the deal slipping away. 'Is it worth having a call? Can we salvage this?'

'My intel,' Hugo said, with none of Rupert's delicacy, 'is they've got a few options on the go, and another party is much more open to their terms given, shall we say, the *unique* financial position they find themselves in.'

'Firm as jelly,' Rupert said. 'Giving them anything they want. Makes it hard to go up against.'

Kit crossed her arms and shook her head. She had really thought this was going to happen. There had been so many meetings, so much back and forth, so much optimism from Clay and Seth . . . and she'd been played. *Probably all Max's doing*, she huffed. She felt like a fool. She was far too green, far too soft to be in this world.

'Kit,' Rupert said kindly, 'even if I was conceited or foolish enough to think I could convince you to sell them the seventy percent, I could *not* in good faith sign off on those terms. That's more appropriate for a company in deep distress, who will do anything to stay afloat. You are several galaxies away from that.'

'You'll find a partner, Kit,' Hugo said matter-of-factly. 'This is a profitable company with proven growth and strong potential, and there's still plenty of interest.'

'The fact that these bidders want to buy more is a positive thing for you,' Rupert added. 'Selling down when the valuation is this high makes good business sense. The winds are blowing the right way: bull market, the beauty industry boom, the fascination with digital-first brands with a strong community . . .' He looked at her affectionately, paternally. 'This will be a material transaction. Why not take advantage of it?'

Hugo jumped in. 'I've seen businesses worth two hundred million drop to twenty million in twelve months. I'm not suggesting that is *your* arc, but there's a window open right now and it won't stay open forever.' The way he looked at her made Kit feel slightly stupid. 'Selling on the way up is the way to do it. If you seize the moment, and understand how fleeting and incredibly rare that is, you're ahead of ninety percent of the field.'

Kit began to feel like she was being ambushed. Like they'd planned this.

'He's right in that sense, Kit,' Rupert said. 'Most businesses never get this shot. They just peter out, or wind down, or end up selling for an iota of what they were once worth.'

'And even if they get *do* get a solid transaction,' Hugo took over, 'there's no certainty they'll get the next one. Oh sure, an exit is always planned, but who knows what the market, the industry, the world will do? What is certain is *this* deal, this cash, now.'

'Bird in the hand, et cetera,' Rupert finished.

'Did you two script this?' Kit asked suspiciously.

'Look,' Hugo said, ignoring her, 'it's simple. At thirty percent, buyers are simply not as motivated. Take Cosmetic Haus: the reason they were acquired for three hundred and fifty million dollars is because four years earlier they took on a majority partner who invested heavily, took them into new markets, put them on TV and billboards, built experiential retail concepts . . . All of that takes money and experience, and with all due respect, that's not something you and your team have right now.'

Kit stared at Hugo, half-offended, while also embarrassed that she *was* offended.

'Who said we want to be that aggressive, or we're just chasing the big exit?' Kit said defensively. She did want to grow, but not at any cost.

'Sure,' Hugo said, shrugging. 'But why only go halfway? Why not shoot the lights out? You have your house in order, your team are firing, you have momentum: with the right partner, *anything* is possible. The chances of your exit being worth five times what the company is valued at today goes up exponentially if a motivated partner who spent a lot drives it. They're going to work much harder to get that return in a few years—see what I'm saying?'

Kit studied him as he spoke: his bald head, his stubble just so, his thin puffer vest despite it being high summer.

'I've heard stories about investors coming in and firing staff and reducing quality and cost-cutting to get sales and EBITDA up,' she said. 'I don't want that for my company. Or brand.'

'That's why you do your due diligence,' he replied, nodding. 'They're not all bad guys.'

'No, they're just full of shit,' she retorted.

'Kit,' Hugo said, head tilted, looking directly at her, 'now is the time to start acting less like a founder and more like a shareholder. Founders are always too emotionally attached.'

'Now, Hugo,' Rupert interjected, 'you've made some salient points and I, like everyone here at Linley Advisory, am in awe of your brilliant deal-making and negotiation skills. But part of your responsibility as an adviser is to read the room.' He nodded at Kit as if to say, *I've got you.* 'This is *not* a textbook build-and-flip business. This is not some faceless company. This is a small team of people with a brand they care about and a founder who is acting with consideration and care. That's *not* something to deride.'

'Understood,' Hugo said, looking very much like he did not. 'But as Kit's advisers, it's also our job to make sure she is considering every option, every pathway. With all due respect, these shares are being valued far, *far* beyond what they are worth. Capitalising makes sense.'

'Gee, thanks,' Kit said, starting to get annoyed.

He smiled; it was the kind of smile that showed both rows of his teeth, like Britney Spears. 'I'm just saying: you've said you want someone to supercharge your growth, but I wonder if you understand what that takes, what that means in practical terms.'

'Hugo,' Rupert said, leaning forward in his chair, 'Kit is our *client*, need I remind you.'

'What's so bad about wanting to play it safe?' Kit said, arms folded. 'Do fewer things better? Be a solid, consistent business? Not everyone has a big risk appetite, you know. That doesn't make me stupid.'

'No one is calling you stupid, Kit,' Hugo said firmly. 'But you are at risk of losing the best opportunity that will ever come your way if you don't play this right.'

'Jesus, you sound like one of *them*,' she muttered.

'He used to be one,' Rupert explained. 'Hard to shake once you've had the disease.'

Well, Kit would not be bullied by Hugo, or by Blue Tree.

'No deal,' she said firmly. 'Who's next?'

22

KIT WALKED INTO GRETEL'S ROOM in her robe, sipping her coffee. Her daughter was busy reconnecting with her army of glittery, bug-eyed plushies after having been away with Ari. She had also carefully arranged her crystal collection—Rat had collected them for her while on her van trip; Dawn had doubled that amount—on one of Kit's old silk scarves, and was assigning a crystal to each toy. Kit kneeled beside her daughter and commented on how wonderful they looked.

'We have to moon shower them,' Gretel said.

'Oh yes, you do need to cleanse them under the full moon,' Kit said, remembering she did that as a teen with her best friend at the time. That they'd shoplifted the crystals may have negated their magic.

'Can you play with me, Mummy?' Gretel asked, as she meticulously lined the rose quartz in a row.

'Oh, honey . . .' Kit said. That question hit the deepest mothering nerve she possessed, guilt and shame intermingling with deep love and affection for her baby, whom she was acutely aware would not always be young and keen for her company.

'I can and I will . . .' She took a breath and rushed the next words out. 'Mummy needs to get ready first, but then I will.'

Gretel looked at her mother's face. Kit had given Gretel a short fringe, and it was the best thing she'd ever done, accentuating her daughter's enormous brown eyes.

'You never play with me,' she said sadly.

Gretel was easier to absorb when she was angry. It was more predictable in a way. When she was disappointed, Kit felt untethered and powerless.

Kit pulled her daughter close. 'Baby girl, did you know you're my favourite person in the world? I *love* playing with you. Remember how I said I am doing a big project, like how you did your space one for school last year? Soon it will be over, and I will go back to normal not-always-busy Mummy.'

'But I have no one to play with,' Gretel said, expertly breaking her mother's heart.

Kit squeezed her tight. She had no answer for that. 'I'm sorry, baby,' she said. And, oh, she was. She was angry at herself for allowing this deal, work, the endless meetings to rise to the top, while spending time with Gretel so easily slipped down to the bottom because she took for granted that Gretel would always be there. But what could she do? The urgent stuff always outweighed the non-urgent. Gretel would always come second for as long as Kit put Second Day first. *Well*, she thought to herself, *there's your problem right there. So fix it.*

'I love you so much, baby. More than any stupid work. Hey, Rat will be up soon, and she's going to take you swimming, but until then I thought you could maybe watch *Trolls*?'

Gretel's eyes lit up: morning TV was still a unique and special treat. She yanked herself free of her mother's hold and tore down the hallway to the living room. Within seconds, Kit heard the familiar *buwbuw* of Netflix starting up. That Gretel knew how to turn on the TV and cruise through all the various streamers mortified Kit, but she had to admit it was efficient.

A text from Rupert came in as Kit headed to the kitchen.

Good luck today, I trust it will all go well. Forgive me for not being there—I'd rather not be having a colonoscopy, for what it's worth.

Kit was meeting with Pinnacle this morning. She was worried they were heading for another eleventh-hour arm wrestle à la Blue Tree, but Marty and his wild ideas kept her positive. Kit had been fantasising about the crossover products they could make for hair growth *and* styling . . .

They know it's a minority stake right? Kit replied. *No tricks this time?*

They've been clear from day one they want more, Kit, so we know that conversation is coming. But they're playing nice. If anything, they are keener than us to close. Go in today and get them excited. To get the deal you want you need to make them believe in your plan, and passion, and the future of Second Day. Leave no doubt in their mind.

Got it! Kit wrote back. *No pressure!*

Kit tossed her phone on the kitchen bench and took a deep breath to calm herself. There was a hum of nervous energy in her chest and stomach, something she'd enjoyed a blissful break from during her time up north. She sighed, looking around at her pig sty of a house: the beat-up old couch, the chequerboard rug she'd thought was so chic but now made her cringe. She and Gretel had moved here when Ari and Kit had separated, since Kit couldn't afford the rent on the house they'd lived in as a trio. This little semi held so many memories: Gretel losing her first tooth, the first Christmas she really *got* Santa, learning to scoot down the hallway . . . but Kit realised they needed to move on. Time for a fresh start. She dreamed of a home that had a proper space for Rat, an office for Kit, and was wider than seven metres. She was nearing forty: it was time to *buy the damn house*! A house with a garage, so she didn't have to fight the rest of the neighbourhood and diners at nearby restaurants for a parking space every day. A house with some grass. A house close to the sea, maybe . . .

Kit snapped to attention: she needed to get out of her head, get dressed and go. She thanked the gods Rat was here: Gretel was still on school holidays but Lily was away and Ari had gone to New Zealand on a road trip with 'the boys'. The boys were just one guy, Dean, but he was called the boys because whenever he entered a room he brought the energy and volume of several men. He was newly divorced and needed some bro time, Ari explained. How delightful for them to be able to just spontaneously road trip. Kit couldn't imagine. She thought about all the finance guys she'd face in the meeting this morning; they just threw on a suit, said goodbye to their partners and/or kids, and *left the house*. Kit, on the other hand, had to organise child care, find the perfect outfit—not too corporate, not too playful, always polished and chic—do full hair and make-up, make sure her nails were done, dazzle everyone in the meeting, ask the right questions, get her head around impossible concepts that would directly impact the rest of her life, go into the office and do actual work, think about dinner, buy the groceries, take Gretel on her play date, then cook the fucking dinner. And *then* read and digest all the latest documents and updates once she had fed-homeworked-bathed-and-read-to Gretel. No wonder she was stressed. Kit felt a fizzy little tingle on her lower lip and raced to the bathroom. *Fuck.* It was there already. The cold sore she one hundred percent knew was due. *She couldn't have a cold sore in these meetings!* She slammed her bathroom drawers open and closed, looking for the magic tablets to stop it, but she hadn't replaced them when she'd last been afflicted. She quickly dabbed some nail polish remover on a cotton pad and pressed it hard against the red splotch. *Great,* now she'd have to find time to go to the chemist on the way.

Kit quickly did her face and pulled her hair back into a sleek, high bun, with a centre part. She used Second Day pomade and a teasing brush so it was locked in place, then slipped some large mismatched gold hoops with multicoloured glass charms into her ears. She walked out of the bathroom and tapped lightly on her bedroom door before pushing it open. The darkness was disorientating.

She went over to the window and opened the blinds and heard Rat snuffle in bed.

'What are you doing?' she said, her voice croaky. Rat moved from her trundle in Gretel's room to Kit's bed once Gretel woke up so she could keep sleeping.

'Rat, get up, it's nearly nine. I have a meeting, I need to get ready . . .'

Rat rolled over and dug her face into the pillow. 'Mmpft,' came the response.

'Coffee machine is on. Could you make me one, too, please? Long black. Come on, chop chop!' Coffee was forbidden with cold sores and a terrible idea when you were already feeling anxious. Kit did not care.

She began sifting through her wardrobe furiously. She had used up all her corporate looks, every single one of her blazers, suits and shirts had had a run. All that remained were a glut of vintage tees, baggy trousers and fruity dresses. She pulled out a striped, boxy long-sleeved button-down dress with a modest neckline and decided that would do. She added some pretty red Miu Miu heels and a mashup of rings and bracelets.

Fifteen minutes later, Rat stood leaning against the kitchen bench in a singlet and undies, drinking her coffee, watching Kit tear around the kitchen in her heels, wolfing down toast and coffee at the same time as writing a shopping list. Gretel was still happily watching *Trolls* on the couch; Kit trotted over and gave her a squeeze and kiss goodbye.

'That dress is ugly as shit,' Rat commented, taking a sip of her coffee. 'Love you, though.'

Kit looked down. Was it? No! It was chic in a shapeless, Danish-influencer kind of way.

'Don't be a bitch. I need to feel powerful today; I'll be the only woman in the room, as per usual.'

'No one will even know you're a woman under that, don't worry.' Rat smirked.

Rat hadn't been this cheeky in a while, so even if Kit was her target, she was relieved.

Kit gestured to the mess around her as she gulped her coffee down. 'Can you clean this up and make sure Gretel has some fruit and a healthy lunch? Tell her she can have a jam sambo *only* if she eats an avocado one first.' She lowered her voice. 'But she should be so full that it won't actually happen. Okay, I'll be back around four—please *saturate* her in sunscreen if you go out, and do *not* take your eyes off her if you take her swimming. Remember, she is overconfident, but she cannot swim at *all*, so don't let her go further than an arm's length away, and stay between the flags. There's some watermelon that's about to turn, please eat that, turn the aircon off when you leave and text me if you need anything. I love you both to death, see you soon, *mwah mwah mwah*!'

Kit grabbed her water bottle, her handbag and raced out. She checked her watch: late. Even if traffic was good, late. She'd have to go to the chemist after the meeting, by which time the cold sore would have its own star sign and postcode. She jumped into the driver's seat and turned the car on, then reached into the back for her sunglasses, which Gretel had been wearing. As she plucked them from the back seat, she heard a terrible rip. She sat facing forward and felt under her right armpit with her left arm. Skin. She'd ripped a huge hole in the dress. She sat totally still, the only sound her breath, considering her two terrible options: being *very* late, or being someone with holes in her clothes. She figured if she held her handbag on that shoulder and stood with her arms down and her back against the wall, no one would see. Plus she would be sitting anyway. Fuck it. She put the car into drive and sped off.

An hour later, and only three minutes late, Kit was seated in the most spectacular room she had ever seen—possibly that had ever been built. It was long and narrow, with glass walls and ceiling, and jutted out from the skyscraper over the city, like a pier.

'Out-of-the-box thinking, blue sky ideas, get it?' Omari had said when Kit arrived. 'Malcolm commissioned Luis Garcia to design it.'

'Clever,' Kit said, lowering her head self-consciously and covering her growing cold sore with her hand. 'Though it makes me a little nervous,' she added, unable to shake the feeling that the weight of their bodies would trigger its collapse.

'Oh, it's triple-reinforced, don't worry,' Omari said with a laugh. 'And climate-controlled with touch-button window tinting if the sun gets too much. It has its own microclimate basically. Speaking of climate, god, it's muggy today—this summer has gone from impolite to downright aggressive . . .'

'It's foul,' Kit agreed. 'I need to make an anti-humidity serum; none of them work.'

Malcolm was not in attendance, and neither was Marty; they were in Aspen together as a family. *Of course*, Kit thought. Why be in feral, stormy Sydney when you could be skiing? Marty had sent talking points and questions, which had been printed out and which Kit read with a mix of confusion and great interest. He was treating Second Day like a unique engineering project, and Kit was here for it. She'd read somewhere that companies such as Apple and Spotify often brought in people from an entirely different industry with a different mindset, just to mix things up a bit. Marty could be an amazing asset . . .

Hugo had come into the meeting hot. No weather foreplay, no holiday chat: he was on a mission. As soon as they were seated, he began pressure-testing Omari and his offsider, who were accompanied by one of their in-house legals. Arthur, who was in his late sixties, half-man, half-beard, was visibly confused by the fact that there was a young woman in the room.

'What we are keen to understand,' Omari was saying, once Hugo finally let him speak, 'is the size of the prize here. Where do you want Second Day to be in three to five years?'

'Well, as you've seen in the projections,' she said, remembering to present a problem they could valiantly come in and solve, 'we are nowhere near where we could be domestically. We are tracking at around twenty percent brand awareness, so there are—'

'It could be four times as big, no question about it,' Hugo interrupted.

Kit looked at him briefly, then back to Omari.

'Kit,' Omari went on, 'forgive my bluntness, but do you believe the brand can stand without you? Will it have a life span beyond your involvement?'

'I do and it will. I mean, half of our followers don't even follow me, so there's—'

'Kit recognises the value and importance of stepping aside and letting the brand forge its own path,' Hugo said.

'Gosh, if only Kit could say that herself . . .' Kit remarked facetiously. She knew she was being spicy, but she'd had enough of Hugo's mansplaining.

Omari laughed and, to his credit, so did Hugo.

'Boys, if you don't mind, we're running short on time and we're yet to get to the meat in this sandwich,' Hugo said. 'Can you give us some colour around the equity piece? In your last mark-up you inferred it would need to be around seventy percent. Now, you and I both know that's not what was on offer, and other parties have been removed from the process on that exact ask, so perhaps you could give us your updated thinking on that.'

Omari and his colleague looked at each other.

'Well,' Omari said, 'we did actually jump on a call with Malcolm this morning and, look, this will all come through via email later today, but there's what we believe to be a very competitive offer coming. It is for seventy percent, though. That's our directive. Pinnacle's cheque sizes begin at circa a hundred, as you know, but Marty has convinced Malcolm this is not one to miss. We need certainty around exit time frame, founder involvement beyond that, and there are some stipulations around board make-up and executive hires, but nothing too onerous.'

Kit's heart began to beat fast. It was happening *again*.

'Kit has made it clear from day one this is a minority sell-down,' Hugo interjected, not looking at Kit.

'Kit,' Omari said, twirling his pen and looking directly at her, 'do you mind if I speak frankly?'

She wished Rupert were here. Her fear was rising. Her cold sore was tingling.

'Go ahead,' she said.

He leaned forward, placing his elbows on the table, making a steeple with his hands. 'Second Day is a great company,' he said. 'Obviously, or you wouldn't have folks like us trying to buy in.' He smiled. 'Now. You could stick to your path, growing incrementally, enjoying healthy dividends and enough challenges to keep you interested. Or you could reach.' He looked at her, expression serious, brown eyes boring into her, challenging her to break his gaze.

'You could bet on yourself, Kit,' he said. 'Show the world you mean business. Take Second Day to a whole new level. Imagine how proud you will feel when you see your brand soaring, when you allow your team and products to reach their full potential. Imagine what an inspiration you will be to other female founders.'

'Jeez, Omari, you could run for prime minister with a speech like that,' Hugo said, chuckling.

Omari didn't smile, nor did he take his eyes from Kit.

'We can make that happen,' he said, almost whispering. 'We've done it for others. We can all walk away with a very tidy sum in a few years' time.'

Kit blinked. This was a lot for ten thirty am.

'Kit, we don't work with just anyone,' he went on. 'We see something in Second Day, and that's why we want to go in so hard. We can't do what we do best if we can't do what we do best, you know what I'm saying?'

'Not really,' Kit said honestly.

'He's saying that the reason they buy majorities is because then they can really steer companies,' Hugo explained.

Kit nodded. 'Exactly what I don't want.'

'I am not here to cajole or put on the pressure, Kit,' Omari said, hands in the air. 'I recognise there are other bidders in the process, but I urge you to really think about our offer, which telegraphs how serious we are. There may come a day when your brand tapers off, or macro conditions suffer and your customer can't afford you anymore, or they switch to one of the numerous legacy or influencer brands vying for attention with a far bigger spend. How will you pivot from creative founder to considered steward? How can you ensure the ship stays its course? With help. *Our* help.'

'Correct me if I'm wrong,' Kit said, flattered by his speech but enraged by his hubris, 'but isn't your *main* priority to get the highest possible return for your investors, not see that a bunch of hair creams do well?'

'It is,' he said.

'At any cost?' she pushed.

'No,' he said earnestly. He sat back and crossed one leg over the other. 'What good is it if we buy into a company then drive it into the ground? Toxic workplace, unhappy team . . . Why mess with a proven thing? We know you feel strongly about protecting your brand and retaining a large shareholding, and frankly that makes us more excited to partner with you, because we know *you* feel there's more to be done, too.'

Fair point, Kit conceded.

'Our hope is your original shareholders sell out, and you retain thirty percent. We want to work with *you*, Kit. Create something incredible.'

This was the part where Rupert usually stepped in and made it all friendly and normal again, something Hugo showed no signs of doing, so Kit stayed silent. There was power in the pause, Priya had taught her. Don't speak simply because no one else is.

'Thanks, Omari,' Hugo said finally. 'Lot to digest there.'

Kit coasted through the farewells and back to her car in a daze. Despite his theatrics, Omari had ignited something in her. Was he just giving her the hard sell? Or was he genuine? Was it safe to feel excited? She no longer trusted her instincts. He'd basically mirrored Hugo's sentiments last week: that Kit was taking the easy road by only selling down thirty percent. Like she was hedging. Like she could achieve so much more if she just let them do their thing. As she drove along, she wondered if she *was* giving Second Day the best possible chance by settling for a minor investor to cover Toni's holding, then chugging along as they were. Shouldn't she be aiming higher, rising to the moment, seizing this opportunity? It *did* feel like this was a once-in-a-lifetime moment. She remembered Ron telling her not to mess this up, thought about how her life might look and feel if she sold the bulk of her shares to these guys and handed over control. Let *them* run things. Maybe *then* she could play with Gretel when she asked.

She needed to talk to someone about this, and she knew just the person.

'Hello?' a groggy voice answered the phone.

'Oh god, Priya, did I wake you? Oh shit, you're in Vietnam, I forgot. I'm so sorry—I'll hang up, you go back to sleep.'

'No, no, I should be getting up now,' Priya said, her voice husky. 'What's going on?'

'I'll keep it brief: Pinnacle are making an offer for seventy percent. Omari just gave me the full sales pitch.'

'So they didn't listen,' Priya said.

'No, but we expected that. Thing is,' Kit went on, 'he kinda got under my skin. Saying I was doing Second Day a disservice if I retained the majority, that nothing would change, and we'd see none of the growth we aspire to. He argued that I'd be giving Second Day a *real* chance if I partnered with them, and—'

'Kit,' Priya said patiently, 'I'm sure he was very convincing. But that's exactly what he's supposed to be. If it triggered something in you, gave you some clarity, well, that's wonderful, but remember: these guys are big business; they eat small companies and spit them out if they don't do what they need them to. There will be pressure and the brand may suffer; who knows what levers they'll be able to pull with that much ownership?'

Kit sighed. Had she even wanted real advice? Or just reassurance she should take this risk, do the thing. Honestly, if Priya had said go for it, she would sign today.

'And wouldn't we reconsider Blue Tree, if you are now open to selling seventy percent?' Priya added.

'Yeah,' Kit answered. 'I thought about that, but we can't accept their preference share thing. I don't know—I'm so confused. Maybe I *should* just let go. Why am I holding on so tight? What even is my endgame here?'

'Only you know that, Kit,' Priya said kindly. 'But it's not a decision to make rashly. When are they submitting their offer?'

'Later today,' Kit said flatly. She turned on her wipers to see through a sudden downpour.

'I'll reserve my judgement until then. You liked Blue Tree until this point, too, remember.'

'You know what it was?' Kit said. 'I think I was just excited to hear a clear vision. The others are so vague, like, "whatever support you need, blah blah blah," but Omari spelled it out. He kind of made me feel like a world-beater. And you *know* I love mad Marty's ideas.' Kit was surprised to hear herself selling Priya on this. Selling her on a seventy percent selldown. *What was she doing?*

'I'll schedule a call once we've received the offer and we've all had time to digest it. This is a big decision, Kit. Let's not throw out everything you care about because of one impassioned speech.'

'I won't. It's just . . . it's hard is all.' Kit heard a whine in her voice, and instantly regretted it.

'Business is hard. Deals are hard. Trusting people is hard. Forgoing growth and opportunity is hard. Scaling up and risking big is hard. Choose your hard.'

'Yeah, true. Thank you, Priya. Sorry for waking you.'

'No problem. Bye, Kit.'

Kit sat at the traffic lights, chewing over what Priya had said: the calm voice of patience and reason. She *was* being utterly reasonable, of course. Rational and reasonable. But some part of Kit was annoyed. The glacial pace of it all was killing her; she wanted to move forward. There'd been a call to action today; she felt different. She thought back to what Piper had said, that the best time to sell was when it felt a bit early. A bit uncomfortable. *That* certainly rang true. Kit was so envious of Piper's clarity, her laser focus. She knew her path and lived by it. Kit flitted around here and there, unsure and unconfident, guessing and hoping it would just magically work out. Maybe someone coming in to help her steer was what she needed. It would allow her to go back to being a creative, spending time on the vision and the strategy instead of faulty pump lids. That could only be a good thing. And, of course, she would have enough money never to have to worry again. In this life or the next.

Her thoughts were interrupted by the phone. Rat was calling. That was never good.

'Rat? Is everything okay?'

'Gretel is fine, if that's what you mean, but the house has kinda flooded and fuck me if I know what caused it cos the rain doesn't seem *that*—'

'WHAT?! What do you mean?' Kit yelled, getting beeped from behind for not moving fast enough on a green light.

'We came home from the beach cos it started pissing down, and there was water everywhere when we walked in. All through the kitchen and living area. It's, like, an inch deep? Also, your room and Gretel's are *not* good.'

'*Fuck!* Have you called a plumber?'

'No,' Rat said. 'I called *you*.'

'*I* can't fix it. Call a plumber, *now!*' Kit yelled.

'Which one?'

'Oh, for fuck's sake, I'll do it. Just get anything good out of there, please, and put Gretel up high—I don't know, on the bench or something.'

Rat began laughing hysterically, infuriating Kit even more. Then she heard the words she'd never thought she'd hear. 'Of course I called a plumber, you psycho. He's on his way.'

23

FEBRUARY

FEBRUARY WAS FEBRUARY-ING TO THE best of its humid, frizzy, chaotic ability. The whole of Australia had returned to work to discover the year, and indeed the rest of the world, was already well and truly firing, and they needed to *catch up*. Kit felt it. She'd wake up too early, cortisol firing, and feel instantly aggravated and on edge, like she would never get through her to-do list. She'd weave manically through her day like someone on cold and flu tablets, the air so thick you could chew through it, everyone irritable, then go to bed with a few wines under her belt and a heavy dose of CBD and melatonin to stop her overworked brain from waking her up with three am thoughts about what an ESOP was, because Priya said she needed one in place for executive staff and to attract good talent ... and that she needed to buy Gretel new goggles because she'd left them at the holiday rental ... and that she also needed new sneakers because she'd had a growth spurt . . . and a new excursion bag because her old one had ripped . . . Kit felt trapped in her busyness; she couldn't see a way out. Sure, the deal was temporary, but bedding in a new partner and board was going to take work. And then there was the ludicrous new product release schedule they'd promised said partner . . .

With Priya's cautious approval and a firm nod from Piper in her back pocket, Kit had tentatively agreed to move to the next stage with Pinnacle. Toni was beside herself, Simon was happy to sell down five of his ten percent and Kit had agreed to selling down thirty-five of her sixty percent. Pinnacle's indicative offer had valued the entire company between eighty and a hundred million dollars. If young Kit, even Kit from last year, was told her company would be worth that much, she expected she would very likely scream and jump up and down and quite possibly cry. It was, in any language, at any level, by any stretch, a *ludicrous* amount of money. But Kit didn't scream or cry, because some part of her didn't, *couldn't*, believe it would eventuate. She took it all very seriously, and yet a real and serious outcome still felt inconceivable. So, she told no one, and pushed it to the back of her mind.

Pinnacle had demanded exclusivity, which meant no other active bidders, which meant Rupert was treading a very careful line. He was positive about the deal overall, but to Kit's relief remained focused on ensuring Kit wasn't signing her company away to a pack of wily devils in sleeveless vests. He'd warned her the activity would ramp up now it was getting to the pointy end, and he wasn't kidding. These deal guys lived and breathed this stuff, it was their full-time job, but Kit was also trying to parent, direct the marketing campaign for their new product, and create chirpy, cool and informative content for customers. Every time Kit received an email from Rupert or Curtis or Hugo, and there were plenty, she felt her heart quicken with anxiety, and a voice in her head said: *It's over.* She couldn't help it: this process had conditioned her to expect bad news. A push-back. An untenable new clause. A threat to walk. Kit would be in the middle of herding a slippery, wet Gretel from bathroom to bedroom, and a text from Rupert would arrive asking her to phone him immediately. It was never to say, *Everything is going great, nothing to do for now!* It was invariably to tell her that what-ever point of certainty they had reached even hours earlier had been superseded. Time and time again this would happen, just when they were getting somewhere: Pinnacle would say or do something that undid all their previous good work. Last week she'd had an exciting chat with Omari about bringing on the ex-skincare buyer at Sephora USA as an advisory board director. She'd felt genuinely thrilled . . . then his people sent an updated term sheet indicating Pinnacle's returns at exit would need to be three times everyone else's.

At least Gretel was staying with Ari now, which gave Kit some breathing room. She was back at school, confident and resplen-dent in all her year one glory, Shona was back on WhatsApp asking if school finished at the same time as last year, even Rat was busy with some casual nannying, but instead of a calm, child-free household, Kit had a home full of industrial-level humidifiers blaring all day. The insurance people were concerned about the mould that had kicked off following a week of nonstop rain, and had asked the Cooper girls to vacate. So, along with Rat, Kit had been staying in an Airbnb a few streets away—once again, miraculously organised by Rat. It was a very small, very miserable home with two huntsman sightings and counting, but at least Rat was trying. Ari kept telling her they should just stay with Gretel and him at the Tamarama mansion, but Kit explained in no uncertain terms that she a) didn't want to, b) would just end up parenting, and c) didn't want to. Living in a dank, arachnoid-infested rental only just pipped living with Ari, but it still pipped.

'These shots aren't giving; if anything, they're *taking*,' Hyun muttered, his expression the visual representation of *ew*. Second Day were days off launching their repair hair mask and the shots that had come back for the campaign were unusable.

'They're gorgeous—they're maybe just not completely right for *this*,' Kit said quickly, not wanting the team who had worked so hard on them—mostly because she and Camille had been absent, working on the deal—to feel bad. One of the models clearly had hair extensions—a big no for a hair shoot—while the other couldn't have been older than eighteen, with perfect virgin hair. This would have been fine for a styling product but made no sense when advertising a mask for over-processed, dry and damaged hair. She wanted to kill Toni for sending these models; she'd known Kit's team weren't confident enough to push back.

'What if we used graphics and art over the top, make it look cool, like we meant it?' Hyun suggested, thumbs looped through the belt loops of his floor-length denim skirt.

'We aren't selling eyeliner or nail gems, Hyun,' Kit said. 'We're selling hair masks to the kind of woman who spends six hundred dollars getting her hair coloured every six weeks. It needs to be glossy and beautiful.' Kit sighed. 'We need to reshoot. Jordan, I'm sorry. You and I both know this is not going to work.'

'Understood,' Jordan said meekly. She knew she was partly to blame. Jordan had taken two weeks off to spend with her fling before he flew back to Brazil, gone from her life and vagina forever. That was fine, of course it was fine, but she'd not even glanced at the mood board or models before she went and now they needed a full redo.

'It's okay,' Kit said. 'We will sort this. Just use product shots for the teaser. So how can we best organise a reshoot quickly?' She looked at each of the team in turn.

Jaz popped up out of nowhere, as content creator types were wont to do. *'I* have a little ideasicle,' she said, eyes shining. 'What *if,* instead of models, we shot some micro influencers? Those girlies *love* modelling, and they share *everything* on their socials. They're the *best.* Plus it gives us extra bang for buck.' Jaz flashed Kit a dazzling smile. She might have been a personality hire originally—and her optimism, can-do attitude, smile and liberal compliment-spreading buoyed the whole office—but she had made herself indispensable with her quick thinking and smarts.

Kit considered her idea. 'I like it; clever. Someone over the age of thirty, please.'

Hyun and Jaz looked at each other. *'Paola!'*

'We need three, a range of ages and looks: can I have six options by this afternoon? Hyun, can you ask Camille if she has time to slip out for a coffee with me?'

As Kit walked back to her desk, her phone vibrated: Priya.

'Hello, Kit, how are you?' she asked.

'Hey, Priya.' She sighed without meaning to, slumping into her chair. 'I'm okay . . . Things will calm down soon.'

'I've heard that one before,' Priya said, chuckling. 'Kit, I wanted to check in and gauge how you're feeling about Pinnacle. I can see it progressing quite quickly, and it's easy to feel steamrolled in these things . . .'

'Well,' Kit said, as she tried to ignore Delilah and Jordan speaking animatedly a few metres away, 'I'd be lying if I said I was one hundred percent convinced. But I haven't felt one hundred percent about anything during this whole process.'

'You can pull out at any time,' Priya reminded her. 'It's always your call. They *are* asking a lot.'

'Right?! I feel like I've made so many concessions,' Kit said, lowering her voice. 'It makes me worried about going into business with them. Will they always be like this?' She watched Jordan jab her finger at something on Delilah's screen. If Kit had to guess, Jordan was asking Delilah for a tube 'exactly like this', which was Delilah's least-favourite directive.

'Part of that is simply the nature of the deal,' Priya said. 'Try not to view it as an indicator of what they will be like to work with.'

'I just feel like I change my mind, even my *deal-breakers*, so quickly. How can anyone take me seriously if I keep moving my own goalposts?'

'Evolving your thinking is critical in business but *especially* around deals,' Priya said. 'Strong views, loosely held, as they say. Be flexible on some things but keep what is really important in sight.'

'That's the bit I worry about,' Kit admitted. 'Knowing what's really important.'

'Protecting your brand, your team and company,' Priya stated. 'You've been clear on those things from day one.'

'I guess I mean overall,' Kit said. 'You know—in life. How can I know what I want in three or five years? I don't even know what I want for *dinner*.'

'I've never known you to coast for even a moment, Kit,' Priya said. 'Don't sell yourself short.'

'Also, the money,' Kit said, turning to face the wall to be less audible. Was she *really* about to complain about banking thirty million dollars? 'Being rich was all I dreamed of as a kid, Priya. I grew up with very little. But now I feel . . . I don't know . . . guilty about it? Like I don't deserve it. It seems crazy, too much. *Greedy*. Plus I'm worried about what it says to my team, even my customers.'

Kit could hear Priya's husband chatting and laughing with someone in the background, the first time Kit had had a glimpse into Priya's personal life.

'Business is transactional by nature. Entirely neutral. People bring their own feelings to it, whether they're watching or partaking. You *do* deserve this, Kit.'

'I'd be in the foetal position without you and Rupert. In fact, I wouldn't have even considered going through this process.'

'Business is not a charity. You make and sell things every day; this is just an extension of that. Feel proud. There's nothing honourable about refusing money,' Priya said sagely.

'Yeah,' Kit said. 'If Toni gets some, why not me, I guess . . .'

'Kit, you could've already sold to Blue Tree and been a very wealthy woman, but you declined. I think it's fair to say money is not your true motivator. You care about what you have created and its future.'

'If I *really* cared, though, wouldn't I refuse to sell the majority? Keep control?'

'You do need to feel comfortable with the level of control you are ceding,' Priya said. 'And this is no small amount, Kit, let's be honest. If they are buying seventy percent, you're saying you're happy to let them take the reins.'

Kit felt a queasiness in her lower stomach.

'Am I making a huge mistake?' she asked Priya outright.

'It's not so black and white,' Priya said, after a pause. 'Take your time and go over every little detail. Ask every question you think of. Imagine the worst-case scenario with the new terms and understand that it's possible. Consider a universe where the people—be that your customers or your staff—are left vulnerable or worse. There are some things you can't undo.'

Kit covered her eyes with her left hand and inhaled and exhaled deeply. She wasn't in the mood for a full doomsday assault.

'We have a shareholders' call tomorrow but you can message me anytime,' she said. 'I mean that, Kit. I know this is a lot.'

Kit hung up the phone just as Camille walked over. Kit wanted to talk to her about Pinnacle, see how she was feeling about it all. She wanted her take on things. Even better, her buy-in. 'Let's get a coffee,' she said, standing.

'And this is really what you want?' Camille said after Kit had walked her through the latest update. Camille was sitting across from Kit at Poor Pluto, a hole-in-the-wall joint with coffee so good that no one minded sitting on a crate to drink it. Camille wore a fitted ankle-length black dress and Chanel ballet flats, a single gold cuff on her arm. Her black Wayfarers were classic, resisting both time and trends, and she sipped on a long black. Of course.

'I think what is possible is really exciting,' Kit said, aware she sounded just like the people who had convinced her this was a good idea. 'It feels like the option that leads to more options.' There she went again.

'They will be able to do whatever they want with the brand, the products, the team, the retailers . . .' Camille said. 'I don't understand why you would let that happen if you don't need to.' It was a reasonable statement. Camille regarded Kit carefully, her head cocked on an angle.

'That's why we created the brand-integrity clauses,' Kit reminded her. 'They can't mess with the stuff we really care about, like our marketing principles, or our formulation credo, our sustainability charter or our sales channels . . . We have put *so* many protections in.' Kit felt like she was defending herself, even though she was Camille's boss. Camille had that power.

'I don't understand why we cannot revert to Blue Tree,' Camille said. She had ended up liking them a lot.

'I liked them, too,' Kit said, 'but they had a terrible preference share scheme. Fatal incompatibility, Rupert called it. Anyway, they've bought some self-tan brand, apparently.'

Kit was strangely heartbroken when Rupert had told her. Like she'd turned a guy down but now that he'd moved on she wanted him back. Also, there was Max. She'd never see him again. This was for the best, she concluded. He'd gotten under her skin by being mean, like she was twelve years old and pining after the school jock who'd teased her about her shoes. Ridiculous. Camille said nothing, just sipped her volcanic coffee.

'They will be able to choose things like exit timing, investing profits into growth, international channels and so on,' Kit went on. 'I am as freaked out by that as you, so trust me when I say I am carefully looking over all of it. But we definitely fenced off the critical stuff, the DNA of the company. You were part of that. You know.'

Camille nodded but still didn't respond. Kit was growing annoyed. She was doing everything she could to ensure the safety of this company, the company *she* had started, and which *she* felt a very real pressure to protect. Why did Camille care so much? She could leave and get another job; the responsibility and risk here were all Kit's! She took a small breath to compose herself before speaking.

'Camille, I wouldn't be going down this path if I didn't think it was a genuine opportunity.'

'We'll become all about profit,' Camille said. 'You know that, right?' She shook her head slightly, clearly upset. 'You don't get it. This will change everything. All the heart and soul will go.'

Kit had known Camille would have notes, but that didn't make this conversation any easier.

'Can you be specific?' Kit asked.

'The reporting,' Camille said. 'The *constant* reporting. The pressure to make huge KPIs and sales targets. And if we don't do it? They replace us. They'll start changing suppliers and materials, ruining our products to get costs down. They'll get rid of me the moment they can, you'll see.'

And there it was, the heart of the issue. 'Camille, on what planet would I allow that?' Kit asked incredulously. 'You are *vital* to this company, to *me*!'

'You won't have a choice!' her CEO shot back. 'Don't you see? You won't be in charge anymore, what *you* want doesn't matter!'

'Just so you know,' Kit said calmly, 'I've told them there needs to be a unanimous board vote to remove any of the executive team.' Rupert had said it was highly unlikely Pinnacle would approve it, but Kit was dogged. She needed Camille. She couldn't work with some cookie-cutter CEO bro they dragged in. Then again, if Rupert was right, what could she possibly do? Was she going to throw the whole deal away because they—the seventy percent shareholders, the overwhelming majority—had veto over senior staffing appointments? These were impossible questions; she pushed them to the back of her mind.

'It's your company,' Camille clipped. 'You don't have to justify anything to me.'

Kit changed tack. She needed Camille on side.

'You weren't in that first meeting,' Kit said, 'but something sparked. With the co-manufacturing and the other brands in their stable and the innovation piece . . . I felt real excitement.' She paused. 'Camille, we have made something amazing. Now it's time to take it to the next lev—'

'Yes, yes,' Camille interrupted. 'Spare me the jargon. I just hope you're right about them.'

She finished her coffee and stood to leave. Kit frowned as she hurriedly drained her own coffee. *Fine, Camille. Be that way. I am doing my best here. You think this is easy? You fund and start a company and work your arse off day and night for years and then it can be your decision. Oh sure, everyone comes in hot with an opinion, but they don't actually have to make any decisions or live with the consequences, do they?*

The two women walked back to the office in silence.

Later that day, still feeling uneasy after her talk with Camille, Kit received an email from Rupert that did nothing to assuage her nerves.

> FYI overnight Pinnacle denied our request for Priya as ongoing chair but accepted the licence deed so long as percentage drops incrementally each time and additional 5m in sales reached.
> They will accept executive hire/fire clause so long as exec reaches at least 80% of KPIs.
> Given our phone call yesterday, I will assume you are agreeable to these, Kit.
> Curtis—please insert into mark-up and revert asap.
> Fondest,
> Rupert

Kit gasped. No Priya? Why? What threat could she possibly pose? She wrote back:

> Hang on, Priya is non-negotiable.

Rupert responded:

> Noted.
> Remember, she can always act as your personal mentor if she cannot fulfil chair duties.

Kit chewed her lip in thought. Going into this without Priya in her corner was unthinkable. Although, maybe she *could* just employ her as a personal mentor . . .

The next morning Kit was on set early for the make-good mask shoot, styling the hair for the 'after' shot on Paola, a striking Columbian woman in her early thirties. Paola was a yogi-wellness influencer wielding a very specific, raw-food-diet kind of power over two hundred and ten thousand highly engaged followers. She had naturally dark hair but had been dying it blonde for a long time, making her a fantastic candidate for a repair mask.

'This is good,' Jordan said behind Kit, as she watched her work. '*Really* good.'

'It is, isn't it?' Kit said proudly. 'Man, I've missed doing hair,' she added wistfully as she put the finishing touches on Paola's glamorous, swishy blow-out. She hadn't done any proper styling for what felt like months. It seemed a lifetime ago that the full extent of her job was doing people's hair. *How* easy *I had it*, she mused, recalling how fun it had been: the chaos on set, the rushing, the hip-hop playlist the photographer's assistant snuck on before anyone noticed, the thrill of seeing the photos come through on the laptop in real time.

'Sorry,' Paola said, looking at Kit in the mirror. 'I don't mean to be a weirdo, but can I just say I am totally starstruck right now?'

Kit immediately deflected. 'I'm starstruck by your *hair*! I mean, I know our products work, but seeing the instant effect, I get these moments of pride, you know?'

'Oh, you *should*!' Paola said emphatically. 'Your stuff is fantastic. I bought the cream when you first launched years ago. Still buy it. And this mask . . . it basically performed CPR! I hope you don't mind me asking, but . . . how do you do it all? Like, the brand is going bananas, you do all those tutorials on Instagram, that magazine cover last month, plus you are a mother . . . I can barely manage my content and workouts!'

'I'd be lying if I said it was a breeze,' Kit said. 'But I feel lucky, you know? It's all good stuff I get to do. I'm not down a coalmine or arguing for human rights.' The minimisation just rolled off the tongue. If Paola only knew how much self-medicating and drinking and nervous pooing Kit was doing.

'You're such a girl boss,' Paola said admiringly. 'It's *nothing* compared to what you do, but I'm starting my own brand of yoga mats. They're fully recycled and antibacterial, because let's be honest, how often is anyone cleaning their mat?'

Kit laughed. 'So true . . . *Really* good idea, Paola. Solid point of difference.'

'Did you take investors at that early stage?' she asked. 'I was thinking about bringing one in, just to help me get it all up and running . . .'

'Can you do it alone?' Kit queried. 'Can you afford to, I mean? Can you cover the first run?'

'Well'—Paola laughed nervously—'I guess, maybe . . . ?'

'Try,' Kit urged. 'Take out a loan if you need to. Borrow from the bank of mum and dad. Treat your equity like gold when you're starting out; you never know what it could be worth one day. Plus, you know, if you wait until you have some success on the board, you'll be able to value your company higher, and ideally sell less equity for more money.' Was that paying it forward, she wondered, or just dishing out unsolicited advice?

'Wow, yeah, thank you. Good food for thought.'

Kit fluffed the ends of Paola's hair and stepped away so Paola could stand up. 'Good luck with your mats. DM me anytime you need an ear.'

'Thank you so much . . . Can I grab a selfie before I go?'

'Of course,' Kit answered. They mushed their heads together and smiled as Paola artfully took a succession of selfies.

'Thanks! So good to meet you!' Paola called as she rushed over to the set.

Kit was on a high. The hair, the chat . . . *I will* do more of *this once this deal is over,* she told herself.

As if on cue, her phone chimed with a message from Rupert.

Hello Kit, can you jump on a call when you have a moment?

How did she go from not even knowing this man a year ago to speaking to him twenty times a day?

Am free in 10, she replied, and wandered over to the catering table for a jar of yoghurt and some coffee. Kit knew Pinnacle's final *final* offer was likely coming through today, and she was grateful for the distraction of being on set. She had slept badly, mind racing, and was now on her third coffee. What if they just flat-out denied all of Kit's requests? What would she do? Did she have the confidence to walk? She grabbed a chunky mystery muffin and thought about it as she chewed. Yes, she confirmed to herself. She *did* have the confidence to say no.

Another text, this one from Rat.

the insurance nobs just said we cant move back in tmrw

Fuckers. Leave it w me, Kit replied, cursing them and their endlessly shifting finish date. The rental smelled, and it was on a busy road, plus Gretel was due back in two days. She wanted to welcome her daughter *home.*

'Hey, Rupert,' Kit said, answering his call. Her stomach flip-flopped in anticipation of what he was about to tell her.

'Hi, Kit—give me a sec, I'm going to dial Priya and Curtis in.'

'Hello?' Priya said a moment later.

'Can you hear me?' Curtis asked.

'Hi, everyone!' Kit sang chirpily, her nerves making her silly.

'Good, we're all here,' Rupert said. 'I'm about to send around the documents, but the offer is in, and I'm pleased to report the number is markedly higher than we predicted: a total EV of ninety-five million, making it sixty-six and a half million for a seventy percent holding in Second Day Pty Ltd, to be segregated into the proportionate shareholdings.'

'*Fuck me*,' Kit whispered.

'That equates to thirty-eight million for you personally, Kit,' Priya said. Rupert spoke M&A, but Priya spoke Kit.

Kit felt completely overcome. She pushed her back against the wall and slid down until she was sitting on the floor.

'Kit? Are you there?' Priya asked.

'I am. I'm just . . .' Kit closed her eyes and took some deep breaths. She felt sick, weightless, dizzy, all at once. She placed the phone down on the concrete floor and covered her mouth with her t-shirt to get more from her breaths; she couldn't get enough air suddenly. After a few seconds, she opened her eyes, inhaled and picked up her phone.

'I'm here,' she said. 'I'm here. I was just absorbing what you said.'

A chuckle followed from both Rupert and Priya.

'It's a tremendous offer, Kit,' Curtis said.

'You should feel terrifically proud,' Priya said. '*Especially* as a female founder. Did you know less than three percent of investment goes to women-owned businesses? Appalling, given what these businesses inject into the economy . . .'

'Maybe it's because there aren't enough women investors,' Kit suggested.

'Anyway, we're very close,' Rupert said. 'They really have their rockets on; I've never seen anything quite like it. However, there *are* a couple of outstanding issues.'

Here we go, thought Kit. *The bit where they ask for my firstborn.*

'They're holding firm on four directors and options for each of those directors,' Rupert began. 'They're also pushing back on some of the brand integrity elements—they want global retailer discretion, which I know you were steadfast about retaining, and our request to lower those aggressive executive KPIs has been rejected, placing your team in a vulnerable position. We will go over it all in depth later. I'm sending an email now. Please read it promptly, as they want our mark-ups this afternoon. Provided we can find a middle ground on these items, we should be set to send the revised shareholders' and licence deed for you, Simon and Toni to approve this evening.'

'Dammit,' Kit said. *Here we go again.*

'When investors spend that much money they need to feel they're getting a good deal,' Rupert reminded her.

'Take your time and go through all of it carefully, Kit,' Priya interjected. 'That's *their* timeline, not ours. You need to feel comfortable with every single term. This is not something to rush.'

'I'm here shooting till two, but I can give it my full attention after that. Are you lads free then?'

'Of course,' Rupert replied.

'Standing by,' Curtis added.

'Take all the time you need,' repeated Priya.

'It's the usual flotsam at the finish line,' Curtis said reassuringly. 'I'm confident we will get there.'

'Indeed we will. Bravo, Kit,' Rupert said, his voice full of pride. 'Execution is what separates the wannabes from the did-its, and you're about to do it.'

Kit went through the rest of the shoot in a dreamlike state. Never, *ever* in her life had she imagined a world where she would have tens of millions of dollars in her bank account. She felt like she was the lead in a Disneyfied rom-com with an unconvincing and overly contrived ending. Like it was all a trick, and Rupert would send a text saying *GOTCHA* any moment now, because *Kit Cooper wasn't supposed to be rich.* There was no way she could get used to this idea! It would never feel normal. As she walked out to her car, she felt the same as she had when she lost her virginity to Kurt Harris in year ten: like everyone would be able to see on her face that she had changed. *She was different now.*

At home, after a futile attempt at a power nap—buses, neighbours, garbage trucks and nerves colluding to keep her awake—Kit made a little nest on the couch with tea, water, popcorn, Maltesers and extra pillows, trying to make it cute and fun to drown out the voice in her head that said, 'You are so wildly, wildly unqualified for this.' She opened her laptop and read over Pinnacle's mark-ups, which were both blunt and unforgiving. Maybe *they* were tiring of the process, too. After all, what was this, the eighth round of mark-ups?

Her phone buzzed.

Hi everyone! I'm Georgie, Henley's mum, your class parent for 1B, hope I can make this year a little easier!!

Thank you Georgie, thankless job ☺

Thank you Georgie, we love you!!

Thx Georgie does anyone know if chess club is on this week?

Georgie you will regret this LOL

Chess club starts wk 3 it was in the email from Ms Piper

Claudia said parents are meant to be at assembly this Friday is that true?

Does anyone have the number for after school care we need to swap Ivy's days

Hi Georgie, thank you for your service! We'd—okay I'd—be lost without you! Kit wrote, happy for the distraction. She would be completely at sea without a class parent.

A text came in from Rupert.

Been talking with Pinnacle's advisers, Kit, I'm afraid they are not going to budge, and they are not accepting further changes. Or in plain terms: we agree to THIS deal, or there is NO deal. I believe they're serious. Will call in 30 minutes.

For fuck's sake! Kit cursed aloud. *Really?* This is what it all comes down to? An ultimatum? *Okay, calm down,* Kit told herself. Think big picture. Is this really that bad? Or are you just pushing back for the sake of it now? *What are you afraid of?* Her advisers had done everything they could to safeguard the brand, it was going to be fine. Pinnacle wanted the best for Second Day, they were investing so much, they *had* to make it work! They wouldn't do anything to get the founder offside, that made no sense. Everything was going to be fine. It was just business! No need to be so emotional! She had found herself in a uniquely fortunate position and she'd be a fool to let it slip by. She didn't want to keep shuffling along. She was ready. Piper wasn't the only one who could make big moves. *It was going to be fine.* People brought investors into their businesses all the time. She was not breaking new ground. *It was just business!*

She picked up her phone and called Rupert, praying he would answer before she chickened out. Her hands were trembling.

'Am I mad if I agree to this?' she said when he answered.

He chuckled. 'I think most people would say you'd be mad to *not* agree, but Kit, only one opinion matters, and that is yours. I support whichever way you decide to go. All this last-minute rushing is very unpleasant, and I'm genuinely puzzled by it.'

'Hmm,' she said, nibbling on her left thumbnail nervously.

'Do you feel confident you understand the—'

'Let's do it,' she interrupted. 'Enough of this. I just want it done.'

Once they'd hung up, Kit threw her phone onto the cushions and looked around. She felt shaky, fidgety, restless. She let her eyes close and rubbed her temples. *She should go for a run*, she thought, *that would help settle her*. It occurred to her, if this was supposed to be the biggest moment in her life—birth of child aside—shouldn't she feeling elated? Why wasn't she sharing this enormous news with anyone? She felt an unexpected wave of sadness and loneliness wash over her. Who was she supposed to tell? Who was she supposed to be enjoying this with? Who was proud of her? *Who was in her front row?* Ron was no good; he would be on her doorstep with his hand out before she could even say 'selldown'. She didn't have a boyfriend to buy her flowers and lift her up and yell, 'YOU DID IT!' She didn't have a mother to squeal with her, and to brag to all her friends about her daughter's success. She didn't have a business partner with whom she could celebrate their shared achievement; Toni had contributed nothing to this deal, nor to the company as a whole, so there was no way in hell Kit was going to pop a cork with her.

Kit had felt alone raising Gretel, and raising Second Day, even raising Rat, which she was still doing. Had she always worked so hard and made herself so busy because she was avoiding feeling this loneliness lurking just below? As she sat in the moment, and really allowed herself to feel the pain, Kit realised she had always been lonely. Doing big and hard things exacerbated it, because those were the moments you needed your people, your partner, your parents to help you through and then celebrate with you when you pulled it off. Kit had a brilliant team around her to make it happen, but she alone had made the decision. And she alone would live with it.

'Jesus,' she whispered aloud. 'This is a *good* thing. Get a grip.'

She needed a drink, she told herself. And someone to drink it with.

THE THING HAS FINALLY THINGED AND WE MUST CELEBRATE, she texted Maggie. *I don't care what you had planned. Rat can babysit if you need her.*

Maggie replied almost instantly.

Holy fuck done deal??????????

Maggie was very excited by the prospect of her best friend being a multi-millionaire. She'd been sending Kit links to fifty-six-million-dollar NYC apartments and enormous superyachts with the words: 'Add to shopping list.'

As good as . . .

As Kit added a barrage of dancing-woman-star-lightning-bolt-nail-polish-sparkles emojis, she suddenly had the ridiculous thought that she was jinxing the deal by celebrating before she'd signed.

MY LOVE!!!!!!!!!!!!!!!!!! I am so proud of you my sultan biz queen, followed by a succession of stacks-of-dollars emojis. *I'm in meetings til 6. Meet you at Oyster in the Pearl at 7. Dress up! Have a champagne! We're rich, for god's sake!! ILYSM! We're RICH!!! xxxxx*

Five hours later, as Maggie and Kit finished off a four-hundred-and-fifty-dollar bottle of Krug that Kit had uncharacteristically splashed out on (a dangerous game given they'd only ordered fries and olives to soak it up), Kit glanced around at gamine twenty-five-year-olds wearing literal bras for tops, and handsome boys in suits laughing and having fun. *Is* this *where people went?* Kit thought. *Is this what people did?* Even on a Thursday? Was this what she had been missing out on while she madly businessed and mothered?

She looked at her friend mischievously. 'This champagne tastes like I'm a good dancer. Would be a shame to let it go to waste . . .' Suddenly she elbowed Maggie hard in the ribs. 'Oh my fucking *god!*' she gasped. 'D'you remember I told you about that arsehole in one of the meetings but he was a really hot arsehole? He's over there. No *way* . . .'

'Where?' Maggie said loudly, swinging her head around to see.

'Suit, tall, glasses . . . *glasses?*' Kit frowned. 'He doesn't wear glasses.'

'Oh, you beautiful bastard,' Maggie said. '*He's* what we were promised with genetic engineering.'

Max Darling was standing in a trio of suits, talking animatedly—far more animatedly than Kit had thought possible—looking like a normal, extremely handsome man out at a bar, not a bad-tempered meeting disruptor.

'Let's go!' Maggie said, jamming the half of her phone that would fit into her tiny glittery clutch and collecting her glass.

'What? Where are you going?' Kit yelled over the noise of the crowd and the music.

'We're goin' to say hi!' Maggie said, but as she attempted to slide down from her stool her heel got caught on the foot bar, and she stumbled forward a few steps. Amazingly, given her blood alcohol levels, she managed to steady herself before stacking face first.

Kit leaped up to help her, laughing hysterically.

'Oh my god, oh my god,' she said, grasping Maggie's arm and pulling her upright. 'You're so fucking ham . . . ham'—she gasped for air between bursts of laughter—'*hammered*!' Which only set them off again.

They had just resumed their seats to recover their composure, when Maggie's eyes lit up at something over Kit's shoulder. '*No!*' Her jaw dropped, and she started waving furiously.

Two shiny-skinned, stylish men in their fifties came over and each gave Maggie a three-kiss hello.

'As I live and breathe,' the smaller one said. 'How *are* you? Oh, I love this.' He fingered the fabric of her tasselled dress. 'Very Gaga does Vegas.'

'Kit,' Maggie said excitedly, 'this is Alejandro and Ethan— they're the ones whose house I did in Coogee, remember? With the underground sauna?'

Kit smiled and greeted the pair, compliments flying around like missiles.

After a few minutes of listening to the three of them verbally salivate over a twelve-globe ceramic lamp from Mexico, Kit excused herself to go to the bathroom. As she made her way down the long, dimly lit hallway to the bathroom, trying to read a text from Jordan, she almost bumped into someone. Without looking up, she issued a, ''Scuse me,' and kept going.

'Is that all I get?' she heard and swung around.

It was Max, smiling broadly as though they were long-lost best friends.

'Thought it was you,' he said, as usual stopping a sentence or two before any regular person would.

'It's me-ee,' she said, waving with her phone in her hand, brows high, smiling tipsily.

'So you ditched us, eh?' he said, leaning against the wall, his head narrowly missing a wall sconce emitting a tea light candle's worth of illumination.

'What?' she said.

'Our offer? It was politely declined?'

'Yeah, but you politely declined *my* offer first, so even stevens.'

'Touché,' he said, laughing good-humouredly.

He was definitely less of a jerk out of the boardroom, Kit thought. *Still a jerk, though.*

'Anyway, shame,' he said. 'We could've been really good together.'

Still holding her gaze, he took a slow sip of what Kit assumed was expensive whisky. He wasn't even trying to hide the double meaning behind his words. The balls on this guy! She shook her head at him.

'What?' he asked, feigning innocence.

'You're unbelievable,' she said. 'You know, you were such a prick in that meeting. That was my first presentation, and you tried to derail me at every turn. You give finance guys the rep they deserve.'

'Kit, Kit, Kit,' he said, shaking his head. 'That's deals. We're not braiding each other's hair; we're calculating the risks of expensive and time-consuming mergers.'

'I know what deals are, ding-dong, I'm in the middle of one right now,' she shot back.

He threw his head back and laughed. 'Ding-dong. Good one. I must say I prefer it to "prick".'

Kit, feeling excessively bold and flirtatious, said, 'You and your foul mood were a hot topic after that meeting, let me tell you.'

'*Not* that I need to disclose anything of this nature to you,' he said, 'but I'd had a rough day. So, I apologise. As it turns out, today I have had an *excellent* day. So, here is me after an excellent day. Better?' He smiled.

Kit turned and flattened her back against the wall to let a succession of giggly women pass, then swivelled her body towards Max again, deliberately swinging a little closer this time.

'Well, I should go,' she said, looking into his eyes.

'You should go,' he said, returning her stare.

'I *really* should go,' she said.

'You simply must,' he said.

'Off I go then,' she said, not moving a muscle.

Neither of them spoke for several seconds.

'Where are you headed after here?' he said. 'Same place as me?'

'Hang on,' she said, snapping out of the trance. 'We are, like, *in business together*. We can't do this.'

'Ah, but we're *not* in business together, are we?' he said significantly. 'Blue Tree is out. No conflict of interest.'

Kit could only shake her head. Never in her life had she been so directly propositioned. It was very, very hot. She just couldn't believe it was *this guy* doing it.

'I just . . .'

'Oh,' he said. 'Is there a boyfriend? Sorry, I thought . . . Rupert had mentioned you were a single mother.'

For some reason, the fact that he asked if she was involved, and that he knew she was a single mother, was far hotter than anything else he had said or done. She looked at Max—those silly eyelashes, that giant hulking form, the dark hallway—and recognised this moment for exactly what it was. An absolute one-off, never-to-be-repeated chance to create a filthy core memory.

'No boyfriend,' she said.

He took a step towards her. 'No girlfriend. And no deal.'

'Then I guess . . . no problem?' she said, just before his lips met hers.

The kiss was soft at first, but quickly built in intensity.

'GET A ROOM, GET A ROOM, GET OUTTA THE WAY, GET LAID, GET A ROOM,' a drunk guy sang happily as he pushed past them.

Kit pulled away. She felt completely reckless. *Never* had she felt so devoid of reck. This was unquestionably permitted, she decided. This was *living*. This was what she had shelved for years. So this was happening.

'I need to use the ladies and then put my best friend in an Uber. I'll meet you out front in ten.'

'Taking charge,' he said approvingly. 'I like it. Hope you're like that later.' He raised his eyebrows suggestively.

Kit rolled her eyes. 'You speak as though you've been scripted by a rom-com writer.'

'See you soon,' he said with an exaggerated wink, before striding off down the hallway.

Kit walked quickly to the toilet to do a wee and freshen up. Despite the thick fog of champagne clouding her mind, she felt the flutter of nerves. Was her bikini line in okay shape? What undies was she wearing? She sniffed her pits and tried to catch her breath in a cupped hand.

You won't believe this but sis has picked up, she texted Rat at record speed. *will text u his name n address in case I don't come home cos he cut me up and put me in freezer xxxx*

Rat replied immediately. *Make me proud.*

Kit laughed. It was only ten thirty pm, she noticed. Jesus, talk about an efficient night. She would be laid and home in bed by midnight at this rate.

24

KIT WAS *NOT* HOME IN bed by midnight, but she did make it in before the streetlights went off. It had been so long since she had done anything even remotely in the category of carefree, and it felt *incredible*. Who would have guessed the antidote to her freakout yesterday was getting hammered and having a one-night stand? Her head was hard at work accommodating her post-sex giddiness and a life-threatening hangover. She knew which would triumph; she desperately needed ibuprofen and sleep. Kit smiled to herself, thinking about Max's apartment—though apartment seemed too poky a word for the top-floor deco oasis he called home. Even in her disorientated state of mind, she could tell some energy had cleared last night. She was a mess, but she definitely felt lighter. Her dry spell had been broken. She had let off some steam with her best friend. There were a few creases still to iron out before signing the deal, but it was as good as done. She felt weirdly serene. Happy. Excited.

She walked in the door, removed her shoes and tiptoed straight to her room, having already had a shower—a very X-rated one to begin with—at Max's. She unzipped her leather minidress and fell into bed. She was grateful Gretel wasn't here right now to see this but, oh, how she missed her little girl. She would be back this afternoon. Life couldn't get much sweeter.

Kit woke to her phone blaring two hours later. She was in such a deep slumber that she couldn't for a moment place where she was. She stared at her phone, trying to work out what was happening; it was her alarm. It was automatically set for six thirty each morning when Gretel wasn't around to wake her; she'd forgotten to turn it off. She stopped the awful noise and flopped back onto her pillows. She had *planned* to allow herself a sleep-in, lie to everyone about a doctor's appointment, but she knew she'd never get back to sleep now. She took a swig from the giant water bottle next to her bed and thought about what her day held. Or tried to: her mind went immediately back to Max, and the very unexpected turn last night had taken. 'Stunning,' Maggie had said when she told her she was leaving to one hundred percent have sex. 'Absolutely *stunning*.'

She texted Maggie. *Home and the satisfied recipient of exactly the kind of pounding you'd wish for your bestie. Why did we drink so much? Why didn't we eat any dinner? Where are my sunglasses? Why did I wear sunglasses?*

Maggie sent a screen full of eggplant emojis and just as many question marks.

Kit got up to make a fizzy vitamin B drink in the kitchen and saw Rat's room was empty as she walked past. That wasn't right. Where was she? She went to the living room and to her relief saw Rat's legs curled over the sofa.

Kit stood peering at her sister. She'd become so thin, she realised. Her perpetual tan had gone, and there were dark circles under her eyes. *You need to spend some time with her,* Kit scolded herself. She's by herself all day while you're busy with the deal and work and the groceries and . . . As she bent further over her sister's sleeping form, her phone fell out of her robe pocket and landed on the floor with a loud clunk. Rat woke with a start.

'Fuck—sorry, Ratty,' Kit whispered. 'Go back to sleep.'

Rat rubbed her eyes and looked up at Kit. 'You look like shit,' she said, voice croaky.

'I *feel* like shit,' Kit replied.

'How was it? He didn't give you a black eye, I see. That's always a good start.'

'*Rat!* Don't say things like that.'

'I cope how I cope,' Rat said, shrugging. 'So, was he hot or was he just in the same bar as you?'

'He's . . .' Kit blushed like a teenager. 'He's *stupid* hot. He's actually a private equity guy I met a few months ago . . . I did think he was a bit of a fuck-knuckle at the time.'

'Oooh, hate sex,' Rat said, yawning. 'Best kind.'

'It's pronounced *chemistry,* I think,' Kit said. Then she smiled goofily. 'It *was* kinda electric, though. Full post-sex jelly legs.'

'Gonna see him again?' Rat asked.

'Oh god, no,' Kit snorted, because she had already made it very clear to herself that she wasn't. 'This was just a moment in time. He's not my type. He had *self-help* books on his bedside table. So ick.'

'Good dick can offset the ick,' Rat said. 'Just saying.'

'Nah, not interested,' Kit said. 'Can we go have a disgusting breakfast? Bacon, pancakes, all that shit. I might vom if I don't get some grease soon. Come on, get up.'

The two sisters had a long, overpriced breakfast in Bondi, then walked along the promenade before collapsing on the grassy hill to people-watch for a while. It had been years since Kit had just flopped around on a weekday, and it was long overdue. She needed some junk time with her sister without the constant diversion of Gretel, just the two of them. They were both feeling a bit tender, but they had each other. Rupert had texted Kit to say he had chased Pinnacle about Second Day's mark-ups, but Pinnacle were yet to reply. Their lawyers had said the paperwork should be ready for signing on Monday, at which Kit breathed a huge sigh of relief. She could barely tie up her sandals today, let alone sign away the controlling stake in her company. She was operating on twelve percent battery. Even the photos Jordan sent through from the reshoot, which were some of the most gorgeous, dynamic imagery Second Day had ever produced, could barely hold Kit's interest. She was just so happy lying on the grass in the sun with her sister, knowing Gretel would be home in a few hours, and aside from moving back home—finally!—the three girls had a whole weekend of absolutely nothing ahead.

'How's your head?' Rat asked, a lazy hand flung across her face to shield her from the sun.

'Never drinking again,' Kit replied.

'I don't mean that—I mean after your bumpy cuddles. Killing you he hasn't texted, isn't it?'

Kit thought about this. Once the dust settled, one-night stands had a habit of turning her a bit inside out, like a puzzle put back together incorrectly. That it was *Max* put it on another level entirely. In the harsh light of day it all felt like a fever dream. She could *never* tell Camille and Jordan, but man, she wanted to. Only they would understand how insane it was that she'd ended up sleeping with him. She felt something like panic, maybe a close relative of panic, wash over her as she thought about Rupert ever finding out. Not that it was his business, and not that Blue Tree were relevant anymore, but just because, well, she kind of thought of Rupert as a dad figure. *Daddy issues*, she thought. *What a cliché.*

'Nah, I'm okay,' she replied finally. 'Definitely worth it. I'll need memories like this when I'm seventy-five and can't remember what sex is.'

'Will he text?' Rat asked. 'Or is he old and prefers to call? *Gross.*'

'Didn't give him my number,' Kit said, ignoring her jibe. That was no accident. Better to leave it as a sexy little memory. And anyway, he might still be a jerk. 'He has clearly slept with a *lot* of girls . . .' she mused aloud.

'I can't see why people think that's a bad thing,' Rat said. 'Like, honestly, you wouldn't want an inexperienced mechanic, so why would you want an inexperienced root?'

Kit was lost in her own little world. 'His *skills*, though. I've never . . . What he did was . . .'

'I should get back on the horse, I suppose,' Rat said. 'They must be missing me out there.'

Kit turned her head to look at her sister. 'I think you just needed to go into your shell for a while. Self-protection, you know?'

'Yeah, prolly,' Rat said, eyes closed, looking blissful in the morning sun.

'Hey, want to go see a movie?' Kit asked, with as much enthusiasm as she could muster. 'Get our nails done?'

'Yes to nails, no to movie.'

'Hey, Rat?' Kit said, coming up to rest on her elbows. 'If shaving your head was meant to make you unattractive, you failed. You've never looked more beautiful. You're fully in your Cate Blanchett elf era.'

Rat sighed. 'It's tough being this gorgeous.'

'I wouldn't know,' Kit said, laughing.

'Be grateful.'

'Guess I'll go cry into my millions,' she replied. It all still felt like a funny joke. Utterly surreal.

'*Our* millions.' Rat was very much in the 'for' camp. 'Gotta hand it to you, sis—smashing the patriarchy and sleeping with them on the same day? Pretty sick.'

25

THREE DAYS LATER

KIT PEELED HER EYES OPEN and blinked a few times, feeling like concrete had been poured into her brain. Almost instantly her breathing quickened, and her heart began to flutter, just as it had done all night. Fuck it! Her anxiety just would not fucking *quit*. Maggie said she might be perimenopausal—all this not-sleeping and anxiety. Kit just hoped it wasn't a sign she was making a mistake.

The weekend had been golden. Kit and Rat had packed up their stuff, said goodbye to the spider cave, and arrived home to find it smelled of damp and looked like they had been burgled, or were mid-renovation, or both. They tidied up and opened all the windows before Gretel arrived after school on Friday, and the three girls celebrated being home with a couple of fat pizzas. Early Saturday morning Kit had loaded the car with towels, swimming costumes, cookies, sandwiches and fruit, and they'd set off to Palm Beach for the day. A mellow Sunday morning making pancakes followed, Gretel happily covering her entire bedroom with some stickers Rat had bought her, but by mid-afternoon Kit's Sunday Scaries were in full effect. To her embarrassment, she was wounded that Max hadn't somehow worked out her email address or DMed her, even though she had told herself he wasn't going to and she didn't want him to. And, of course, she was incredibly excited and anxious about Monday. THE day. Signing day. Curtis and his team had been working hard all weekend, Kit had carefully read over the shareholders' agreement for the seven hundredth time, along with the share transfer form and the share purchase agreement, and that, apparently, was that. Curtis had warned Kit to clear her schedule from eight am, which she had.

She flopped a hand onto to the bedside table and circumnavigated around earrings, melatonin pills, hand cream and a pile of Gretel's picture books until she found her phone. It lit up: *6.19 am*. The last time Kit had seen its stupid face it was 4.42 am, at which point she had actually—to her mortification—begun to cry with anguish and fatigue. She'd done the thing she swore she would not do and taken temazepam at one am, figuring that if she got five solid hours, she'd be fine. Of course, she'd forgotten the dense mental fog she'd have to fight her way through this morning. That *none* of it even worked, that her anxiety was so powerful it could break through her entire stable of medicinal weaponry, made her furious. Kit swiped the phone off flight mode and was just about to put it down again when it began ringing. It was Priya. Kit sat up immediately and cleared her throat.

'Oh, thank god you're awake,' Priya said.

'What's going on?' Kit asked, sounding like she'd smoked a pack of cigarettes overnight.

'Curtis's been trying to reach you for hours. We all have. We need you to sign now. Did you check your email?'

'What? No, hang on, *now*?' Kit blinked furiously as if it might help her to understand what was happening.

'Did you see my texts last night? I said you should stand by until you heard from us. Pinnacle need to move fast; we're not exactly sure why.'

'I'm sorry—I put my phone in flight mode at ten thirty,' said Kit, taken aback. Why was everything so urgent all of a sudden?

Call waiting beeped. Kit looked at her screen; it was Curtis. 'Oh, Curtis's calling, Should I—'

'Answer that. And run a brush through your hair.'

'Huh?' Confusion was layering upon confusion. But Priya had hung up.

Kit answered Curtis's call while self-consciously touching her hair. 'Curtis?' she said.

'Good morning, Kit,' came a deep, melodious voice over the phone. (Kit always felt he'd missed his calling as a late-night slow jams DJ.) 'Forgive my calling so early, but Pinnacle's lawyers have asked us to execute this as soon as possible. We'll be doing it via video link now, given that Malcolm is overseas and it aligns with his time zone. Could you get your laptop, have your phone with you, and wait for an invite? Video is required. Thank you.'

'What are—' she began, but he'd hung up.

Kit jumped out of bed, grabbed last night's bra, which was still on the floor, threw off her giant bed t-shirt, put the bra on and then the t-shirt back on, all in a state of complete bewilderment. There was just-woken-up confusion, there was sleeping-pill-just-woken-up confusion, and then there was sleeping-pill-just-woken-up-and-about-to-sign-away-your-company confusion. She decided not to bother with undies; this was a purely waist-up affair. She bolted to her wardrobe, threw the tee off again, and pulled a button-down shirt from a hanger. She looked in the mirror and saw a face she really wished she hadn't: puffy, creased, black smudges under the eyes, and roughly three hundred years older than yesterday. Kit had taken great care to always appear polished and professional in front of her advisers, lawyers and any potential partner—and now *this*?! She ran some red lipstick over her lips and yanked her hair out of her sleeping bun, fluffing it up and pulling it forward to cover most of her eyes and cheeks. She would just have to have hair for a face, she decided. No, wait, her frames—she'd wear those! She didn't actually need them, the lenses were glass, but they were vintage Givenchy and Kit loved how they looked. Plus, they obscured most of her eyes. She put them on and hurried down the hallway to the dining room table, where her laptop sat next to several dirty plates and coffee cups, against a backdrop of total domestic chaos. Gretel's toys, dinner plates and her drink bottle sat on the breakfast bar; there was a basket of washing on a stool; and the milk had been left out next to the coffee machine so there would be none for breakfast. *Perfect*, Kit muttered to herself.

She positioned her laptop so the kitchen wasn't in the background and entered her password. She could still smell that bloody damp. She was about to text Curtis a thumbs up when she realised her laptop was dead. *Fuck! Not now! Fuck!* She sprinted to her bedroom—on tiptoes, so as not to wake Gretel—and yanked the power cord out of the wall, then raced back to the dining room, rammed the charger into the device, then climbed down under the table to plug it in to the wall. She smashed her head on the underside of the table as she came back up and let out a quick, sharp, 'Fuck!' *It wasn't meant to be like this!* she thought angrily, dangerously close to tears. They'd been inching towards this moment for months, and *this* was how it was going to go down? Shaking, head throbbing, she took a deep breath in and then let it out. *Think calm, be calm. Control the controllable*, she told herself, before resorting to ominous positivity: *This is a fucking awesome moment and you* will *enjoy it.*

Her phone chimed with a message and then another, each electronic chime compounding her panic. She crawled up into her chair and texted Curtis—*2 m*—while she waited for the laptop to power up. The second it was online, a Microsoft Teams video call invite popped up. She accepted and saw Curtis and his associates in their boardroom, looking calm, professional and composed. How, at this hour? *How?* Had they been there all night? Kit answered with audio only, hoping they'd forget to ask her to switch on her camera.

'Okay, Kit, please go into your email and click the one sent just after five am,' Curtis said. 'And we do need you on video, please, for legal reasons. Their lawyers are on, and they will be joining us momentarily, I'm told.'

'Yep, right, okay . . .' She ruffled her hair then turned the camera on. Why couldn't they have used Zoom so she'd at least have a filter? She took the brightness on her screen right down, then avoided looking at her herself, figuring if *she* didn't notice how she looked, neither would they. She opened her inbox and found twenty-six emails had come in since ten pm that she had (not) slept through. *Who are these people?! Who does this on a Sunday night?*

She opened the email. 'Okay, done.'

'Kit, is there anyone else at home with you?' Curtis asked.

She snapped her head around, expecting to see a serial killer stalking towards her. 'What?! Why?'

'We need a witness,' said Curtis.

'No, only my daughter,' she said. Rat hated the damp smell so much she had stayed at her friend Margot's house last night. Kit was so thrilled Rat was feeling social again she could almost forgive her for not being home the one morning Kit needed her.

'Okay, in that case you'll have to film yourself signing electronically on your phone.'

'So I . . . sign on my phone?' she asked slowly.

'No. You will electronically sign the document you currently have open on your laptop, but you need to record it using a special legal authorisation application we are texting through.'

On cue, her phone chimed. 'Okay, all right, let me just open this thing . . .' As she waited for it to load, she heard a small voice at the hallway door.

'Mumma?'

Kit whipped her head around to see Gretel peeking out from the hallway. Her hair was wild and puffy on her crown, she was clutching Captain Sloth and she was pants-less. She could not have looked cuter. Every cell in Kit's body wanted to race over and swoop up her little girl. Instead, she blew her a kiss, mouthed, 'I love you,' and held up her hand as if to say *five minutes*, which, of course, would mean nothing to a six-year-old.

Kit looked back at the app. 'Um, okay, it says it needs a passcode?'

'It has just been emailed to you,' Curtis said.

Kit clicked back into her email, and sure enough a passcode email popped up.

'*Please enter the registered phone number for safe two-step passcode authorisation,*' she read aloud. She furiously tapped in her phone number.

'*A passcode has been sent,*' she read aloud. '*Please check your mobile device.*'

She looked down at her phone. A text popped up.

Please click on this link for your passcode.

'Are you guys pranking me?' She laughed, a hint of hysteria coming through. *Oh good*, Kit thought. *Anxiety and sleep deprivation have invited insanity to the party.*

'Just security protocol,' Curtis said calmly.

'*Mummy!*' hissed Gretel.

'Honey, I'm just finishing up here. Pop back to your room and choose a book, and I'll be right there, okay?' she said, equal parts sweetness and optimism.

Gretel glared at her.

Kit turned back to the screen with a wry expression, hoping for an understanding smile in return, but the lawyers stared at her unblinkingly.

She clicked on the link and a nine-digit passcode came up, which she furiously scribbled on her hand using one of Gretel's textas, before finally being able to enter it into the app.

'Okay. Done. Now what?' Kit asked, already exhausted but having achieved zero so far.

'Open the contract and click "Ready to sign",' said Curtis, as calm as a pond.

Kit scanned and scrolled but could not see it. She felt a small, warm body sidle up next to her but couldn't do anything about that until she had mastered the document equivalent of a Rubik's cube.

'Curtis . . . where? I'm sorry, but I can't see it,' Kit felt flustered and stupid.

'Top left, Kit. Above the yellow box.'

'Okay, done.'

'Now, on your phone click "Ready to sign" and angle it so the camera can record you signing.'

Kit didn't understand at all what he meant but was too afraid to ask. This process would be hard after two espressos, let alone minus ten espressos, which was the level at which her brain was currently operating.

'So, like, to my screen.' She hoped her downward inflection would signify confidence.

'Try in line with your body, so your front camera can see your laptop screen,' Curtis advised.

She leaned the phone against one of yesterday's coffee cups, while on her other side Gretel tugged on her shirt. '*Mummy!*'

Kit digitally signed the numerous pages as instructed, her phone filming her all the while, like some kind of pervy contract creep. She *hated* this: this panic, this rush. The vibe was so far off what it was supposed to be. Kit had daydreamed about signing day . . . It was to be a heady mix of glamour, celebration and fulfilment. Kit, sweeping into a boardroom that overlooked a city on a sparkling, blue-sky day, wearing that vintage Prada dress she'd promised herself as a reward for the transaction and some cool black sunglasses, signing a single sheet of paper with a flourish, before being met with applause and the sound of champagne corks popping. Instead, she was on the verge of tears in her living room, impatiently observed by her lawyers, wearing neither undies nor mascara. Kit inhaled and exhaled, pushing her emotions down. She just needed some sleep. Everything was totally in order. Focus to finish. Big-girl pants.

'Okay,' Kit said, scanning her screen furiously to see if she'd missed anything. 'Think we're done.'

'There's one more, on page six,' said Curtis.

'Oh, yup, gotcha,' said Kit.

As she scrolled frantically, a small pudgy hand reached up from under the table. Kit found the final line, signed, clicked 'Finished signing' then took a deep breath.

'Okay. Wow. I think we're done . . . Are we done?' Tears were threatening, but she went on. 'Thank you for being so patient with me. I'm sorry I was scattered and—'

'Kit,' interrupted Curtis quietly.

'I know I haven't been your classic client, and no offence, but I hope not to see you for a while, ha ha ha, because I think I've probably hit my lifetime limit of deal talk and—'

'*Kit!*' said Curtis, louder.

'What?' she asked, surprised by his sharp tone.

'Your daughter took your phone before you finished the final signature. We're going to need to start again from the top.'

One of Curtis's associates walked into the room, and Curtis apologised and put the call on mute. The associate and Curtis spoke intently for a few moments, then Curtis came off mute.

'Please excuse us, Kit,' Curtis said. 'We'll call you back shortly. Stand by.'

An hour later, Kit had still not heard from Curtis. She texted Rupert and Priya, but neither of them knew what was going on. The advisers always handed over to the lawyers at the finish line, Kit remembered Rupert telling her. They'd done their bit. She showered and dressed, made Gretel's breakfast and lunch, got her dressed, created a glorious Elsa braid snaking down her back, and was just about to bite into some peanut butter toast when Curtis messaged.

Kit, I will call in 5 minutes.

That was *exactly* when Kit needed to leave to take Gretel to school. Last night she had promised her a hot chocolate on the way, which was completely idiotic given she had no idea what was happening with the signing process.

She looked at her daughter, who was sitting at the breakfast bar, completely absorbed in making a card for her new year one teacher—*i love you so much miss jeong*—and cursed under her breath. Yet another let-down, another excuse. Gretel deserved so much better.

'Oh, honey, Miss Jeong will be so chuffed when you give that to her. What a day-maker.'

'She will only stick it on her wall if it's *very* good, like Remy's, so do we have any puffy stickers, you know the ones that were shiny?' She paused a beat then looked up at her mother. 'Mum, do you know any wedding girls? I want to be a flower girl.'

'A wedding girl?' Kit asked.

'The wedding girl, in a white dress,' Gretel said, back to colouring intently.

'Oh, a *bride*,' Kit said, smiling. 'No, sorry, darling; no one I know is getting married.'

'Can you then?' Gretel pleaded. 'I want to be a flower girl. Frankie was and she got to wear a princess dress with *real life* high heels.'

'Let me have a think,' Kit said. 'So, honey, I have another quick phone call in a second, but we'll go for your hot chocolate straight after that, okay?'

'*Another* one?' Gretel said, slumping. 'You're *always* on the phone!'

Kit felt that one. 'I know, baby. I've been very, very busy, and I'm sorry. But today is the big day, the last day, the day we celebrate—remember I said it was soon? I even ordered some cupcakes for us to have this afternoon, and Maggie and Beau and Dyl will come over . . . It's actually a really exciting day for Mu—'

'Can I watch *Bluey* then?' Gretel knew her way around these conversations and where they ultimately led: to her being babysat by the TV while Kit babbled on about EVs and SHAs on the phone.

Kit nodded, but Gretel had already jumped down and walked over to the sofa, grabbing the remote control from the coffee table as she went.

Kit's WhatsApp began dinging, startling her.

Can the parents who park in the no stopping zone PLEASE stop! The residents have lodged a formal complaint to the school so we are risking losing the few parking privileges we have. Thank you.

I see parents do it every day it's so rude

Not hard to park a street away and walk people!!

The residents have obviously never had to do school drop off god its only for 30m every day can they relax

We ride to school, kids love it and better for the planet 😊

Kit's phone rang, interrupting the highly emotive parking exchange—Curtis.

'How we going? Track down Aspen Mo yet?' Kit plonked onto a stool.

'Kit, we have just been given some . . . confronting news,' Curtis said, his tone grave.

'Is everyone okay?' Kit asked. Had Malcolm come face to face with a tree while skiing?

'There's no way to sugar-coat this,' Curtis said sombrely. 'Pinnacle Capital has withdrawn their offer.'

'*WHAT?*' Kit blinked rapidly as she tried to process his words. She stood up and began pacing. 'What do you mean, *withdrawn*? Why? I was in the middle of signing! Are they for real? Can they do this?'

'Their board put a halt on all mergers and acquisitions, effective immediately,' he said.

'But *they* were the ones making us sign at cock's crow this morning,' Kit responded. 'Why would they do that if they were just going to call it off? What could have changed in the last hour?' Kit had raised her voice; she couldn't help it. She walked into her bedroom so that Gretel wouldn't hear her swear, which was very much on the cards.

'That is the only information we have been given, I'm afraid,' Curtis said. 'However,' he said, lowering his voice, 'I have heard confidentially that the two partners, Ian and Malcolm, are feuding, and Malcolm did not have approval to acquire this stake. He was rushing it through before Ian could stop it.'

'Are you *serious*?' Kit asked, in disbelief. 'We're caught up in some playground fight?'

'Unfortunately, there's likely very little we can do to resuscitate the deal as it stands. After an unholy flurry of activity last night, the silence now is deafening. Malcolm and Omari aren't answering, and neither their advisers nor lawyers will take my calls or respond to emails. If Ian has blocked it, I'm afraid I can't see a scenario where this deal is happening—at least, not in the near future.'

'*Fuck!*' Kit said. 'Sorry, Curtis, but I don't know what else to say.'

'Kit, I am sorry,' Curtis said. 'I'm shocked, to be honest. This is extraordinarily unprofessional.'

'It's me,' she said, feeling sorry for herself. 'I'm cursed.'

'I'll speak to you when we know more,' Curtis said.

The second that call ended, Priya phoned. Kit answered, primed for a hearty common-enemy download.

'Kit,' she said, 'I'm calling to see how you're holding up.'

'It's, well, yeah . . .' Kit said, swallowing back tears. *Kindness! Her kryptonite.*

'We mustn't downplay the enormity of this. Your life was about to change in many significant ways.'

'Mm-hmm,' Kit said, sniffing. Was it her imagination or was Priya being more brusque than usual?

'Now, Kit'—Priya's voice was gentle but firm—'I'm going to say something that I hope I don't regret, but I believe this is worth saying.'

'Go on,' Kit said grimly, lowering herself heavily onto her bed.

'It may not feel like it in this moment, but there *are* upsides to this deal collapsing. It was incredibly rushed, and well, to be frank, I was baffled by some of the things you agreed to in the end.'

Kit frowned. Hang on, what?

'For one, there was no time frame around Pinnacle's drag-along right, which meant they could have forced you into selling the whole thing in six months' time if they wanted to—'

'Rupert said they would *never* do that so soon after an acquisition,' Kit rebutted.

'Their options created a disproportionate upside for them at exit,' Priya went on. 'Their covenants regarding manufacturing costs had the potential to dramatically lower the quality of your products, which I know you care about, and having retailer control could have seen Second Day in the Kmart bargain bin by Christmas!' She paused. 'Kit, they could have fired your executive team if they didn't meet those huge targets. That's a big one. Camille may have been gone within months.'

As Kit listened to what Priya was saying, she became light-headed, like she had been about to step onto a freeway and had been yanked back at the last second. *She had agreed to all these appalling things!* She'd been impatient, and so fatigued, and she'd cut corners and made poor decisions. How was that any better than her first run at a shareholders' agreement? Had she learned nothing?!

'Camille saw it, you saw it, I should have listened,' Kit said, shaking her head in disbelief.

'Deals are designed to wear you down so that you just give in to their demands,' Priya said.

Kit swallowed slowly; her mouth was suddenly so dry. 'How did I let it go so far?'

'There were benefits, of course—financially especially—but I must admit I felt a wave of relief when Curtis filled me in,' Priya confessed.

'Yeah, well,' Kit said, wounded by Priya's admission, 'feel free to let me know if I am making a shitty decision next time, okay?'

'This stuff is really challenging, even for those of us who have been doing it for decades, but I feel I should make you aware of what you were prepared to sign away,' Priya said.

Kit inhaled and exhaled by way of response. She hated thinking that Priya was disappointed in her.

'There is still a partner out there for you,' Priya said kindly. 'We will find them. Maybe we revisit some of the bidders you flushed our earlier.'

'Mm-hmm,' Kit said, taking a long blink and wishing she could unsleep with Max.

'You are not facing this alone, Kit,' Priya said. 'We are here for you. You are a brilliant young woman, doing incredible things. You're in some very rare air. And it's far from over.'

'Thank you, Priya,' Kit said, her voice breaking.

'I'll schedule a call to debrief later today. Take care, Kit.' Priya ended the call.

Kit let the hand holding her phone fall and stared blankly at the space in front of her, trying to come to terms with what had just unfolded.

'Mummy?' said a soft voice from the doorway.

'Yes, honey?' Kit said on autopilot.

'Can I have my hot chocolate now?'

26

ONCE GRETEL WAS HAPPILY HOT-CHOCOLATED and delivered to school, Kit could finally allow her facade of Everything Is Fine to crumble. She walked inside, dumped her bag on the bench, took off her frames, sat on the lounge, and she cried. She cried hard and ugly, and she gave it everything she had. She cried because today was supposed to be a momentous occasion, a new chapter, and instead she'd wasted months, and tens of thousands of dollars in fees, and so much energy—oh, the *energy* she had expended on that deal! She cried because Priya had revealed what a selfish, impatient fuckwit she'd been, how she had lost her way and almost her company. She cried because she felt tricked and naive. She cried because she had foolishly allowed herself to believe this would *actually happen*. Of course, it wouldn't: she was never going to pull something like that off. She'd known in her heart all along that ludicrous amount of money was never going to be hers, it was utter fantasy. She cried because now she would have to tell everyone there was no deal, everything was going to stay exactly as it was. She cried because she had ruined any chance of crawling back to Blue Tree since she'd got drunk and slept with one of their analysts. She cried because her house was small and smelled of mildew, but there would be no buying a new place now. All she had was disappointment, sunk costs, and the interminable problem of Toni's *goddamn fucking stupid fucking shares*.

Fucking Toni, she thought savagely. *She* had started all this. Kit had been fine, happy, loving her work and her life, then Toni blew everything up. Her phone pinged.

Your cupcakes are ready for pickup! Love, Cupcakes and Gems.

Great, Kit thought bitterly. *Let's celebrate my failure with some overpriced cupcakes.*

She heard a key in the door. Rat was back; Kit had her first customer. She wiped under her eyes and stood up, walking to the bench to clean up Gretel's pencils and crayons, something to keep her busy.

'So?' Rat said, brows raised. 'We buyin' Chanel handbags today or what?' She was wearing a pink silk cami with no bra, baggy denim shorts and Crocs, an old tote bag of Kit's slung over her shoulder. She dumped it on the floor and grabbed a plum from the bowl on the bench, taking a huge bite.

Kit looked at her and tried to blink away her stupid tears. 'It fell over at the last moment. They didn't have full board support.'

Rat's shoulders dropped along with her jaw. 'You're fucking kidding me. They can't do that!'

'They really can,' Kit said. 'It's over.'

Rat put her keys and phone on the bench and walked over to give Kit a firm hug. 'You know I hate hugs; this is big for me.'

'It is,' Kit sniffed.

Rat pulled back and put her hands on her hips. 'Well, this is some fresh trauma, isn't it . . . Those shitsacks. Can't believe we're not gonna be millionaires now; I'd banked on that cash for my inheritance.'

'I knew I'd mess it up,' Kit said glumly. 'I chose the wrong guys.'

'And now you must choose violence,' Rat said, as fired up as Kit was dazed. 'Can you sue them?'

'Nope. Until it's signed, the offer is non-binding.' She took an unsteady breath. 'The whole thing has been one let-down after another. I honestly wish I'd never bothered. Just call me Icarus.'

'Who's she?' Rat said frowning. 'Anyway, I'm really sorry, sis,' Rat said, uncharacteristically earnest. 'You work so, so hard—like, early-grave level. Look at all the new wrinkles you have . . . You deserved this, and they stole it, the dirty dogs.'

'I know that it's the champagniest of champagne problems,' Kit said, putting on an affected voice. '*Oh, my big deal collapsed so now I don't get millions of dollars, waah.* But I was so excited for Second Day Version 2.0—fresh people, new products, experience . . . Some grown-ups around the table.'

'Nah, you dodged a massive bullet, I reckon,' Rat said flippantly. 'Can't you just go back to the runner-up?'

'Um, I slept with one of them,' Kit said curtly, 'so, no.'

Rat tried very hard not to smile. '*Second* runner-up?'

'They weren't right,' she said. 'Square peg, round hole.'

Rat stood back and looked at Kit ruefully. 'So, look, I don't wanna add to your super shit day, and I really wouldn't if wasn't urgent, but I spoke to Dawn last night . . . she called like, *mad* late, and when I called you your phone was already off—'

'Rat?' Kit asked. 'What's wrong?'

Rat screwed up her nose. 'Look, I know he's basically an NPC to us, but . . . he's dying.' She paused. 'Like for real this time.'

Kit's hands flew to the back of her head, and she linked them as though she were doing sit-ups. She exhaled slowly, loudly. *Okay*, she thought, *this is a lot. Big day, lots of challenges. But you can handle it.* The news about Ron flicked a switch within her, putting things into perspective. There was far more important shit going on than a business deal.

'Cancer's back?' she asked.

'Yeah, with, like, supervillain vengeance. Stage four. Dawn has switched from giving him wheatgrass juice to meditating for him, so you know it's serious.'

'Fuck,' Kit said despairingly, closing her eyes. *Why* now, when he was just starting to open up? Or was that *why* he had started to open up? He must have known he was sick again; she *knew* he was acting differently. She felt anger bubble up. If he'd known he was dying and didn't tell her and Rat, that was weeks or months they could have spent with him, letting Gretel get to know her grandfather better; they could even have helped Dawn care for him. Instead, he dropped the bomb when it was too late. *Why was he like this?!* Why couldn't he just be a normal human? Was he that terrified of feelings? Of love? She suddenly remembered his recent attempts to call, and it took her breath away. He *had* tried to tell her. She just hadn't answered. She felt queasy with guilt.

'Okay,' Kit said, choosing to act rather than feel things. 'We need to get up there asap.' Her brain, already ten steps ahead, was asking who would look after Gretel.

'Yah,' Rat confirmed.

'Is he still at home?' Kit asked.

'Hospice. Mooloolaba.'

'*Hospice?!* Fuck, that was quick . . . Okay,' she said. 'Can you look at flights up there today while I see if Maggie can take Gretel for a couple of nights?'

'Not Ari?' Rat asked.

'New Zealand.'

'Well, he needs to fly back,' Rat said, annoyed. 'This is a family *crisis*. For god's sake, Kit, stop pandering to him. He needs to grow the fuck up. Tell him to be *better*—'

'Oh yes,' Kit said, 'this feels like a good time for you to tell me how I should live my life. Please, I'm all ears.'

Rat rolled her eyes. 'Calm down—I'm on your team, bish.'

'Just find some flights to the Sunshine Coast, please,' Kit said briskly. 'And text Dawn to say we're coming and *not* to let him die before we get there.'

This day, Kit thought, shaking her head as she waited for Ari to answer her call. *The fucking audacity of it.*

'Kitty, hey, what's up?' Ari answered, sounding out of breath. 'Sorry, just out riding.'

'Hi, hey, look, I'm calling with an SOS,' she said. 'Dad's cancer is back and he doesn't have long. He's in a hospice in Mooloolaba, and Rat and I need to get there fast, so could you come back to stay with Gretel for a few days?'

'Oh, man,' Ari said. 'I'm so sorry. That's really heavy. I didn't know he was sick again. Didn't you guys see him in—'

Kit knew he was being kind, but she didn't have time for it.

'We did,' she cut him off. 'He went downhill fast, so we've got to get up there. Can you come back?' she asked.

'Yep, yep, I just'—he paused, his breathing still ragged—'I wonder if . . . I hate to do this, sorry, but is there any way Maggie could maybe step in?' His inflection was sky-high.

'Why can't *you* do it?' Kit was on the cusp on pulling the trigger. It wasn't even his fault; he was just a safe space for her to shoot.

'Shit, it's just that Pam and Colleen have planned this whole thing . . .'

'What thing?'

'Oooh, I don't think now is a good time to talk about it,' he said uncomfortably.

'Ari, what's going on?'

'Nothing, nothing, I'm just—Nothing. You need to focus on Ron.'

'I *can't* focus until you tell me whether you're coming back to look after Gretel,' she snapped.

'They're throwing me and Wren an engagement party, okay?' he blurted. 'It's not what it sounds like . . . It's silly, and small, and it's nothing. I was going to tell you about it but—'

'*What?*' she hissed. 'You're getting *married*?' Kit stopped just short of looking for a hidden camera. 'You were right,' she said. 'It's not a good time to talk about this.'

'Unbelievable,' she muttered, as she stared at the phone she had just slammed down onto the counter. 'Un-be-*lievable*.' She was not going to make the mistake of relying on him *ever* again. He was a selfish, ridiculous excuse for a man. She dialled Maggie but got no answer, so texted instead.

Ok long story, headline: Ron is on deathbed, Rat and I have to fly up today, would you have space for Gretel for a couple of days??? Don't think she should come. Ari is in NZ.

Then, in a separate text, she added: *Also the deal collapsed. No deal. All that for nothing. This day is too much. I cry. A lot.*

'Flights are *so fucking expensive*,' Rat yelled from her trundle in Gretel's room. 'Is there some music festival on up there we don't know about?'

'Doesn't matter, just book it!' Kit replied.

Nervous energy was fuelling her breakneck dishwasher unload and reload. Next she would clean the kitchen, then pack both her and Gretel's bags. Organisation was Kit's safety net when she was spiralling; she needed to be very busy and very fast at being busy to stop the disorientated, spacey, scared feelings taking over. In such a short space of time so many things she had thought were certain had buckled . . .

Kit's phone buzzed. She glanced at the screen: it was Toni. *Not now, Satan*, Kit thought to herself as she let it ring out.

A text from Maggie popped up: *My darling!!! Of course, we will take baby girl. I fucking love you so much. I'm leaving work to see you, be there in 20.*

One from Toni. *What happened?!! What went wrong??? Call me asap xxxx*

A WhatsApp from Shona. *Is Ms Jeong pregnant?? who will be the teacher if she goes??*

27

TWO DAYS LATER, KIT SAT in a small plastic chair, almost certainly an outside chair, next to the single bed housing her very frail, very ill father at the hospice. He had dropped considerable weight since she'd seen him, even though he'd had little to lose. He looked nothing like the handsome, overbearing man she'd grown up with.

As he slept, Kit scrolled on her phone, occasionally looking up to examine him curiously. Who was this man, who was her flesh and blood but whom she felt no strong attachment to—didn't even love, really? How could the two of them be so comprehensively different?

His hair was sparse and greasy, sitting flat against his head, his skin was red and blotchy from years of heavy drinking and the Queensland sun, and grey hairs sprouted out of his nose and ears. His eyebrows had gone wild. Kit had half a mind to give him a quick grooming session, extend him some dignity in these final days. Why hadn't Dawn done that? She had floated in earlier with an update, her demeanour a confusing blend of contempt for modern medicine and genuine sadness. A passing remark about how it was 'good that you made time' quickly put Rat offside. Not because Dawn was wrong, per se, but because Rat had no time for what she called a 'basic witch' who'd only known Ron for a couple of years but acted as if they were lifelong partners. To Dawn's credit, she read the room, leaving to organise the burial ceremony—which, Kit understood, involved a death walker, a biodegradable coffin and a lot of sage.

Rat had left soon after, off to the beach for a swim. She was going mad cooped up in the hospice, which smelled like disinfectant and linen starch at best, cooked cabbage and urine cakes at worst. 'If he gets chatty text me,' she said and loped off.

Kit knew Rupert was doing his best not to bother her, but he *had* sent a debrief of the collapsed deal: Malcolm had driven and almost closed two sizeable acquisitions, Second Day being one, without Ian's sign-off; Ian was calling for Malcolm's removal from the board and wanted to buy him out . . . blah blah blah. Kit could not care less about their rich-boy in-fighting. She was done with them. Rupert, who was keen to act while they still had momentum, had compiled a shortlist of candidates to approach. When was Kit available for a meet-up?

'You came,' a raspy voice said from the bed, and she snapped her head up.

'Hey, Dad,' she said, reaching over to hold his hand. He didn't move his to meet her, so she left it sitting awkwardly on top.

'You came,' he repeated.

'Rat and I arrived yesterday,' she said, wanting him to know they did care, and they were here for him. 'Soon as we heard.' With her other hand she tapped out a text to her sister: *he awake*.

'I worry about you girls,' he said uncharacteristically.

'We're fine,' she said, wiping a tear from her cheek. 'We're worried about *you*.'

'Don't waste the energy. I'm on my way out.'

Kit nodded, sniffing.

'Did you sell the company?' he asked, eyes closed. 'You never said.'

She took a beat before replying. 'Sure did,' she said, feigning positivity. 'Just finishing up the paperwork . . . Your daughter is now a very wealthy woman.'

He smiled; his expression was one of relief and peace. 'Now we're talkin'. Good job, kid.'

A fast-moving nurse wearing an unholy amount of eyeliner barged in saying, 'Knock-knock,' instead of knocking. She checked the clipboard on the end of Ron's bed, looked at her watch, glanced at the monitor, then walked out again.

Rat barged in next, dress damp over her swimming costume, hospice bath towel around her neck, feet covered in sand, panting.

Kit patted her father's hand, then stood up and kissed him on the forehead. 'Love you, Dad,' she said. 'I'll give you two some time.'

Kit went out into the foyer, helped herself to a cup of water from the cooler near the entrance and walked outside. Her heart was racing. Why had she lied? *Because it could be the last time you ever talk to him, and you want him to die knowing you are a success and you're going to be fine*, she reminded herself. It cost her nothing but meant a lot to him. She stood by her decision.

A text had come in from Piper while her phone was on silent. *$95m!!!!!! jdskla djskldjsakl!! OMG Kit!!!!! I am SO sorry it fell over, friggen slimeballs! But that ev is INSANE!! Everyone will remember* *that, puts you in good stead for REAL buyer ;) Good luck. You WILL find you perf partner xxxx*

How did Piper know all this? Priya wouldn't have said anything; she was far too professional.

Piper sent another text, this time a link to an article in the *Financial Times*, with the headline: PINNACLE SET TO INK $95 MILLION DEAL WITH HAIR BRAND BEFORE INTERNAL BUST-UP. And right next to that was Kit's smiling face.

Oh, Kit realised. *That's* how she knew.

Part three

FOUR MONTHS LATER

28

KIT OPENED HER EYES, BLINKING in the light streaming through the vertical blinds she was intent on replacing. She stretched and looked around at her bedroom, which was bare save for her bed and an old wooden sideboard heaving under the weight of books, candles, jewellery, her iPad and three chargers. She didn't mind the empty space. At Maggie's insistence, she was taking her time to decorate. 'You always end up with shit furniture because you can't wait the eight-week lead time, so you just buy whatever nasty floor stock is available,' she scolded. Maggie was right, Kit did rush, and despite being such a visual person, she had never made the time to decorate *properly*. She had lived in tiny flats with cheap stuff she'd collected over the years, then she'd moved in with Ari and had a baby, and suddenly it was all woods and whites because Ari's furniture was better, so they used his. Those bits and pieces had followed her to the semi she'd lived in since, but they were not invited to this house. Kit was finally ready for a beautiful home. A grown-up, considered home, filled with joy-sparking chairs, rugs and lamps. She'd enlisted Maggie to create the vibe and help with the furniture and colour scheme, and Maggie had run with that ball at full speed. Kit's role at this stage was mostly paying invoices for wildly exotic pendants and dreamy wallpaper that wouldn't arrive for months, maybe decades.

Kit got out of bed, threw off her giant sleeping t-shirt and pulled on the underwear, leggings and crop she'd laid out the night before. It was six thirty am, Gretel and Rat should both still be asleep; she had time for a run.

Kit warmed up a little; she felt great. She now took magnesium glycinate instead of melatonin for sleep, she'd stopped drinking through the week, quit vaping once and for all, and best of all both the small girl and the tall girl now slept through the night, in their own beds, in their own rooms.

After the deal collapsed and her father died, Kit had the worst flu of her life. She spent two sweaty, achy weeks in bed, thinking she might actually perish and that would be an improvement on how she felt in that moment. When her health returned, it was as if she'd shed her chrysalis and it was time to start living *right*. The first thing she did was pay herself and Simon some long overdue dividends and put down a deposit on a three-bedroom townhouse in Coogee. The new place had such a light, happy energy. It was full of enormous windows, surrounded by trees, had a small yard and garden plot, and was on a cul-de-sac, so there was almost no traffic. They could walk to the sea, they could walk to cafes, and Kit had her very own garage. Life was sweet.

Kit walked downstairs to the living room to get her AirPods from her handbag, and saw Gretel was in fact already awake and watching a show about unicorn tweens dealing with crushes and socially awkward school fallouts when they weren't cooking cupcakes or fighting demonic dragons.

She walked over and plonked down next to her daughter, kissing her on the cheek and ruffling her hair.

'Hi, schmoops. How'd you sleep?' Gretel had been sick earlier this week and still had a rotten cough.

'Mum, can I have some toast?' Gretel said, not taking her eyes off the screen.

'Banana and honey?'

'Yes, please, Mum,' she said.

Kit stood up and headed to the kitchen. 'Hey, I was thinking we should go to the museum today; there's a wildlife photographer exhibition on, lots of amazing photos of baby lions and scary spiders and cute foxes . . .'

'Mum?' Gretel called.

'What's up?' Kit replied.

'Can you eat smoke?' her daughter asked, apropos of nothing.

Kit smiled. 'Um, well, not really, because it's not a solid or liquid, it's a—'

'*Remy* said she ate smoke; I knew she was lying.'

'Ah, okay. Well, maybe she did, or thought she did,' Kit said. 'We weren't there.'

'She always lies. She told me that her mum lets her have ice cream every day!' Gretel said.

'Well, we don't know, maybe her mum *does* let her have ice cream every day; that's not really any of our business,' Kit said vaguely, mashing the banana together with honey and cinnamon in a bowl.

Gretel began coughing.

'Ooh, honey, that cough doesn't sound so good . . .' Kit grabbed some vitamin C melts and placed them on the plate next to the smashed banana toast.

'Can you come eat at the table? You'll make a mess on the couch.' Not that it mattered; it was filthy and old, and would be put out for hard rubbish once the velvet oxblood sofa Maggie had selected arrived.

Gretel sighed and dragged her feet over to the table, as though Kit had asked her to clean the entire house then mow the lawn.

'Mum, I hate this cough. It deletes my good times.'

Kit tilted her head. 'Deletes your good times?'

'Because I can't laugh,' Gretel said with frustration, before coughing again. 'I did at school yesterday and it hurt.'

Kit managed to repress her giggle. 'I'm sorry, honey.'

Her phone chimed, but she ignored it. Those days were over: no phones at the table or during meals.

Only once Gretel was fed and back watching TV did Kit collect her phone and AirPods and step outside into the frigid morning air. She read the text that had come in.

Kit it's Francis. The space in Darlinghurst I was telling you about has finally come on the rental market, and they have agreed to let me show it this afternoon, are you free?

Kit gasped. She had been waiting for a text from this real estate guy for *months*. A friend who worked in the building—a stunning, fully fitted-out, polished-concrete dreamhouse—had given her the heads-up that one of the fashion brands there was relocating. Part of New Kit's charter was finding a new Second Day HQ; she wanted a clean, fresh slate for their clean, fresh outlook, but she refused to settle for anything other than perfect. It had to inspire her and the team, it had to have room for them to grow, and it had to be beautiful enough that they could shoot content and host meetings, even events. This building offered all of that.

Finally my office is ready for me! Shall we say 2?

Two hours later, Gretel and Kit were admiring an aerial photo of hundreds of frogs on hundreds of lily pads, marvelling at the colours and patterns, when Kit heard someone behind her say, 'Kit?'

She turned to see who it was, and inhaled sharply.

'Max!' Heat spread up the back of her neck, and she tucked her hair nervously behind her ear, smiling. *Get your shit together*, she instructed herself. *What are you, twelve?* She was glad she'd worn her new trench and made an effort with her hair.

'Thought it was you,' he said. 'And who's this?'

He crouched down to Gretel's eye level; her expression made it clear she was annoyed at him for interrupting.

'This is Gretel,' Kit said, rubbing her daughter's shoulder.

'Hi, Gretel,' Max said. 'Are you a frog enthusiast?'

She stared at him, saying nothing.

'Did you know the biggest frog in the world weighs as much as a human baby?' Max continued, refusing to give up. 'It eats snakes and turtles for dinner. Shell and all.'

'You *shouldn't* eat turtles,' Gretel reprimanded. 'Miss Jeong says they'll go exstink.'

'Not even turtle ice cream?'

She opened her eyes in shock. '*No!*'

'Fair enough. Anyway, I'm Max. Hi.'

Gretel just turned to Kit and said, 'Can we look at the polar bears now?'

'One moment, honey. I'm just saying hello to Max.' She was quietly proud of her daughter for giving Max absolutely nothing. He'd have to work harder than that to win Gretel over.

'How have you been?' he asked, looking at her intently, placing his hands in the back pockets of his jeans. 'Recovered from the Pinnacle mess? What a circus. That must have been awful. I was going to reach out,' he said, then stopped. 'I should have.'

Kit looked at Gretel, happily playing an interactive touch-screen game about endangered animals.

'It wasn't fun,' she said. 'But I think it was all meant to be.' She wasn't going to go deep on it with *Max Darling*, a guy whom she'd last seen naked, sprawled across his bed, and who hadn't sent a single message or email since.

'I hear you've parked the process for now?' he said.

'Had a rethink. There's no need to rush it,' she said. A line she'd trotted out a million times.

'The market says otherwise, but it's your call, obviously,' he said.

She bristled. He wasn't going to come and deal all over her, was he?

'So what brings you here?' she said. 'Frog enthusiast?'

He smiled. *And what a smile*, Kit thought. He was wearing an olive-green long-sleeved t-shirt and black jeans with brown boots. He dressed well, she admitted. Simple, but well put together.

'I do photography on the side,' he explained.

Of course, *you do*, Kit said to herself. Next he'd probably say he loved to cook and give foot rubs. How was this guy even real? There must be something very wrong with him. The fact that he was single—if he still was—served as a huge red flag.

'Would we ever go for a drink?' he asked.

She realised he never looked around, just held her gaze. It was slightly unnerving. Or hot. Maybe both.

'I don't know,' she said. 'Would we?'

'I liked our last one,' he said.

'Not *that* much,' she muttered.

'I didn't catch that. Or was I not supposed to?'

'If you liked it so much,' she said, 'you probably would have called or sent a text.'

He looked at her in astonishment. 'Are you *serious*?' he said. 'You can't be.'

'What?' she said, affronted.

'You told me to never, ever, ever call or contact you,' he said. 'You even wrote it on the notepad I have next to my bed: *Do not contact Kit.*'

'Oh, I did *not*,' she scoffed. But she may well have. She *was* pretty drunk.

He exhaled, smiling broadly. 'You're nuts. You honestly don't remember, do you?'

'You can't tell people they're nuts anymore,' she said, avoiding the accusation. 'It's not PC.'

'Mummy, can we *goooo*?' Gretel whined, tugging on her mother's hand.

'Okay, well, I humbly request permission to contact you,' he said.

'Pass me your phone,' she replied, holding out her hand for it, repressing a grin.

He handed it to her, still smiling, and she entered her own number, then called it. A shrill ringtone emanated from her bag. 'There. Done.'

'Now I might not call just to spite you,' he said teasingly.

'Your loss,' she said, with a confusing amount of confidence for someone who was unquestionably happy to see this man again. 'Catch you later, Mr Darling.'

She took Gretel's hand, and they walked off into the crowd.

29

KIT STUDIED THE DOZEN OR so pieces of giant red curved acrylic in front of her, trying to imagine how they were going to come together tomorrow. The production company they'd hired to design and build the Second Day stand were the very best and very expensivest, so she trusted it would look incredible. It had better: they had invested a lot of time and money into this glorious, glossy beast and its premium positioning.

Second Day were sitting front and centre at the entrance of the Shine lifestyle festival, a three-day beauty-wellness-fashion expo designed to showcase brands, where excited crowds could try and buy things between listening to creators, CEOs, stylists, founders and celebrities talk about Their Journey. It was Kit's idea that they exhibit; she felt they needed to be out there creating excitement and memories for customers, both new and loyal—especially after the press about the failed deal. She wanted to reassert the brand: show everyone they were doing great, kicking goals, et cetera. All that aside, Kit had missed talking to people, and educating, and doing what she was good at: hair.

'Hey, what time do I need to arrive tomorrow?' she asked Jordan. 'Have we confirmed Ava as the model?'

'Um . . .' Jordan scanned the running sheet. 'Yes, she's confirmed. We need you here made up and ready to go at nine forty-five: masterclass is at ten, Q and A at ten forty-five, and the meet and greet directly after.'

'Okay, roger that.' Kit began unloading products from one of the numerous boxes at her feet. 'Do you remember when we could only afford that cardboard stand at the hair expo?' Kit asked, feeling sentimental. 'It was so bad. And then the lady I chose from the audience to style had *head lice!*'

'Oh my god, *yes*,' Jordan said, clapping her hands together at the memory. 'And you were, like'—she put on a voice—'*Deanne, you know what? I think you'll look* great *with a slick ponytail!* And you put that hair up in twenty seconds flat.'

'The dangers of live styling,' Kit mused. 'I wouldn't care now—Gretel and I have had nits twice already this year—but back then I was a precious princess.'

Hyun materialised with a tray of coffees. His new perm looked immaculate, and somehow his oversized denim jacket—'thrifted, obvs'—remained cast sexily off one shoulder even though he was running errands and definitely needed both hands. He tipped his head behind him to the Jellymin vitamin stand, which was one million times more complete than Second Day's.

'You've got some fa-aans,' he singsonged at Kit as he handed her a coffee.

There was a group of four or five women giggling and looking over at them.

Kit didn't miss a beat; she grabbed a bunch of samples from one of the boxes and walked directly over to them, smiling.

'Hello, ladies,' she said warmly. 'Nice stand you've got there. I like how . . . finished it is.'

They all laughed.

'I thought I'd pop over with some samples of our repair mask,' Kit continued. 'Use it when this is all over and you're back in your soft clothes on the couch.'

'I *love* your texture cream,' said an attractive blonde woman wearing a slouchy oversized cream suit. She touched her hair. 'Blow-dries always look terrible on me,' she confessed. 'I always feel like a newsreader . . . I much prefer an air-dry . . . Oops, sorry!' She rolled her eyes. 'Where are my manners? I'm Flick from Basil PR—we look after Jellymins.'

'Hey, Flick. Nice to meet you.'

'*Loved* your piece in *Forbes* last month,' she said. 'Such a fascinating ride you've been on . . . Let me know if you're in the market for PR, won't you?' Flick gave her a cheeky smile.

'We actually do it in-house,' Kit said, 'but thank you.'

'Oh, can I ask why? Have you had a bad experience with an agency?'

Kit thought of Toni; 'bad experience' was putting it mildly.

'I'm just a control freak,' she said lightly. 'I prefer to have a handle on everything. So,' she went on, changing the topic, 'excited for a wild few days? I heard they sold sixty thousand tickets . . .'

'But *such* a worthwhile branding moment,' Flick said. 'Once we're unpacked, I'll drop over some caffeine and B vitamin gummies: you're going to need them.'

'Um, can I just say,' interjected a woman who looked exactly like Salma Hayek, if Salma Hayek was six foot tall, 'your dry shampoo is the only styling product I use now since you did that video showing that you can use it on wet hair: *total* game-changer.'

'Thank you,' Kit said, beaming. 'I'm so chuffed to hear that. Feedback—good or bad—truly fuels my fire. Remember to really massage it into the scalp, won't you?'

'*Phew*,' said a small woman entering the group. She was very thin, in her fifties, wearing black leggings and a Lululemon jacket, her blonde hair pulled up into a messy butterfly clip. Her skin was shiny, plump, meticulously tended to. 'Hope we've got enough stock,' she muttered. 'We ran out last time so I upped numbers but still . . .' She peered around at the chaos of the convention centre. 'Anyone see Susan? She said she was on her way.' She noticed the stranger in the group. 'Oh, hi, I'm Bec.'

'Oh, yes!' said Kit, recognising her. 'Bec Holmes. You started Jellymins because your ill husband wouldn't take his supplements and had a sweet tooth: genius idea . . .'

'Thank you,' Bec replied warmly, and then her gaze shifted to look over Kit's shoulder. 'Susan! Over here!' She waved madly.

Kit turned to smile at the new arrival before making a polite exit, when she realised it was the woman she'd chatted to after her panel on the Gold Coast last year. She wore a shirt dress in an abstract black-and-white pattern and black ankle boots, her expression warm and friendly.

'Oh, hi!' Kit said, smiling. 'I'm Kit, we met—'

'At the conference last year,' Susan finished. 'Nice to see you again, Kit.'

'Susan is our chair,' Bec explained. 'Well, she's our owner now, too, but mostly I think of her as our chair because she's so damn good at it.'

Kit sensed Bec was the kind of founder who took it all in her stride, a calm, down-to-earth woman who knew what mattered in life, and worrying about a faulty jar or Reddit trolls was not it . . . Hang on. *Susan* owned Jellymins?

'Wow!' Kit said, looking at Susan. 'That's . . . Wow, congratulations, that's super exciting.' Kit smiled widely, the sting of this perfect acquisition not unlike seeing a happy couple when you're going through a break-up. Also: who the hell *was* Susan? Why did she now own a vitamin gummy company? Kit would be frantically googling all of this the second she was back at her stand.

One of the men setting up the stand interrupted, and he and Bec began an urgent discussion about the positioning of a giant inflatable strawberry.

'I read about what happened with your deal, Kit,' Susan said discreetly. 'What a disgrace.'

Kit shrugged. 'Just one of those things,' she replied. 'What can you do?'

'I'm sure there was a slew of investors ready to step into their shoes,' Susan said, peering at Kit as if trying to read her expression.

'Yeah. But I decided to park the process. None of them felt right and I had run out of steam. Hindsight made me realise Pinnacle probably would've destroyed the company . . . I really lost my way for a while there, so for the moment sitting tight feels right.' Why was she being so candid with Susan? *That was definitely TMI*, Kit thought.

'A deal like that is about more than just business,' Susan said. 'And more than the bottom line. It's a decision about how you want to spend your life. With whom. Doing what. Considering how every day would look. That can't be rushed.'

'Exactly,' Kit agreed. 'And honestly, I needed a breather. Some big family stuff went down, and the idea of a new process then the stress of new investors coming in: I didn't have it in me.'

'Can I ask why you were selling such a large stake?' Susan probed gently. 'It's a very good time to sell. I should know; I'm one of the idiots who bought in at the top'—she gestured good-naturedly towards the Jellymin stand—'but handing over all that control and equity . . . I'm worried you're not getting good advice.'

'Didn't Bec hand over all her control and equity to *you*?' Kit asked cheekily.

'Fair call,' Susan conceded, 'but she was desperate to sell. Her husband died and she lost her motivation. She wanted out. The company is in terrific shape so she seized the moment. But I get the sense you're not even close to that point. You have more to do.'

Kit glanced back at her stand. 'I do, and I am really happy. I'm back to being creative, doing all the hands-on and education stuff. I'm shoulder to shoulder with my team, not absent and distracted with the deal, plus I'm available for my family. Things are good.' She smiled. It had taken time to work through her feelings about the deal, to recognise and also forgive herself for how much she'd lost her way, but she felt she was finally moving on. 'I realised that if it all comes to nothing—there's no deal, or big exit—well, I went into it all with nothing and I was happy, so I can keep going with nothing, too.'

Susan smiled. 'Very wise, Kit. Although I don't think you've closed the door on deals just yet . . . How did your other share-holders react? Any pushback on not selling?'

Kit's smile faded. 'That's an understatement. The whole process kicked off because one of them was in debt and needed to sell. The bank had taken control of her shares.' *This is confidential information*, Kit reminded herself. *Stop!*

'Tricky,' Susan said. 'How did that work out?'

'The company ended up taking out a loan to buy her shares,' Kit said. 'I've been assured it's very common, but I hate it. I hate *any* kind of debt.'

Toni had tried to insist her thirty percent had to be sold at the Pinnacle valuation, twenty-eight and a half million dollars, but was quickly shut down by Rupert. If she wanted to sell now, he told her, she could take the money on offer or she could leave it. She settled for eight million.

Susan raised her brows. 'Smart move: it buys you time, and now you can transact on your terms, when you want to. Autonomy and agency are very important for founders. And some debt can actually be a positive thing.'

'Oh, it wasn't my idea,' Kit assured her. 'I have a brilliant mentor; she reminds me of you, actually. Really took me to task for rushing that deal despite the shitty terms on offer. And as well she should have.' Kit smiled bashfully. 'Also the boys at Linley are amazing.'

'I'm glad you have good people around you,' Susan said, returning her smile.

'Well,' Kit said, 'I suppose I should get back.' She felt a weird reluctance to leave, like Susan was her business crush and she wanted more time with her. 'So lovely to chat again. Bye, Bec. Bye, everyone.' Kit waved and walked back to the Second Day stand.

'Damn it,' she cursed under her breath. Why hadn't *Susan* invested in Second Day? Why hadn't Rupert found *her* and given *her* the IM? Kit would've killed for a partner like that: someone wise and rational, who could see things from the founder's perspective and not just the buyer's perspective. Also: *a woman*.

'They didn't give you any gummies,' Hyun observed with disappointment.

'They're sending some over later,' Kit said. 'Hey, do you have my looks for the weekend with you?' Kit had started using a stylist for her media appearances; it saved so much unnecessary stress. 'I've got to pick up Gretel but I want to try them on tonight so I don't wig out in the morning when they don't fit or make me look like a cartoon character.'

'I dropped them at your pad,' he said. 'Rat told me all about her new job. Wholesome.'

Rat had taken a position at a local day care centre. It made no sense to Kit, but also a lot of sense: she was great with Gretel, loved making up games . . . and was part child herself.

'So, how are you feeling about tomorrow?' Kit asked Hyun. He was hosting a live event, his first in front of a large audience. She was pushing him to be more front and centre, so that Second Day was not so reliant on her. It had come through again and again, from every bidder: the brand needed to be able to stand alone without Kit.

'Like I'm gonna eat it up and leave *zero* crumbs. I'm wearing a pink silk suit, Jaz is doing my make-up; did you know she's a make-up artist? *And* she was on *Bake Squad* last year. *And* she is dating a Formula One mechanic.' He paused. 'I thought she was just the office golden retriever, but she's *actually* amazing.'

'How generous of you to say,' Kit said, with exaggerated earnestness.

'Naww, thanks,' he said, missing the sarcasm by a mile. 'My LED facial awaits, call me if you need.'

Kit collected her daughter at the school gate at four minutes past three: late enough to warrant a scowl from Gretel. She gave her a kiss and a hug, and then handed her a bag of popcorn to munch on.

'Hey, guess what?' Kit said. 'We're going to Lucky Bamboo for dinner!'

Gretel did a little skip as she walked. 'Yum! Can I have three—no, *five* springy rolls? And an apple juice?' She broke free of Kit's grip and ran ahead to press the pedestrian button. 'Is it a fancy night? Is Daddy coming?'

'He going to try, if he finishes work in time.'

Ari was living right on Bondi Beach with Wren in a brand-new, freestanding house, paid for with Wren's phenomenal income as a gaming influencer and energy drink ambassador. Gretel's father was still travelling a lot, but he was a much more constant and consistent presence in her life now. To their credit—and Kit's undying gratitude—Wren had helped him to understand that he was being a selfish jerk and needed to get his shit together for the sake of his daughter. For the first time ever, Kit had a mostly reliable co-parent, Gretel had her dad around, and Bondi had another rad guy wearing artfully placed beanies and exciting loafer-and-sock combinations.

Kit was clipping Gretel into her car seat when she heard her phone ringing. She checked the caller ID: Rupert. Her curiosity was instantly piqued. From speaking to him three or four times a day at least, now she never heard from him.

'To what do I owe this pleasure?' she asked, returning his call once she was in the car and driving.

'How on earth are you, Kit? We really miss you around here. Have I caught you at an inopportune time?'

'Who's that, Mum?' Gretel hollered from the back seat. 'Is it Dad?'

'No, it's a work call, honey. Give me a sec.' To Rupert she said, 'I'm good. What's up?'

'I just had the strangest call,' he said. 'A cold call from Catteridge Capital, asking to set up a meeting.'

'Okay,' Kit said cautiously. 'More information?'

'It's a private fund owned by Susan Catteridge. She's an interesting one. She doesn't accept IMs, which is why she wasn't part of our process; she waits to find investments she likes and reaches out.'

'Oh my god, *Susan*!' Kit said. 'I chatted with her today at this expo we're doing. She just bought a vitamin gummy company so she was taking a look at their stand.'

'Ah, *that* makes more sense then,' Rupert said. 'She knows you.'

'Well, we've only met twice, but yes.'

'I wish you'd mentioned her earlier,' he said, chuckling. 'She's a gold-standard investor.'

'I had no idea who she was when I met her last year. But she seems super smart. Warm. Wise. Reminds me of Priya.'

'I think we can safely assume she is interested in investing in Second Day, Kit.' He paused, giving her a moment to absorb what he'd said. 'She wants to meet with yourself, me and Camille next Wednesday. How are you placed that afternoon? Four pm?'

'No *way*!' Kit exclaimed, excitement coursing through her.

'Why are you yelling, Mummy?' Gretel said.

'Sorry, honey. It's happy yelling. Oh my god. One *million* percent yes!' she told Rupert.

'If she owns a vitamin company, you still might be able to create those hair vitamins you were excited to do with mad-dog Marty. I wonder what he's up to now . . .' Rupert mused.

'Um, Rupert? Do I have permission to be excited about this? Could this actually happen?'

'From what I've heard, she's shrewd but fair,' he replied. 'She's not the type to overspend or put her money into black holes, but she doesn't have a returns-at-all-costs mindset. She's customer-focused and builds in time to grow her investments meaningfully. Plus, she's very comfortable with a minority stake.' He paused. 'So, yes, Kit, I would say you have permission to be excited.'

'Great. Because I am really, *really* excited,' she said. 'Consider Wednesday four pm *locked*.'

Kit ended the call, a huge grin plastered across her face. '*Fuck* yeah,' she whispered, bumping the steering wheel in joy with the heels of her palms.

'Who *was* that, Mum?' Gretel asked.

'That was Rupert, a man I work with,' she replied as they slowed for a red light.

'The man who used to always be on the phone,' Gretel said.

Kit frowned; she hadn't realised Gretel had even clocked his name. 'Yes, sweetie, that's Rupert.'

'Why is he calling?'

Kit turned to look at her daughter. Gretel's brows were knitted together in concern.

'Honey, what's wrong?'

Gretel frowned hard and lowered her chin.

The light went green, and Kit drove on.

'Will he call tomorrow?' Gretel asked.

Now Kit was really lost.

'I don't know, honey. He might. Why?'

'So you will be on your phone again all the time?'

Kit manoeuvred her rear-view mirror so she could see Gretel's face. Her little mouth was turned down.

'Hang on one second.' Kit took a left turn and pulled into a no-standing zone. She got out of the car and pulled Gretel's door open. Kneeling on the pavement, she took both her daughter's hands in her own and looked up into Gretel's eyes. 'Honey, Mum will *never* be on the phone like she was before. Ever. We have our phone rules, and they're real. Even Rat knows the rules.'

Gretel looked at her mother suspiciously.

'It won't be like last time, pinkie promise.' She extracted her right hand from Gretel's, and held up her right pinkie finger for her daughter to entwine her own around it. Gretel slowly, eventually gave up one limp pinkie.

'You know I won't break *that* promise,' Kit said. 'Rupert will call. There will always be work and always be calls because I am the boss of the company. But I am also the boss of *when* that work and those calls happen. Okay?'

Gretel nodded infinitesimally.

'Know what? I'm going to turn my phone off right now, okay?' As Kit stood up, opened the passenger-side door and grabbed her phone from her handbag, her brain quickly spat up all the texts and calls she was waiting on or needed to make that afternoon. But no: this was important.

'You want to do it?' she said, returning to Gretel's side and handing her the bright pink phone.

'Can I send Remy some emojis first?'

Kit laughed. 'I think that's missing the point. Here, you hold down that button and I'll hold this one . . . ready?'

Gretel's chubby little finger pressed on one side of the phone, and Kit's did the same on the other. A text suddenly bloomed on the screen.

'Who's Frog Man?' Gretel demanded as the screen went black.

Acknowledgements

WITHOUT A WOMAN NAMED Karen Crawford, this book would not exist, and I would not be who (or where) I am today. When Karen came in as the chairperson at Go-To, I woke up. Karen gently, firmly pushed me into the guts of the company, encouraging me to pay attention, learn, ask and, most critically, think much, *much* bigger. She was fluent in both finance *and* creative founder, and she was masterful in guiding me down a path while making me believe I had arrived there myself. She was so generous with her wisdom, experience and network, so open-hearted with her advice. Karen was a tremendous advocate for women in business and made me feel like I belonged at the table, by skilling me up, and then reminding me I *was* capable when things got hard.

Karen died of brain cancer in 2022. Her husband John lost his childhood sweetheart, and her children, Ben and Claire, lost their mother. I lost my mentor, and the world lost a very special human, with so much life and love owed. My purpose with this book was singular: to channel Karen's guidance, her encouragement and her superpower to make extremely complicated things understandable. To write about business as an outsider *and* an insider, which is how I feel, and maybe others do, too. To encourage people to go forth with confidence and purpose. (And great hair.)

Mike Symons, thank you for being the most supremely patient, good-natured and reassuring adviser a young woman hurled into M&A could hope for. You know the game inside out, you play it respectfully and carefully, and you make me think anything is possible. I wish everyone had someone like you in their corner when shit gets real. Greg Hipwell—careful: you give lawyers a good name. You are an exceptional legal bodyguard, and the sultan of common sense. (And contracts.) You and your team excel at gentle, considered and intelligent advising. Thank you. Paul Bates, Peter Lehrke and Stef Drury, thank you for allowing me to do what I need to, for trusting me. Your support and help in the early days were especially instrumental; I think of you like family. Brad Dransfield and Leonie Faddy, thank you for being such formidable, brilliant, empathetic people, and for coming in at an A+ *every single time*. I respect and appreciate what you bring, what you give and who you are more than you know. Thank you to all the founders and business owners who have generously shared their insights and learnings (and mess-ups) with me. I'm paying it forward, and always will (with pleasure). Special, deep thanks to every Go-To staff member since day one, and also every customer: a business without a strong team or a loyal customer isn't a business for long.

Similarly, a novel without a good editor sucks. Eyes closed and hand-on-heart thanks to Cate Paterson, for pushing back and challenging me, and for doing it with kindness and encouragement because: snowflake author. Your attention to detail, eagle eye, curiosity, passion and care shine through—I feel wildly lucky and grateful to have worked with you on this novel.

Thank you, Ali Lavau, for revealing a sparkling spring beneath the dense, wordy mountain. You're a true master at your craft. Thank you, Tara Wynne, for being my long-time cheerleader and first reader sense check, and for somehow always keeping it both real and optimistic.

Thank you, Hame. Your love is such supportive, solid ground when I stumble, fall and collect myself, and your sounding board is the only one I care about. You gifted me precious space to dedicate time (I didn't have) to write this, at a time when life demanded so much of me. The title of this book is something I say to you all the time, and we both know it's a lie, but listen, I swear, things *will* calm down now. Rudy and Sonny? *Mum's finished the book.* It's done. I'm back. I love you. Now let's go get a friggen milkshake.